Gallery Girl

By Wendy Holden and available from Headline Review

Simply Divine
Bad Heir Day
Pastures Nouveaux
Fame Fatale
Azur Like It
The Wives of Bath
The School for Husbands
Filthy Rich
Beautiful People
Gallery Girl

Wendy Holden

Gallery Girl

headline review

First published in Great Britain in 2010 by
HEADLINE REVIEW
An imprint of HEADLINE PUBLISHING GROUP

1

Cataloguing in Publication Data is available from the British Library

ISBN 978 0 7553 4258 7 (Hardback)
ISBN 978 0 7553 4259 4 (Trade paperback)

Typeset in AGaramond by Avon DataSet Ltd,
Bidford-on-Avon, Warwickshire

Printed and bound in Great Britain by Clays Ltd, St Ives plc

Headline's policy is to use papers that are natural, renewable and recyclable
products and made from wood grown in sustainable forests. The logging and
manufacturing processes are expected to conform to the environmental
regulations of the country of origin.

HEADLINE PUBLISHING GROUP
An Hachette UK Company
338 Euston Road
London NW1 3BH

www.headline.co.uk
www.hachette.co.uk

To The Turtle and The Toad
with love

Chapter 1

Below the glitter of chandeliers in the ornate room, starved cheekbone hit surgeried temple as fake air kiss met fake air kiss. Celebrities and socialites had fought capped tooth and tipped nail – and that was just the men – to be in the very front, on the row of gilded and red-velvet-cushioned seats that would provide the closest view.

But the front-row seats had gone to the most powerful people in the business: the market-makers, the movers and shakers. This row of billionaires, collectors and connoisseurs, men in the main but with a sprinkling of women, were noticeably less animated than those behind them. They exchanged a few nods, a few measured words, but their eyes were suspicious, their jaws were set. They clenched their catalogues and paddles with whitened knuckles. For them alone, this was a competition, and only one of them would win.

At the front, shining brilliantly, was their prize. Mounted in the centre of the platform, before a specially contrived mirror background designed to deepen its dazzle, the about-to-be-auctioned artwork flashed tantalisingly, turning slightly in the eddies of warm air.

Prostheseus Bound consisted of five prosthetic limbs, bandaged, sprayed gold and hung along a gold-sprayed plastic washing line.

The artist behind this creation was nowhere to be seen. Rumours as to his whereabouts swept the crowd from time to time, like the wind sending ripples across the surface of the sea. He was the guest of royalty. He was sailing with a megastar. He was on location. He was staying away deliberately; a modest man, he was shunning publicity. This last rumour was the only one that no one believed.

The event was ticketed, strictly for registered bidders, but soon so oversubscribed that a satellite room had to be set up across the hallway. Here, women with beige hair and high cheekbones milled around with slim, smart men smelling of expensive aftershave.

Now the master of ceremonies appeared and a hush fell on the room. You could have heard a Van Cleef tiepin drop, or a Tiffany diamond cocktail ring bury itself in the red plush of the carpet.

Every eye was on the distinguished figure taking up his position behind the pulpit-like wooden rostrum bearing the auction house logo. He was a man whose very presence signalled, resoundingly clearly, that this was an art event of supreme importance.

Master auctioneer Jeremy Silk did not, after all, bring his gavel down on just anything. He presided only over sales which achieved into the millions. With his trademark tall figure, saturnine looks and laid-back cool, he was almost as much of a pull as the pieces he was selling.

Jeremy was a master of rostrum theatricals. When things really got going, he danced round his pulpit like Carlos Acosta, and the way he crinkled his eyes regularly got excited female collectors bidding beyond their better judgement. His smile, it was said, could melt credit cards.

Today, as usual, he was impeccably pin-striped, side-parted and signet-ringed. His hand-made leather shoes shone like mirrors. Every aspect of his appearance had been carefully choreographed, even the inside of his suit. Especially the inside of his suit. The inside of his suit was Jeremy's sartorial tour de force. As the bidding hit the first million, he liked to mark the event with a flash of bright satin lining. It never failed to send the crowds wild.

Turning his sharp, elegant profile to the side, Jeremy now cast an eye over the brigade of assistants surrounding him on the platform. It was a look that the maestro of an orchestra might sweep over his musicians before raising his baton.

Outwardly calm, each assistant betrayed tics of tension. The suave young men with laptops, in charge of fielding internet bidders, blinked and licked their lips. The peach-skinned girls handling the phone bids, slender in black miniskirts and high heels, nervously tucked thick strands of glossy black hair behind shell-like ears.

Jeremy's dark brows drew together in a slight frown. He twisted his long, sensual lips. Were there as many girls as there should be? Wasn't one missing? Augusta? He remembered her earlier, struggling to connect to a client in the British Virgin Islands. It turned out that she hadn't switched on her mobile.

These girls were so dim. Pretty, but dim. An advance bid for a million had come through on Ariadne's phone, but she had confused the noughts and told him it was ten thousand. However, punters expected to see glamorous babes in high heels manning telephones, and so, Jeremy knew, he was stuck with them.

The giant screen behind him, which would flash up the bids as they came in in five separate currencies, lit up. USD, CHF, GBP, euro, rouble.

Where the hell *was* Augusta? Behind his calm mask, Jeremy was infuriated. Besides the small matter of her handling the Moscow bids, he liked his assistants ranged symmetrically on both sides, like the backing band they effectively were. Hugo, Milo and Romeo were on his left with their laptops, but on the right there was still only Ariadne and Anastasia.

Jerking suddenly backwards in a manner that would have had his Harley Street osteopath rolling his eyes, Jeremy beckoned Hugo. 'Tell someone to bloody well find Augusta,' he snarled.

Jeremy allowed a few minutes for the search, during which he smiled and nodded at the front row, the regular bidders. They smiled and nodded back, aware of the value of the acknowledgement in such circumstances. The art world rumour was that Jeremy Silk's levels of greeting were calibrated to what you had spent last time round. A million got you a nod, two million a nod and a smile. Five million and over got the full Silk monty: a nod and a smile plus a lean over the rostrum and a murmured word.

Working his way along the front row, Jeremy reached a well-preserved blonde with Ivana Trump hair and a white Chanel suit.

He smiled, nodded and bent forward. 'Mrs Klumpp. Delighted to see you here,' he murmured.

The blonde's face remained expressionless, although she inclined her head and revealed, somewhat stiffly, a set of very white and very level teeth. Jeremy was experienced enough in the art of high-society facial deciphering to recognise that on anyone less Botoxed, this would be the broadest of smiles.

Mrs Herman T. Klumpp III, to use her full title, regularly spent millions of her husband's billions pursuing her interest in seeming interested in contemporary art. Along with a handful of others at the same exalted financial level, Fuchsia helped keep the art galleries and auction houses of London standing, not to mention those in Geneva and New York.

All good news for Jeremy, who had a serious vintage wine habit and a third home in Tuscany after the first and second in Chelsea and St Mawes. Currently the Tuscany place needed reroofing, and there was an Aston Martin he had his eye on as well.

He wondered if the rumours were true about Fuchsia Klumpp unfastening articles of clothing in lieu of waving her bidding paddle. Surely not. No one he knew personally had ever seen it; Fuchsia, despite being a legend in London auction rooms, at auction rooms throughout the world in fact, rarely appeared in them. Collectors at her level seldom materialised bodily, preferring to send a functionary to do the hard work of sitting and bidding.

The fact that she was here today seemed, Jeremy felt, to

confirm the art world's favourite long-standing rumour. That Fuchsia was conducting a passionate affair with the artist whose false legs now dangled tantalisingly before them all.

Behind him, Hugo murmured something. The search for Augusta, Jeremy gathered, had proved fruitless. Before him, the crowd was getting restive. The big gold clock at the back of the hall had passed eleven. In the front row, one hand patting her immaculate blonde up-do, Fuchsia Klumpp's spiked red heels were tapping with silent impatience on the carpeted floor.

The show, Jeremy recognised, had to go on. Well, Ariadne would just have to manage Moscow as well. There was no chance of Anastasia doing it: she thought CHF was something to do with China, not the Swiss franc, and imagined KFC was a unit of international currency.

He muttered the new instruction, then, maestro-like, raised his long, well-kept hands. The crowd, who had begun to murmur amongst themselves, instantly quietened down.

'My lords, ladies and gentlemen, welcome,' Jeremy began in his trademark tone – drawling, patrician and with a suggestion of amusement. 'Without further ado, Lot One.'

He raised manicured eyebrows roguishly at the front row. 'We start the bidding at one million. I have a telephone bid for one million.'

Gasps and cheers from the crowd. The screen behind him rippled with figures. Seeing the expectant eyes upon him, Jeremy lost no time obliging with his party trick. Deftly unbuttoning the front of his suit with one practised hand, he jerked out an equally practised hip. Out swirled the side of his jacket, revealing a flash of tangerine silk lining. There was a roar of applause.

Jeremy raised his hands again. Immediately the applause died down, to be replaced by respectful silence. 'One million I'm bid. One million, two hundred and fifty thousand I'm asking . . .' He looked confidently round, revelling in the familiar feeling of being utterly in control, of having the crowd eating out of his hand.

His control wavered as he saw, below him, Fuchsia Klumpp casually unfastening the topmost of the many large gold buttons on her jacket and then fixing him with her eye. Jesus H. It was true!

Jeremy forced himself to concentrate. 'Thank you, Mrs Klumpp, for that bid.' He was always scrupulously polite. It added, he felt, the all-important personal touch. 'Three million two hundred and fifty thousand I'm bid. Three million five hundred thousand I'm asking . . .'

'Come on! *Come on!* Get your fucking wallets out!'

The impassioned growl came from some thirty feet above the Silk rostrum. Up here, unbeknown to the crowd below, the star of the show had concealed himself in a cubbyhole set behind the mouldings of the classical frieze running round the top of the main room.

From the tiny room's grille window, cunningly hidden among the Greek plaster crests, he had a grandstand view. He looked down on the excited crowd, on *Prostheseus Bound*, on the screens of the laptops, on Fuchsia Klumpp and on Jeremy Silk, who, from this angle, could be clearly seen to have a bald spot.

The artist shook back his long, straight, Apache-black hair and curled his lip, amused. He had no love for Silk. He loathed the auctioneer's ludicrous showboating, but not as much as he loathed the cut Silk's auction house took from sales. Given the publicity they got for an event like this, the artist thought, *he* should be bloody charging *them*.

As for Fuchsia, his patron and mistress, he'd like to see her put her money where her mouth was, or had recently been. Surprising, he thought, how groomed she looked now compared to the gasping, grinding, greedy cat she had been only an hour ago. It helped to have a personal hairdresser and stylist on tap at all times, of course.

'Ohhhhh. Mmmmmm.' Something warm and naked moved beneath him.

The artist blinked. In contemplation of the scene below, he had almost forgotten what he was engaged in up here, but then he had always been able to compartmentalise. The particular compartment to which he now returned his attention was an attractive, dark-haired young woman rubbing her naked body suggestively up against his.

The extent of his own undressing had been to pull open the fly of his skin-tight black jeans; now, rubbing her dark nipples with the heels of his hands, he thrust powerfully between the slender white thighs wrapped around his black-denimed buttocks.

'Oh! Ooohhhhhh!' Her head was flung back, her short black dress, ripped summarily off – he couldn't remember if by her or by him – flung on the dusty floor a few feet away.

'I shouldn't be doing this,' she gasped. 'I'm supposed to be down there. Working.' She tossed her shining hair in the direction of the scene below and gave a snorting, rather horsey laugh.

'You're doing a great job up here,' the artist grunted. Probably better than what she would have done down there. He'd found her in a back room before the auction had begun, trying cluelessly to set up some telephone link. The sight of her bottom, tightly clad in black, had provided the answer to what to do with the excess of testosterone which the prospect of a sale sent coursing through him. It had been the work of a moment to persuade her upstairs.

She was laughing horsily again. He tried to remember what her name was. Anastasia? Augusta? Aurora? A roarer was about the size of it. He was famously hot stuff in bed, but he had never heard anyone make this much noise.

'You're fantastic,' groaned the girl, her eyes closed in ecstasy as he thrust into her again.

No, it wasn't Aurora. It was something else. Augusta? What did it matter; these auction-house girls were all the same. All girls everywhere were the same. Available. When you were the bad boy of the British art scene with the looks, money and success to go with it, no one ever said no.

Silk's assured voice drawled its way upwards. 'Four million I'm bid. Four million, two hundred and fifty thousand I'm asking . . .'

'*Mmmmmmm*,' gasped Aurora/Augusta/whoever/who cared. '*Amazing*. No one's ever done this before.'

He wondered briefly what was amazing her. His technique, or the money being offered for his art? They were both pretty mind-blowing, it had to be said.

'Five million I'm bid . . .'

'*Uhhh. Ooohhhh!*' Her fingers dug into his back. Her heels were excitedly bashing the sides of his calves. What did she think he was, a bloody horse?

The tension in the hall below matched the acceleration of pace in the storeroom. Jeremy was whirling his orange lining like a toreador as the bidding started to exceed even his wildest expectations. One by one the front row had dropped out, as had, to Jeremy's fastidious relief, the spoddish man in the creased raincoat in the third row who had repeatedly stuck up his paddle as if asking the teacher if he could go to the toilet.

People were jostling excitedly, although in the main being careful not to wave their numbered paddles too animatedly. That could be an expensive business.

In fact, the only paddle moving was in the front row, attached to another well-known billionaire art collector, a large, dishevelled man in a loose white shirt. He was battling it out with Fuchsia Klumpp's Chanel buttons and a third party on the other end of Ariadne's phone whose identity was strictly secret.

'Eight million I'm bid, eight million two hundred and fifty I'm asking . . .' exclaimed Jeremy in disbelief, his famous cool rapidly evaporating. He had expected three million, tops, for *Prostheseus Bound*.

'Yes, no . . . yes, no?' he pressed. 'Mrs Klumpp, are you out?'

Fuchsia Klumpp was not out, although she was certainly half out of her jacket. And while she wasn't, strictly speaking, Jeremy's type, there was no doubt her method was distracting.

Upstairs, the artist thrust again into the melting loins of his conquest. The white thighs clasped tighter about him. 'You've got a good grip,' he muttered into her hot, sticky neck.

'Pony Club,' she gasped, grasping the front of his black mesh vest like reins. For a moment he staggered to keep upright in his high-top, thick-soled, unlaced black trainers.

'Nine million I'm bid . . .'

There was a roar of applause as, downstairs, Jeremy Silk removed his jacket altogether. Another cheer greeted the loosening of his tie. 'Come on, Jeremy! Get 'em off!' shouted a large, overexcited lady in orange who evidently cherished the hope that he would strip completely. For his part, seeing Fuchsia now extend a stick-like leg and shake off one very high, spiked red heel, Jeremy hoped very much that *she* wouldn't.

'Ten million . . .'

The boys at the laptops were practically bouncing in their seats. The girls' lips moved fast against the telephones.

The crowd's cheers gathered strength as the numbers drove upwards. As the eleven million mark was passed, they gave a visceral roar. The room was febrile, volatile. It felt as if it could explode at the application of a lighted match.

'Twelve million I'm bid,' gasped Jeremy. It was his finest professional hour, but he was beginning to wonder if he would personally survive it. He must, though. He could not go down in history as expiring at the sale of five gold false legs, however much of an auction record they had set.

In the room upstairs, the girl was lashing her head from side to side, whipping the artist's face with her hair.

'*Thirteen* million . . .' The man in the white shirt had dropped out. It was now Fuchsia Klumpp's buttons versus Ariadne's man of mystery.

'Oh! *Oh!*' Upstairs, she was bucking and thrashing beneath him. Pony Club was right. He was the rider. She was the horse. He was riding this whole damn thing, this whole auction room.

'*Fourteen* million . . .'

The artist ground into the girl. She was bouncing against him and making a neighing noise.

'*Fifteen* million . . . thank you, Mrs Klumpp.' With a teasing circle of the button with her red-tipped fingernail, Fuchsia pulled the jacket open. Jeremy's eyes skated over a bony ribcage and a very small red lace bra.

In the cubbyhole, the girl shrieked. Downstairs, the crowd roared; clapping, stamping, wanting more.

'*Sixteen* million from the telephone,' gasped Jeremy, as Ariadne nodded her glossy head. He, who never perspired, who smelled always of Trumper's West Indian Limes, was now breaking into a muck sweat. He yanked at the buttons of his shirt.

'That's the stuff!' shouted the woman in orange.

Upstairs, he drove into her. Deeply, powerfully, savagely. She rose in ecstasy. Downstairs, the crowd yelled. Mrs Klumpp extended the other leg and shook off the second shoe.

'*Seventeen* million from Mrs Klumpp . . . do I hear eighteen million?' Jeremy groaned. He was certain of the Aston Martin now. But would he live to drive it?

Upstairs, the artist's bottom was a leather-clad blur. Sweat poured from him. Downstairs, Mrs Klumpp pushed her skirt up a thin thigh to reveal cream suspenders.

'*Eighteen* million from the telephone.' Jeremy Silk was mopping his streaming brow. 'Do I hear . . .' He could hardly think of the figure.

Pony Club was shrieking; her cries mingled with the noise from the crowd below.

'*Nineteen* million from Mrs Klumpp . . .' As the thin, red-tipped fingers rolled the other stocking off, Jeremy feared he was going to burst. His heart drummed. He could feel the veins pulsing on his forehead. Surely it could not go on much longer? Fuchsia Klumpp was practically undressed . . .

Oh, but damn it, it could. Ariadne was nodding. 'Nineteen million five hundred thousand from our telephone bidder . . .'

Upstairs, the artist gathered his flagging strength for one last push. Pony Club bucked and shuddered beneath him. Downstairs, the auctioneer saw Mrs Klumpp start to unbutton her skirt.

'*Twenty million*,' he yelped. 'All done at *twenty million*. A record for this artist at auction.'

'*Oh Christ* . . .' Upstairs, with the smack of Jeremy's gavel against the desk, the artist released himself in a long, sweet, hot, triumphant rush.

Jeremy raised his shaking hands. Immediately the noise subsided.

'My lords, ladies and gentlemen,' the auctioneer gasped. 'May I offer my humblest congratulations. Not only to Mrs Klumpp, who placed the winning bid, but to every one of you. Here, today, you have seen history in the making. You witness a landmark moment for contemporary art. A record sum for this artist, indeed for this auction house, has been achieved. *Prostheseus Bound* by Zeb Spaw. Sold for twenty million pounds!'

Chapter 2

'Prostheseus Bound *by Zeb Spaw was yesterday sold at auction for twenty million pounds . . .*'

Alice, who had not up until that moment been really listening to the radio, now found herself sitting bolt upright in the tepid water of the bath.

Twenty million pounds! She blinked her eyes hard and stared in disbelief at the small grey transistor sitting on the battered sill below the partially cracked bathroom window.

'*. . . an all-time record for the auction house and marking a personal high point for Spaw's artwork,*' Sarah Montague was continuing. '*Zeb Spaw himself was not available for interview, but we have here Jeremy Silk, the auctioneer who presided over the sale. Welcome to the programme, Mr Silk. Expect it's still sinking in, isn't it?*'

'*Ha ha, yes, well thank you, Sarah,*' a polished male voice replied. '*It's a delight to be on the programme, which if I might be permitted to say, I'm a great fan of myself.*'

'*Mr Silk,*' the presenter continued briskly, ignoring this blatant attempt to suck up, '*there are people listening out there who are wondering how a price tag of twenty million for what is in essence five false legs on a washing line can ever be justified . . .*'

'It can't be justified!' shouted Alice from the bathwater.

'*That works out at four million pounds per leg, doesn't it?*'

'*If I might be permitted to say, Sarah, your argument is a little reductive. If we pursued that line, even Rembrandt wouldn't amount to anything more than daubs of paint and some canvas.*'

'Bollocks!' Alice yelled at the radio.

'*So you're really saying, Mr Silk, that* Prometheus Bound—'

'Prostheseus Bound, *my dear Miss Montague. Referring to the prosthetic limbs round which the work is centred. A title that, while acknowledging the classical heritage of contemporary art, is nonetheless unafraid to have a little fun with it.*'

'*Fun!*' fulminated Alice, who was now, thanks to some recently applied facewash, foaming at the mouth both literally and metaphorically. 'The entire art market's being distorted – *ruined* – by reptiles like you and Zeb Spaw and whatever utter numpty actually bought this heap of crap. And you call it *fun*!'

'*Can you tell us anything about the buyer, Mr Silk? A Mrs . . .*' Here there was a rustle as the presenter evidently consulted her notes. '*A Mrs Fuchsia Klumpp?*'

'*Mrs Klumpp is an extremely important and knowledgeable collector with a great interest in contemporary artists . . . in contemporary art, I should say.*'

'*Evidently very rich, anyway,*' Sarah Montague stated briskly. '*What do you say, Mr Silk, to the suggestion that people like Mrs Klumpp, paying enormous prices for works, encourage a situation in which prospective artists feel that traditional methods and styles are not worth learning or pursuing and only work that shocks and bewilders is of any interest and value?*'

'Good question!' Alice exclaimed, as the auctioneer cobbled together a defence making Fuchsia Klumpp, whoever she was, sound a more important patron of the arts than Lorenzo de Medici.

'*In that case, Mr Silk, the sixty-four-thousand-dollar question – although in this case it's actually the twenty-million-pound one: five gold-sprayed prosthetic legs on a washing line. Is it art?*'

'*No!*' roared Alice with every fibre of her being.

The small, rickety sliding door that divided the bathroom from the hallway was now wrenched open. A head of tousled dark hair appeared, beneath it a swarthy face still crumpled and flushed with sleep. David. She'd woken him up, Alice realised, reddening. Here she was, hair in rats' tails, sitting in a cold, greyish bath and shouting at the radio.

'What's up?' her boyfriend asked. Noticing that he looked very tired, Alice felt guilty as well as silly. He'd come back late from the hospital, probably not more than three hours ago, judging by the fact that the water tank had not had the chance to heat up after his usual post-work shower. This was why her bath was cold, but it seemed churlish to berate him about that now. Better to channel her indignation into the news story.

David pulled open the battered bathroom door as fully along its broken rollers as it would go – just past halfway – and inserted his tall, naked frame – he never slept in clothes – through the resulting aperture. In the cramped, steamy space of the bathroom he looked huge; as always, Alice marvelled proudly at the scale of him. So tall, so broad, so handsome, so clean-cut, like the sculpture that might be his namesake. David was solid without being fat, miraculously muscular considering how little exercise he did.

Like many doctors, he led an almost wilfully unhealthy lifestyle. He couldn't help working appalling hours, but he could certainly help, Alice felt, his appalling diet. It was not unusual for her to get up in the morning to find the congealed remains of an Indian or Chinese feast scattered unappetisingly across the kitchen table, alongside an empty bottle of corner-shop Chianti.

Her warnings never had any effect, however, other than to make him laugh and call her the health police. Besides, his habits left no physical mark. David, who had never in his life got on an exercise bike or running machine, was in far better shape than, say, Rafael, the husband of Alice's friend Suki. Rafael and Suki were rich and had a gym in their Notting Hill basement. Not that you could tell by looking at Rafael, who, for all his genuine charm and infectious *joie de vivre,* was nonetheless broad of beam and short of leg.

'Someone's bought five gold-sprayed false legs for twenty million pounds at auction,' Alice reported indignantly.

'So that's why you were shouting at the radio,' David observed, perched precariously on the edge of the bath. 'I thought it was Mrs Nutt for a minute.'

As well as being their irascible downstairs neighbour, Mrs Nutt was also their landlady, a fact which had prompted David to christen their tiny, dusty flat the Nutthouse. Sometimes, when feeling especially critical, he called it the Workhouse, a tribute to its unrelieved gloom and the fact that the last new stick of furniture had apparently been purchased back in the 1950s. If it had been purchased at all; an alternative theory of David's was that the entire contents of the Nutthouse had been procured by Mrs Nutt from a skip. He also claimed to believe that her flat downstairs, which neither of them had ever entered, was a Barbara Cartland paradise with marabou feathers, four-poster beds and a fridge full of pink champagne.

'Can you blame me?' Alice said, attempting to shake her wet hair defiantly back. Cold drops from the ends ran unpleasantly over her breasts. 'Five prosthetic limbs going for twenty million. It's crazy.'

David rubbed a hand over his tired eyes and blinked blearily. 'You're right. Actually, I feel pretty furious about it too.'

'*Do* you?'

Alice looked at him in surprise. For all the fact that she worked in an art gallery herself, albeit one dealing in much older, more traditional works than the one under discussion, David remained essentially uninterested in the subject central to her life. Just as, while she admired his work in the hospital, medicine was never a subject that had attracted her. She was squeamish, for a start.

David, however, had never wanted to be anything other than a doctor, just as Alice herself could hardly remember a time when she had not loved paintings. Art, she sometimes felt, was the force that sent the very blood rushing round her veins. A really wonderful portrait, a miraculously observed landscape, a powerfully evoked genre scene had the power to move her to tears.

But they had no such effect on David, whose essential view of art was that it was something to hang on the walls. So to hear him, now, sharing her view that contemporary art as typified by *Prostheseus Bound* was both dangerous and disingenuous was as unexpected as it was gratifying.

He was nodding and grinning at her. 'Course I'm cross. Here I am, working all bloody hours for crap pay as a junior doctor, when I could have got some prosthetic legs from the hospital store, painted them gold and become a billionaire overnight.'

'Oh, David!' He was only teasing her. How could he not take this seriously?

Alice rose out of the bath, the tremendous noise of the water echoing her own feelings.

As she searched for a towel, she felt him looking her up and down appraisingly. While Alice had a good figure and was proud of it, she had the pale skin of the true redhead, which, under the single bulb of the flat's grotty bathroom, tended to acquire an unpleasant grey cast.

'Must make *you* think, though, this false leg business,' David remarked as he followed Alice down the tiny hall to the bedroom. It was so small that a double bed and a wardrobe, both in a state of collapse, was all that could fit into it.

She turned, a frown puckering beneath her straight red-brown brows. 'Of course it does. That sort of crap going for that sort of price has nothing to do with art. It's not good for the market.'

David rolled himself back under the rumpled sheets and duvet. Propped against the pillows, he pushed his hands behind his head and regarded her lazily through his thick-lashed eyes. 'Yeah, but it's the way it's going, surely. Look at that gallery you work in. It hardly sells anything.'

'That's not true,' Alice said hotly. She had now discovered, to her fury, that her clothes were no longer waiting on the hanger on the wardrobe door where she had put them the night before.

David had evidently knocked it off when blundering in from work. Her freshly pressed white shirt and black trousers now lay in a heap on the carpet with his doctor's scrubs on top of them. And wet towels on top of those; no wonder they had been in short supply in the bathroom. She opened her mouth to complain, but David was still in full flow.

'Admit it,' he urged from the bed. 'You're working at the wrong end of the art business. Who's buying the stuff you and Adam sell? Contemporary's where the money is.'

'It's crap, though,' Alice protested. 'Mendacious, exploitative, Emperor's New Clothes . . . and speaking of clothes . . .' She held up her creased and damp trousers. 'Thanks *a lot*.'

David did not look at the trousers. His eyes remained on her own. 'Have you seen those places in Gold Street? Those hip galleries full of rich and famous people fighting over the Tracey Emins?'

Alice was sufficiently surprised to let her ruined work wardrobe drop from her fingers. She had of course seen the Gold Street galleries many times: the shining, glass-fronted establishments with the white interior walls and the beautiful girls at the front desks, stretching along the Mayfair street which was London's contemporary art epicentre. She disliked what they sold but she knew it was part of her job to keep abreast of the art market. Unlike her employer, Adam, who preferred to pretend contemporary art did not exist, she was not an ostrich.

But she had no idea that David had ever seen the Gold Street galleries. He had been there physically several times, with her. But she had not realised he had taken anything in. He had seemed completely uninterested at the time.

'When was the last time the Palladio Gallery sold anything for twenty million?' David pressed.

'We sold a Ben Nicholson for two thousand last week,' Alice retaliated.

'Ben who?'

'An important British modernist painter,' Alice began defensively.

'A member of the St Ives school and formerly married to the sculptor Barbara Hepworth . . .'

David was waving both hands from the bed. 'Spare me the detail. That's not the point.'

'What is the point then?' Alice asked, stopped in her tracks, her mind still racing away on Nicholson, on delicate etched circles on prepared paper framed in glazed boxes.

'Two thousand quid! Probably doesn't even cover the weekly running costs,' David chuckled.

Remembering that this was exactly what Adam himself had observed, somewhat wearily, at the time, Alice was temporarily lost for a reply. David jumped into the breach.

'Come on. You know what I'm saying. Why stick around with that clapped-out old gallery and clapped-out old Adam when you could be where the action is? Where the money is? Don't you fancy sitting in one of those Gold Street windows, trussed up in a tight skirt, tossing your romantic red hair about and waiting for the next oligarch to come through the door?' He raised a suggestive eyebrow.

Listening to him speak, Alice had become steadily angrier. Now she exploded. '*What?* Are you *joking*?' She was torn between amazement and absolute fury. David of all people knew how she loved her job and her gentle old employer.

He was grinning back at her, unrepentant. 'OK, OK. Calm down. Just being devil's advocate.'

'What?'

'Keeps you focused,' he returned easily. 'You've got to ask yourself hard questions sometimes.'

Do you? Alice thought, continuing to stare angrily at the worn grey carpet.

'Come on,' came the warm voice from the bed. 'Forget it. I was only teasing. I'm sorry, OK?'

Mollified by this rare apology, Alice glanced at David and saw that he was smiling his special smile, full of promise and suggestion. She had forgotten, in her surprise and outrage, that she was standing before him naked. Her own misgivings about how she must look – the light that struggled through the dusty windowpanes was hardly more flattering than that in the bathroom – faded as she saw the unmistakable message of approval rising beneath the bed sheet.

She grinned suddenly. 'You're joking. I'm about to go to work.' But she was smiling as she raised her hair with her hands and let it fall heavily about her white shoulders. One of the tumbling long red locks brushed her stiffening nipple and sent a pulse of pleasure through her.

'Come here, you goddess,' he growled.

Chapter 3

Alice had read somewhere that the best sex was either three minutes long or thirty minutes, nowhere in between. This was the former category, fast, hot and furious and from which she emerged flushed and with the ends of her hair practically sizzling and restored to its full red, if unbrushed, glory.

'I love you, you crazy ginger nut,' David murmured into her neck. He was holding her tight in his strong arms, and the feeling of security was blissful. Alice wanted to lie there for ever. However, there was work: the gallery, wrong end of the art business though it apparently was.

She dressed, tugging out the creases as best she could. As David watched her, half dozing, from beneath his heavy lids, Alice suddenly remembered something.

'We're going to supper at Suki and Rafael's tonight,' she reminded him, busy with her buttons. She did not meet his eye. She knew what the response would be.

'Do we *have* to?' he groaned, on cue, from the bed.

'Yes we *do*,' Alice said firmly.

'Suki's a complete geisha,' grumbled David, by which Alice knew he meant that Suki was a frivolous woman who did not work and was entirely supported by a man. And while this was an uncharitable view of her oldest friend, it was not, she knew, entirely an unfounded one.

'She's a good cook,' Alice reminded him.

'So she should be,' David riposted. 'She's been on cooking courses with everyone from Rick effing Stein to Raymond bloody Blanc.'

This was true too. In Suki's huge kitchen, on the shelf above the brushed-steel six-ring professional stove, was a row of pristine cookery books in which current high-profile princes of the culinary arts had inscribed messages to Suki, some surprisingly gushing.

'Make a change from takeways anyway,' Alice retorted, squinting at her reflection in the clouded mirror of the utility wardrobe provided by Mrs Nutt. David had really messed up her hair, damn it. Unless, after shampooing, she got straight to a hairdryer with her serum, it always reverted to its default setting of tangled frizz. Although David seemed to like it like this. His idea of her, inspired by her red hair, as some wildcat he had to tame had endured from the beginning of their relationship.

Just as well, Alice mused as she took a hairband from the supply inside the top wardrobe drawer next to her make-up bag and restrained her mane from her face. Personally, she could not see, and particularly not this morning, what David found so irresistible. Unmade-up as she was, she looked ghostly pale, with hollows around her eye sockets and beneath her cheekbones. With all that hair forming a backdrop, she looked, she thought, like a Victorian corpse.

Perhaps that was the real reason why Adam called her Beatrix. He claimed, with characteristic whimsy, that it was because she looked like the famous painting of Lizzie Siddal, red-headed muse of the Pre-Raphaelite Dante Gabriel Rossetti. But Lizzie Siddal, of course, had been just as famously and rather less romantically dug up by her erstwhile lover so he could remove the poems he had previously thrust in her coffin and publish them to make a bit of money.

Behind her, David was still muttering about Suki. 'I'll have to meet you there. I'll come from the hospital,' he was saying ungraciously.

Alice, applying her mascara, raised a russet eyebrow to herself in the mirror. She knew this trick. 'I hope that doesn't mean you're planning to dodge the whole thing.'

'Course not,' David said, not particularly convincingly.

'Have you got the new address?' Alice turned from the wardrobe door with her lipstick in her hand.

'New?' David exclaimed sulkily. 'She's only just finished bossing designers around the last place.'

Alice smiled. It was a fact that Suki never lived anywhere that could not have made a feature in *World of Interiors*. Even her student rooms had been carefully colour-coordinated. 'New, yes,' she said. 'Rafa got another big promotion. Then they found . . .' she raised her voice in a comically accurate imitation of Suki's high-pitched, breathy and somewhat affected voice, 'this *perfect little place in Notting Hill*.'

'Perfect little place,' snorted David from the bed. 'You just know it'll be the size of Buckingham Palace.'

'Only without the bad taste,' Alice replied. She had been to see the Royal Collection with Suki recently. While she herself had swooned before the Rembrandts and Van Dycks, Suki had recoiled in horror from the red carpets, chandeliers and gilt that provided their setting. 'It's like a Muscovite brothel!' she had shrieked.

'I'll see you later then.' Alice finished her face, planted a kiss on David's head and, ignoring the arms which reached up as if to pull her down again, hurried out of the flat. She was late already. Adam was an almost comically relaxed employer, but even he had his limits.

Dodging the puddles in the passage leading to the lift – there were always puddles, even in summer – Alice reflected that David would no doubt be sound asleep again already. His hours at the hospital were brutally long. He was working for promotion, for the next step on the ladder. But it was a particularly steep and difficult ladder, and getting up it was a struggle.

Even so, Alice had never doubted, any more than David, that

he was doing the right thing. It would be years before he saw any significant money. He didn't earn much more than she did.

So why, Alice now wondered, had she not turned on him during their recent conversation, claimed to be devil's advocate too and asked why he didn't give up NHS medical work and become, say, a plastic surgeon in a top Californian clinic?

Because, she realised, it had simply not occurred to her. Why would she want to encourage him to doubt his convictions, or shake the foundations on which he had built his career? In which case, Alice wondered, why had he felt the need to do just that to her?

The lift juddered to a halt at the floor below. The doors crashed back to reveal standing on the landing an irascible-looking old lady in a grey wool hat, a big dark coat and zip-up fleece-lined ankle boots. Beside her was a battered shopping trolley. Mrs Nutt. Alice's heart sank.

'Nice day,' she ventured, nonetheless. Although in truth, thanks to Mrs Nutt's refusal to pay a window-cleaner, the outside of the Nutthouse's sixth-floor windows were so dirty she had no idea what the day was like. Exterior conditions tended to remain a mystery until one was on the other side of the main downstairs door. And while this added an element of surprise to the morning, it made getting dressed something of a guessing game.

However, as it was early summer, a nice day seemed quite likely. The fact that Mrs Nutt was dressed to go on expedition with Shackleton was irrelevant; she dressed like that whatever the weather.

'Call it nice, do you?' Mrs Nutt grumbled in her throaty cockney, shuffling in backwards and pulling in her shopping basket. Alice had originally thought this was black, but she could now detect about it a faint hint of green. Black Watch? she wondered. Or just mildew? 'You can keep your nice weather,' Mrs Nutt added, grinding her wrinkled lower jaw against her top plate. 'Didn't get a wink o' sleep last night, I didn't.'

'I'm sorry to hear that, Mrs Nutt.'

From her wrinkled yellow eye sockets the old lady rolled a surprisingly bright glance at Alice. 'So you bleedin' well should be. Someone in your flat. Bangin' around at Gawd knows what time o' night.'

Alice pulled an apologetic face. Admittedly David could clump around a bit sometimes on return from the hospital. But this was nothing to the volume from the booming television that could be heard through the floor some nights from Mrs Nutt's. Saturdays especially; you wouldn't think it to look at her, but Mrs Nutt was an avid fan of *The X Factor*.

There was, Alice knew, no point suggesting the installation of heavy carpeting in the Nutthouse to absorb some of the sound from both establishments. Their last request – for a gas cooker that actually worked – had resulted in the appearance at the door of an ancient man in the company of a second-hand cooker they subsequently had to connect to the gas main themselves.

Alice reminded herself that Mrs Nutt lived on her own and was probably lonely. She must be nice to her; few other people were.

'I'm very sorry, Mrs Nutt,' she said humbly.

The old lady cast her a malevolent glance from under her grey wool hat. 'And then just as I'd got off to sleep, there's all this shouting from your bathroom.'

Alice bit her lip. The *Today* programme. 'I'm sorry,' she repeated. 'That was me, shouting at the radio. There was an item about how five gold-sprayed false legs had been sold at an art auction for twenty million pounds.'

She had hoped Mrs Nutt might see the funny side. But the old lady just looked shocked. Her yellow face turned grey and her saggy old mouth drooped open. 'Twenny . . . ?'

'Million, that's right. I know. It's just ridiculous.' Alice shook her head impatiently. 'Modern art makes a fortune. It's incredible.'

The old lady was chomping her jaws again, her wrinkled cheeks puffing rapidly in and out in agitation. She cast Alice another piercing, assessing glance. 'You work in one o' them art galleries, don't ya? Should put your bleedin' rent up, I should.'

Alice was too astonished at the avaricious speed of the old lady's mind even to be indignant. 'Not one of those sort of galleries though, Mrs Nutt. We don't sell anything worth twenty million pounds. Frankly,' she admitted ruefully, 'twenty pounds is more our level.'

The lift had stopped at the ground floor. Alice jumped to push the heavy door open for the old lady, whose mouth remained unsmiling amid a riot of wrinkles. 'Well what you're working there for?' demanded Mrs Nutt.

'Sorry?' said Alice, as the old lady, her hat, coat and shopping trolley passed beneath the arm holding the door open and into the front lobby.

Mrs Nutt paused in her progress across the shining floor tiles to the front door. She turned. 'You're working in some gallery sellin' twenny-pahnd pictures when you could work somewhere sellin' ones for twenny million. Sahnds like a waste o' time to me.'

Alice stared. *Et tu*, Mrs Nutt.

'Well, I like it,' she said defiantly, opening the brass front door latch and ushering the old lady into the outside world. With difficulty she resisted the temptation to push her off the front step and into the road. Mrs Nutt was lonely. If you were unhappy, it made you nasty.

Mrs Nutt paused outside the door and sniffed. Her bright little eyes turned up at the London sky. 'Nice day, you said it were,' she remarked accusingly.

'Yes.' Alice looked up. There were clouds, admittedly. But also the odd patch of blue.

'Well it ain't.' Having delivered herself of this, Mrs Nutt eased herself off the step to street level. Her trolley thumped down after her.

Alice, who was going in the same direction, stomped across the street and marched down the pavement on the other side, burning with self-righteous indignation. As tenant of the Nutthouse, she was a *customer* of Mrs Nutt's. Had the old bat never heard of service with a smile? Was belittling and criticising her clients really the best way forward?

She longed to be able to move from the Nutthouse to somewhere more salubrious. She had been there for years as it was, ever since she had moved to London from university. The problem was, the Nutt flat had location in its favour – convenient not only for Adam's gallery, but for David's hospital, which was one of the reasons he had moved in so soon after meeting her. The other reasons had been a mutual physical attraction so powerful that it had seemed pointless not to live together practically from the start. How much of their sex life, Alice suddenly wondered, could Mrs Nutt hear from underneath? All things being equal, she was probably lucky not to be attacked in the lift about that too.

How wonderful it must be to have a whole peaceful house to oneself, as Suki and Rafael had had from the start. Thanks to Rafael's job in some obscure yet immensely well-paid echelon of the banking industry, they had never even lived in a flat; in fact they avoided them if at all possible. It had been years, for example, since they had visited the Nutthouse, Alice thought. Suki had no doubt long since banished the memory from her conscious mind, consigning it to a world of Dickensian squalor where people shared bathrooms, no one had dressing rooms and footwear was stored in a crushed, smelly heap at the bottom of the wardrobe. Rather than, as were Suki's, in individual Perspex boxes with a picture of the shoes on the front.

Alice's thoughts now turned to the evening dinner party. The new Notting Hill house was certain to be as perfect as bricks and mortar could get. Everything in Suki's life was, especially Albertine. Alice smiled as she thought of her goddaughter, an adorable five-year-old moppet with big eyes, Alice in Wonderland hair and a nursery full of tasteful wooden toys whose pastel harmony David liked, to Suki's horror, to disturb every Christmas with violently coloured plastic.

Stumbling over a piece of raised pavement, Alice's attention snapped back to the here and now. Her annoyance with Mrs Nutt and the speed with which she had consequently walked had, she now saw, got her an astonishing distance. From her starting point at the Nutthouse, near St Pancras, she was now almost the other side of Russell Square. She paused in both her thoughts and her walk to admire the sunshine on the tall London planes with their camouflage trunks and wide, leafy branches lifting to a pale blue sky across which stretched the chalk trails of aeroplanes. Below stretched a sea of green grass, swirling around the bright flower beds that Camden Council tended so assiduously, lapping up to the ornate black railings separating the square from the surrounding pavement and the ring of chugging taxis and vans beyond.

The bright morning light sparkled on the fountain in the centre of the main route through the square. The benches encircling it were already filling up with the teenagers bound ultimately for the nearby British Museum. And not just teenagers either; coming towards her now, Alice saw with interest, was a positive battalion of Chinese visitors, walking four abreast behind a tour guide holding a Burberry umbrella aloft. Possibly they had just emerged from the Russell Hotel, whose red-brick façade, chateau-like and fantastical with its witch's-hat turrets, stretched along almost one entire side of the square.

Alice continued down past the grand-townhouses-turned-hotels of Montague Street, the name as usual provoking the thought that there should, by rights, be a Capulet Street nearby as well. With this reflection, she realised that she must be calming down. Her state of mind, after the agitation of David's devil's advocacy and Mrs Nutt's unwelcome remarks, was returning to normal. The leafy squares of Bloomsbury had exerted their customary magic.

Turning the corner into Museum Street, she met, as she often did, a fresh crowd of jeaned and trainered international students newly disgorged from their tour bus. They were milling outside the spiked black iron gates, waiting for the museum to open.

Feeling a drop of rain on her nose, Alice looked up to see that the weather had changed. The formerly cloudy blue sky was now angora grey, and the raindrops were becoming harder and more frequent. She felt sorry for the students. As it was only half past nine, and the BM didn't open till ten, they faced thirty minutes of getting wet. Mrs Nutt was right. It wasn't all that nice a day.

Chapter 4

The Palladio Gallery was contained in a tall Bloomsbury townhouse painted a pale primrose yellow. This had undoubtedly looked startling in the sixties when Adam had first opened it. Even now, cracked and peeling, the building could still raise the spirits on a drab morning. The colour made you think of sunny days and southern Italy, and there was something of the pantomime backdrop about the elaborate façade; four arches with moulded frames forming the main window, with thin barley-sugar-twist mullions dividing the panes. There were moulded ovals and decorative sills elsewhere on the front, and the door was sunk deep into a panelled entrance with original fanlight and bootscraper.

The street Palladio was on had come up in the world recently. When Alice had first begun working for Adam, the ground floor of the building on the right had been occupied by a snack bar called Extreme Sandwiches and the ground floor on the left by an estate agent called Motley Properties. Garish backlit plastic fascias and windows full of stickers had characterised both establishments. By contrast, the faded elegance of Palladio had stood out.

The last twelve months had, however, seen a surge in gentrification in the area, partly fuelled by the Eurostar terminal at St Pancras. Extreme Sandwiches, which had catered mainly to taxi drivers and tourists, had removed its plastic sign and substituted it with a tasteful sage-green one on which was painted in swirling black letters its new name, Bella Umbria. Instead of hot dogs and bacon sandwiches, it now sold paninis, wraps and stuffed focaccias. More taxi drivers seemed to come than ever before.

Motley Properties, meanwhile, was now Tomley's of Bloomsbury, also with a hand-painted sign, this time calligraphed white against a soft grey background. The result of all this was that Palladio, which had been the smartest shop in the row, was now the scruffiest, and the manager of Tomley's was always complaining about the peeling paintwork.

Alice rummaged for her keys in the no-logo leather bag that David had bought her for her last birthday. As always, she was the first to arrive at the gallery. Today, she would be the only one: Adam was going to one of the country-house auctions at which the gallery obtained a great deal of stock. Most of the house owners were personally known to Adam: acquaintances who had struggled on in the family stately until the roof was literally falling in and who were now forced to sell an etching or two to pay the gas bill. They were, despite this, lucky, Alice considered. Adam always paid them a fair price for their art treasures, and sometimes, his soft heart touched by their plight, he paid considerably over the odds.

Alice preferred not to think about the over-the-odds price Adam would probably pay today. The friend in need, Binkie, who lived as they all did in some rotting pile in the Home Counties, apparently had a collection of one hundred and seventy original Hogarth prints. They would be a wonderful addition to the gallery, but could they, she wondered, afford the outlay? Let alone the storage space.

She knew, and suspected that Adam knew too, that the Palladio Gallery was not really in need of new stock. It had plenty; far more than it could store. What it desperately needed, on the other hand, was customers.

Sales were down, down, down. The gallery's average weekly take now barely covered the heating and lighting bills. The business would no doubt have closed down years ago were it not for the fact that Adam owned the freehold of the building.

She inserted the key carefully; the lock needed persuading. More than that, it needed coercion, pleading, soothing, affection, even. Especially in the morning, after a cold or damp night, it needed jollying into the day.

With a final wriggle of the handle, she got it to open. It wobbled forth with a rattle, and the familiar smell from inside – musty, slightly mouldy, slightly dusty; of aged paper and aged building – rushed into Alice's nostrils. She switched on the lights and carefully twisted the bamboo pole that opened the ancient and delicate blinds on the tall windows. Palladio stood revealed, at the beginning of yet another week.

It was a gallery that dealt in pictures of all types – oils, watercolours, drawings, engravings, lithographs – dating from the early eighteenth century to the mid twentieth. Owing to the damp condition of the upstairs rooms, which could otherwise have been used for storage, almost all of the stock was on display.

The result was a phantasmagoria of images. There were watercolours of fantastical plant life alongside castles by lakes; Gwen John-ish oils of pale girls alongside vastly inflated eighteenth-century farm animals or Cubist cyclists of stupendous proportions. Every wall was crammed with framed oils and watercolours, chained together in lengths that hung suspended from the picture rails and rattled in the draughts like Marley's Ghost.

Even so, more room was still needed. There was no chair that lacked a stack of prints, pencil sketches and watercolours, all mounted on thick cream card. More pictures, framed and unframed, were ranged on the mantelpiece, along with volumes of art history and ancient auction catalogues; the whole held in place by carved marble bookends and shadowed by skew-shaded lamps. Yet more pictures were crammed into the great flat drawers of mahogany chests. Alice suspected that Adam would have displayed work on the ceilings and floors if gravity had not ruled out the former and good sense the latter.

She was switching on the lights in the small back kitchen when she heard the gallery door rattle. Surprised at a customer at this hour, she darted into the shop to find, to her surprise, the threadbare tweed jacket and baggy brick-red corduroys that comprised the uniform of her employer.

Adam's hairline receded from a domed forehead, from which sprung wild, unbrushed grey hair. He smiled when he saw her and extended both long arms, which his jacket sleeves never quite covered, in a gesture of courteous delight. 'My dear Beatrix! How are you?'

'Fine.' Alice smiled. Adam always believed in a proper greeting, just as he believed in tea in proper cups and saucers and always washing his hands thoroughly before lunch, even if lunch was only a sandwich from Bella Umbria. A special sandwich, nonetheless. In despair at the range of modish breads that had recently arrived there, he had somehow managed to charm the staff into providing a unique-to-him daily service of one plain ham sandwich on white bread with the merest dab of Colman's.

'I thought you were going to a house sale,' Alice said.

Adam's tall, baggy frame now heaved in a sigh and his kindly face clouded. He pushed his half-moon glasses back up his nose with an unhappy air and looked forlornly about him. Guessing he wanted a seat, Alice darted forward and moved a pile of mounted sketches from the nearest one. Adam sank down, placed both his large hands on his long legs and looked at her miserably.

'What's happened?' Alice gasped.

'Binkie died, poor old chap.' Adam removed his glasses, sniffed and sorrowfully shook his large head with its straggly grey hair.

'Oh Adam. I'm so sorry.' Instinctively, and even though she knew he was not the touchy-feely type, Alice had laid a hand on his graph-paper-pattern shirt. Although, indeed, he was not the touchy-feely type, Adam did not shake it off. His wide, disingenuous eyes, as he raised them to hers, were shiny with tears.

'They found him this morning in his library. He was clutching his Hogarths to his breast. Dead as a doornail,' Adam added, suddenly putting a hand to his mouth and rubbing it.

Alice was trying to imagine clutching one hundred and seventy large prints. If they were all framed, it was possible Binkie had been crushed to death.

'What about the pictures, though?' she pursued, curious. 'Are they not for sale any more?' She realised that despite her considerable reservations, she had secretly longed to examine a set of over a hundred original Hogarth prints. Eighteenth-century cartoons had, after all, been the subject of her MA dissertation.

Adam shrugged. 'Binkie has a somewhat go-ahead son,' he said delicately. 'He has other plans, it seems.' He spoke lightly, but Alice sensed he was deeply upset.

'I thought Binkie especially wanted you to sell the Hogarths for him.'

'He did.' Adam nodded, blinking energetically. 'He knew I would make sure they went to good homes.' He seemed about to say more, but didn't.

'I'm sorry,' Alice said, aware she was repeating herself. But what else was there to say? Besides, she *was* sorry.

'A bad start to the day,' Adam said, nodding deeply. 'I've known Binkie all my life. We were at prep school together, you see.'

Alice nodded sympathetically, trying and failing to picture Adam in shorts and a blazer.

'They're all going, one by one,' Adam said softly, his eyes misty with memory. 'Everyone I used to know.'

'Oh, Adam.'

He rallied at that, and smiled. 'And then,' he added, with a touch more spirit, 'coming here on the bus, I read *this*.' There followed a rattle of newspaper as he excavated a copy of the *Daily Telegraph* from somewhere about his person. He shook it out and held up a front page dominated by five gold false legs dangling on a washing line. 'They sold it for—' he began in astounded tones.

Alice held up her hand. 'I know. I can't believe it.'

Adam looked back at the paper. 'This chap Spaw,' he said, sounding bewildered. 'He says that when he's working he puts a group of systems in place. It rather makes him sound as if he's installing computers.'

'Yes,' said Alice, nonetheless wishing Adam would install some computers himself. She had, several times, forcibly made the case for one, but Adam had no interest in what he called newfangled contraptions. He had, he said, always managed perfectly well on paper. This was, Alice now knew after more than a year getting to the bottom of the hopeless mess that was the gallery's client list, something of an exaggeration.

But not, however, without its interest: the many addresses and phone numbers written on the cards of racy-sounding sixties Soho clubs seemed to indicate that Adam had quite a past. One of the addresses was 'HRH Princess Margaret, Kensington Palace, SW1'. Most, however, were scrawled indecipherably on cigarette packets and the backs of old envelopes. Some of the customer telephone numbers still had the old London exchange districts, and Alice suspected that many of the people they had belonged to were dead.

Adam was reading on, shaking his head sadly. 'Spaw says here that he was encouraged from the very beginning,' he remarked in his gentle voice. 'He seems to have won competitions and been given grants left, right and centre.' He looked up over his half-moons and fixed his myopic gaze consideringly on a distant Augustus John sketch. 'You know, my dear Beatrix,' he added wonderingly, 'I can't help but feel what a mistake that is. Surely young artists should be discouraged?'

'How do you mean?' Alice asked. Certainly Zeb Spaw should be discouraged, and in the strongest possible terms. But *all* young artists?

Adam pushed up his glasses. 'All great art is revolutionary,' he explained. 'It's about being misunderstood, about being an outsider. If you're celebrated and given money from the start, what's there to rebel against?'

'Nothing,' Alice agreed.

'Take Michelangelo,' Adam continued. 'His father used to beat him mercilessly because he wanted him to be a lawyer. And yet he became the greatest artist that ever lived. It is my considered view,' he added, folding the paper and laying it at his feet, 'that it would be better to have grants to *dis*courage young artists. Pay them to do something else.' He smiled at Alice. 'Don't you agree?'

She grinned back. 'Absolutely. I think you've hit the nail on the head there.'

'I'm old-fashioned, I know,' Adam added, rising on his long legs to his full six-foot-plus and walking over to the nearest wall to examine what hung there. 'But I have never been able to see what is so wrong with pictures that are beautiful, that actually look like something or someone and don't cost a fortune into the bargain.'

Alice felt a lump rise in her throat. Palladio was run strictly on the principle of affordable art. 'I'm not trying to make money,' Adam had said at her interview. 'What I want to do is simply encourage the love of art. Palladio's aim has always been that: whatever your means, you can find something here. Art doesn't have to be impossibly overpriced.'

It had all been music to Alice's ears. Adam's belief that beautiful things made for a better society exactly echoed her own. 'I'm a child of my times, I suppose,' he had added, shaking his head ruefully. 'Just an old hippy, really.'

With his half-moon spectacles, tweed jacket and worn cords, he looked to Alice less hippy, more retired brigadier. She could not imagine him dancing naked at Woodstock. But there was no doubt about his gentleness and the wholeheartedness of his belief that art healed social wounds and ought to be as available to as many people as possible.

He was, he had explained, about to retire and wanted to hand over the gallery he had spent his life building to someone as passionate about his favourite periods of art as he was. Someone young, with energy, who could develop the business.

And yet he hadn't. Admittedly he had, some months ago, raised her title to that of deputy manager. But her salary and actual level of responsibility remained as low as ever. Meanwhile, Adam remained in daily attendance, obstructing all the reforms that Alice longed to make. Had to make, if the gallery was to survive.

Time and time again she had been about to broach all these fermenting thoughts, but had always drawn back at the last moment. Adam was so gentlemanly, so kind, and she was so fond of him. How could she tell him he had to go so she could install computers and send e-mail newsletters? He needed to make the decision in his own time. The trouble was, as the weeks and months ticked by, as the takings dropped and the stock mouldered in the drawers, his time was eating into hers.

Now she could only watch as, free hand clutching the banister, Adam stomped up the narrow staircase with its threadbare runner to his office in a corner of a storeroom on the floor above. It was not a chamber into which Alice was encouraged to venture, still less Mrs Shanks, the cleaner. What Adam did up there amid the dust and the cardboard boxes and beneath the giant damp stain on the ceiling was unclear. Whenever she came in, he seemed always to be reading the paper.

Alice went to complete the task she had been originally engaged in: making a cup of tea in the tiny scruffy kitchen at the back. Now that Adam was here, of course, that cup of tea would take a different form. The tea bag in a mug would become loose leaves from a Fortnum and Mason tin spooned into a pre-warmed teapot and poured into the thin white china cups and saucers sprigged with pink roses that had apparently belonged to Adam's mother. As she sloshed the hot water on to the fragrant leaves, Alice wondered briefly about calling David.

A quick exchange of words with him, just now when she felt so uncertain, would be a ray of sunshine amid the pounding rain. He had been discouraging earlier, admittedly, but he had said he was teasing. And she knew from many, many occasions in the past that when she really wanted cheering up, there was no one better at it. Perhaps he could meet her for lunch.

Of course, he would probably be asleep still. But once he had gone to the hospital later, Alice knew, her chance to speak to him would be gone. At work, he was uncontactable. He had always been categoric about the fact that the time and attention he gave to unnecessary personal phone calls was time and attention he was not giving to a needy child.

Alice poured the cups of tea and took Adam's up, wobbling slightly in its delicate saucer as she negotiated the piles of books and other debris littering the stairs. It was a daily wonder that Adam did not fall down and break his neck.

She stopped before his office door and was about to raise her hand to knock when a sound from within froze her wrist in the air. A gulping sound, racked and broken. There was no doubt what it was.

Alice scuttled back down the stairs, the teacup swaying wildly. Adam, of all people, was crying.

Bewildered, upset and not a little frightened, she fled to the kitchenette and rummaged in her bag for her mobile. She desperately needed to speak to David now. The Nutthouse phone went to answerphone, however, as did David's mobile. Somehow, she had missed him.

Chapter 5

Suki and Rafael's new house stood alone at the end of a wide west London street. Suki had warned her to look out for a big yellow skip outside; it certainly was big, Alice thought, seeing the vast container on the road heaped with old pipework. Suki had evidently ripped out every bathroom in the house.

The sweep of wide pale steps to the portico was so long it reminded Alice of the one Cinderella ran down on her exit from Prince Charming's ball. She pressed the shining brass bell on the glossy black door. There were footsteps, a fluttering laugh and immediately it opened into a hall so big the entire Nutthouse could have fitted in.

'Alone?' Suki smiled, her teeth dazzling in the sunny evening. Either the weather had improved since she left Bloomsbury, Alice thought, or else people in Notting Hill paid for an upgrade.

'David's coming later, from the hospital,' she explained, hoping he was. He had better. She was desperate to see him after what had happened at the gallery. Adam had disappeared shortly after the tea incident; to where, Alice had no idea. He did not say and he did not come back. She had locked up after a largely uneventful day, having sold a postcard, price 50p and a small print of a rose, price £50. Before leaving, she had tipped Adam's *Telegraph* in the bin and reflected gloomily that Palladio's trading day had fallen somewhat below the level enjoyed by the auction house that had sold Zeb Spaw.

Suki, on the other hand, seemed in higher spirits even than usual. Her customary look, parties included, was dressed-down glamour: white jeans, bare feet, grey pashmina and pencil twisted casually in her tumbling blond hair. Tonight, all smoky eyeshadow and heavy kohl, she was positively Elizabeth Taylor, *Cleopatra* era.

Alice stared. Suki's long-limbed and fabulous figure was shown off to perfection in a bolero top embroidered with pink sequins, below which she was plainly not wearing a bra and which stopped well short of her tanned and toned tummy. She wore filmy pink chiffon trousers, faintly see-through and caught at the ankles with a circlet of bells which tinkled when she moved. The look was finished off with silver high-heeled mules and lots of jewellery.

Alice suddenly felt dowdy and self-conscious in her own fitted black shirt and Capri pants. Adam's salary permitted little beyond a monochrome, functional wardrobe; she relied on her hair to provide colour. Her hair, however, for all her post-work efforts at the Nutthouse, was still not behaving, and compared to Suki's exotic make-up, her own lick-and-a-promise approach looked slapdash and underdone. At least her ballerina flats were new and shiny, although, as Suki was certain to notice, also cheap imitations of a more expensive make.

'Have you brought your costume with you?' Suki asked brightly.

'Costume?'

'Didn't David tell you it was fancy dress?'

'David?' Alice blinked. Why would *David* tell her? He never spoke to Suki if he could avoid it.

Suki rolled her eyes. 'Honestly. I rang yesterday to tell you. You were out and David said he'd pass it on.'

Alice tried to remember where she could possibly have been.

Yesterday had been a Sunday; she and David had been in the flat most of the day, as he had been working the night before She had gone to fetch milk and Sunday papers at about eleven, she remembered. But David had not mentioned Suki's call when she returned.

Suki's expression was scornful. 'Does he ever think of anything apart from that bloody hospital?'

'Not really,' Alice acknowledged.

'Poor you, darling.' Suki rolled her eyes. 'Hope it's worth it.'

'What was the dress code, anyway?' Alice said fiercely, not wanting to be drawn into discussion of the less perfect aspects of her relationship; particularly with someone for whom life obviously could not be more perfect.

'Arabian Nights.' Suki shrugged. 'Oh well. Never mind.'

She turned to go inside; before following, Alice gestured at the skip on the pavement behind her. 'What are you building?'

'Not us, the neighbours,' Suki said, nodding towards the identical large white house next door. 'They're putting a private spa in their basement. Swimming pool, whirlpool bath, treatment rooms, the works.'

Alice absorbed the fact that these houses were so big you could build an entire health club in the cellar alone. The money involved must be colossal. How did people earn so much?

'The guy owns an art gallery in Gold Street,' Suki added carelessly. 'Cornelius Sump, his name is. But of course, you must know him,' she added excitedly. 'You being in that world and everything.'

Not *again*. This was getting tiring in the extreme. Alice forced a weak smile. 'I don't know him, actually.'

Suki pulled a face. 'But surely you meet everyone who's everyone in the art world?'

'Er . . . nope. Not as such.'

'Never met Damien Hirst?'

'Um, no.'

Suki rolled her thickly kohled eyes. 'Honestly, darling,' she trilled. 'Only *you* could work in the million-dollar glamorous art world and never have any of the fun!'

'I'm not really working in the million-dollar end of it,' Alice said wearily, thinking that Suki really ought to know this. She had been her friend for half a decade, and Alice had been working with Adam for two years. On the other hand, if your conversation didn't involve large sums of money or famous people – which conversation concerning Palladio obviously wouldn't – Suki tended not to listen to it. It was, Alice supposed, strange that they were still friends, considering how little they had in common these days.

Suki, however, had returned to the subject of Cornelius Sump. 'One of his artists is that gold-false-leg guy Zeb Spaw. Twenty million quid!' Suki whistled. 'Can you believe it?'

Alice shrugged. This morning, in the bath, she couldn't. But it now seemed mere miserable fact.

'Cornelius is probably going to build a rooftop helipad with his cut from that.' Suki grinned, her green eyes alight with the reflected glory of living next door to someone so lavishly successful.

'I doubt it,' Alice said drily. 'The false legs were sold at auction. Spaw bypassed his own gallery, by the sound of it. I shouldn't think your friend is all that pleased about it.'

Whether Suki had heard this, Alice wasn't sure; she now found herself being ushered into the enormous hall. It was covered in a wallpaper Alice felt she did not immediately understand.

'Fabulous, isn't it?' Suki enthused, following her eyes. 'It's hand-made, hand-laid and printed with sepia holiday snapshots from the fifties. It's made by a friend of mine. I met her at the University of Life.'

'The University of Life?' Alice echoed. She had always thought this a figure of speech, but Suki made it sound like a real place.

'Oh, it's a sort of collective of artists, poets and philosophers.' Suki smiled serenely. 'We meet in a pub in New Cross – all *fabulously* basic – and they sort of give lectures about living wisely and well.'

And you end up with hand-laid sepia photograph wallpaper,

Alice thought, trying not to giggle. 'So what did you learn from the University of Life?' she asked, with as serious a face as she could manage.

'That I should downsize,' Suki explained, also with a serious face, as she waved a jewelled hand round her colossal hallway.

'*Downsize?* But you've just moved into the biggest house in the world!'

Suki tapped her shining hair. 'Downsize in my *head*, darling. Satisfaction doesn't come from material things. I need to think about enrichment, rather than just being rich. I need to live more for others, not for myself all the time.'

Alice regarded her in amazement. Satisfaction for Suki had *always* come from material things. She was living proof that money absolutely did make you happy.

'So I'm helping develop a line of knitwear made from wool from a sheep sanctuary in Wensleydale.' Suki beamed.

As Alice continued to stare speechlessly, tinkling laughter came from the kitchen. A cork popped.

'Come and meet the others,' Suki said cheerfully, leading the way lithely down a strange woven carpet that looked as if it might be made of bulrushes. By someone else from the University of Life, possibly.

'Everyone, this is Alice,' Suki announced, as she turned right at the bottom of the staircase into an enormous, wooden-floored, open-plan kitchen. The room stretched backwards past various brushed-steel units and state-of-the-art gadgets to a pair of floor-to-ceiling French windows overlooking what was, given the location, one of London's most prestigious garden squares.

Everyone else, Alice saw glumly, had been appraised of the dress code. Three other couples, all glittering and glowing with Oriental satins, embroidery and jewels, stood in the kitchen like planets surrounding Rafael at the centre, a sun radiating bonhomie and champagne. His stocky, muscular frame was encased in a gold brocade coat, and his thick, curly brown hair was topped off with a squashy gold turban. His tanned, smooth, plump elastic face stretched in impish delight as he swooped on Alice. His hug was hearty and smelled deliciously of expensive aftershave.

'Come as an untouchable, have you?' He grinned, his round brown eyes dancing beneath the purple jewel at the front of his turban. Rafael had all Suki's insensitivity; fortunately, he also had her thick skin. Perhaps, Alice reflected, it was one of the reasons they got on so well.

'Oh ha *ha*.' She grinned. 'Got it in one, and while we're at it, here's my begging bowl.' She reached into the no-logo bag and pulled out a crumpled Tesco's carrier, from which she produced a box of Bendick's Bittermints.

'David didn't tell me about the dress code,' she explained.

'Too busy saving lives, I expect,' he said.

'Come over and say hello.' Suki suddenly reappeared. 'The Luke-Warms have arrived.' Rafael made some humorous mock-helpless gestures as his wife dragged him away.

A blank-faced girl in a brass-buttoned white jacket glided to Alice's side with a bottle, its neck wrapped in white linen. Alice watched the fizzing golden liquid pouring into her glass and took one of the complex-looking canapés from the passing tray of another white-liveried flunkey. 'Miniature omelette Arnold Bennet, made with quail's egg,' this second flunkey intoned in an East European accent as expressionless as her face.

Alice felt a pang of sympathy for her. She was probably a brain surgeon in Poland.

Something low and pounding murmured on an invisible music system somewhere. There were, Alice observed, no pictures on the wall; all decoration in the kitchen was supplied – somewhat improbably, given the predominance of stark metal – by a vast and intricate glass chandelier whose multiple coiling arms were tipped with coloured glass flowers. It should have been hideous, Alice thought as she looked up at the great writhing, knotted, coloured glass ball. Overblown as it was – and as it were, being blown glass – it worked.

'Don't you love it?' Suki trilled from behind her. 'It's Murano glass. Rafa and I picked it up in Venice when he whisked me off to the Cipriani last month as a pre-birthday treat.'

Before Suki realised that materialism didn't make her happy, presumably, Alice thought wryly, noticing the sparkle in her friend's eyes. Personally, she could hardly imagine the fabulousness of David whisking her off to the Cipriani for a pre-birthday treat. He was too busy to whisk her anywhere at the moment, even for a walk on Hampstead Heath.

Chapter 6

The flunkeys were back again. 'Soya-marinated cube of ahi tuna and wasabi,' recited the Polish brain surgeon, proffering a tray of precisely arranged squares of something purplish-pink.

Alice took one, still looking around. She could not see a spot of dirt anywhere. Suki must have an army of cleaners.

'Alice!' Rafael exclaimed suddenly. Alice whirled to see her friend, arm clamped round a diminutive but determined-looking woman with a short dark bob. 'This is Caroline. Caro, meet Alice.'

Alice rather liked the look of Caroline. Her eyes were frank and friendly and had a magenta-jewelled bindi between them. Her handshake was firm and businesslike, even if her hand was decorated up to the elbow with henna tattoos.

'Alice works in art. Alice, Caro's a documentary superstar. Works for the BBC. You must have seen that incredible series she did about gang culture. Earned a fistful of awards.'

'Enough already, Rafa!' Caroline protested, laughing.

'You work in art?' A man had joined them and was looking straight at Alice. He wore a peacock-blue silk coat and pink silk turban, and looked remarkably at home in them. Alice sized him up. He was handsome in a smooth way, slightly tanned, wealthy-looking. The hair that could be seen beneath the turban was fair, and he had a slight foreign accent and vaguely formal air. Russian? she wondered. She hadn't met him before; he must be one of

Rafael and Suki's smart new friends. To go with their smart new house.

Rafael had swooped back, throwing out a signet-ringed hand on the end of a gold-brocade arm to introduce the man in blue and his very thin, fair-haired wife. 'Alice, Caro, let me introduce you to Nikolai and Elena. They live a few doors down from us.'

'Elena,' Suki added, swooping past, 'has been to the University of Life too. We went together, in fact. She's developing a range of low-additive, low-calorie, hand-cast, vegetable-flavoured children's ice lollies.'

Caroline's eyes, Alice saw, were dancing with amusement. Alice wanted to smile back but instead politely concentrated on shaking Elena's limp, chilly wrist.

'You are an artist?' Nikolai repeated to Alice. He seemed entirely uninterested in Caroline.

'No, I work in an art gallery.'

'How fascinating,' Nikolai replied with scrupulous politeness. There was, Alice thought, something very focused about him, those light, intent eyes, the clipped voice. 'I'm very interested in art,' he added, rather unexpectedly.

'Are you?' Alice asked, relieved. If he was Russian, they would have a lot to talk about. Palladio had recently bought some rather charming nineteenth-century views of St Basil's Cathedral from another of Adam's recently deceased former schoolmates, 'an old Moscow hand', as Adam described him.

'Yes,' Nikolai explained in his rather flat voice. 'I have a weekend house in Suffolk near the celebrated contemporary artist Zeb Spaw.'

Spaw again. Alice's heart sank. Was anyone in London talking about anything else?

'His house is near a village called Aldeham. Very charming. The village is very desirable. Our house,' Nikolai concluded proudly, 'has doubled in value since we bought it, which is very satisfactory.'

'Um, great,' Alice said.

'Spaw's house is quite marvellous,' Nikolai continued in his heel-clickingly formal way. 'A handsome Queen Anne residence worth at least eight million. He has made a fortune. A fortune.' He shook his head admiringly.

'But his art's not all that good, is it?' Alice put in, irked by this wholesale admiration merely for someone's money.

Nikolai looked at her strangely, as if trying and failing to work out what she could possibly mean by such a remark. He seemed to decide, in the end, to ignore it. 'Spaw also has an interest in performance cars, and is often to be seen putting them through their paces in the country lanes surrounding the village.'

'He does *what*?' Alice exclaimed. 'He drives sports cars round a country village?'

'Indeed.' Nikolai nodded eagerly, and his glassy eyes sparkled. 'Some of the cars reach speeds of up to one hundred miles per hour!'

Alice shook her head. Clearly Zeb Spaw's dreadful artwork was only the start of his failings. He sounded like an utter philistine.

'You know Spaw, of course?' Nikolai was watching her closely, blinking and twitching. 'You deal in his art?'

'No, thank goodness,' Alice said feelingly.

Nikolai looked taken aback. 'But why thank goodness? Surely, with prices of twenty million, he is an art dealer's dream?'

Alice explained about the auction cutting out the gallery. Nikolai shrugged. 'It's a free market.'

'For that sort of art, yes,' Alice said hotly. 'But the problem is that that kind of thing gets all the attention and the money and nothing else gets a look-in. No one's interested in any other type of art.'

Nikolai's pale eyes were unsympathetic. 'Market forces,' he said. 'What sort of art does your gallery sell?'

'Eighteenth to mid twentieth century.' Alice suddenly remembered Adam explaining, at her interview, that even though he had opened Palladio in 1969, nothing later than the 1950s was permitted on the walls. She was about to add this, fiercely, to Nikolai, but then thought better of it.

'And it doesn't sell?' Nikolai's smile was pitying.

'Not as well as it might if . . .' Alice hesitated on the brink of another outburst against Zeb Spaw and his ilk, but managed to stop herself. She seemed to have spent most of the day engaged in such outbursts.

Nikolai's eyes remained on her. His expression was now curious. 'So why not sell what sells? You have heard the expression, if you can't beat them join them, no?'

'Yes, of course,' Alice said tensely. 'But I don't want to join them. I think what they do is rubbish. I think—'

Perhaps fortunately, she was interrupted by Rafael bouncing up. 'Isn't Alice heaven?' he exclaimed to Nikolai. 'She's the only person I know who works in the art world and doesn't make a fortune. She does it for love, don't you, darling?' he added, as he swept off again.

Nikolai looked astonished. 'For *love*?' he echoed, as if this confirmed his worst fears. Giving Alice one final, doubtful glance, he moved off too.

Caroline, who had wandered away to join another group, now floated back. 'As I meant to say before we were, um, *interrupted* . . .' She cast a stern glance at Nikolai, now in the opposite corner with Suki exclaiming all over him. 'I'm researching a documentary about Britart,' she added in her warm, deep voice. 'About how sexy art is now, how London's the centre of it, all about the fame, the personalities, the incredible amounts of money, the fact that art's the new theatre, the social glue . . .'

'Well you're talking to the wrong person in that case,' Alice cut in. Although, she reflected, Palladio could definitely do with some glueing. As well as plastering, pointing, plumbing and completely repainting.

'Hey, steady on.' Caroline grinned. Her face, Alice thought, was not especially beautiful, not when compared to an acknowledged stunner like Suki, for example. But it was strong-featured, with intelligent eyes, and a long, straight nose which, with the wide mouth and tawny skin, gave it a Spanish air. 'I'm not suggesting I interview you. Your gallery's obviously . . .' she raised a considering eyebrow, 'different from the kind of place I'm concentrating on.'

Alice nodded. She felt vindicated, yet, she realised, slightly disappointed. A spot of TV coverage would do Palladio no harm at all.

'What I was about to say was that I might be able to help you,' Caroline said.

Alice started with surprise. 'Help in what way?' Her mind began to tumble. Was Caroline offering to inject some capital? Persuade the BBC to do some corporate art investment? Either would be fantastic.

'I've got lots of contacts in the art world.' The other woman smiled. 'If you ever wanted to move to a different sort of a gallery. One in Gold Street, say.'

'*Gold* Street?'

Caroline nodded. 'You'd learn a lot there, no matter what you thought about the art. They know how to sell, those people. Great experience.' She pressed Alice's arm encouragingly. 'I don't like to see a good woman held back, you see.'

Alice shook her head slightly. Held back? But Adam was going to hand the gallery over to her. Soon. Any day now, in fact. She just needed to push him harder on this point.

'I don't feel held back.' She raised her chin proudly. 'And I'm not sure Gold Street's my sort of place . . . Oh, excuse me . . .' she added in relief, as out of the corner of her eye she saw David appear – finally – in the sitting-room doorway.

'Sure,' Caroline said lightly, turning away to join the group with Rafael and Nikolai.

Alice, meanwhile, eagerness making her clumsy, plunged towards her boyfriend over all the feet in her way. 'Careful!' tsked Elena, fastidiously moving her silver heels out of danger.

Kissing David hello, Alice caught the familiar whiff of

antiseptic. She noticed his eyes dilate in alarm over her shoulder; turning, she saw Suki swooping and twittering about the dress code.

'Well, I *can* manage Arabian Nights, as it happens,' David said reluctantly, shrugging off the work bag on his shoulder, and pulling it open. From the very bottom he dragged out something white and scrunched-up and shook it out. 'If I button it to the top and put the collar up like this, I'll pass for a wife-murdering sultan anywhere.' He gave Suki a malicious grin.

'Your doctor's coat?' Suki sounded doubtful.

'Well we don't really wear these any more. It's probably been in here years.' David was shrugging it on.

Looking at him, Alice felt a pang of lust. David, thanks to his thick black hair and intensely dark colouring, always looked so handsome in his white doctor's coat. He looked good in his green scrubs too, come to that. He looked good in anything. Even with a slight shadow round his chin, revealing that he had not had time to shave. Of course, Alice thought proudly; he had had more important things to do.

'I hope there's nothing nasty on it.' Suki was shuddering.

'Probably. But hopefully nothing lethal,' David remarked airily. Alice wanted to shriek with laughter at Suki's horrified expression.

'Personally I don't know how Rafael stands it,' David said later, as they lay in bed, in the orange glow that was the nearest London got to darkness and with the thump of Mrs Nutt's TV from below. 'Suki's insane. She spent ages telling me about that University of bloody Life she's been exploring her hidden shallows in. I told her, if she wanted a sense of perspective, she should have told me. There's way too much bloody perspective at my hospital.'

Half beneath the duvet, Alice nodded. It was true that it had not been the best of evenings. All anyone seemed to want to talk about was Zeb Spaw; amazement that she worked in, that *anyone* worked in, any branch of art other than the headline-grabbing contemporary seemed universal. This depressing fact had sent her ever deeper into the champagne bottle, and now she felt drunk as well as depressed, and with the beginnings of a migraine. She should, she knew, get out of bed and drink two pints of water, but the effort felt so enormous, the undoubted hangover that would follow in the morning seemed mild in comparison. Tomorrow was another day.

'She's developing knitwear with some sheep sanctuary in Wensleydale.' David shook his head. 'She'll be opening a bloody cheese sanctary next.'

Alice groaned in reply.

There was a sharp beep from the sitting room. Alice stirred, vaguely recognising the sound. 'Text?' she muttered.

David was already on it, bounding out of the room. It seemed to Alice a long time before he was back, but in the gloopy, underwater world of inebriation, perspective could appear oddly stretched.

'Who was it?' she murmured.

'Work.'

'Everything all right?' She poked her head from out of the duvet, anxiously scanning his face. There were, she knew, one or two young patients he was particularly worried about at the moment.

She was rewarded with a melting smile. 'Fine,' he said, his eyes glowing as he looked at her.

Chapter 7

While not as bad as she had anticipated, Alice's hangover was, however, bad enough. Bad enough to prevent her getting out of bed in time for work. Lying against her pillows, gingerly sipping Alka-Seltzer, she remembered with vague relief that Adam was away at a country house sale today and would not be aware if she arrived at the gallery late. Adam's most pronounced virtue as a boss – besides his belief in absolute artistic standards and steadfast principles of art and democracy – was that he was not the clock-watching type. Or watch-watching type, for that matter; he did not even wear one.

David, whose head for drink was somewhat harder, was predictably unsympathetic. 'It's all self-inflicted!' he chortled as he left.

'That's precisely what's so awful about it,' Alice murmured, turning her hot head on the pillow, trying to find a cool spot and glad for once that Mrs Nutt's filthy windows restricted the light. The fact that, given the state of the panes, she could actually tell it was a sunny day gave an indication of just how sunny it must be.

It was mid-morning and even hotter than she had imagined when Alice reeled past the head-splitting road-drilling that seemed always to be going on in the vicinity of Palladio. She was holding her breath in an attempt not to inhale the stomach-churning scent of toasting cheese which flooded from the entrance of Bella Umbria.

After a worse-than-usual struggle with the lock, she was desperate to release her bursting lungs, but the door, as it shook and rattled open, stuck on the pile of junk mail that had dropped the other side. But finally the door was free and Alice scuttled gratefully into the cool darkness, inhaling the dusty air in great gulps, which made her cough. Deciding to leave the opening of the shutters until such a time as her stomach had calmed down again, she went to the back kitchen, fishing out another sachet of Alka-Seltzer as she went.

Bang!

She stopped, mid step, and looked up at the cracked and dusty ceiling.

Bang!

What was that? It was coming from Adam's empty office.

In the deafening silence that followed, Alice became horribly aware of how absolutely alone in the gallery she was. It was dark, it was quiet; even the road drill in the street outside seemed suddenly miles away.

The urge to run away consumed her. She felt vulnerable and ill, as well as fearful. She tiptoed swiftly from the back kitchen to the front door. Better leave. Now. And once outside, call the police.

But with her hand on the latch, she paused. Would the police come? And by the time they arrived, might not the intruder – always presuming he was an art thief – be long gone? With the best of the shop's stock.

Alice glanced back into the gallery. The faces in the paintings hanging from the chains on the walls gazed at her appealingly out of the shadows. *Save us*, they seemed to say. *You are our only protector*.

She put both hands to her burning forehead and groaned. Why now? Why today? A break-in would be fine any other day of the week. Just not today, when she felt as awful as self-infliction could make one feel. Not now, when all her courage, resilience and strength were needed just to keep her upright and prevent her being sick.

Reluctantly, she retraced her footsteps across the gritty wooden floor and moved resolutely towards the bottom of the steps. She could hear nothing at all now, especially as the road drillers had stopped for one of their frequent breaks. Perhaps, she allowed herself to think, something had just fallen off a table in that crowded clutterhole of an office. Yes, surely that was it.

Bang!

The sudden impact made her heart leap painfully, followed by a hot rush of fear.

Morbid fantasies crowded her fragile and throbbing brain. Who was up there? An aggressive crack addict? A murderer with a knife? Would anyone hear her if she screamed?

She looked longingly at the front door of the gallery. The drilling had started again, and the thought of outside's pressing heat and toasted cheese stink made her wilt. It might be scary in here, but it was also dark and cool. It didn't smell wonderful, admittedly; a Diptyque candle or two would not have gone amiss. But at least the smell was only dusty, not Dolcelatte.

She took a number of deep breaths and willed herself to calm down. The something-fallen-off explanation had started to gain the upper hand again when a scrabble began above. There was no doubt that this hinted at something more animate. But surely just that: an animal. A rat, possibly, or one of London's millions of ragged pigeons, come in down the chimney.

David, Alice knew, would not have hesitated. As a doctor, he faced difficult situations every day of his life. Surely, she berated herself, it was not beyond her merely to walk up a flight of stairs?

She put a hand firmly on the banister. Not too firm, however; the fitting was far from secure and might fall off altogether if someone really grasped it hard. Slowly she hauled herself up the dusty wooden staircase to Adam's office. Visions of blood-soaked murderers jabbed before her eyes as, having gained the small landing, she took a painfully deep breath, put a trembling hand on the loose and rattly door handle, turned it, swallowed and pushed it open.

No wild-eyed figure waving a knife greeted her after all. Her hysterical gaze rested on her employer, flat on his back, his spectacles even more wildly askew than usual and his collar undone, rolling around on the floor like a beetle unable to right itself.

'*Adam!*'

Her initial fear that he was hurt evaporated as he caught her eye and gave her a delighted grin. 'Oh, it's you, Beatrix. How awfully nice to see you.' It was as if they were meeting at a garden party.

'Are you, um, all right?'

'Fine,' Adam said, against all evidence to the contrary. Cheerfully he scrambled to a sitting position.

She could see that he was wearing the same clothes as yesterday. Of course, he always wore the same jacket and trousers, but the shirt and tie were usually clean. Or cleanish. But the grubby and crumpled graph-paper shirt before her, Alice could see, had not been donned fresh this morning.

He had spent the night on his office floor, she realised. The sounds she had just heard from below were those of someone waking up in an unexpected place and thrashing clumsily around, trying to work out where they were.

She noticed that Adam's face, normally creased and yellowish, was a brilliant shining red. Then she spotted the empty Gordon's bottle he was endeavouring to hide by clamping it under his arm.

'Are you drunk, Adam?' Alice asked quietly, trying not to concentrate on the irony of one in her condition asking such a question.

He had managed to lurch to his feet now and was whistling hard and tunelessly, frantically shuffling some papers on his desk as if the circumstances were the most natural in the world.

'Not at all, not at all,' he said.

There was a crash as the papers slapped to the floor, followed by the telephone.

'Although,' he added, flicking her a doleful, apologetic look, 'there's a distinct possibility that I was some hours ago.'

'Why?' Alice asked, as he fumblingly picked up the telephone with its dangling cords. She was puzzled as well as shocked by this departure from the norm. Adam had never been a drinker, in her experience. Although now she came to think of it, there had been occasions very recently when he had left the gallery just before lunch and returned late in the afternoon without any particular explanation. Had he, she now wondered, been to the pub? There were many in the vicinity; not all of them gastropubs with sawdust floors, reclaimed furniture and Latin background music. Some were still actual Edwardian boozers, their outsides all opaque glass, tiles and hanging baskets, places where people like Adam could disappear into the sticky-carpeted interior and pass a lost afternoon very easily.

Standing amid the rubbish-piled middle of the room, Adam met her stare. His eyes, bloodshot, slightly rheumy, wavered, then steadied. He sighed hugely, almost visibly inflating with the effort, his spine straightening and stiffening. Then, as he let the air out, he seemed to crumple before her. His shoulders sloped sideways, his spine curved, he withered away before her. It was, Alice suddenly thought, like looking at the dried, crumbling, yellowing husk of something that had once been vibrant, colourful and alive.

'Because there isn't any point,' he said. All the friendliness and apology had gone from his voice. He spoke clearly and slowly, and with a dreadful tone of finality.

'What do you mean?' Alice squeaked, standing before him with her fists clenched. She felt more genuinely fearful now than she had been even before climbing the stairs. 'What do you mean, there isn't any point? No point in what?'

They faced each other across a few feet of dusty floorboard. His eyes remained on hers, flat, steady. 'In trying to run a gallery,' he said in the same ghastly monotone. 'No one wants the stuff we sell.'

Surprise and annoyance had momentarily driven Alice's hangover from her mind. Now, however, it came rushing back, with redoubled and painful force. She winced, and shaded her eyes. It was only for a matter of seconds that she looked at the dusty floor, during which time, at lightning speed, a great many impressions raced through her head.

The feeling that she had, for all her protestations, taken a terrible wrong direction in life seized her with terrible force. She and Adam had been united against an encroaching world of awful art, but now, it seemed, she stood alone. He was a drunk under whose retrogressive hold a business and a career – *her* career – were dying. It seemed a watershed moment, or perhaps a gin-shed one.

'Why bother?' came Adam's mournful voice. He sounded utterly defeated. 'Why bother when someone can sell five gold false legs for twenty million pounds?'

The thought of Zeb Spaw caught Alice's downward thoughts. They swung, stabilised, then started to reverse upwards. Was Adam saying – was he *really* saying – that he was prepared to abandon a lifetime of artistic endeavour because of five plastic legs on a washing line? It was unbelievable. Yet as he was speaking with obvious conviction, it was also true. Which meant, she decided suddenly, grimly, that it had to be fought.

'No point crying about it,' Adam observed wearily. Alice realised he had mistaken her downcast mien for tears.

'I'm not crying,' she said fiercely, jerking her chin up. 'I was just thinking. You can't give up now, Adam.' She stared steadfastly into his wavering eyes. 'If Palladio goes—'

'What does it matter if Palladio goes?' he burst in, passionately. Alice stared, amazed; her boss, always scrupulously polite, had never interrupted her before, ever. This more than anything revealed how extremely upset he was.

'It matters very much.' She forced her voice not to shake. 'We sell great work. Wonderful pieces.' Then, as this had not caused Adam's expression to alter in the least, she added, more nervously, 'And it matters because there's hardly anywhere in London where people can afford a piece of proper art, for a start.'

She did not add that it mattered particularly to her because her future as a gallerist hung in the balance. If Palladio closed, what, exactly, would she do?

What would Adam do, come to that? She pictured him alone, in some brown mansion flat – interesting: after all this time together, she had no real idea where he lived – drinking cold tea from a dirty mug and thinking about his lost gallery. No. It could not be. She could not allow it to happen. She went to seize his hands, impulsively, and then thought better of it. One did not seize Adam impulsively; he was not, for all his gentleness and sixties idealism, that sort of person. She might have found him drunk on the floor five minutes ago, but he had regained his dignity and distance in an amazingly short space of time.

'You can't give up now,' she said urgently, aware that she was repeating herself. As Adam's haunted eyes seemed to beg to differ, she cast around desperately for reasons to support her contention. 'And especially you can't give up because of *Prostheseus Bound*.'

An expression of puzzlement rippled across Adam's creased and despairing features. 'Prometheus what?'

'*Prostheseus Bound*,' Alice corrected. 'It's what the artificial legs were called.'

'That – that – was called . . . *Prostheseus Bound*?' Adam's voice was trembling, but there was more fire in it, Alice noticed. More heat. More life than the awful dead flatness of before.

Her hopes began to rise. He was angry . . . could she make him angrier? She racked her brains to remember what that slippery-sounding auctioneer on the radio had said about it. Surprisingly, given her depleted physical state, she found she was able to recall it in word-perfect detail.

'Referring to the prosthetic limbs round which the work is

centred. A title that, while acknowledging the classical heritage of contemporary art, is nonetheless unafraid to have a little fun with it,' she recited.

As he listened, Adam's eyes seemed to change shape. They contracted, grew rounder and more protuberant. 'Is that really true?' he said slowly, his tone cracking with incredulity. 'I couldn't bear to read the full report in the newspaper. But is that really what the artist said about it? That five gold false legs were somehow . . . classical?'

Alice nodded. 'It's what the auctioneer who sold it said about it on the radio the other day.'

Adam's face now purpled with emotion. She had never before suspected the rainbow of colours it was capable of. He looked down; his balding head was purple too. 'Monstrosity . . . slur on art . . . outrageous,' she heard him mutter. His voice gurgled with anger, like a volcano about to explode.

'So you see, you can't give up now,' she prodded gently, sensing she had the advantage.

Adam flung his head up. His eyes burned, his nostrils flared wide; you could, Alice thought, almost see the steam coming out of them. She had never seen her mild, courteous boss so angry. She watched as he walked over to the table and banged on it. A cloud of dust flew up.

'By God,' he stormed. 'You're right. I will never give up. While people like Zeb Spaw walk the earth, I will *never* give up.'

Alice let out a long, low sigh of relief. Thank goodness. Execution seemed, for the moment at least, stayed. She still had a job.

Yet any hope that the morning's dramas might curtail Adam's secret visits to places of refreshment were dashed by the sound, at one on the dot, of the shop bell jangling and the door swinging shut, and the sight of a pair of battered cord trousers heading up the street at speed.

Chapter 8

The fizzing sound of a lark, faint but unmistakable, drifted to Dan as he cycled slowly along the deep and ancient lane. He thought immediately of Vaughan Williams, whose *Lark Ascending* had been playing on Radio 3 when he left the cottage.

He closed his eyes for a few seconds as he cycled along, recalling the climbing notes of the violin. Many people regarded the piece as being too popular to be a work of genius, but Dan loved it. He loved most classical music. He was an artist, but while his own skill was in his pen and his brush, he never worked alone. Radio 3 was his constant companion.

He opened his eyes to see that he had just emerged from the cool shadow of a clump of oaks. He stared, amazed, at the sunlit fields, blazing yellow with dandelions, as if some huge and unseen hand had scattered yellow paint powder on the grass. After many days of hot weather, there had been rain the night before, which had brought a freshness to the air, and the impression that everything was washed and sparkling.

Dan pedalled happily along, at peace, exulting in the magnificence of nature and feeling his appropriate tiny significance amid the infinitely old Suffolk landscape. His eyes now took over from his ears. Looking up at the sky, he felt he had never seen so many blues in it before. And they changed all the time: now, for instance, the teal blue of the centre faded to pearlised violet at the edges. In autumn, he knew, there would be purple and orange sunsets, and in winter, skies anywhere from palest duck-egg to deepest rose.

And the greens! The countryside round here, curving, intimate and tufty, was green in so many different ways. The summer fields were a bright, rich green against which the black and white cattle showed particularly well. The gorse that edged the fields was a deep, blackish green that was the perfect foil for the blaze of yolk-yellow flowers it produced in the late spring. This landscape was, Dan thought happily, an artist's paradise, even if one was a portrait painter like himself, specialising in people rather than views.

At the sound of something very powerful and fast rounding the corner behind him, Dan scrambled hurriedly down from his bicycle and pressed hard into the hedge. Just in time: the shiny red Lotus, filling the lane, shot by with an expensive roar. But not before its fat front tyres had ripped through the puddles and splattered Dan from head to foot with thick black mud.

There was, of course, no doubt as to who the driver was. Zeb Spaw, *enfant terrible* of contemporary art, obviously returning to his magnificent Queen Anne mansion after a roar round the surrounding countryside in one of his many performance cars.

Dan looked hotly after the vehicle, reflecting not for the first time about his own hapless choice of village. He had left London to escape high rents and a high-pressure London art scene increasingly skewed to lionising ever more ludicrous contemporary artists. He had hoped to paint cheaply and in peace in the countryside, only to discover that the artist epitomising everything he most disliked owned an estate just down the road.

'Wanker!' he yelled after the departing scarlet beast, shaking his fist while being depressingly aware that he could not be heard or even seen. The red top of the car was now five fields away and moving rapidly out of sight.

'That's the spirit,' said a voice from behind him, and Dan, who had removed his glasses to wipe off the spatters of mud, hurriedly replaced them. He found himself looking at a familiar figure wearing a broad-brimmed black hat over long grey hair. Roger Pryap. A student in the weekly life-drawing class Dan ran for the local authority's further education programme in order to supplement his meagre income as a painter.

'I'd like to run that bastard Spaw over with his own bloody car,' Roger Pryap remarked violently. 'And then I'd peel him up from the bloody road and enter his corpse for the bloody Turner Prize.'

Dan grinned. 'Hello, Roger.'

Roger Pryap, however, was in no mood for polite salutation. His mind was still churning angrily on the subject of Spaw. He pushed up his hat brim and glared at Dan. 'You heard that he just sold some work at auction for twenty million quid?'

Dan hadn't heard. It was facts like these that he had come to the country to escape. He gasped. '*Twenty million?*' It was hard to compute such figures, even when the work in question was an acknowledged great; a Picasso, say, or a Raphael. But a *Zeb Spaw*? 'What was it?'

'Five false legs attached to a washing line,' Roger snarled.

The sun chose this exact moment to slip behind a cloud and the bright countryside around Dan darkened. 'Five false legs . . . ?' He shook his head. It would be unbelievable, except that it was only too believable.

'Sprayed gold,' Roger added sardonically.

Dan looked down at his trousers. Sprayed with mud, he thought, and by the same great artist. Did that make them a work of art too? Of course it did; who was to say it didn't? Worse still, *Muddy Trousers*, created in a nanosecond, and its companion piece *Muddy Bike Seat* would be worth far more than anything he could produce himself, painstakingly, lovingly, over several months.

It was so unfair.

'Out for a walk, Roger?' he enquired of the other man, wanting to change the subject.

Roger looked triumphant. 'Bit of sketching, actually. Like you said.'

Watching him produce a small pad from beneath the flap of

his shirt, Dan remembered that he had, indeed, during the last life class, recommended that his students went out and drew from nature. He had not expected Roger to take him up on it, Roger's interest being specifically in the human form. Perhaps too specifically.

'Very good, Roger,' he said brightly, examining the sketches. Roger had evidently spent a considerable part of the morning roaming the local countryside. The results were surprising. The surrounding land was low-level and rolling, but Roger had exaggerated and extended any upward feature to achieve a series of swelling hills looking remarkably like bottoms and breasts; adding strategically placed cairns to the latter for good measure.

'A very individual interpretation, if I may say so,' Dan remarked, handing the notebook back and wondering whether he would ever look at the local beauty spots in quite the same way again.

When interviewing life models, Dan had always been at pains to stress that the atmosphere in his classes was pure and respectful. Improper thoughts, he had assured them, never entered the heads of the art students, who saw the models before them not as naked women, but as forms; as light, shape and shadow, pure and simple. This certainly had been the case throughout his own training at the Royal Academy Schools. The life classes he ran at Aldeham village hall were a different matter; at least since Roger had arrived. His enthusiasm for art, Dan suspected, was at least equalled by his enthusiasm for seeing bare breasts on a weekly basis only yards from his own front door.

It was precisely this situation that had prompted two models to resign their posts in quick succession. Before Zeb Spaw had struck with his Lotus, Dan had been on his way to interview a third as their replacement. Now, splattered as he was from head to toe in mud, he would have to go home and change. Defiantly, he wiped the mud off the seat crossly with a scrunched tissue, not caring if he was wiping away his pension plan.

Chapter 9

Behind the electric double gates guarding the mile-long tree-lined drive leading to Blackwood Park, Zeb Spaw was in a scarcely better temper.

'Whaddya mean, Bigsky wouldn't go the full four mill?' he snarled into the phone. 'I thought these oligarchs were made of money.'

He tossed his long black hair angrily as he spoke, wincing behind his wraparound blue sunglasses as a wave of pain coursed through his head. The spin round the lanes in his newest Lotus, intended to shake off the hangover from the night before, seemed only to have made it worse. And what his dealer and representative Cornelius Sump, of the Sump Gallery of Gold Street, London, was saying was not making him feel much better.

Spaw's butler, Toombs, stood nervously nearby, clutching the silver tray on which he had brought the mobile and a glass of hair-of-the-dog Ruinart champagne. Zeb snatched it from the tray and downed it in one.

'After *Prostheseus Bound* went for twenty mill,' he fulminated, 'you'd think Bigsky would be less of a tight-fisted git.'

At the London end of the telephone, Sump, natty in his grey cashmere checked suit behind his flat white desk, drummed his brown, sockless feet in their Gucci loafers on the gallery's wooden floor. He did not relish his client reminding him that his most expensive work had been sold through an auction house and not the gallery representing him. But when he had raised this with Spaw, he had been told in no uncertain terms that Damien Hirst had had an auction sale, and that anything Hirst could do, Spaw would outdo.

'Bigsky offered three point five mill for *The Right Hand of the Father*,' Sump explained. 'I thought that was reasonable. You've got to remember that even oligarchs aren't as rich as they were.'

'Reasonable!' exploded Spaw, his handsome face dark with anger. Agitatedly he raked a tanned hand through his shoulder-length black hair and shot a contemptuous glance through his shades at the painted ceiling featuring Helios driving the sun chariot across the sky. On buying the house, he had planned to paint the neoclassical Robert Adam hall entirely in black, ceiling and all. But English Heritage had come down like the ton of Grade One-listed bricks they pointed out that Blackwood was. In vain had Zeb argued that time was up on all that eighteenth-century crap and people like him were the artistic future.

'I wanted four mill at least,' he raged petulantly to Sump. 'Doesn't this tosser realise he's buying a piece of art history?'

From his position right at the back of the gallery, Sump adjusted his lenseless red Prada frames and gazed at the piece in question, an NHS regulation wheelchair which had been sprayed gold and was now occupying the front window in solitary splendour.

He was not asking himself whether *The Right Hand of the Father* was worth four million pounds. Or whether Zeb was as important an artist as he claimed to be. Only time would tell on those points. All that mattered now was what anyone was prepared to pay for them.

And on the question of whether he could have driven the oligarch collector any higher, Sump knew the answer was no. 'Three point five was his limit,' he averred.

'You're fucking joking!' Zeb yelled, stomping his trainers

on the hall's black and white marble floor – the floor he had originally planned to cover with red rubber. Frustratingly, they made no sound whatsoever. 'And what about the bed?' he demanded as he strode angrily yet silently about. 'Did you show that to Bigsky?'

'I did,' Sump admitted. 'But he wasn't keen.'

'*Not keen!*' Zeb raged. 'He's been given the opportunity to make the art purchase of a lifetime, and he's . . .' He paused before echoing sardonically, '*Not keen?*'

'That's right.'

'*Why* wasn't he bloody keen?' Zeb pressed, his outraged ego demanding an explanation.

'I'm not sure.'

'Yes you are,' Spaw snarled. 'So bloody tell me.'

Sump sighed. 'You might not like it.'

'Look, I can handle criticism, OK?'

There was a doubtful silence from the Sump end.

'I'm waiting,' Zeb said testily.

'OK. He said the bed was too much like the wheelchair.'

'Like the wheelchair?' Zeb exploded. 'It's *nothing* like the fucking wheelchair.'

'It's possible that there are *some* similarities,' the gallery owner pointed out delicately. '*The Right Hand of the Father* is an NHS wheelchair sprayed gold. *The Right Hand of the Father II* is an NHS hospital bed on wheels sprayed gold.'

'Well so what?' Zeb snapped. 'What's wrong with similarity? Monet painted that bloody cathedral in Rouen millions of times.' He sensed Sump was holding something back and was determined to know what it was.

Sump sighed, then let go. 'Bigsky also said the gold bed was like a blinged-up Tracey Emin: not very original and a bit passé.'

In the hallway of Blackwood Park, Zeb reeled across the chequerboard marble floor. His breath came hot and rapid from his distended nostrils and his brain felt about to explode.

'You can't be serious,' he roared.

'Look, it's just the one guy, all right?' Sump assured him. 'And he's wrong, of course he is—'

'Wrong!' Zeb screamed. '*Wrong!* You bet he bloody is. He's so wrong he's almost right.'

'Look, he's Russian, OK? What do Russians know about culture?'

Something about that sentence did not sound quite right to Zeb, as names like Chagall, Tolstoy and Tchaikovsky galloped briefly across his memory. But he was disinclined to think deeply about it; about anything, in fact, but his own pounding rage.

'A work of mine's just gone for twenty million at auction,' he roared. 'What's fucking passé about that?'

'Nothing,' Sump assured him, choosing not to revisit his own personal ire about the matter; choosing, too, not to reveal to his client that the extortionate sum achieved for *Prostheseus Bound* had been seen in certain quarters as proof of the beginning of the end for its artist. As the tipping point. Zeb Spaw, people were saying, had got as big as he was going to get, and it was all downhill from here. There had even been suggestions that, far from being the trailblazer of before, he was now behind the times; that gold-sprayed limbs and hospital beds were more than a bit ten minutes ago.

Sump had naturally refuted such claims – and they were as yet only whispers – whenever he had heard them. The Cornelius Sump Gallery, after all, stood to lose if Zeb's market price dipped. But the possibility of Spaw being taken down a peg or two undoubtedly added a touch of sugar to the bitter prospect of reduced profits.

'What sort of a dealer are you anyway?' Spaw was ranting in his ear. 'Letting people say that about my work – *my art*. God knows why I stay with you.'

Sump had heard this before, as had most other galleries in Gold Street. Zeb Spaw was famous for his defections. That he had walked out on every gallery who had ever represented him had always been officially ascribed to differences of artistic viewpoint.

But no one in Gold Street was under any illusion that money wasn't the main factor. Spaw was famously greedy.

Sump, all the same, did not intend to let Zeb leave *him*. He was arrogant, grasping and ungrateful, but so were all the other artists Sump represented. And at least, unlike the others, Spaw was prestigious, famous and sold. Whatever people were saying – and it was only a whisper. The most pathetic, inaudible whisper, Sump reminded himself, when compared to the great shout of twenty million pounds. Even if it wasn't a twenty million he would be seeing any cut of.

'Just wait and see what we've got lined up for the street party,' he soothed. 'Ours is going to be the best bash on the block. Everyone who's anyone will be there, and you, as the featured artist, will get all the attention.'

It was a tradition that the most famous artist represented by each gallery was given the window during Gold Street's celebrated annual street party, an occasion when, as celebrities rubbed shoulders and the international press and art media looked on, each establishment pulled out all the stops to outdo the others.

'Obviously it goes without saying that you'll have the entire front window at Sump—' Cornelius promised.

'Yeah, yeah,' Spaw interrupted rudely, yawning.

'And of course we'll be putting your hottest and newest work in there—'

'*Sponge*.'

'*Sponge?*' Sump repeated.

There was, Zeb detected, a grain of disappointment in the dealer's voice. Indignation surged once again within him. '*Sponge*, yeah,' he snapped defensively.

There was a silence from the dealer's end.

'Does *Sponge*,' Sump asked carefully, after some seconds had elapsed, 'involve, by any chance, video?'

'No.'

'Mmm. I see.' Sump cleared his throat. 'It's just that . . .' he began, then stopped.

'Just what?' growled Zeb.

Sump took a deep breath. 'Just that I was wondering whether video shouldn't be your next move, Zeb. Installations. You haven't, um, expressed yourself that way yet.'

'I don't do video installations,' came the uncompromising reply.

'Sure, sure,' Sump soothed.

'I don't know why you're even mentioning them.'

'Well, because everyone's doing video now. Full-on films, even. McQueen, Taylor-Wood, those guys.'

'Sam Taylor-Wood is not a guy,' Zeb pointed out irritably.

'You don't want to get left behind,' Sump warned.

A freezing silence greeted him. Then a drawing-in-of-breath sound, like the sea receding before a particularly violent wave crashed on the shore.

'Left behind? *Left behind?*' Zeb's voice was hitting counter-tenor levels of indignation.

'Or maybe found objects?' Sump went on, deciding he might as well be hung for a sheep as for a lamb. 'That's pretty hot now as well. Stuff you find in the street. Army greatcoats, tissue boxes, whatever. You arrange it to make a statement.'

'I'll give you a statement,' Zeb roared. 'I'm not a bloody tramp. I don't pick things up from the street. *Fuck off.*'

'OK. OK,' Sump said hurriedly. He had gone too far. Now he sought to claw some ground back. 'So – great. *Sponge*, fabulous. So how's it going?'

'Fine,' Spaw said, looking angrily round for Toombs. He needed another glass of champagne. Where was the lazy bastard?

'When can I see it?' Sump pressed.

'When I'm good and ready,' Spaw snapped, his bad mood back with a vengeance. 'You get on with selling what you bloody well have. Four million for that wheelchair or I'm crossing the road to OneSquared.'

'You wouldn't do that!' Sump exclaimed with such shock in his voice that the gallery assistant, Portia, a dim but amiable twenty-year-old currently gazing blankly out of the window, glanced at him in mild surprise.

'You watch me,' Spaw sneered.

'Hello? Zeb? Are you there?' Cornelius Sump realised that he was speaking into nothing. His star client had rung off.

Chapter 10

'So you think you'll be OK taking your clothes off?' Dan asked the young woman in an undertone as he poured her a cup of tea.

'Will I be OK taking my clothes off?' she repeated loudly, shaking her hair back over her plump shoulders. 'More than OK. Actually, I find nakedness empowering.'

Dan sensed, but did not see, this piece of positive reinforcement electrifying Mrs Mullock, the tea-shop proprietress and the only other person in the room. From her surveillance point at the back of the shop she was ostentatiously polishing the cake display cases and hanging on to every word. No doubt she was wondering what he was doing here with this skimpily dressed woman, all black eyeliner and black lace-up Dr Marten boots, and only a scrap of clingy black jersey dress to fill the space between. Some of Bo, admittedly, was covered up by slightly matted purple-dyed hair which ran like red wine stains over her shoulders. Much of her exposed plump and slightly yellow-tinged flesh was covered by various tattoos that Dan longed to stare at, but out of politeness didn't.

'I feel absolutely in control when I'm naked,' she stated in her decisive, fruity voice, stretching her arms in the air in a gesture that pushed her large yellow breasts forward. 'I feel very sexually powerful, as if I'm connected to feminine energies everywhere, and I find that a very rewarding experience.'

There was a crash from behind. Dan looked round to see Mrs

Mullock crossly picking up shattered pieces of cake stand. Nonetheless, he was glad to hear that Bo felt empowered naked. There were, after all, female-nakedness-disempowerment issues in the life class, and he had not yet brought them up.

'I guess it's because I'm pagan.' Bo nodded seriously.

'Pagan?' Dan echoed.

Bo seemed surprised he was surprised. 'Sure. I worship Gaia, the earth goddess. My tattoos,' she added, making a gesture down her body, 'represent the five elements: earth, fire, water, air and wind.'

Five elements? 'I didn't realise,' Dan said, 'that wind was a separate element.'

'Yeah,' Bo said carelessly. 'So I've got leaping flames on my tits, a cloud on one buttock, a ploughed field on the other and a waterfall going into my pubes.'

Another crash from Mrs Mullock's end of the shop.

Dan blinked. He had advertised the post in the local authority magazine, and on her application Bo had mentioned a job at the council planning department. He had been expecting a mousy bureaucrat, not a sexually empowered pagan with a pubic waterfall.

'I got really into paganism after I went to a workshop at a climate camp,' Bo was explaining, pulling her tart apart with black-painted fingernails and staring at it quizzically. Looking for the filling, Dan guessed. Mrs Mullock's meanness with icing, jam and buttercream was legendary in the village. It was rumoured that each rock cake contained an exact number of currants – three, Dan guessed. No wonder an increasing number of locals preferred the café at the nearby mega-Sainsbury's.

He would not be here himself, he knew, were it not for the fact that Ye Olde Village Tea Shoppe's unpopularity made it perfect for this afternoon's meeting. Taking Bo home was impossible; the cottage was tiny with just him and Birgit, his housemate, in it. And despite his efforts to clean up, it was always a mess.

He had considered taking Bo to the local pub. But her

unconventional appearance would only have sent yet more rumours round the village, and he and Birgit generated enough of those as it was. The degree of surveillance under which he had felt himself since moving to Aldeham seemingly increased all the time. Just stepping out of the cottage's tiny front door felt like walking on stage at the O_2. You couldn't see anyone watching, but you knew they were, and somehow that made it more intimidating.

He cleared his throat as he brought himself back into the present. There was of course something he needed to discuss with Bo. But would prior warning about Roger Pryap put her off? And if so, where would he find anyone else? Bo had been the only applicant for the post.

Nonetheless, he pressed on. 'There's something else I need to tell you,' he muttered, looking down at the fingers he was twisting about each other. 'About the classes.'

Bo looked him in the eye. 'Spill,' she commanded. Her frank pagan gaze terrified Dan. He felt his resolve waver, then disappear altogether. 'Er . . . do you like classical music?' he asked brightly. 'I, er, like to have it on in the background. For the, um, students to listen to. As they, er, work.'

After Bo – who was fine about classical music – had driven off in a markedly un-pagan Mini Cooper, Dan walked meditatively home along the village street. He hoped that he had done the right thing in engaging her without flagging up the real issues. On the other hand, he had the powerful impression that if anyone could cope with Roger, Bo could.

The way home from Mrs Mullock's tea shop went through the top end of the village, near the church. This was the end where the Aldeham wealthy lived; where, as it happened, Dan had recently been spending a considerable amount of time painting a portrait of Kevin Swift. Swift was a former four-wheel-drive concessionaire who had sold out just in time, made a fortune and now lived in splendid circumstances in the Dower House, the second biggest house in Aldeham.

Yet Swift's abundance of good fortune had, in Dan's view, done little to make him a likeable person. He was also exceptionally unpleasant to look at, with a fat red face whose broad and turned-up nose was irresistibly reminiscent of a pig's.

Dan reached the Dower House gates. These comprised a recently installed automatic monstrosity of gold and black iron wrought into pseudo-heraldic contortions which he suspected contravened planning regulations. The house behind it was a lovely Jacobean building in the local pretty golden stone, retaining as much grace and dignity as was possible given that Kevin Swift had seen fit to pick out the frames within the mullions in sage-green paint and placed bays trimmed in ball shapes in silver pots either side of his sage front door. The glaringly new brick drive hardly helped either.

Dan hurried past, not wanting to be seen either by Swift or his neurotic wife Toni, who looked like a frazzled bird and seemed to drink like a fish. Dan had never seen her without a glass of champagne in her over-manicured claw, no matter what the time of day.

Next to the Dower House was the vicarage, whose run-down, mossy appearance contrasted wildly with the newness next door. Dan had occasionally glimpsed the vicar: a bald man of downbeat appearance who looked as if, far from being certain of eternal salvation, he worried a lot. Next to the vicarage was the church, St Botolph's, pleasant sixteenth-century Perpendicular from the outside but inside, as Dan had found, restored by the Victorians to within an inch of its life. He never went past without wondering who St Botolph was and resolving to look him up, but somehow he never got round to it.

Aldeham Manor, next to the church, was the largest house in the village and had always been mysterious at the end of the tree-obscured drive behind its gates. In winter, when the leaves were gone, it was possible to glimpse, at some distance, a mullioned house built of honey stone with barley-sugar-twist chimneys and balls on top of the gables.

But Dan had not glimpsed this often. Not being a churchgoer, the ecclesiastical end of the village was not one he tended to frequent. Until the Swift commission had materialised, he had known no one there.

Nor had he been an especially regular pub-goer. While the Star Inn, across the green from the church, looked pretty enough from the outside, all thatch, brick-and-flint and tiny windows, it was cramped, messy and dark inside and therefore not all that different from his own cottage. In addition, the largely charmless landlord liked loud rock music; the last time Dan had been in he had nursed a pint to the strains of Rainbow's 'Since You Been Gone' at earsplitting volume on an endless loop that seemed to have got stuck somewhere in the mid 1970s. He had not been back since; the best beer in the world wasn't worth such a sacrifice, and the Star's was far from that.

Besides, some instinct had warned Dan against large gatherings of villagers, or becoming too close to the heart of local affairs, though from overheard conversations in the post office – Mrs Snitch being the busiest body in Aldeham – he had gathered that someone, although no one knew who, had recently bought the Manor and was having it done up.

Determinedly un-nosy though he was, Dan could not help pausing now as he passed the front of the Manor gates. They were open; vans were up the drive. It was possible, if one craned one's neck slightly, to peer round the bend in the drive, and see furniture being carried up the sweep of elegant front steps before the great ornamented, wide-open front door. Presumably the Manor was done up now, and the rich person was moving in.

As, some ten minutes later, Dan reached his own front door, he tried not to notice the weeds flourishing in profusion around the front step. It would be nice, admittedly, if Birgit would stir herself to clean up the place in which she lived entirely supported by him, but the thought had evidently never occurred to her. Birgit didn't do thinking, as such. Her cognitive processes seemed to consist of waves of impressions and impulses, the most recent eradicating all earlier ones.

She was wandering around the sitting room when Dan pushed open the door, singing along in her flat Dutch voice to some very loud jazz emanating from the CD player. She was also stark naked.

Chapter 11

'Hi,' called Dan, wincing at the din, as if this and the nakedness were the most normal thing in the world. Which, up to a point, they were. Wandering around unclothed to loud music, perilously near the open windows, was something Birgit did a lot in good weather. Just as well, Dan felt, they did not live in the centre of the village, but at its most unfashionable end, where the property was cheapest.

It was the cheapness of the property, rather than any romantic notions about rural life, that had brought Dan to the countryside. Realising he could no longer afford to live in London – not on what he was earning as a portrait painter anyway – he had chosen Aldeham entirely on the basis that it had a house he *could* afford to rent.

Milkmaid's Walk sounded picturesque but was in fact a run-down row of cottages at the end of the main street. It was at the opposite end of the village from the church, green, pub, rectory, Dower House and Manor. There was no one with money on Milkmaid's Walk. The four red-brick-and-flint cottages with their ridge-tiled roofs were home to himself and Birgit and an old lady with cats called Mrs Minchin who lived next door but one. In between them were Tadeusz and Stamina, a pair of Lithuanians who had recently moved in.

They were polite but distant; their English was not good enough to permit more than an awkward hello. Mrs Minchin, meanwhile, was much given to bursts of angry dialect delivered in a strong Suffolk accent which was less intelligible even than Lithuanian or Dutch. The result was that no one on Milkmaid's Walk could understand anything anyone else said. It was, Dan reflected, like living in the Tower of Babel. The fourth cottage was, in theory, a holiday cottage, although no one ever appeared to take holidays in it. As it was next door, Dan mourned the wasted space on a daily basis; how useful it would have been as a studio. As things were, however, he was forced to use his cottage's tiny second bedroom as a place to work. And the top of his easel with a canvas on almost touched the ceiling. The light, too, was restricted through the tiny windows, which was giving the more recent of his portraits a somewhat crepuscular look.

Birgit nodded her shaggy blond head in acknowledgment, waved happily at him, and continued her out-of-tune caterwaul. Singing was also something she did a lot of. She had told Dan she was a jazz singer the night they had met at a trendy Hoxton art party, although this had struck him as unlikely. Then she had taken him home to her flat and given him the sex of his life. After that, establishing the veracity of her professional claims came a definite second place.

Dan had soon found out that sex was very important to Birgit. For a while, as she took him through her extensive repertoire, it had been important to him too. These days, however, he felt exhausted at the mere thought of it. The problem, he knew, was that he didn't love her, any more than she loved him, and without love, even the best sex in the world could pall. Although not for Birgit, it seemed, whose appetite remained undimmed. For her it was a physical requirement, like eating or drinking, and with approximately the same level of emotional attachment. Dan was incapable of replicating her matter-of-factness. Increasingly he dreaded the moment when, rolled over on his side and pretending to be asleep, Birgit tapped him on his arm before, with the peremptory efficiency of a male nurse, slamming him abruptly on his back, sliding her naked and athletic form across him to straddle him and setting to work.

Sometimes he wished that Birgit would move out and find someone else whose carnal interests matched her own, but she seemed disinclined to do so and he didn't have the heart to make her leave. He would worry about her if she did, he knew; she possessed to an even lesser extent than himself the qualities required to survive in the real world. Including fluent English, although hers was getting better slowly. Hopefully she would go of her own volition eventually.

In the meantime, he was resigned to having her around. He even quite liked her; she was a crazy but well-intentioned Dutch person with whom he had nothing in common but who was company of a sort. He thought he would probably go mad otherwise, stuck in this village on his own, and she certainly kept the locals talking. Ironic, that. He was the artist; one might have expected him to be the exhibitionist.

Dan's style was, on the contrary, as shy and soft-spoken as he was himself. He had short-cut black hair, long only in the glossy lick that fell over his geekish black-framed glasses. Sartorially, he was old-fashioned, his habitual uniform being black gym pumps and baggy trousers, bought from charity shops along with their overlarge jackets. Sometimes these suits came complete with braces which, as Dan was tall and skinny, held the trousers up over the white T-shirts he generally wore. He knew that most artists looked infinitely more exciting. Zeb Spaw, for example, with his long, glossy hair and exotic, high-cheekboned, almost Native American handsomeness. Not to mention his tight black trousers and T-shirts and trademark high-top black trainers.

Birgit's lithe, slender-hipped, small-breasted figure twirled before him round the tiny sitting room, colliding with the chairs and falling over the piles of local newspapers and junk mail that lay around the floor. It seemed unlikely that she was, as she had once also claimed, a trained classical ballet dancer. But she had an extremely good figure, one Dan had tried once or twice to paint, although not with much success. She was constitutionally incapable of keeping still, required the radio on at shattering volume throughout the session and ate an endless sequence of bags of crisps. It was for these reasons that Dan had ruled her out as a model for the art class.

He noticed now, in the pile of junk mail nearest to him, jutting out between the supermarket flyers and local freesheets, an item of mail that did not look like junk. It was a thick cream envelope on which his name had been carefully hand-written in neat italics. The postmark was over a week ago. Opening it, he found he had been invited to the Federation of Portrait Painters' Annual Dinner after all.

As the usual card had failed to arrive, he had imagined his quitting London to be responsible for this evident falling off the art radar. In Aldeham, he felt as if he had fallen off every radar going. And yet here it was – the dinner invitation – for tomorrow night. He had found it only just in time.

He waved the card accusingly at Birgit, who was undoubtedly responsible for shoving the envelope into the junk pile. But as she was lost in music, there was clearly no point trying to interact with her.

Dan stared at the invitation. Did he really want to trail all the way to London to go to the portrait dinner? Tomorrow night had been his scheduled night for taking the finished work round to Kevin Swift. On the other hand, the annual dinner of the Federation of Portrait Painters was an important industry event – in as much as portrait-painting could ever be called an industry – and as such was a valuable opportunity to make contacts and gather information. Dan, never the most confident of networkers, was nonetheless aware that one had to tout oneself to some extent, and some of the old stagers present tomorrow night might have some good tips for increasing trade.

Besides, the delivery could easily be brought forward a day. The portrait was practically ready. If he went upstairs now and applied the finishing touches, it would be dry by the evening. And as the sitter lived only at the other end of the village, it would be the work of a few minutes to take it there and hand it over.

His boots echoed on the dusty wooden treads as he climbed the narrow uncarpeted stairs to the second bedroom. He switched on Radio 3 and felt immediately soothed by a Debussy piano prelude he particularly loved. Slow, bell-like, deep and an invitation to forget everything and anything that was ugly and annoying.

He took some deep breaths and looked round. He did his best to keep his studio tidy, but the small metal tubes in which paint came could not be stacked easily and were necessarily scattered over every available surface. And sometimes, the excitement he felt when a picture was going really well was not of the sort that could stop paint dripping everywhere as he seized tube after tube in his enthusiasm. The result was work he was pleased with, but also a floor that looked like a million seagulls had pooed in every colour imaginable. Sometimes, when his palette was not to hand, Dan, possessed by the urge to get his idea down on canvas as quickly as possible, had been known to mix paint on the top of the chest of drawers. He felt guilty about it afterwards, even though the landlord never came near Milkmaid's Walk and the chest actually looked better with colour on it.

However, this was no excuse or explanation for the heaps of yellowing newspapers, curling magazines and other rubbish piled in every corner, along with rags used for wiping paintbrushes. Canvases, some complete, some half worked, were stacked against the skirting boards, and a number of easels with more canvases stood conversationally about, at angles, like groups of people at a party.

The fact that all his art paraphernalia was in here meant Birgit could not use the room and had to share his double bed in the main bedroom. It had been a close call between her sexual demands, which he could have avoided with separate bedrooms, and the demands of art, which also required a room of its own. But in the end, art had won.

Chapter 12

As the spotlights faded and the screams of the teenage girls died away, Siobhan lowered the hands she had discreetly raised to her ears. Then, as the lights went up, there was a thump of music and the band suddenly appeared again, running on from the sides of the enormous stage. The screams redoubled in volume and Siobhan tugged hanks of thick brown hair over her ear lobes. At thirty, she was too old for this.

She wondered if Ciaran, her forty-year-old husband, felt uncomfortable as well. He was standing, just as she was, but instead of swaying, clapping and shouting along like the rest of the overexcited audience, he was perfectly still, staring at the four men on stage with an intensity that struck his wife as bordering on the violent.

Siobhan wondered what he could see. To her, the re-formed Take That's performance had been fine, absolutely great, if you liked that sort of thing. And clearly, the screaming, cheering crowd – both men and women – did. They were delighted to see the band back together. Some obviously were fans from the first time round: *They May be Old, They May Be Fat, But We Still Love Take That*, read the banner being hoisted aloft by a group of well-built blondes on the other side of the stadium. Siobhan smiled. None of the men on stage looked old or fat to her; they looked, on the contrary, athletic, well-preserved and excited. Very excited. And they had performed well; she had enjoyed it, even though boy bands weren't really her thing. Classical music, on the other hand, was. She had thought it was his thing too; they had met at a concert of music by the Elizabethan composer William Byrd. She had been an art student; he had introduced himself as a mature music student. The concert had been candlelit and atmospheric and she had been enchanted to hear that Ciaran was planing an album of seventeenth-century lute songs.

Only later, after several dates, had he revealed that he was in fact a former pop star, had been in a boy band, and the lute songs were part of a new musical direction. Siobhan had been more interested in this than perturbed about the pop star past – it was over, what did it matter? The lute idea had, however, never really come to fruition, Ciaran apparently finding it difficult to master the chords.

They had married a mere few weeks afterwards. Siobhan had been surprised to discover that he required her to leave art college. 'There's only room for one artist in this relationship.' He had grinned, and she had grinned back, not taking him seriously. Who would say such a thing and mean it? Nonetheless, she *had* left; and shortly afterwards they had moved to America, where Ciaran intended to pursue another new musical direction and she intended to find a new art course.

This had proved impossible, because they had moved about so much. Ciaran had decided to follow several different musical directions, one after the other, and had shot around the country recording solo albums everywhere from Nashville to Detroit, trying to hit on the winning formula each time. Then, quite suddenly, a mere few months ago, he had given up trying to crack America and decided he wanted to return to the UK.

Take That, waving and grinning, now began their encore. There was a howl of delighted recognition from the audience. Ciaran remained tense.

Siobhan studied him covertly. Of course, she had an artist's eye and could see loveliness in everything. But you didn't need this to appreciate the astonishing extent of Ciaran's handsomeness. Even after ten years of marriage, she doubted she had ever seen anyone so good-looking. He had the kind of smile that made one think of choirs of angels and sunbursts through clouds.

That easy smile, the clear skin as fresh as Irish rain, the wide-set eyes, green as the hills, fringed with lashes as black as peat and with that suggestive little crinkle beneath them. The waves of dark hair flowing romantically back from his widow's peak and falling about the neat little ears with the small diamond studs she had given him on their wedding anniversary earlier this year.

She admired the way he put his look together with the utmost care and judgement. Those fashionable yet discreet sideburns; the designer stubble. Unlike many men, particularly wealthy ones, Ciaran knew how to dress: tonight he had a classic white shirt hanging out over distressed designer denims, a black leather biker jacket over the top and one of his collection of wildly expensive watches.

Money and success had given him taste and confidence. The only thing money and success had not been able to add was a few inches to his height. Siobhan, who was six feet in stilettos, and rather liked high heels, had nonetheless long since learned to accept that the future was flat.

As the screamers screamed on and Ciaran still did not move, Siobhan wondered what was occupying her husband's thoughts. Surely he wasn't envying the four men on the stage. He hated to talk about his boy band past and she had long since learned not to ask questions. From time to time she had been tempted to seek answers on the Internet, but clearly he did not want her to pry and so, out of love and loyalty, she hadn't. Siobhan was of a fanciful, romantic cast of mind and rather enjoyed this heroic self-denial. But as time went by she had become less interested – as, so she thought, had he.

So why, Siobhan wondered, had he brought her here? A boy band concert was surely a situation which must stir a lot of memories; some perhaps best left buried. Why put himself through it?

It had been a spur-of-the-moment decision. Siobhan had been happy enough to go; while she could take or leave Take That, she loved London and the prospect of a night at Claridge's, which had been their home from home on returning from America. It was all much more exciting than the countryside. Than Suffolk, and Aldeham in particular.

Immediately Siobhan felt guilty at the thought. Aldeham Manor was a beautiful house, surrounded by a lovely garden. It was the archetypal glamorous country mansion. It was just that – well – the whole thing had been rather a surprise. On the morning in their London hotel bedroom when Ciaran had announced he was taking her into the country for a day out with a difference, the last thing Siobhan had expected was to be driven, after several hours, up a long and winding drive to the front of a big house and told that this was, from now on, to be her home.

It was poised in its gardens like a jewel in its setting, undeniably beautiful, a small E-shaped sixteenth-century manor house with sun-warmed granite mullions and winking diamond panes. When people thought of England, Siobhan knew, they thought of places like Aldeham. What she thought herself, though, she was not entirely sure.

'Don't you like it?' Ciaran had asked her, watching her closely in that way he had. 'I thought you loved surprises.'

Siobhan had nodded, looking at the front of the house in wonder. What else could she say but that she was pleased? The drive was lined with suppliers' vans; he had obviously put an enormous amount of money and effort into the place, although how, without her knowing, she could not imagine. 'It's lovely,' she had said slowly. Of course it would have been lovelier still to be consulted. But it was obviously too late for that.

'You can be lady of the manor!' Ciaran had urged her, dazzling her with his smile, and she had nodded again, trying to look as if the prospect filled her with joy as well. What it had actually filled her with was perplexity: why on earth had he done it? Another of his whims, his sudden urges? What was a rock star without a rock star mansion, after all; perhaps it was not so unusual. Nor was it, she knew, especially unusual for him to do something without telling her, although his decisions were not generally on this scale.

She would simply have to get used to it, as she had had to get used to so much over the years they had been married. Did she like this peripatetic existence? They had moved so often, it was difficult to know. And Aldeham, whatever the circumstances of her arriving there, was a stunningly beautiful setting.

Screaming applause interrupted her train of thought. Looking round at the hysterical young girls, Siobhan could not help wondering how good the Take That reunion was for the group's wives and girlfriends. Her eye caught a particularly beautiful blonde two or three rows in front, lissom and pale-skinned and with the most gorgeous bright gold hair tumbling over her slender shoulders. When someone like that was openly adoring your husband, it must take a strong or particularly gorgeous woman not to feel threatened.

With a final flourish of sound, the concert was over; Gary, Jason, Mark and Howard bounded off into the wings for the final time and the spotlights over the huge stage began to dim. The girls around them began to leave, some still gasping and chatting in excitement, some silent and wet-eyed, apparently overcome by prolonged proximity to their heroes.

Siobhan turned back to Ciaran, who had snapped out of his reverie and was pulling the wings of his jacket collar up to his sideburns. In the bright lights of the foyer, he looked irritated. There was a twitch about his eyebrows, a slight pinch just above his nose, as if his otherwise smooth forehead was about to scrunch in anger. What was wrong with him?

She threaded the wide belt of her red leather coat through its big silver buckle. Then she tossed her long dark hair as if she didn't have a care in the world, threaded one slender red-leather arm through Ciaran's black-leather one, and, leather to leather, they went out into the temperate June evening.

Chapter 13

It was hot in the car, and Siobhan let the window down. The air was full of exhaust fumes mixed with the damp, cool, rotting smell of the nearby river. Siobhan glanced past Ciaran's set profile to admire the dancing black water running wide and silent between the illuminated wharves of former warehouse buildings now full of cutting-edge flats and buzzy restaurants.

They had gone to look at an apartment there not long ago. Siobhan, who loved London, had had her hopes high that he would buy the huge, empty top floor of a former sugar warehouse. It was so big, so light, so exhilarating.

The living area had been particularly enormous – 'The kids'll be able to roller-skate up and down there,' the agent had suggested.

'There are no kids,' Ciaran had said quickly, coldly.

Siobhan had blinked away the sudden hot, wet rush in her eyes. Why there were none she had no idea. They were both healthy. She longed more than anything to be a mother. They made love regularly – more than regularly. And yet, each month, the news was the same.

They had not bought the apartment. Ciaran had bought Aldeham Manor instead.

An ambulance screeching past them, sirens in full cry, distracted her as they entered Soho.

'God help whoever that is,' she said superstitiously, as she always did when she saw ambulances.

'Be some bloody drunk or other,' Ciaran remarked uncharitably.

Back at Claridge's, he looked at himself moodily in the mirror as the lift attendant slammed the Edwardian cage doors shut and started the elderly mechanism juddering upwards.

'I don't want anything to eat,' he growled as they entered the suite and Siobhan went to the folder full of room-service menus on the glass-topped desk.

Sensing he wanted space instead, Siobhan headed for the bathroom and a long, luxurious soak. As the water thundered into the big white tub, she glanced round the door to see Ciaran, his back to her, wrenching the top off a whisky from the minibar and pouring it straight down his throat. She watched as he started up his laptop.

She slipped into the perfumed suds and luxuriated in the warmth and scent. From next door there was silence; the London traffic, on the street far below, was a faint hum thanks to soundproofed glass. Presently Ciaran stuck his tousled dark head round the door. 'Going for a walk,' he said tersely. 'Get some air.'

After Ciaran had gone, Siobhan rose from the bath and wrapped herself in a thick white robe. Wandering out into the sitting room of the suite, she felt her wet soles sink into the thick carpet.

Ciaran's laptop remained where he had left it, on top of the desk. The chair before it looked hastily thrown aside, as if this had been his last act before coming to the bathroom to announce that he was going out. There was something brightly coloured on the screen – some people in extravagant poses, wearing black – but the image disappeared almost instantly as the screensaver took over.

At the tap of a fingernail, however, the photograph was revealed again. Ciaran – a very young Ciaran – dressed in a tight black leather waistcoat and shorts, his hair dyed white-blond and his cherubic face plump and shining. He was surrounded by three other handsome youths: the other members of Boyfriend. Ciaran had called up a Boyfriend fan site.

Ciaran had hardly ever, through the entire time they had been married, said anything about his former life in a boy band, apart from that it had been hell from start to finish and he was glad that it was over.

She had not pried. But now, with the website actually open before her, as if left for her deliberate perusal, she saw nothing wrong with scrolling around the site.

Her first thought was how very funny it all was. Ciaran looked hilarious in those tight shorts, and the history of the band was hysterical. Apparently the final split had come about during a tour of Japan. A member of the band called Declan explained to the website how he had got fed up with 'the terrible lyrics and whole screaming teenager thing. So I went off mid-song and stuffed my black leather trousers and silver shirt down the nearest loo. They'd become about as glamorous to me as overalls.' After which, apparently, he had gone off and joined an experimental Japanese orchestra.

Siobhan laughed aloud. Perhaps it was understandable that Ciaran preferred not to talk about any of this.

'What's so funny?' demanded a voice behind her. Ciaran's. He had come in without her hearing.

Siobhan twisted round, still smiling. 'It's hilarious.' She waved a hand at the laptop screen. 'Stuffing his clothes down the loo and everything.'

'It wasn't so hilarious at the time,' Ciaran said grimly.

Siobhan reached out and took his hand. It didn't respond or clasp hers. 'Well it's over now,' she said reassuringly. 'You don't have to do it any more.'

'What if I wanted to?'

Siobhan blinked at the vehemence in his voice. '*Wanted* to? But why would you? I thought you never wanted to walk on a stage again, on your own or as part of a group. That's what you always say.'

'What I always *said.*' Ciaran spoke in a strange, compressed voice that sounded as if it was being ground from between his teeth. 'That was before tonight. And I want some of that.'

'Some of what?' Did he mean . . . some of Take That?

Her heart began to race. A wave of heat suffused her. In the softly lit room, against the silvery twenties wallpaper, she could see the glint of determination in his eyes.

'I want to get the band back together,' Ciaran said, his voice hard, grating, determined and entirely different from the soft Irish brogue he used when he wanted to charm.

'But . . .' stammered Siobhan. 'But you haven't spoken to any of them for ten years. You don't know where they are.'

'I can find out.' Ciaran bit out the words. 'Why not? Other bands have done it, not just Take That. Look at Boyzone and Ronan Keating. They made a great comeback. So why the hell can't I?'

'Er . . .' Siobhan began.

Ciaran slammed the antique writing desk so hard it made her jump. 'God,' he howled. 'I want to be in Boyfriend again. Number-one hits! Sell-out concerts! I miss it. *I miss it.*'

Chapter 14

The blue Suffolk sky stretched away as far as the eye could see. Below it, the crowded wheatfields, just beginning to turn gold, rode the ancient ripples and undulations of land tilled since time immemorial. The air was sweet with sunshine, grass scent and birdsong.

Against this background of lush nature, the elegant Queen Anne mansion of Blackwood Park seemed an essay in pretty logic and restraint. But there was nothing either logical or restrained about its owner, the black figure now marching down the sweep of stairs at its entrance as swiftly as was possible in footwear not securely attached to the feet.

Zeb Spaw had noticed nothing about the beautiful day or the breathtaking view. His attention was entirely turned in on himself. He was rarely in a position that he felt apprehensive, and never in one where he felt fearful. But the fact that he had not heard from Fuchsia Klumpp for more than a week, not since she had bought *Prostheseus Bound*, had made him nervous.

He had been relieved at first. Deep down, Zeb disliked and resented his mistress. She was essentially a cold and calculating nymphomaniac and there was no question that she was interested in his art. Fuchsia's only interest in art was in the social status it gave her, and her only interest in him was physical.

But after a few more days, his relief had turned to a nervousness as new as it was unwelcome.

Normally when she bought a piece of his, she liked him to come to her house and admire it, to tell her the story of its creation. It was the perfect pretext for a visit; her husband, always assuming he was at home, couldn't possibly object. Herman T. Klumpp III probably would object, Zeb guessed, to the fact that, after the work had been publicly admired and he had returned to one of the international conference calls he seemed permanently engaged on, Fuchsia liked Zeb to make energetic love to her on the new purchase: 'Your very personal signature,' she would crow.

As Fuchsia had exotic sexual tastes, and some of the pieces were very angular, sharp, awkward or uncomfortable in other ways, Zeb had more than once come to regret the artwork he had created without considering such eventualities. *Prostheseus Bound* was a good example. He had decided not to think too hard about what might result from congress with that.

But in the past few days he had been wondering whether congress was likely anyway. It seemed increasingly certain that something had happened. Fuchsia's purchase of *Prostheseus Bound* may have been a triumph over her rivals, but her pleasure in it seemed mixed. With a sneaking sinking feeling, Zeb knew she had paid somewhat over the odds. Fuchsia, he also knew, did not like to feel like a mug.

He started to review what he felt about her. Fuchsia Klumpp might be a selfish sex addict, but she also happened to be one of the wealthiest art patrons in London. A world player too, although it had to be said that her passion for international art fairs had been a useful front for her rather more genuine passion for international artists like himself. Such an occasion, Zeb recalled now, had been the cause of the only real lust he had ever felt for her: last year, at the Venice Biennale, he had watched from the biggest suite at the Cipriani – Fuchsia's – while, clad in the tiniest of bikinis, she did deals with the most powerful gallery-owners on the sunloungers around the pool. The sight of her down there, limbs shining with oil, embodying not only the ultimate in the plastic surgeon's art, but also money and power, had had him panting with genuine desire.

Slowly, in his mind, Fuchsia became what she had never been: an object of desire. Sure, she was emaciated, with a strangely stretched face, but she was also on every influential art board and top gallery council. She featured in the 'Gold' section of all the most important lists of art benefactors. She dominated the best art parties and was, thanks to expensive expert advice, ahead of the curve of every art trend. She was in the know, had the skinny, knew everyone and everything.

Zeb's anxiety grew as he considered what he had to lose by falling out of favour. Fuchsia was a patron of such power that a single swoop on one artist's studio could send him – or her – into the stratosphere. And back down again if, as had been known to happen, she changed her mind and dumped her collection of works by that artist back on the market, bringing prices crashing down and ruining careers into the bargain. It was not without reason, Zeb knew, that people said Fuchsia had too much power. It was true that her swoops and dumps distorted and destabilised the art market.

The thought sent a chill through his stomach. Fuchsia's patronage, more than anything else, had helped thrust him to the forefront of Britart, as well as provide him with a great deal of money. After her purchase of what was at that time his most expensive work to date, a gold-sprayed lavatory called *Flash in the Pan*, he had never looked back. Fuchsia had been delighted with it, saying she was the only person in the world who contributed to a work of art every time she went to the john.

But was she delighted with him now? It seemed not, and Zeb, like all tyrants, was on the hunt for someone to blame, and to take his frustration out on.

His heels slipping in his trademark oversized unlaced trainers, he was stalking towards his studio, formerly the hay barn on the Blackwood home farm. He had, when buying Blackwood Park, planned to convert the large stables adjoining the mansion for this purpose, but English Heritage had once again demonstrated their ignorance of contemporary art and its practitioners by refusing to allow him to demolish the Georgian horse stalls.

The result was not only annoyance, but inconvenience. Getting to the hay barn involved the crossing of several annoyingly large fields, and was a considerably longer walk than the one to the stable block. Zeb hated walking. He had wanted to be driven by Toombs to his studio, but a local environmental group had got wind of his plans. On the basis that some exotic frog lived there, they had prevented the building of a road through the fields. Zeb had no option now but to walk – an uncomfortable business in jeans as tight as his, and shoes as loose.

He kept his eyes trained on the ground, as unobserving as he was uninterested in the blues, golds and greens which stretched and rippled all about him. What did he care about landscapes? Only losers painted those.

The group of farm buildings of which the hay barn/studio was the largest also contained a farmhouse which had been patched up for the accommodation of the many assistants Zeb required for his current project. The farmhouse was by no means as thoroughly restored as the barn, and the assistants were unpaid, but they were happy to endure any privation in order to have the magic words 'Studio Assistant to Zeb Spaw' on their CV. It was ridiculous, Zeb thought as he opened the inner door to the studio, how he allowed himself to be used.

Inside, the studio could not have been more of a contrast with outside, where the heritage authorities had insisted on retaining the authentic eighteenth-century appearance. As the barn had not looked particularly eighteenth-century when Zeb had acquired it, having been considerably knocked about and altered through the years, this had been less a case of retaining the appearance than re-creating it from scratch with an extensive restoration project.

Involving as it did meticulous research by any number of historic barn experts, plus the sourcing of authentic materials and craftsmen, the project meant that work on the outside of the studio had cost far more and taken far longer even than the conversion of the inside. The barn's outside, exquisitely restored though it was, never failed to annoy Zeb for this reason. It seemed to him to embody the way that the local authority and the heritage bodies acted against him at every opportunity. They were jealous, of course. The British famously hated success. Worse, in attacking him as they repeatedly did, the various authorities seemed to be ignoring and disrespecting his undoubted importance as an artist.

Almost foaming with anger now, Zeb walked into the large, white, halogen-lit workspace. Without warning, and before he could dodge out of its way, something big, cold and wet came spinning through the air and hit him smack in the nose.

Chapter 15

'What the . . . *fuck*?' Spaw roared, as the big, cold, wet thing slid down his face and down the front of his tight-fitting T-shirt. It was a sponge, he now saw, a big yellow sponge of the type used to clean cars. It was soaked in paint; moreover, the paint it was soaked in was scarlet. Looking down at himself, Spaw saw he was smeared all over in thick, gloopy red, as if he were the victim of a massacre.

Footsteps came hurrying across the wooden floor of the studio towards him. 'Sorry, boss,' said Josh Hazelhurst, Director of Production. 'We weren't expecting you.'

Spaw peeled the sponge off his groin, where, as he scorned underwear, it had stuck with an unpleasant coldness to what lay beneath. 'Weren't expecting me?' he echoed ominously.

'Well – no. Toombs said you were out in your car.' Josh, short, apologetic and eager to please, smiled wistfully. 'Lotus, isn't it?' His eyes glowed.

'Never you mind what it is,' Zeb growled. 'What's going on here?'

Josh blinked in surprise. 'Oh. Right. Well, we've just been getting on with *Sponge*, as instructed.' He extended an arm to the huge, light-filled space behind him.

Some thirty feet above them, the former barn's pitched roof was held up by eight huge cross-beams. Along each one, lengths of stout rope had been attached to large unframed canvases which hung a few feet from the floor, about four to each beam. A couple of metres from each canvas stood a young assistant at whose feet were ranged a number of dark green plastic buckets, each containing a different colour of paint. Sticking out of some of the buckets were the same sort of large yellow sponges that had just hit Zeb in the face; other sponges, meanwhile, were being hurled violently at the canvases by the assistants.

The result was that each canvas was covered with multi-coloured splatters, and the air between and around them was a blur of flying sponges and paint. There were slapping, squelchy sounds as the missiles hit the canvases, which rocked wildly from side to side under the force of the impacts, or else spun giddily round on the ends of their ropes.

'It's just such an exciting project,' Josh said earnestly as he walked eagerly forward in his espadrilles towards the ten or so assistants, Zeb clumping heavily along behind in his unlaced trainers.

Zeb drew himself up to his full six feet and regarded the sponge-hurlers. He had initially intended that only the most attractive young female art college graduates work in his Blackwood Park studio. But Josh, in charge of organising and recruiting them, seemed to have hired a bunch that were mostly male and mostly Japanese. He had assured Zeb that Japan was where the contemporary art action of the moment was, and all the best graduates, but Zeb suspected the fact that he personally could be counted on to have no sexual interest in them had something to do with it too. Josh took his pastoral duties as seriously as he took everything else.

Which was quite a feat, considering how absurd arty Japanese men could look. Most of them had truly ludicrous spectacles, the type the NHS had stopped handing out in the mid 1970s. They had punky hair striped in badgery black and white and wore tight jeans in shades of dazzling neon along with incredibly long, pointy shoes. Their T-shirts, Zeb noticed now, were printed with various slogans. *Show me the Monet*, said one. *I'm only here for*

Vermeer, declared another. Zeb frowned at this evidence of levity. The atmosphere in his studio should be serious. Religious, almost. Important art was being created here.

'We're all really excited about *Sponge*,' Josh added, noticing that his boss's glowering brow had yet to lift.

'So you bloody should be. It's *fucking* exciting,' Zeb returned ungraciously. It had been his idea, hadn't it? And if Josh *had* added certain elements, such as the rope mounts rather than the easels Zeb had originally planned, and also suggested the sponges, it was only because the inspiration of working with a great artist like Zeb had fired him with ideas he would not otherwise have had.

'You don't think we should be doing video?' he asked Josh suddenly.

'Video?' Josh looked at him.

'Video installations.'

Josh looked worried. 'I'm not much of an expert on those, I'm afraid. I'm more your paint-and-canvas man.'

Zeb eyed him disapprovingly. That was a blow. Sump had hit a sore point when mentioning video. Zeb's opposition was not so much aesthetic as practical. He had difficulty working even a normal camera. And he had to ask Toombs for help with sending texts, the ancient butler being surprisingly adept at them.

Perhaps, Zeb thought, his eyes still on Josh, he needed to get rid of his paint-and-canvas man and find himself a techno whiz-kid who could win the Turner Prize by projecting pictures of people wiping their bottoms on to the sides of tower blocks.

'What about found objects?' he growled at Josh. 'You know – you pick things up and make a statement?'

Josh's eyes were wide with panic. 'Look,' he said, slightly desperately. 'I saw some tunnels made out of strips of plastic tape at the Venice Biennale. They sort of wobbled when you walked down them. If you want to do something edgier, we could probably manage those.'

Zeb waved his hand impatiently. For God's sake, he was a leading contemporary artist. He didn't have to stoop to any of this crap. 'Forget it,' he ordered, to Josh's evident relief. 'Let's stick with *Sponge*.'

'The kinetic aspect is a real plus,' Josh enthused as he led Zeb towards the centre of operations. 'It brings an extra dimension of uncertain energy which fuses with the element of surprise implicit in the fact that the colours are applied in random order.'

Zeb looked at him impatiently. 'What the hell are you talking about?'

'The kinetics – you know, the movement.' Josh beamed. 'As the pictures swing from the ropes.'

Zeb's dark eyes flashed in the shadows of his brows. 'I know what kinetic means, thanks,' he snapped. 'I'm one of the greatest artists of my generation, remember?'

The light in Josh's eyes went out and the excitement drained from his face. 'Sorry, boss.'

Zeb thrust his tanned and stubbly jaw into Josh's. 'I'm the creative force round here, not you, OK? If anyone's going to talk about kinetic bloody dimensions, it'll be me, thanks.'

'OK, boss, sorry, boss. I just thought, you know, as you hadn't actually *seen* them before . . .'

'Who says I haven't seen them before?' Zeb snapped, his thick black brows drawing threateningly together. 'Of course I've seen them before.' He tapped his luxuriant hair. 'I've seen them in my *head*, haven't I? When I *invented* this *entire concept*?'

'Yes, of course, boss. Sorry, boss.'

Zeb's sharp black eyes snapped back to Josh. 'How many do you reckon you can knock out . . . produce, I mean?'

Josh glanced at his workforce. 'Well, the first lot are almost complete, as you can see. Each assistant can probably do about three a day.'

Zeb raised an eyebrow. That was good news. They'd be able to produce hundreds of the things at this rate and they'd only need his signature on them to sell for hundreds of thousands. 'Three a day? We can make more than Warhol,' he said, with a triumphant curve to his lips.

'Yes, and what's even better is that each one in the *Sponge* series is completely unique and diverse,' Josh concurred brightly, 'each with a different message about the random nature of existence. I really do think they're among the most interesting things we've ever done . . . *you've* ever done,' he added hastily.

Zeb nodded, his sensual mouth pressed together in satisfaction. His glance dropped to his clothes. With the heat of his body, the red paint was starting to dry and crust over. He frowned. 'Better go and get changed,' he grumbled. 'I look like I've been stabbed to bloody death.'

As the great artist did not look up at that point, he missed Josh's expression. Wistfulness would not have been a bad description.

Zeb stomped away, as well as one could stomp in trainers that lacked laces. As he left the studio, his mobile rang. He glanced at the number and almost collapsed under the impact of a mighty sweep of relief.

Fuchsia. At last.

Chapter 16

'Hello, big boy,' breathed a female American voice.

'I've missed you,' Zeb assured her, injecting a honeyed regret that was almost entirely genuine. 'Where have you been?'

'I told you I was going to Art Wallamaloo,' Fuchsia trilled in reply. Her voice grated on him, as always.

Nonetheless, the sense of ease from torment deepened. Wallamaloo was the newest kid on the international art fair block, and Fuchsia, who as a matter of course went to all the others, had naturally gone there too. Have chequebook, have wall space, will travel, Zeb thought, trying not to worry about the fact she had not asked him too.

He hoped she hadn't bought anything. Fuchsia was *his* patron, and her purchases of other artists always made him feel insecure. More insecure.

'Wallamaloo was awesome,' Fuchsia enthused. 'Great for shopping.'

He knew she didn't mean fluffy toy kangaroos or hats with corks on; nonetheless, he tried to sound casual. 'Who did you buy?'

'A neo-cave-painting triptych by Bimble Bumble and a neon breast sign by Dean Studio,' Fuchsia announced with strident triumph. 'The nipples move from flat to erect. How cool is that?'

'Er, cool, definitely,' Zeb said, wondering what the hell neo-cave-paintings were. Did that make Bimble Bumble a neo-caveman? Or woman? Or were they two different people?

As for Dean Studio, he was bloody lucky to be living in the age of Bruce Nauman and neon as art form. Otherwise he'd be doing signs for chip shops.

'Dean's just so great,' Fuchsia gushed. 'Such an artist. He insisted on being paid in gold florins and on a gentleman's hand-shake. Can you imagine – trying to source gold florins in Wallamaloo!'

Or gentlemen for that matter, Zeb thought sourly. He tried to steer Fuchsia on to the subject of the gold bed at Sump's. While she had a large number of his gold-sprayed household appliances, the thought of snatching it from under Bigsky's nose – if he could persuade her that was what she was doing – might induce her to take yet another, even after *Prostheseus Bound*. Worth a try, Zeb thought. Collectors, especially at the top end of the market, were viciously competitive. 'Bigsky—' he began, but was cut off as Fuchsia gave a triumphant cackle.

'Bigsky was *there*! At Wallamaloo! He wanted the Studio as well, but my private jet got there before his did.' There was a triumphant growl to her voice. 'Serves him right, the asswipe. Always boasting about how his Murakami's bigger than mine.'

'This work of mine—'

But Fuchsia was off again. 'In the end, Bigsky had to settle for a swirling carpet of beer cans by a Greek feminist art collective.'

'I see.'

'*Everyone* was at Wallamaloo. Awesome parties . . .'

Zeb listened as she rabbited on, reflecting that Fuchsia bought art as other women bought clothes – although she bought clothes too. But art was infinitely more expensive and therefore more enjoyable. And unlike buying clothes, buying art made you seem intellectual.

'Free this afternoon?' she asked suddenly.

'Free for what?' Zeb asked innocently.

'Whaddya think!' she growled. 'We haven't christened *Prostheseus* yet.'

Zeb closed his eyes. He was relieved, but dismayed at the same time.

'I've got a window between two and four before tea at Claridge's with Rachel Whiteread.'

Rebellion surged in Zeb, and not just because of Rachel Whiteread. Why waste time with her and her bloody house moulds? Her space under chairs? But what really irked him was not being able to turn Fuchsia down. She used him for sex like she might use a vastly expensive gigolo with a sideline in drawing and sculpture.

He hated being a lackey at the court where she was Queen of Art. He wished he could detach himself from her clutches. But he had bought into her just as she had bought into him. Bought him outright, even.

He toyed with the idea of refusing her, but then remembered the unsatisfactory conversation with Sump. Of course his position was unassailable, but there was no harm in shoring it up further. Fuchsia was a powerful ally. An afternoon spent pleasuring her would not be time wasted.

'I'll be there,' he said, forcing the resentment from his voice.

'Bring the black leather mask and the handcuffs,' Fuchsia ordered. The line went dead.

Role play. Plus the five artificial legs. As he stuffed his mobile back into his pocket, Zeb's heart sank further. With *Prostheseus Bound* he'd made a rod for his own back, he really had, although his back wasn't the part he was most worried about.

He needed to get out of this relationship. But how? He was a big artist, but she was an even bigger collector. Which meant, of course, Zeb thought as inspiration struck, that the way out was to become an even bigger artist. One big enough to escape the most powerful patron.

The Cornelius Sump Gallery clearly wasn't going to pull that off for him, Zeb concluded critically. Sump had failed to sell *The Right Hand of the Father* to Bigsky, which was the equivalent of failing to sell Mars Bars to a chocaholic. A missed penalty shot, in other words.

And *Sponge* was going well, there was no doubt about that. The question was whether Cornelius Sump deserved the great honour of launching it on the world.

Zeb was halfway back to the house now. He had still noticed nothing, however, about the rippling golden fields beyond the barn, nor the graceful spread of Blackwood Park with the sun on it. His thoughts were entirely elsewhere: in the small central London enclave where the prestigious contemporary art galleries were concentrated.

It was time, he decided, to leave the hopeless Sump and start afresh with another Gold Street gallery. And there was only one left on Gold Street that he hadn't already been with. Angelica Devon at OneSquared.

Zeb ran through what he knew of Angelica. She had long, crinkly dirty-blond hair, a leathery permanent tan and was a bit too old to be quite so thin. But then, she had been a rock chick once; had, unlike most, married her rock star as well. She wasn't as stupid as she looked, Zeb was forced to admit.

Marrying Nick Devon had been a masterstroke, even if he had spent the last few years yo-yoing to rehab and fronting various comebacks that never quite came off. But everyone knew Angelica didn't give a stuff about Nick; what she cared about was her gallery and the kudos it gave her. Through a mixture of Nick's dosh and her own knack, OneSquared was now one of the bluest of blue-chip galleries. It operated at the very highest end of the contemporary art market and was a name to conjure with.

As was Angelica's, Zeb thought. Perhaps she *was* the answer. She had a reputation for ruthlessness and the power to make or break artists. Or make artists even bigger. Big enough, possibly, to escape powerful patrons.

Chapter 17

Angelica Devon gazed doubtfully at the display in the window of her gallery. The line of black rubber flags that had looked so arresting at Art Wallamaloo seemed to work less well here. Should she, she wondered, have been quite so keen to snap up the young Australian artist Ryan Houseworthy solely on the grounds that she hadn't any Oz artists and they might become the next big thing, as China and Russia were at the moment?

Should she have read so much into the fact that the very rich, very powerful collector Fuchsia Klumpp had been hovering over Houseworthy at the time, although she had eventually left the black flags and gone to inspect some neon breasts.

The flags had been hell to transport back and there had been some nasty moments at Customs. Reminding herself that Brancusi had had the same problems had been less comforting than Angelica had imagined.

Now the flags were here in the gallery, they looked too big for the space. There was also a problem with the electric fan required to make them move in the desired effect of undulating ripples. The fan in the window was underpowered; instead of making the rubber move boldly as it was meant to, it achieved a mere limp slap against the aluminium flagpoles. She should, Angelica upbraided herself, have bought Houseworthy's fan as well as his installation.

'What did you say?' she snapped, to the woman sitting next to her.

'We need to decide on your party theme solution,' the party planner repeated with a glassily patient beam. She wriggled her Diane von Furstenberg-clad bottom awkwardly on the white fake-fur beanbag, one of a group of four at the back of the OneSquared Gallery. Her plum-coloured nails, painted to match her lipstick, poised ready over the keyboard of her BlackBerry to take the details. 'Do you have a theme in mind?'

Angelica wrested her attention from Houseworthy's flags, crossed her legs and sank further back into her own beanbag to think hard.

Themes were always tricky for a gathering as important and high-profile as the OneSquared annual party. The entire art world came to the Gold Street street party, plus any amount of A-listers. To stand out from all the other galleries, to maximise the publicity that was the whole object of the exercise, you had to hit on exactly the right blend of originality, humour and cleverness. Originality most of all.

Last year, Angelica remembered fondly, her Fuck Me, I'm Famous party had been the hottest ticket on the street. She had been hot, certainly, in the dress that one of her artists, Spike Cattermole, who worked with transparent plastic bags, had designed and made especially for her.

This year, Angelica was toying with several themes, the front-runner being Debauched, Dirty and Decadent, with glitterballs and candlelit boudoirs. She would wear gold hotpants, glo-mesh and a rainbow-coloured wig.

But she had no intention of showing her hand first, let alone her wig. Leaving her theme, as well as her canapé choice, to the very last minute – or, rather, the last few weeks – had been her successful strategy for many years. It allowed spontaneity, topicality and, most importantly, the opportunity to find out what all the other galleries were doing. And then trump the lot of them.

'What's everyone else doing?' Angelica asked.

That Penelope from Diamond Snail would know, she had no doubt. These people always claimed discretion was their watchword, but discretion was no one's watchword when there was money involved.

Penelope tossed back her skilfully highlighted blond bob and stretched her plum-coloured lips in an unconvincing smile.

'Actually, I'm not entirely sure. My colleagues in the profession are a very discreet bunch.'

Angelica sat up, smoothed her hands down her tight brown leather skirt and stared at the buckled Italian biker boots at the end of her bare brown legs. 'Pity,' she remarked lightly. 'It's the kind of information that's really rather useful to have when one's planning a party on this, ahem, *scale of expenditure*.'

She flashed Penelope a swift look and saw her eyes flash in alarm. A direct hit. Penelope was weakening, and now Angelica went in for the kill. 'And obviously,' she continued airily, 'although Diamond Snail has planned the OneSquared Gallery's parties for some years, that doesn't mean to say—'

'OK,' Penelope interrupted swiftly. 'Just a minute.'

Her fingers scrolled hastily down her BlackBerry. 'OK,' she repeated, frowning at the screen and pushing a hank of blond hair behind one ear. 'Here we go. Miroslav Butterworth Fine Art is doing a Venice party. Harry's Bar is doing the catering, they're flooding the inside of the gallery and a couple of real gondoliers are being flown in from the Grand Canal to row up and down singing "O Sole Mio". They have a very large space, obviously.'

Angelica listened in alarm. It sounded more interesting than anything else Miroslav Butterworth Fine Art had displayed in its gallery lately. Its last exhibition had been a doll's house built of blue-whale penis bones, and if there was anything more five minutes ago than whale penis bones, or bits of whale in general, Angelica didn't know what it was.

'Dystopia's doing Sex.' Penelope was still scrolling. 'The waiters will be wearing vagina costumes and sadistic tattoos and there'll be a reverse stripper.'

'*A what?*'

'She comes on naked, pulls her clothes out from inside her and puts them on,' Penelope said absently, her eyes still on the screen.

'From *inside* her?' Angelica repeated, half repelled and half worried. Should she have a reverse stripper too?

'Sump are doing a barbie on the beach,' Penelope went on. 'They're having a mobile shucker . . .'

Angelica wrinkled her small, surgically enhanced nose and indulged in the comfort of contempt. Mobile shuckers were a bit passé, frankly. She'd had someone last year wandering round with metal buckets full of oysters attached to his waist.

'They're flying in lobsters from Maine and sand from the Cap d'Antibes,' Penelope was saying. 'Or is it the other way round?' She frowned at her keyboard. 'I'm not sure they've made their mind up yet.'

Angelica raised an eyebrow. If Portia, the gallery assistant at Sump, had anything to do with it, there wasn't a mind to make up. She was even dimmer than Angelica's own assistant Natasha. Nonetheless, Angelica felt the screw of pressure tighten. Her party *had* to outdo Sump's. The two galleries were the greatest rivals on a street celebrated for the internecine nature of its dealings.

'The Rabid Gallery is doing Russia. They're building a dacha and planting a birch forest.'

'What? In the gallery?'

'At the back of it.' Penelope scrolled down again. 'They're having gold-leaf vodka and dancing under the tsars.'

'Under the stars, you mean,' Angelica corrected irritably.

Penelope looked up and batted her much-mascaraed eyes. 'No, under the tsars. There'll be cages above the guests containing men in gold braid coats, waxed moustaches, thigh-length boots and very tight white trousers.'

Panic surged within Angelica. Would Debauched, Dirty and Decadent be enough?

And that, of course, was just the party theme. The other big question to be decided was which of her artists would get the most coveted display of the year, in the gallery window during the celebrations. There were various contenders, already fiercely jockeying for position, even though the party was well over a month away.

Hero Octagon, one of her pushiest clients, had already made a bid to crowd the window with her papier-mâché phalluses, but Angelica was doubtful. Papier-mâché willies were as five minutes ago as whale ones, frankly; willies in general were just so over. Ganymede Steam and his heads of frozen urine were a possibility, but what if they melted with unpleasant consequences in the heat of the party crowds? No, she needed a big, stand-out, structurally stable piece by a big, stand-out artist. But what? The Houseworthy flags were a worry. Her latest-but-last signing, Kenny Bang, might do, with his freeze-dried sheeps' brains moulded into supermarket logos. But they didn't exactly look exciting. Nor did Kenny, come to that, being small, surly and with an impenetrably thick Glaswegian accent.

'We need to decide on your music solution.' Penelope was looking at her, bovine eyes blinking earnestly.

'What music is everyone else having?' Angelica demanded immediately.

Penelope was frowning into her BlackBerry. 'Sump's having Stunners International and Rabid's having a lesbian string quartet from Ulm . . .'

Natasha, the gallery assistant, came clacking up now in her stilettos. She was holding out the telephone.

'Can't I ring them back?' Angelica asked testily. 'I'm in the middle of a crucial meeting.'

'It's Zeb Spaw,' Natasha gasped with the excitable toothy breathlessness with which she said everything. 'He says it's urgent.'

Chapter 18

As ever in Aldeham Manor, Siobhan was not entirely sure what to do with herself, or where to go. Her preference would be the kitchen, the least ornate of the house's many rooms, with its low beamed ceiling, stone floor and big, approachable, utilitarian wooden table.

But Julie the housekeeper was there, thumping down on the board with the iron, her face, as usual, like thunder.

Siobhan suspected that ladies of the manor were not meant to feel like this, creeping around apologetically and dodging out of the way of the servants. She felt like the heroine of *Rebecca*, with Ciaran as a rock-and-roll Max de Winter. Julie, meanwhile, with her boot face and abrupt manner, made a decent fist of Mrs Danvers.

Perhaps it would help if she knew someone in the village. Aldeham, however, seemed to consist almost entirely of old or middle-aged people. Or else that woman from the Dower House who had come round 'to say hi', as she put it, the morning Siobhan had first been left alone here. Siobhan remembered a tiny, tanned woman in a small and extremely tight black leather dress screeching something about an invitation to her husband's birthday party. When Siobhan had muttered an apologetic refusal, she had insisted she 'pop round for champers sometime and a girlie chat'.

Siobhan was hungry, but not so much so that she wanted to

make a sandwich and eat it under the baleful eye of Julie. She tried to remind herself that Julie was tremendously efficient, a much better ironer than she was herself. It was just that one never saw her without feeling she was about to explode.

She went instead into the house's entrance hall, the huge room on which the front door opened and which, interiors-wise, set the Manor's tone. Her spirits sank, as they always did, on seeing the decor.

'Maximal' was how internationally famous designer Maeve Kandinsky-O'Halloran described her unique take on the decorative arts. Siobhan hated it. It reminded her that Ciaran had not only bought a house without telling her, but had also employed another woman to decorate it.

She had disliked and distrusted Maeve almost as much as her work. She was stick-thin and sly-looking with dyed black curly hair, a croaky, low-pitched voice and an even more low-pitched top revealing two pouting vanilla-scoop breasts supported by a push-up bra. She was tiny, almost pixie-like, the sort that made tall Siobhan feel all fingers and thumbs. But her small stature had not, apparently, stopped her heading up a multimillion-dollar corporation with a celebrity client list, prestige house projects on all five continents and offices in New York, London, Paris and Dubai.

Siobhan's own preference would have been for white walls, simple woven grass floors and handsome pieces of oak furniture that related to the age of the house. Most importantly of all, perhaps, good pictures from all periods. The wealth of white walls all over the house made the showing of a wonderful art collection possible.

Instead she had got maximal, Maeve-style. While Siobhan had never been a fan of minimal, with its muted pebble colours and flat shapes, this, the absolute opposite, was just as bad in a different way. The furniture Maeve had commissioned for the sitting room was huge: a vast oval pantomime mirror like the one Snow White's stepmother had questioned, and colossal cushions set in bulky carved frames like the throne of Old King Cole. Side tables were massive and of glass, like the one Alice had taken the key from. The master bedroom was pink and black, with a Gothic magenta-lined canopy over the bed, a pink carpet so thick it was like walking on sponges and a bathroom with purple strip-lights. The dining room contained so much gold – from the table, the lamp bases, the chandelier, the frames of the mirrors – that it looked as if Midas had run amok.

The worst thing of all, Siobhan thought, was that while she thought the decor hideous and ridiculous, Ciaran liked it. More than that, he loved it. The huge furniture seemed to satisfy some desire for aggrandisement. He even liked the huge and ghastly gold harp Maeve had placed in the hallway – a patriotic Irish touch, allegedly. It did not make Siobhan feel patriotic when she saw it; it made her feel depressed. Ciaran, on the other hand, was so enthused by it, he was, despite his failure with the lute, considering recording with it.

Siobhan climbed the main stairs' purple carpet, woven through with a gold scrolled design, to the master bedroom, which seemed more suited to Morticia Addams than herself. In the adjoining purple-lit bathroom, she went to the basin to wash her hands and face.

She leaned forward and peered into the circular mirror surrounded with lilac bulbs. Her pale oval face was still smooth, but cross-hatched lines were appearing here and there. Her large green eyes, flecked with gold around the pupils, held an anxious shadow and her hair could do with a good cut, although God only knew where you got that sort of thing round here. She had never worn much make-up, but perhaps, she worried, it was about time she did. Uneasily, she thought of Ciaran on tour with the band.

She had hoped that the plan to reunite Boyfriend was a whim, a passing fancy, which would last only as long as the memory of the Take That concert. But ever since they had returned to Suffolk, Ciaran had pursued his new ambition with every ounce of the drive and determination that was his trademark. And with which, of course, he had once pursued her.

'Hey there, gorgeous.'

She turned, surprised, at Ciaran's voice; his soft, playful, Irish one, she noted with relief. She looked up and saw him lounging against the door frame, his eyes, in the purple light, lazy and good-tempered.

She smiled. 'I didn't know you were up here. I thought you were in the studio.'

He looked handsome in his fresh white linen shirt, his worn jeans, his feet bare. He lowered the arm and ruffled his dark hair, flashing at her a grin as dazzling as his shirt.

Siobhan dabbed her face, flinching slightly at the feel of cold water on her hot skin, and reached for the thick purple towel that waited on a pink metal rail under the basin.

'I've found the orchestra,' Ciaran announced.

'*Orchestra?*'

'We're going to have a full symphony orchestra as backing,' Ciaran explained. 'During the concerts.' He grinned. 'Surprised you that, hasn't it? Bet you thought our songs were too crap to get the classical treatment.'

Siobhan did not reply. The fact was, she didn't know the songs well enough to comment. But her guess would have been that no, they weren't good enough for that.

He took her hand and pulled her roughly out into the black and pink bedroom, where he stood against her and pushed his mouth hotly at hers. The urgency of it excited her despite everything; her breath quickened as he pressed against her, pushing her down on to the quilted black counterpane, grinding gently, so she could feel the hardness in his jeans.

Ciaran's face was taut with desire, and yet, Siobhan saw, there was a smugness there, a confidence, a triumph, even.

'What's the matter?' he demanded as she pulled away.

'Nothing. I'm just . . . not in the mood.'

He looked at her in disgust. 'Well, fine,' he said petulantly, coming out again to address her. 'If you're not in the mood, then I'm not either. No wonder,' he snarled, turning on his heel on the thick pink carpet, 'no wonder we've never managed to have any bloody *kids*.'

Chapter 19

In the gloomy bedroom-cum-studio in Milkmaid's Walk, Dan stood before the just-finished portrait of Kevin Swift. A Haydn partita arose from the paint-spattered radio and climbed delicately into the air around him. It added an ethereal splendour to what was already a triumphant moment.

Dan was modest to the point of self-abnegation, but even he had to admit he had done an excellent job. The portrait was a remarkably true likeness; one of his best works, in fact. He could never predict how pictures would come out, and this commission had, at first, seemed particularly unpromising. There had been the way in which Swift had beaten him down on price as if Dan were trying to flog him some old banger, rather than a work of art, and then of course there had been the problem of the unprepossessing appearance.

And yet, after all, it had succeeded. The restricted light in which, after the initial sittings, Dan had worked on the picture at home had toned down the car-dealer's belligerent puce face and given a thoughtful, even monumental quality to his short, bristly fair hair and the pale eyelashes which added to the overall porcine effect. Gentle shadow had also limited the garish effect of the truly hideous costume in which Swift had chosen to be painted: a pink and gold brocade Nehru jacket which had apparently been hand-built at vast expense by some fashionable designer, and in which Swift apparently imagined he cut a Raj-ish dash. As an elephant, possibly, Dan would think as he worked away with the brush.

And yet none of these irreverent reflections had stopped him conferring that most unlikely of qualities on the brash, rude, vulgar ex-motor salesman: that of dignity. Painted from the head to the waist, in profile against a sober grey background, Swift looked cultured, contemplative and intelligent. Everything, in short, that he wasn't.

Yes, he thought, folding his arms, pushing up his glasses and shaking his black flop of hair out of his eyes. The portrait of Kevin Swift really was tremendously successful. Ridiculously good considering the pathetic price he would be paid for it.

He reminded himself that the money had never been the point. It couldn't be if you were working in an area of art as currently unfashionable as portrait-painting. Inflatable lobsters went for fortunes, of course. But beautifully rendered pictures of real people, conveying in one image all the joys, sorrows and complexities of being human; well, you could forget being rewarded for that. Dan, however, was not bitter. He had never regretted his choice of specialisation, and looking at the magnificent work now glowing before him on his easel, he felt more than vindicated. He was what he had always wanted to be – an artist.

The feeling that someone was standing behind him made him turn round. It was Birgit, naked in the doorway, her flat, wide face showing evidence of excitement. Dan's heart sank. Sex was the last thing he felt like at the moment. Nonetheless, he turned down the Bach.

'Tank Gott for dat,' pronounced Birgit, who was not a fan of classical music.

'What's up, Birgit?' Dan said nervously as she stepped towards him through the squeezed-flat paint tubes and brush-wipe rags.

'Tap!' Birgit exclaimed in her abrupt, guttural voice.

'Sorry?'

'Tap he is not working downstair.'

Dan shook aside the black hair that still dangled over his

glasses. DIY was not one of his strengths, which was why the shelves that had collapsed in the sitting room were still stacked against the wall and why the stuck window in the main bedroom remained obstinate in its refusal to open, making it an oven on hot nights. Anything going wrong in the mysterious and complex taps and plumbing area, therefore, made him feel positively panicky. His first thought was to ring the landlord, a short-tempered Ipswich builder, but then he remembered that the phone had been disconnected, owing to an unpaid bill which had lain undiscovered in the heap of junk mail until it was too late.

'What to do, huh?' Birgit demanded from the doorway. 'Is no bath or kettle. And loo no flush.'

Dan dragged his paintbrush through its cleaning rag, perturbed. The loo and the kettle were priorities, certainly. And whilst in normal circumstances he could live without a bath if he had to, tomorrow night's dinner would require a basic level of cleanliness. He had a vague idea that he needed to turn the taps off in order to investigate, and that there was a stopcock somewhere. But where?

Birgit, as ever, was no use in a crisis. Her bare feet were already slapping bad-temperedly back down the staircase. It was now, with a rush of relief, that Dan remembered that Tadeusz, the Lithuanian next door, was a plumber. Granted, he was somewhat alarming both in build, which was muscular and substantial, and manner, which was just this side of abrupt. But perhaps, if he was in, and Dan asked him nicely, he might find it in his heart to help them.

'Don't touch anything,' Dan told Birgit as he pushed his glasses up his nose, went out of the front door and traversed the few steps between his own weed-choked entrance and that of Tadeusz and Stamina, which was a good deal neater. He knocked on the white front door.

There was the sound of footsteps in the hallway and the door opened to reveal Stamina. She was a large, fair girl with a broad, shiny face and a small, unsmiling mouth. In homage to the hot day, she was wearing white shorts that were both too short and too tight. On top she wore a close-fitting top of flesh pink; the effect in general reminded Dan of a strawberry ice cream. An overwhelming smell of frying rushed out of the doorway behind her. She stared suspiciously at Dan.

'Tadeusz?' Dan asked, swallowing slightly. There was something rather terrifying about Stamina, both in her glare and her proportions. He had the impression that she did not respect him.

The large fair head turned from side to side in a negative. Dan's shoulders slumped in disappointment. 'Oh,' he said faintly. 'I needed help.'

'Help?' Her voice was deep and rather grating.

'It's the stopcock,' Dan explained. 'I don't know where it is. I hoped Tadeusz might be able to help.'

'Cock? You want Tadeusz help you find cock?' Her voice had risen an octave in outrage.

Her tone did not register with Dan. 'That's it.' He nodded delightedly. 'Cock.'

Stamina's unsmiling mouth now bunched in fury. The next thing Dan knew, the door was slammed mightily in his face.

He returned to Birgit wondering how on earth he could explain. He decided not to bother, and spent the next hour searching fruitlessly for the stopcock. That the emergency plumber who he eventually contacted via the village phone box and at vast expense could not locate it for some time either was, he supposed, some comfort.

Chapter 20

It was a beautiful afternoon, Siobhan thought as, following the bedroom encounter with Ciaran, she walked through the grounds fanning out around the lovely old house. The back of it – which was, in a formal sense, the front – led out on to terraced lawns, linked by short sequences of shallow steps in the same golden stone as the buildings. Beyond that was the formal garden, patterned box hedges planted with roses and with a sixteenth-century sundial at the centre. Elsewhere was the kitchen garden, the raised beds, the bean rows, the greenhouse. And endless lawns, spreading about the house like a skirt to the outer rim of trees, and beyond them the estate wall.

The colours looked particularly rich and beautiful in the heavy light. Good summer weather, Siobhan thought. All the more reason, one would think, for Bert and Dean, the Aldeham gardeners, to have bothered to turn up today.

But of Bert's tall, stooping form in its greasy navy jacket, and his son Dean's shorter and more thickset figure in his ill-fitting jeans, there was not a sign. Even Dean's builder's bottom, sometimes seen bent over the herbaceous borders like some huge white double mushroom, was not visible.

Siobhan had accepted – reluctantly – that Bert and Dean never worked in wet weather. They evidently did not believe in waterproofs. Assuming they did not own any, Siobhan had bought them each a set. But they had taken them home and they had never reappeared, and nor, when it was raining, had Bert and Dean. Siobhan had the uncomfortable feeling she was being exploited, laughed at, even.

But it was difficult to know what to do. She was supposed to be in charge of the garden, after all. Sensing – unusually for him – that she was less than pleased about Maeve decorating the house, Ciaran had grandly suggested that Siobhan take Aldeham's grounds and do what she wanted with them.

The trouble was that she did not want to do anything with them. She did not feel qualified to do so. Her fingers were not green, and even if they had been, she lacked the faintest idea of where to start in a garden this size. The amount of work was overwhelming.

She noticed a yellow wagtail pecking at the green moss on a stone-tiled roof and smiled. Her fingers itched to whip out the coloured pencils she held in the case under her arm, pressed against the sketchpad, and get it down on paper. Quite suddenly, she was finding she wanted to draw everything.

It was as if the great mistake she had made in giving up her art course had finally dawned on her. It had taken a long time, perhaps forced by the realisation that she and Ciaran were staying put. Now that there would be no more house moves, there was time to think, at last.

But they were uncomfortable thoughts, about the chance she had thrown away. Her tutors had begged her not to leave, telling her she was a promising student, but Siobhan had not listened. She had just met Ciaran, who had blinded her with his charm. The decision not to struggle any longer with theory and technique had been easy when the prospect of a life of glamour and excitement was beckoning. The houses, the cars, the clothes and the holidays all seemed far, far removed from the prospect of penury after graduation. As Ciaran himself had said at the time, art was not a career. Hardly anyone made a living at it.

But Siobhan, even so, had been aware all these years of a sense of something left unfinished. A sense that was now sharpening to a painful point of regret.

Bert and Dean were here after all, she saw with surprise as she ambled round the back of the house. It was just that their familiar blue banger was parked in a different place from usual, although in its usual manner – askew.

Of the actual gardeners there was, however, no sign. And she had walked round most of the grounds just now. No doubt they were malingering somewhere. Siobhan felt a rush which mixed impatience with feelings of inadequacy and despair. She was responsible for their behaviour. The garden was supposed to be her domain.

Just her luck, then, that Bert and Dean were the laziest gardeners in Christendom, although she hesitated to say as much to Ciaran. He would not want to know; she didn't want to seem to be moaning, and anyway, she still harboured hopes that the pair of them might one day actually start working.

She had tried everything with them. She had tried charming them with trays of tea and biscuits in the hope of making them grateful. But this had only encouraged them to sit about for even longer. After a certain interval she would walk past, casting stern, pleading glances at them in the hope it would drive them back to work. But Bert and Dean only looked back blankly, sipping impassively and dunking in another biscuit.

Siobhan considered, now, marching round to beard Bert in the greenhouse, where no doubt he was hiding. But entering the kitchen garden would mean seeing all the weeds, as well as Bert lounging in the greenhouse, only, on spotting her, to jump to his feet with a speed and agility which gave the lie to the affliction of the spine he claimed precluded him from any bending work such as picking up leaves or weeding.

She reminded herself that the whole point of coming outside was to relax. She tried to push Bert and Dean from her mind. Yet, with one savoury tang of smoke, they were back. Round the back of the Manor, near the old brewhouse, was the place where

Bert had his bonfire. He was obviously there, taking an unscheduled break with Dean. The spot had been chosen, Siobhan suspected, as being sufficiently far from her sight to allow slacking with impunity; also, she doubted it was exclusively garden rubbish that he burned there. When Bert and Dean were not 'working' at Aldeham, they had a number of odd jobs, including delivering a local free newspaper. Judging by the large black plastic bin bags Bert seemed daily to turn up with, contents unknown, Siobhan guessed that a great many of the papers were being delivered straight on to her bonfire. She groaned and walked on beneath the trees, kicking dry leaves up in frustration as she went.

Dan had recovered his usual good temper by the time he was due at the Swifts'. Walking down the main village street in the mellow evening sunshine, the portrait swathed in layers of bubble wrap and brown paper, he was gently humming the overture from *The Marriage of Figaro*. The drowsy, sunlit evening chimed perfectly with the humming-bee opening of the piece.

Indeed, the hour was lovely enough to make Dan, for all his recent pipework challenges, feel more than normally content with life. The world was so beautiful, he thought, admiring the rich light on the flint fronts of the cottages and the summer flowers which grew in profusion in the many pretty gardens. Tall hollyhocks lolled against the walls in a profusion of pink and red; acid-yellow dahlias nodded their spiky heads; bursts of white marguerites lined the tiny lawns; cats snoozed on windowsills beside warm terracotta pots from which spilled vivid red splashes of geranium. It was all so simple, yet so pretty and somehow so essentially English.

If Dan looked up the gently winding street, he could see the church at the end, its tall spire just visible above the great green bells of the trees which surrounded it. He could see the ducks on the pond, which appeared an oval of silvery blue beneath the evening sky. At times like this, he thought, the village looked a perfect picture, although not the sort of picture he wanted to paint himself.

He approached the primary school and the post-office-cum-shop. He dipped his head as he passed the entrance of the latter, remembering with a stab of guilt that he still owed Mrs Snitch for some stamps. He had forgotten to take his wallet with him the last time; not that it would have made all that much difference if he had remembered. It wasn't as if there was much in it.

But Dan's memory, poor as it was for wallets, was prodigious when it came to music. Now, having sung his way to Act II of *Figaro* and through the Countess's lament about her husband's infidelity, he had reached Cherubino's love song to the Countess, 'Voi che sapete'. *You who know what love is. Ladies, see if I have it in my heart.* As he walked alongside the mossy, elbow-height wall, which began at the church gate and ended at the entrance to Aldeham Manor, he sang Cherubino's request for emotional enlightenment:

Donne, vedete s'io l'ho nel cor
Donne, vedete, s'io l'ho nel cor
Quello ch'io provo vi ridirò
E per me nuovo, capir nol so

I'll tell you how I feel.
It's new to me, I don't understand it.

Double-checking that no one was around to hear, he drew in breath to sing the next lines. But before he could make a sound, another voice took up the melody.

Sento un affetto pien de desir
Ch'ora è diletto, ch'ora è martir

I sense an affection full of desire
Which now is pleasure, now is agony.

Dan's mouth dropped open. His first instinct was admiration: the person singing had a lovely voice. A light, pretty soprano, and yet full of all the plaintive yearning the song required.

A split second later, he was overcome with embarrassment. Who was it who had heard him trilling away like a pantomime dame, then joined in herself? Possibly mockingly?

Chapter 21

Before he could plunge quickly past and thus pretend it hadn't happened, a woman appeared on the other side of the wall, emerging from the deep shadow of the chestnuts by the gate.

Dan had never seen her before. He wondered if he was really seeing her now. There was something ethereal and fawnlike about her, as if she were a dryad, a wood nymph, pausing about her business beneath the summer trees. Then he noticed she was not wearing traditional wood-nymph attire, but black Capri pants and a white shirt.

She was flesh and blood all right. Only not the sort he was used to seeing in Aldeham. With his keen eye for beauty, his sense of form, line, colour and symmetry, Dan admiringly drank in the woman's heart-shaped, high-cheekboned face. Her shiny brown hair was pulled back into a ponytail and her creamy skin was scattered with gingery freckles. Beneath eyebrows shaped like elegant circumflexes a pair of large green eyes regarded him with friendly interest.

Dan searched for something to say. 'You're a good singer,' he blurted eventually.

'Doesn't everyone sing that one in the bath?' She smiled modestly, revealing lovely teeth. Her low Irish accent struck him as wildly exotic; most people in Aldeham either had gnarly Suffolk vowels or barking country-landowner ones.

'Not as well as you,' he said, blushing as he delivered himself of this compliment.

'Hey, you're not a bad singer yourself, you know,' the woman replied genially.

'I love that song,' Dan confessed. 'It always seems to me so perfect, the way all the melodies resolve themselves. I never get tired of hearing it.'

'Me neither,' she agreed, her shining ponytail wagging its agreement.

They looked at each other for a moment. Dan felt rather breathless. She was so beautiful, standing there with the shadowy trees behind her, a modern goddess of the woodlands with the evening light gilding the topmost strands of her hair.

Then her green eyes jumped away and fixed on the painting he held under his arm. Her face changed immediately from an expression of something like wonder to one more like disappointment. 'Oh. You must be from Maeve Kandinsky-O'Halloran,' she said. Her voice had changed too: the lightness had gone; it now had an accusing note.

Dan was puzzled. Maeve Kandinsky-O'Halloran? What sort of a name was that? 'Who?'

The brunette, who was not particularly tall, jerked her chin up. 'The interior designer,' she said, a slight frown troubling her forehead.

'I've never heard of her,' Dan said. 'Although I have heard of Kandinsky.'

'You like him?' she asked immediately.

Dan considered. As a matter of fact, early-twentieth-century abstract of the Kandinsky school was not his absolute favourite, but he recognised its deservedly important place in the canon.

'You're not keen!' she accused, her eyes teasing. 'You don't like modern art?'

'I prefer it to contemporary, definitely,' Dan said.

'Really?' The brunette looked amused. 'I'm quite a fan of contemporary.'

Dan decided not to pursue this line. He didn't want to disagree with this enchanting creature, and particularly not about so profoundly distressing a subject. Probably just as well not to mention, either, that one of the nation's most famous practitioners of that most degraded branch of art lived a mere few miles away. He felt he could not bear for her to be excited about the proximity of Zeb Spaw.

'Is Maeve Kandinsky-O'Halloran,' he asked, returning to safer if not entirely unconnected waters, 'a relation of Kandinsky?'

The brunette snorted. 'I doubt it.' She smiled. 'So if you don't work for Maeve, what do you do?'

'I'm an artist,' said Dan.

The brunette's face lit up. 'Oh, so that's one of *your* pictures you're carrying?'

Dan confirmed that this was the case.

'Can I see it?'

'Sorry.' Apologetically, Dan shook the flop of hair from the front of his glasses. He wished that he was wearing something less scruffy than his usual second-hand baggy fawn trousers, scruffy tennis shoes and white shirt with buttons missing. This, all that was currently available in his wardrobe, had seemed a reasonable enough outfit in which to drop off a picture – the shirt being a concession to the formality of the occasion.

She was nodding. 'No, I can see you can't. It's wrapped.'

'It's not just that,' Dan confessed. 'I think that the subject should be the first to see the picture of themselves. It doesn't seem fair otherwise.'

'It's a portrait?'

'Yes, so you wouldn't like it anyway.' Dan smiled. 'Not if you like contemporary and abstract art.'

'That doesn't mean I don't like portraits!' The green eyes flashed and she laughed. She laughed beautifully, he thought, smitten. With those pretty teeth and plump pink lips . . .

'I trained at art school,' the brunette said. 'I wanted to be an artist, actually. Once.' Her voice was mildly rueful.

'Really?' Dan pushed his free hand through his hair and stared, amazed. Musical *and* artistic. *And* beautiful.

'But everyone told me it was impossible to make money,' the brunette was saying, her sparkling green eyes clouding.

Dan pulled a face. 'They weren't wrong. On the other hand, it is possible to survive. It helps if you like living in a shoebox, having your menu dictated by the Reduced shelf in the supermarket and your wardrobe by the latest house clear-ance.'

She giggled. 'I think you look very nice. And is your shoebox here? In the village?'

'Yes. But not at the smart end.' He decided not to mention Birgit.

'This is the smart end?' She looked at her surroundings. The idea did not seem to give her much pleasure.

'Yes,' Dan confirmed. 'You've bought the Manor?' he asked curiously.

'My husband has,' she said quickly. She had, he noticed, involuntarily glancing, pale and very pretty fingers. There was indeed a wedding ring on one of them. He felt a powerful wave of disappointment.

My husband has. It seemed an odd thing to say, Dan thought. Distancing. As if the decision was nothing to do with her, which surely it had to be. 'You'll be lady of the manor,' he said encouragingly.

When she did not respond to this, he felt foolish. His ears and face burning, he only heard the very end of the next sentence, in which she seemed to be asking, straight-faced, what the village was like.

He shrugged awkwardly. 'I'm probably not the person to ask. I'm not very involved.'

'Sounds like a good idea.'

Their eyes met again, and this time he found it even harder to detach his. 'Couldn't you,' he found himself asking, suddenly, 'take it up again? Art. If you want to?' The question had been burning within him. 'It's not too late,' he added.

She smiled and tossed her ponytail. 'It probably is for me, sadly. I'm Siobhan O'Sullivan,' she added.

He noticed that she was looking at him almost fiercely, as if anticipating some reaction, as if the name should mean something. He racked his brains, but he had not heard of Siobhan O'Sullivan any more than he had heard of Maeve Kandinsky-O'Halloran. He looked back at her apologetically.

He wondered if she were a model. Or even a film star; new ones were minted all the time, after all, and it had been a year since he lived in London. He realised, rather glumly, that he had no idea what was going on any more. Anywhere, not just the capital. No one could phone him. And if anything arrived in the post, Birgit immediately lost it in the junk pile. Radio 3 was his main source of information, and more often than not he was absorbed in work during the news bulletins and paid attention only when they were playing music he liked.

Siobhan was, Dan now noticed, holding out a hand to shake across the lichen-encrusted top of the wall. Taking it in his, as delicately as one might handle a fragile bird egg, Dan had the fleeting sense that he was making contact with another world, stepping into an enchanted realm.

'Dan Hart,' he muttered.

He wanted to ask why it was too late for her to be an artist, but lacked the courage. She might tell him it was none of his business, which was undeniably the case.

'So who have you painted round here?' Siobhan broke the short silence.

He raised his eyes from her hand, blushingly conscious that he had stared for a long time at the wedding ring. 'Kevin Swift. He lives at the Dower House.'

Siobhan's expression became secretive. Amused, even. 'I think I've met his wife,' she said.

'You'd know about it if you had,' Dan remarked, then instantly felt disloyal and blushed.

'A very tanned blonde woman who wears incredibly high heels

all the time?' Siobhan's eyes flashed naughtily. 'She invited me round for some Dom Perignon.'

She pronounced it phonetically, as Toni undoubtedly had, and Dan suppressed with a mighty effort the urge to burst into maniacal laughter.

Siobhan was looking around her, back in the direction of the Manor. 'I'd better go,' she said. 'It was nice to meet you.' She hesitated, glanced at him, then, seemingly about to take a step away, apparently changed her mind and remained. It was as if, Dan thought, she did not know quite what to do. He could not help her; he was standing there, staring at her like something turned to stone.

'Hope they like the picture,' she said.

'Actually, I think they will,' Dan said truthfully. 'It's one of my best ones. At least, I think it is.'

'I'm sure it is, then.' Siobhan nodded. Still she did not leave.

Dan racked his brains for something to ask her. He had never been any good at small talk. 'Until you said you had trained as an artist,' he began awkwardly, 'I thought you must be a musician. Your singing was lovely.'

Siobhan shook her head in modest denial, her ponytail catching the dappled sunlight filtering through the trees. 'I love music, but I'm not a musician.' She paused. 'My husband is, though.'

Chapter 22

Dan floated on a cloud to the Swifts, his thoughts full of the romantic newcomer. Now he was no longer before her, gazing into her eyes, he could think of any number of amusing remarks. *L'esprit de l'escalier*, he knew it was called. The wit of the staircase, that came to you only when it was too late, when you were leaving. He reached the Dower House to find the gates unexpectedly open. Whenever he had come for portrait sessions, he had been obliged to negotiate a web of security that would not have disgraced the White House. But tonight the ornate black and gold arms were flung open and the glaringly new brick drive was almost invisible beneath the host of cars, mostly shiny four-wheel-drives with personalised number plates, that crowded before the building.

Wondering what was going on, Dan went up to the Dower House's front door, whose ancient studs had been thoroughly Farrow-and-Balled, and lifted the venerable knocker with difficulty. New paint had rendered it stiff to the point of unusability.

A downtrodden-looking woman opened the door.

'Hello, Anita,' Dan said. The woman, he knew, was the Swifts' cleaner. He looked her up and down in surprise. Her usual uniform was baggy black leggings, large pastel-coloured T-shirts and a mop and bucket. Now, however, her barrel-like body was firmly zipped into a tight black dress and bound by a frilly white apron. In her weathered hands was a small pewter tray bearing two enormous black glass objects which Dan thought at first were vases and then realised were champagne flutes. She proffered the tray to Dan.

'What's all this?' he asked.

'They're having a party,' Anita stated, her hamster-like features glummer even than usual.

Shouts of laughter, dominated by the dinosaur roar of Kevin Swift, echoed round the hall. The party, Dan realised, was being held in the drawing room, a chamber as hideous as it was expensive. He had painted Kevin in this room and remembered the enormous fat leather sofas standing like cows in the corn amid the prairie-like swathe of thick yellow carpet. He recalled the armchairs of huge proportions, covered in a mock-tapestry material that, along with the aggressively ornate new marble fireplace, was evidently meant to suggest centuries of fine baronial living.

The pictures were of the variety Dan always thought of as antique landfill: wide, overdecorated gold frames containing tiny oils of distant mountains or unremarkable woods. Curving over them, as if what lay within the frames was worth illuminating, were shiny brass picture lights.

'You'd better go in,' Anita said, pushing the tray at him again.

Another terrifying roar came from down the hall and made Dan jump. 'I'm not invited,' he said, alarmed. 'I didn't know there was a party. Toni never said when I rang up. I've just come to drop something off.' He swung his portrait-bearing arm in Anita's direction. 'Perhaps I'd better just leave it somewhere . . .'

A high-pitched giggle followed by the sharp clack of heels on marble interrupted him. Dan looked over Anita's shoulder and saw Toni Swift emerging into the hall.

She spotted him mid-titter, and her face shut like a trap. She glared at Anita, who, as official door bitch, should presumably have prevented his entry, Dan realised. He also realised that Toni did not recognise him, which was odd, as he had been a constant presence in the house for a whole week recently. But perhaps she didn't have much of a memory. An essential condition, he imagined, of being married to Kevin.

Toni clacked towards them, her eyes – or what could be seen of them within the heavy make-up – narrowed in suspicion. As always whenever Dan had seen her, she was dressed to the nines, although tonight it was more like the tens. Her auburn-and-blonde-streaked hair spilled over her deeply tanned shoulders and she wore a red satin dress, bits of which stuck stiffly out. It was very short and showed a pair of rather gristly knees, which, like the shoulders and every other exposed part of her, were dark brown.

As Toni's skin tone had been rather more normal when he had seen her last week, and she had not, to Dan's knowledge, been to Barbados in the interim, he concluded that the colour was more salon than sunshine. But he was fascinated by the precise shade nonetheless. It hit a register on the brown scale he found it hard to categorise exactly. A sort of gingery mahogany, he concluded as she braked on the marble a foot or two in front of him.

'Can I help you?' she demanded haughtily, swapping what he knew to be her normal Estuarial for lady-of-the-manor tones. 'We're 'aving a private party 'ere this hevening.'

'I've brought the picture . . .' Dan explained, gesturing towards the large brown parcel he had been holding under his arm for what seemed hours now. He could no longer feel his fingers, he realised.

The penny dropped and Toni's cross expression gave way to one of ecstatic excitement. He watched as she totter-scampered back into the drawing room.

'Kevin's picture's come!' he heard her shouting to the assembled throng in her normal voice. 'This portrait of 'im we've 'ad done. 'Oo wants to see it?'

There was a clamour of baying affirmatives. Dan, in the hall, gazed at Anita in fright. Was it possible he would actually have to go into that room and unwrap the picture in front of everyone? Like a party entertainer?

Only he didn't feel like a party entertainer. As the whoops and shouts next door dinned in his ears, he felt like a Christian about to be thrown to the lions. But perhaps this was what party entertainers felt like, especially children's ones.

Slowly, and with trembling hands, he picked up the portrait. Anita proffered the tray of champagne again. 'It might help,' she advised. 'Good for nerves, that stuff is.'

'Who said I was nervous?' Dan squeaked.

Anita gave him a look. 'Go on,' she urged. 'I'll have the other. Down in one.'

As they chinked the vast black glasses and threw the fizzing wine down their throats, Dan felt, despite himself, a surge of something like courage. On the other hand, what had he to fear? The picture was excellent, the best he had ever done. Even a bunch of braying drunkards should be able to see that.

He went into the sitting room. Kevin Swift, buttons straining on his Raj party jacket, was standing in the forefront of a great many other people who looked oddly like him; the men all thickset and bristly and the women either the same or of the trussed, tanned Toni sort.

A woman in a black dress and white apron, who Dan dimly remembered carrying piles of ironing about the Dower House, was stumbling around in the restricted space between the big people and the big furniture carrying two plates of cocktail sausages. These were being grabbed at greedily as she passed.

It was very hot, both from the people and from the rows of thick scented candles with which Toni had crowded the marble mantelpiece. It was ablaze with flames and hot wax and looked like a fire hazard to Dan. The space above it was bare, waiting, he knew, for the finished portrait of the master of the Dower House.

He nodded awkwardly at the assembled company and at Kevin, one of whose great meaty fists was clamped round not a glass, but a magnum of champagne. It wasn't clear to Dan whether he was pouring it for someone or swigging from it; either was possible. Kevin, his face flushed with heat and beaded with sweat, pointed a finger at Dan. ''Ere,' he shouted. 'You. Let's have a look at it, then.'

Feeling the expectant eyes of at least forty Swift acquaintances boring into him, Dan bent reluctantly over the parcel beside him. Nervousness coursed through him. It was tricky, with suddenly shaking fingers, to unpick the Sellotape holding the bubble wrap together. He heard Kevin tsking impatiently. 'Come on, boy,' he snapped. 'Can't imagine what sort of bleedin' picture you've painted if you can't even open the packet.' A wave of appreciative laughter followed this remark.

Ignoring the jibes, Dan continued to unwrap. He would let the quality of his work shut them up. He peeled the final piece of bubble wrap away.

Standing the picture carefully on its side – the frame along the bottom edge disappearing almost entirely into the carpet – he placed his hands in position, turned it round and held it up to the crowd.

The room was absolutely silent. So silent that Dan could almost hear Toni's heavily mascaraed eyes batting. Excitement or anxiety? It was difficult to tell.

Kevin took a step forward. His brow was furrowed, his lips thrust forward and his enormous forearms folded ominously. 'I'm not entirely sure,' he said heavily, 'that it does me justice.'

'It doesn't, Kev,' a fat woman standing behind piped up sanctimoniously. 'You look awful in it.'

Dan threw her a furious look. What bloody business was it of hers?

'It doesn't, you're right,' chimed in someone else. 'You're a lot better-looking than that.'

'I don't mean the bleedin' picture,' Swift growled savagely at his acolytes, who fell back in alarm. 'I haven't even bleedin' well *started* on that yet. I mean . . . this.' He prodded the frame.

'What's wrong with it?' Dan croaked from a dry throat. He felt devastated. Of the many scenarios he had imagined, that Kevin Swift might not like the portrait had never occurred to him. The image was so wildly flattering, even more so now as he stood next to it, sweating, pig-like and revolting. Dan forced down jabby feelings of giddy hysteria.

'Bit bleedin' plain, ain't it?' Kevin accused, stabbing at the understated wide black wood surround with its linen inner border, a frame that Dan felt set the image off to perfection. 'I were expecting summink like one of them,' Kevin snarled, pointing at the gold horrors beneath the picture lights and taking the opportunity to swipe at the sausages as they passed. 'Summink classy.'

'And what,' Dan asked tremulously, 'do you think of the portrait?'

Kevin, his jaws working greedily over the sausage, took a step back and squinnied at the image of himself. 'Hey,' he said, noisily swallowing the masticated meat. 'What's that?' He lurched forward and stabbed at the canvas with a thick finger on which the grease from the recently consumed item could be seen shining.

'What's what?' Dan asked, wincing.

The shining finger was prodding at the painted front of the Nehru jacket. 'There's no way, *no bleedin' way*, that my gut's as big as that.'

Dan was silent. The painted Kevin was at least two stone thinner than its real-life counterpart. What could he say?

'It's not, you're right,' said the fat woman, who had come up once again from behind. 'Not an ounce of spare meat on you, Kev.'

'Not since he went on that Atkinson,' chirruped Toni.

Dan stared furiously at the corn-like waves of carpet, in which his black gym shoes were completely buried.

'*And* me nose doesn't look like that,' Kevin added indignantly. 'You've made it look like . . . I don't know . . . a snout or summink.'

Still Dan did not respond. A tremendous feeling of anger was building within him. It continued to build as he stood there and listened to everyone in the room join in. 'His hair's not like that . . . Look at that background. Very *plain*, isn't it? Not very fancy . . . You'd think 'e'd have put a bit of a pattern in there, jazzed it up a bit. You'd think he might have made an effort. Kev's bound to be paying him a fortune . . .'

Dan's hand was in the pocket of his big baggy jacket. He was not in normal circumstances a violent man, but he felt he would like to smash the picture – work of art though it was – over Kevin Swift's fat and stupid head.

As his hand closed over a cylinder, and then another one, and a thin piece of wood next to it, another desperate notion came to him. He raised his head and drew his hand out of his pocket, his fingers clasped around a number of tubes of paint and a paintbrush. Thank goodness he never left home without some materials at least, even if, forgotten in his pocket, they occasionally caused havoc in the washing machine.

'Just tell me what you want me to change,' he said to Kevin in a flat voice that betrayed nothing of what he felt. 'And I'll go next door and do it. I'll fix it on the spot.'

The car dealer nodded, apparently satisfied at this, and, with the vociferous aid of his guests, began enthusiastically to reel off the long list of inaccuracies that made up Dan's masterpiece. From which Dan gathered that, while to him Kevin Swift looked like Kevin Swift, to himself, his wife and most of his guests, Kevin Swift looked like Brad Pitt.

Dan, briefed on Kevin's revised expectations, gathered up paints and painting and set off wearily into the next room, another sitting room smaller but no less hideous than the first. Here he propped the painting up on a desk, and, after Toni had fussed around removing green marble dogs and elaborate ormolu clocks from its surface, set to work.

Or pretended to. As Toni waded through the heavy pile in her stilettos on her way out, his brush was licking the edge of Kevin's nose. What Toni did not realise was that there was no paint on the brush. Nor, after she had closed the white door with its gold-scrolled fingerboards and elaborate handle, did she see Dan sink into one of the many wide-legged, heavily stuffed blue damask chairs that squatted about the room and spend the next half-hour doing absolutely nothing.

When thirty minutes were up, Dan re-entered the main drawing room. Here, clearly several more glasses – or possibly magnums – of champagne to the good, Kevin was trying to dance with the fat woman around the edge of a glass coffee table. The candles on the mantelpiece had lowered to a single sheet of flame. 'I've finished,' Dan announced flatly. 'You can come and have a look if you like.'

Five minutes later, the entire company was crowded into the blue damask sitting room. 'Bloody marvellous,' boomed Kevin, as soon as his eyes made contact with the canvas.

'Much better,' pronounced the fat woman.

'A masterpiece,' agreed Toni.

Kevin turned to Dan and clapped him hard on the back with a force that almost knocked him over. 'You see. All you needed was a bit of advice. Pointed in the right direction.'

'Yes,' said Dan quietly. 'I see. Thank you.'

Chapter 23

It was twelve noon, but Zeb still lay amid the black Italian linen sheets of his enormous four-poster bed. He had designed it himself; encrusted with stag teeth and antlers, it was a visual reference to his potency, both as an artist and as a man.

He felt less than potent this morning, however. He felt horribly, crushingly bored. He stared up into the canopy and considered his life.

He was handsome, rich, famous, and his career was going from strength to strength. Especially now he had carried out his threat and dispensed with the services of the Sump Gallery in favour of Angelica Devon at OneSquared.

Angelica, as expected, had welcomed him with open arms. More importantly, she had welcomed him with her entire front window in which *The Right Hand of the Father II* had not only been immediately installed but hailed as a seminal and deeply significant work which Angelica had no doubts she would sell at the asking price.

The move to OneSquared had definitely been a good one, Zeb thought, mildly cheered. Angelica had also been ecstatic to hear about *Sponge*, for which she had unhesitatingly promised him the window and the rest of the gallery during the upcoming party season. She had not once mentioned video installations. Let alone neon tits or cave-painting triptychs.

Angelica clearly regarded him as the supreme artist of the moment. She shared, she told him, his indignation that he had never been asked to do the Turbine Hall commission at Tate Modern. She found it as incredible as he did that he had never been awarded the Golden Lion for lifetime achievement at the Venice Biennale or nominated for the Turner Prize. With regard to the latter, she had assured him that she had friends on the judging panel and would do everything she could to see that *Sponge* received appropriate consideration.

She had, in short, said everything he most wished to hear. There had also been a very sexy gallery assistant slinking about in a tiny skirt and very high heels. No doubt she would be happy to oblige him; gallery girls always were.

Zeb sat up in bed. Through the distant windows, a prime view of the lovely old park spread to the horizon. It gave him no pleasure to look at it, however. Was it the countryside, he wondered, that made him feel so restless? He had never been the rustic sort; why the hell had he bought a mansion in the middle of nowhere?

Various reasons, he knew. A country house had seemed de rigueur once you had reached the level of wealth that he had. His accountant had strongly recommended investing in property. And the estate agent had been very slick, glowingly describing the fantastic parties that a house such as Blackwood would be perfect for.

Only after he had bought it did Zeb think it through sufficiently to realise that he didn't, actually, have any friends to have parties with. Nor did he even like parties, not all that much. They had been vital at the beginning of his career, when he had ruthlessly used social occasions to mix with influential and powerful people. But now that he was one of the influential and powerful himself, and people used parties in order to try and mix with him, they were not nearly so enjoyable. As for the idea of entertaining the crowd of freaks, hangers-on and general art vultures who swelled most artistic London gatherings and constituted, in the widest sense, his acquaintance, it was unimaginable.

The mobile phone on his bedside table beeped to alert him to a new message. Zeb picked it up. It was Dirk Finkelstein, his manager.

In line with most artists at his level and in his position, Zeb had recently hired a powerful global entertainment agency to represent him in matters other than the purely artistic ones handled by his gallery. The agency was called Global International Talent, and his new manager wanted urgent meetings about certain pressing projects. Dirk's voice, being nasal, fast and American, was difficult to follow on a crackling mobile message, but Zeb gathered that requests had recently come in for him to mastermind a one-day flash installation, direct a ballet, design a garden and endorse a range of underwear. 'We gotta talk soonest,' Finkelstein's message ended.

Zeb closed his eyes. He felt, briefly and rebelliously, that he didn't want to talk to Finkelstein soonest. Or indeed ever, which was odd, as he had hired him and he was only doing his job.

Zeb fell back on his bed and groaned. He hated the silence of the countryside; his ears felt taut and twitchy, as if they were constantly trying to find something to listen to, like a radio trying to tune itself. And there was nothing to see, either – just endless stretches of fields and sky and the occasional glimpse of sea. It was a hopeless place to be an artist.

He didn't really want to be in the country, he now knew. And yet he didn't want to be in town either, despite the penthouse he kept by the Thames. The truth was, he didn't really want to be anywhere.

Zeb rolled over, stretching his arms out into the emptiness of the bed. There was, of course, another reason why he had bought Blackwood: to escape from Fuchsia. She never set foot in the countryside on principle. She could not get him when he was here. But what Zeb had never bargained for was that there might come a time when she might not want to get him any more.

Fuchsia had just jetted off to Art Timbuctu, another recent fixture on the international art fair merry-go-round. But she had been scheduled to return a day ago, and she had not been in touch.

Zeb forced his thoughts away from Fuchsia. It was a novelty to force his thoughts anywhere – to think at all, in fact. That was another inconvenience of the countryside – far too much time for consideration. He had penetrated sufficiently far into his consciousness to start to wonder whether another, hidden reason for the Blackwood purchase was the hope that out here, in the rolling Suffolk countryside, he might find some woman he actually wanted. Form some sort of relationship away from the jealous eye of his mistress. When it had been jealous, that was. He was not so sure any more.

Whatever the state of Fuchsia's eye, the fact remained that Zeb's secret hope had been dashed. The local village had a dearth of the colt-limbed colonels' daughters he had seen in the frontispiece of *Country Life* when he had been shopping for his mansion.

He thought again, longingly, about Angelica's gallery assistant. Another problem with the country was that slinky *metropolitaines* like that, with high breasts and Bambi eyes, were in short supply. He stared around the vast master bedroom and back to the fabulous four-poster. But there was no one here to share it with.

He stretched his lean and muscular forearms out in front of him. What should he do today? Work in the studio? But what was the point? The whole *Sponge* process, as had been the intention, went along perfectly well without him. And the sponge that had hit him the first time had not been the only one. He was beginning to wonder if they weren't being thrown deliberately.

He stared, bored, at the wall to the right which doubled as a cinema screen. Zeb himself, however, could not work a projector, and although Toombs would have been willing to oblige, the pleasure of a late-night porn movie would have been somewhat compromised by the presence of an elderly butler.

The bedside landline rang. As this was the private number that not even Dirk was allowed, there was only one person it could be. Zeb rolled over the vast black linen distance to the antlered bedside table and reached among the spikes for the receiver. He sent his hand gingerly towards the instrument, which was encrusted with shark's teeth and tended to sharpness on impact.

'I'm ready now,' he snapped to Toombs, indicating that breakfast could be served. Or lunch, or whatever it was.

'Hey, baby. I'm ready too.' The voice was not that of Toombs. It was female, American and full of teasing laughter. He'd forgotten she had the landline too. It seemed a while since she had used it.

Fuchsia. Zeb closed his eyes and swallowed; whether in relief or despair he could not quite tell. Perhaps something in between.

'I missed you, baby.'

'How was Art Timbuctu?'

'Amazing. Bigsky and I fought tooth and nail over this awesome tent installation smeared with goat dung.'

'Who won?' Zeb asked curiously.

'I did,' Fuchsia said with satisfaction. 'It was a dirty fight, though. I hit him. Anyway,' she added, changing the subject abruptly. 'I'll expect you at three. I've got a window between Nick Serota and Larry Gagosian. Three until five, and bring the diamond whip.'

Chapter 24

The excitement – if that was the word – of finding Adam incapacitated in his office had faded. The brief spike in their mutual sense of purpose had, it seemed, faded too. Alice, waiting for the lift on the landing of her flats a week or so after the drama, was thinking about the list of development objectives which, fired with hope and consumed with enthusiasm, she had composed the evening after persuading Adam that he must keep Palladio open. She had presented him with the list the next morning. It had never been mentioned since.

The familiar juddering, grinding machinery of the lift wheezed to a halt at her floor and Alice hauled the door open to get in. She hardly noticed the metal door scraping back into place and, after its usual uncertain pause, the conveyance beginning its downward motion. She was thinking about the development objectives and wondering what, given past form, she had been expecting from her employer. Had she really imagined that Adam would seize with enthusiasm on her suggestions for advertising, expansion of the mailing list and so on and rush off to implement them? Well, yes, frankly. Certainly she had never imagined that he would simply take her paper, shove it absent-mindedly in his pocket and then head out to the pub, never mentioning her efforts again.

When she had asked him about them, a couple of days later,

he had looked at her blankly. 'Oh yes,' he'd said vaguely. 'I'll look at them.'

So far as Alice was aware, the only thing Adam was looking at at the moment with any real interest was the gin optics in the nearest pub. Of her development objectives she had heard not a word. She may have persuaded him not to physically close the gallery, but it was all over in his head, she sensed. He no longer saw the point of going on in the current art environment. Zeb Spaw and *Prostheseus Bound*, damn them, had dealt him a death blow.

The lift stopped on the floor below and the door opened. So lost in her thoughts had she been, Alice realised now, that she was unprepared for the appearance of Mrs Nutt on the landing.

'Ah,' said the landlady, her wrinkled face screwed up against the light, even though little light ever reached the dank interior of the stairwell where the lift shaft was located. 'It's you.'

'Yes,' Alice agreed, bracing herself.

'Nice day,' Mrs Nutt stated unexpectedly.

Alice blinked in surprise at this, the first positive thing she could recall Mrs Nutt ever saying.

She noticed that Mrs Nutt remained on the landing instead of getting in the lift and that, moreover, she had no coat on. The weather must be blazing in that case, which was odd, as even through their own grimy panes it hadn't looked that great.

Alice had never seen her landlady without an outer covering before and had occasionally discussed with David what hidden sartorial gems must lie beneath. Persisting in his professed belief that Mrs Nutt had privately luxurious tastes, David claimed she wore nothing but vintage Dior beneath her winter coat, but Alice could see now only a rather stained lilac polyester twinset and a brownish pleated skirt. Mrs Nutt was also alone, in the sense that the grimy Black Watch – or mouldy – shopping trolley was not present. The door of her flat, moreover, clearly visible just across the landing from the lift, was open wide, revealing a dark rectangle of unlit hall.

'I wondered,' Mrs Nutt said, with a strange creasing of the face that Alice realised after some seconds was meant to be a smile, 'whether you'd mind coming into my flat for a minute.'

Alice stared. The unwonted politeness and effort at friendliness was positively unnerving. 'If this is about the rent, Mrs Nutt . . .' She did it by standing order; had there been some oversight at the bank?

Another strange creasing of Mrs Nutt's face. 'Don't be silly, dear. I want to ask you something, that's all.' She was halfway across the concrete landing now, beckoning with her claw-like forefinger.

'I . . .' Alice was about to say that she would be late for work, but what did it matter? No one would come into the gallery for some hours – lunchtime, these days, being the only time anyone did. Adam, too, was unlikely to be around until early afternoon; what he did in the morning was not entirely clear, although she suspected it possibly involved something entirely clear, in a bottle marked Gordon's.

'Just for a minute, then,' she said. Curiosity as to what the old lady wanted, and, more to the point, what the inside of her flat actually was like, had started to gain a footing.

Mrs Nutt had disappeared inside. Alice followed, taking care to wipe her feet thoroughly on the mat.

Mrs Nutt's apartment was not, as David liked to think, redolent with the scent of exotic perfume, but rather that of bacon, with a musty undertone of cabbage. Nor was there, Alice saw as she followed her landlady down a small, dark hall exactly the same as their own, any evidence of one of David's other pet theories. He had claimed in the past that Mrs Nutt owned the other flats around hers and had knocked the walls through to create a film-star apartment painted pink, primped with marabou feathers and full of chandeliers, sparkling Venetian mirrors, antique furniture, sculptures and priceless paintings.

'Want a cup o' tea, dear?' Mrs Nutt rasped, from the gloom in front of her.

This, too, was an unprecedented offer. What could it mean? Was the landlady about to evict them? 'Er, no thank you, Mrs Nutt, I've got to go to work—'

Mrs Nutt cut in. 'After what I've got to show yer, yer can give up work, dear.' She cackled.

Alice smiled to cover her amazement, but felt a pang of apprehension. Had the old woman gone mad? What was she going to show her? She remembered that no one had seen her go into the flat. David had left for the hospital an hour before. She began to think of excuses to leave, but Mrs Nutt was entirely in command of the situation.

'Come an' sit darn,' she ordered, in a voice that brooked no argument.

Alice followed obediently. Mrs Nutt's sitting room was, in reality, cramped, dark and, in what light could struggle through windows grubbier even than their own, seemed mostly brown. This effect was intensified by the fact that it did not look terribly clean. There was a small sofa with some dark, time-faded pattern and a ragged antimacassar. Next to it, a matching armchair with worn and shining arms was parked opposite the television. From its volume, Alice had always imagined this to be a colossal plasma with surround sound, but it proved in reality to be a small and distinctly old-fashioned twelve-inch which lacked even a DVD player facility.

There was a bare, plain wooden table of the utility type on which the remains of a bacon breakfast sat next to a bottle of Henderson's Relish. Of the mirrors and pictures to which David had alluded, there was little evidence; over the table there was a mirror, admittedly, although it was far from Venetian. Rather, it was the frameless sort that hung on a chain and was often to be found in junk shops. On the opposite wall hung a small picture, or what looked from where Alice stood to be a small picture. It was hard to determine either size or subject because Mrs Nutt, who had shot across the room, was now energetically climbing on a chair in front of it and wrenching it from its moorings.

'Careful, Mrs Nutt,' Alice cautioned, moving swiftly across the room. 'You might fall.' The old lady, struggling with the picture, looked more than precarious. With a grunt, she finally extracted it from its attachment, revealing a wealth of fine black dusty cobweb between picture and wall in the process. A number of small insects scuttled downwards to sanctuary behind the back of the sofa.

'There,' Mrs Nutt grunted with satisfaction, blowing on the top of the frame. She held it out to Alice, who took it, wondering what she was supposed to do with it. Had Mrs Nutt called her in in order to ask for assistance in a house move? A furniture change-round?

'Er, was there anything in particular you wanted me for, Mrs Nutt?' Alice spoke gently – while obviously she had never believed David's fantasies, neither had she imagined Mrs Nutt's flat to be quite so smelly and grim. The sight of it provoked an unexpected tenderness for the cantankerous old lady, who appeared, for the first time, in a vulnerable light. The jokes at her expense no longer seemed quite so funny.

Mrs Nutt squinted at her. There was a flash of amber from the depths of the wrinkles. 'You're 'oldin' it,' she chortled, in tones of delighted disbelief.

Alice looked at the picture in her hands. Given the dust on the glass and the general murkiness of the colours behind it, it was hard to tell what it was exactly.

'My 'usband came by that,' Mrs Nutt elucidated. ' 'E always said it was worth summink. So I reckoned, after what you were saying the other day, about that twenty million . . .'

The penny dropped, crashingly, in Alice's head. Zeb Spaw! Again! Was there any part of her life to which his vile tentacles had not stretched? First Adam, then Suki's party guests; now even Mrs Nutt, fired by the exchange in the lift about *Prostheseus Bound*, was now trying to stake her own place in the great art gold rush.

'Um,' Alice said, trying to control her annoyance. The old lady was looking at her expectantly. She could make out mountains and a gabled building in the foreground that might be a chalet of some sort. It didn't look like a Van Gogh, that was for sure. Still less a Zeb Spaw.

'Give to my 'usband, it was,' Mrs Nutt repeated. 'Been in the fam'ly for years, it 'as. What's it worth, do you reckon?' She stabbed at the picture glass, her eyes bright with speculation as she looked at Alice.

'Er . . .' Mrs Nutt's stabbing finger had removed some of the dust, and Alice could now see, beneath the oil paint thus exposed, a small printed shape with some figures in it. She bit her lip and wondered how to explain that painting-by-numbers works from the – at a guess – mid 1970s – weren't exactly at a premium at the moment.

Some half an hour later – Mrs Nutt had not taken the news well, and Alice doubted that her gabbled and garbled explanation of the workings of the contemporary art market had helped much – Alice was outside and walking down the street. She felt guilty and angry, with herself, and furious with Zeb Spaw. That the hopes of a septuagenarian pensioner had been raised and dashed entirely because of him seemed yet another of his unspeakable crimes against art and society.

The mobile in her bag rang, and Alice felt relieved at the distraction. She would be glad to talk to anyone, even a courtesy call from her mobile phone suppliers.

'Suki!' she gasped with pleasure. Far better than a courtesy call. 'How lovely to hear from you!'

'Oh, darling. It's not lovely at all.' Even allowing for Alice's tinny mobile, Suki's voice sounded thin and strained. Alice felt a clutch of concern. Had something dreadful happened? Had the bottom fallen out of the sheep sanctuary market?

'What's the matter?' she gasped, as Suki gave what sounded like a suppressed sob. 'Is it Rafael? Has something happened to him?'

'Not Rafael, no,' Suki said hurriedly. 'It's Albertine. I'm really worried about her.'

'What's the matter with her? Is she ill?'

'I think so. She's . . .' Another choked-back sob from Suki.

'She's what? Look, if you're worried, you should call a doctor,' Alice instructed fearfully.

'But the doctors round here are so hopeless, and I don't want to be hanging on for hours waiting for NHS Direct . . .'

'I would call them if you're worried, though,' Alice said gently. 'They're very good.'

Suki did not appear to have heard this. She seemed to be continuing with her last sentence. '. . . thought if I called you you might be able to give me some advice – you know, because of David. You must have picked something up from living with a doctor,' she gabbled.

'I know he'd say call NHS Direct.' Alice could only repeat her advice.

'Actually . . .' A new note had crept into Suki's voice. 'I wondered if I could talk to David? I don't have his mobile or anything, but . . .'

Alice chewed her lip. The last thing David would want in the middle of a busy day was a call from anyone, Suki least of all. 'I'm really sorry,' she said gently, 'but he just can't be called at work. I mean, even I never call him.'

'But I need his number!' Suki cried. 'You're my friend – my closest friend. You've got to give it to me.'

'What's wrong with Albertine?' Alice asked, narrowly avoiding walking into a bollard. She felt panicked by her friend's agitation.

'She's all hot and floppy and there are spots on her chest,' Suki shouted.

Alice gasped. These were the classic signs of meningitis. Her protective wall around David sank instantly into the ground.

'Call him, call him,' she spluttered, racking her brains to remember the number she knew by heart.

'Thanks,' Suki said, sounding relieved. 'I mean, I may be overreacting, but . . .'

'Call him *now*,' Alice ordered, knowing that every second counted and social niceties were irrelevant.

'Thanks,' Suki gasped, and rang off.

To relieve her feelings of panic, Alice walked at speed through Russell Square and down into Bloomsbury, picturing what was happening. Suki would be calling David now. She imagined him answering his mobile, his face first annoyed, then concerned as he realised what the reason was. Then concentrated, as he told Suki what to do. She could see this very clearly and started to feel calmer.

As she reached the locked, closed door of Palladio – no Adam – Alice had found a new cause for anxiety. Would David actually answer Suki's call? What if he looked at the number, decided he did not recognise it and ignored it? As swiftly as her shaken fingers allowed, she texted him: *Did Suki gt you? Axx*

She let herself in and went to the kitchen at the back. The roar of the kettle echoed the roar in her own brain as she imagined the enormity of what Suki must be suffering. Little Albertine, so fond of her dolls and dressing up . . .

She felt hot and cold and a terrible tension gripped her from her stomach to her throat. Until she had heard that all was well, she thought, hands shaking as she tried to navigate the kettle towards her mug, she would never be able to relax.

Chapter 25

Dan had come up early to London on the day of the painters' dinner. He had been seized by a longing to visit the National Portrait Gallery and, on arrival, found his feet making their way there almost of their own accord.

They had been there often enough before. Both during his years as an art student, and afterwards when he launched himself as a professional. And while he had never felt entirely at home in the thrusting, competitive London art world, with its in-crowd and its outrages, he had always felt both comfortable and understood in the NPG; the people pictured there were more familiar to him than photos of his own family, and had been infinitely more inspirational.

Especially the Tudors. The earliest pictures in the gallery's collections were his favourite. From an early age he had been fascinated by them, their pale, impassive faces contrasting so strikingly with their colourful and violent lives.

He stared down at his battered tennis shoes striding over the concrete blur of the pavement. He was walking quickly – quicker than he ever did in Suffolk. The countryside made you amble – although there were moments, walking through farms, for instance, when he strode. But London made you rush. He had always walked fast in the city, and now, without any conscious direction from himself, his feet had started to move quickly again. Deliberately Dan slowed himself down. There was no need to rush. There never had been; none of that hurrying he had done before had ever got him anywhere.

His thoughts drifted to their default subject: Siobhan O'Sullivan. Although he had met the new chatelaine of Aldeham Manor only once, her face had glowed in his dreams ever since, her eyes huge and green, her creamy skin surrounded with a halo of soft brown hair. He had even found himself wandering up to the Manor end of the village to remind himself exactly how pretty she was, to check that he had not imagined her in the first place.

All he had actually been reminded of was the existence of Toni Swift, tottering across her brick drive to her vast deluxe off-roader with its blacked-out windows. She had waved at him enthusiastically.

Of course, his interest in Siobhan was purely artistic and professional. It had to be. She was married, and to a musician, which of all types of man had to be the best. Apart from an artist, of course. He wondered what sort of musician Siobhan's husband was, what instrument he played. Or perhaps he sang, which was how Siobhan knew her Mozart. 'Voi che sapete' was hugely famous, obviously, but not everyone knew the whole thing in Italian.

Dan had now reached Trafalgar Square, with Nelson shooting into the air on top of his fluted column and the fountains sending great plumes of water up after him. He contemplated the beauty of the light through the pouring water, creating a powdery haze of rainbow brilliance that seemed a realm apart from the taxis and buses chugging dirtily around the outside of the square.

He glanced in dread at the latest contemporary installation on the square's controversial Fourth Plinth – a pile of beer cans, by the look of it – and hurried past the porticoed front of the National Gallery. Around the corner and up the pavement was the altogether much quieter and more modest entrance to the NPG. Dan felt a surge of satisfaction at the sight of the familiar red walls behind the glass entrance door and the guard sitting in uniform; against the crimson background, he was rather like a portrait himself.

Dan smiled at the guard, who nodded back. He strode under the Romanesque arches of the foyer and took the steep escalator up to the Tudors. There they all were still: Thomas More and his family arrayed soberly at the entrance, then, in the gallery itself, the characters who eventually did for More: Henry VIII and Anne Boleyn.

Dan gazed, fascinated, at Anne Boleyn and tried as usual to imagine this pale, plain woman with the small, secretive mouth as the flashing-eyed seductress who had thrown a kingdom into turmoil and persuaded a monarch to break with the Pope. As always, and even taking into account changing ideas of beauty, it was difficult.

Thomas Cranmer was easier to read, tense and apprehensive in his billowing lawn sleeves. As well he might be – this Archbishop of Canterbury had ended up burned at the stake on the orders of Henry VIII.

And here was Henry himself, massive as a wardrobe, legs apart, arms akimbo, gazing fiercely out from beneath his jewelled cap. Was Holbein, Dan wondered, thinking of Kevin Swift, told to reduce the king's stomach, slim down the king's legs, enlarge the king's codpiece? Almost certainly. Portrait artists, however famous and talented, had always been subject to the whims of the people they painted. Even Sir Joshua Reynolds had had to recast members of various family groups who had not felt his version of them flattering enough. I'm not alone, Dan thought, feeling brighter. Better men than me have had to put up with the likes of Kevin Swift.

And worse, much worse. Henry VIII, for example, was Kevin Swift in a crown and with the power of life or death. Portraiture was a much riskier business at his court; after all, Henry had agreed to marry Anne of Cleves on the strength of her picture alone. When she had arrived from Belgium and he had decided the portrait was over-flattering and rejected her, how terrified the painter responsible must have been. On the other hand, Anne, knowing the fate of her predecessors, was probably enormously relieved.

The backgrounds were so interesting too. The Tudors' unashamedly arriviste penchant for soft furnishings, for example: violently patterned carpets clashing with embroidered cushions and chairs with gold tassels so big and heavy they could probably ring Big Ben. And yet sometimes, for all this bombast and show – indeed, perhaps because of it – vulnerability still shone through. As in the portrait of Edward VI, the king's weakling son. His imitating the same confident pose as his father only underlined the physical difference between them.

Dan looked and looked, drinking in the detail. These images were so famous – and yet almost all by unknown artists. Unknown *portrait* artists. It seemed it had always been the fate of the painter of people to be obscure. On the other hand, fads came and went, but pictures of people always had currency. He felt a flash of triumph at the thought.

Ping. Alice's ears pricked up. Her mobile. Heart in mouth, she picked it up.

It wasn't a text. It was actually ringing. Her jangling nerves, her scrambled ears, had been unable to make the distinction.

'David?' she gasped, her voice sharp with worry. 'Is it—'

'It's fine.'

Alice felt weak with the miracle of disaster averted, and at such speed. 'Did you talk to Suki?'

Now that everything was all right, she allowed herself to revel in David's low, warm voice giving her the good news. 'I would have gone over, but it was pretty obvious from what she said that there was no need,' he reported in his capable way. 'A viral rash by the sound of it, nothing serious.'

'You could tell that just from talking to her?'

'Something and nothing,' David insisted cheerfully. 'She could have picked it up off the floor. Those bulrush ones, maybe.' He snorted.

Alice could not quite bring herself to laugh. Doctors, who dealt in life and death all day, had an almost bizarrely cavalier attitude to it at times.

'But I thought rashes were quite difficult to diagnose,' she persisted. 'Suki thought it was meningitis.'

'Hey, who's the doctor here?' David shot back genially. 'Me or you?'

'Nothing. It's just . . .'

'Just what?' he pressed.

'Well . . .' Alice hesitated. 'Are you *sure*?' David had no time for Suki; would he have listened carefully to what she said? If he had jumped to a conclusion, was it the right one? She searched for a way to put this diplomatically.

There came a sigh from the other end. 'Look, I'll tell you what. I'll go over to Suki's when I finish here and see how things are. OK?'

'Great,' Alice said.

'Just don't blame me if I'm back even later than usual.'

Dinner alone again flashed though Alice's mind, but she pushed the thought firmly away. It was on the tip of her tongue to ask David to give Suki and Rafael her love, but the phrase remained unuttered. David's visit was not a social call.

Chapter 26

The rug was small, red, rectangular and said *Fuck Off* on it in black letters. 'It's a Sharon Aura original,' Fuchsia announced, matter-of-factly unhooking her bra to reveal a pair of breasts that looked rather younger than the rest of her. 'She calls it an Unwelcome Mat.' Fuchsia gave one of her strange mirthless titters. 'That's so funny.'

Zeb did not agree. He did not find the mat funny. Not in the least. That Fuchsia had started to collect and patronise Sharon Aura was not good news for him. Goat dung from Timbuctu and Wallamaloo cave paintings were one thing; the artists were miles away. But Sharon Aura was, like him, at the epicentre of Britart – or thought she was.

'Aura's an up-and-coming name,' Fuchsia told him. 'I'm not missing out on her like I did on Quinn and Turk.'

'I wouldn't call that missing out,' Zeb retorted huffily. 'Anyway, you didn't miss out on me,' he added.

'*That's* for sure,' Fuchsia said heavily.

'An also-ran, Sharon Aura,' Zeb remarked loftily. 'She's not represented on Gold Street.'

'You think so?' Fuchsia threw him a look. 'For your information, she's just been taken on by Cornelius Sump. He's given her his whole goddam window.'

A rush of searing fury burned up Zeb's throat and sizzled at the back of his eyes. He clenched his fists as he struggled to believe it.

That bastard Sump had replaced him with his most hated rival? *Fuck* him.

'Hey, you're not *jealous*, are you?' Fuchsia's voice was mocking.

'Of course not,' Zeb snapped, quite truthfully. He was far more than merely jealous. He was homicidally furious. Frantically he tried to calm himself down. He'd get erectile dysfunction at this rate.

Of course, Sharon wasn't a real threat. She would never supplant his position. But there was no doubt she was having a damned good try, as she had been ever since her breakthrough show earlier in the year. The centrepiece, *My Saturday Night*, had been a city-centre paving stone the artist had vomited over during the course of a drunken evening before levering it up and putting it on display to earn instant notoriety and widespread acclaim.

Fuchsia, stepping out of the French knickers she always wore, went over to the sofa and lay down. 'Hey,' she admonished. 'You taking off those boxers or not?'

Was Sharon Aura providing Fuchsia with sexual services as well? Zeb wondered in panic as he peeled off his tight black jeans. Aura swung both ways, even three ways, as she had once told a journalist. The papers had been full of speculation about what the third way could possibly be.

Zeb approached the sofa reluctantly. Did he really have to do this?

Of course, it could have been worse. Fuchsia was in good shape for her age; few women with her kind of money weren't. She was one of those antelope women, all long, thin limbs and wide eyes. Fragile to look at, which was a joke given what a ball-breaker she was.

Too thin, though. He looked down at her skinny body, naked apart from the high heels she always kept on during lovemaking. Probably the only food she ever ingested was through her hair; she had once told him that she put caviar on it to make it shine. Wasn't there, Zeb suddenly remembered, some sea animal that ate through its hair; the anemone, was it? But Fuchsia, in the way she wrapped her legs round you, more resembled a sexually voracious octopus.

Ten minutes later, Zeb was having the utmost difficulty keeping his eyes away from the top-of-the-range Rolex on his wrist. Fuchsia was taking longer even than usual.

Her eyes were closed in ecstasy, and she was moaning. Zeb almost envied her. His own eyes rarely closed in ecstasy, and certainly not with Fuchsia. This was strictly business, which was purportedly what Fuchsia's billionaire husband thought went on in her office anyway. This huge chamber, stretching over the whole top floor of the Klumpps' vast white-stucco Regent's Park mansion, enjoyed every state-of-the-art convenience. But the only one Zeb had ever known Fuchsia use was the large and roomy sofa on which they routinely made love.

Interestingly the room contained no art whatsoever. He had once asked Fuchsia about this and she had demanded, with considerable scorn, what the point would be of hanging her collection in a place where no one could see it but her.

Fuchsia's fingers, which had worked their way up beneath Zeb's shirt, now dug sharp nails into his back. He stifled with difficulty an unmanly, cat-like yowl. She was grinding her pelvis upward into him, so he felt as if he were being devoured from beneath. By way of a final effort, he drew himself out almost entirely before plunging downward again. Fuchsia loved it when he did that, and now, at last, she began to shout, 'Yes, yes, *yes*.'

It was over, thank God.

'You're the best,' Fuchsia sighed.

'And you take me higher than anyone, baby,' he assured her dutifully. Well, she certainly paid more than anyone for his work; there were no mates' rates on Spaws. And they always had sex at the top of the house, so there was some truth in his remark.

'Do I?' She fluttered her eyelashes.

'You're amazing. *Amazing*,' he assured her. He always felt, at this point, like the mirror on the wall in *Snow White*. Only a less frank version.

As Fuchsia smiled, satisfied, Zeb pulled himself away. Knowing it didn't do to look too keen to escape, however, he licked his finger and circled her small brown nipple with it. 'Jesus, you're insatiable,' she growled in delight.

Oh no. She was taking him at face value. He groaned as her long-nailed fingers scratched insistently at his willy. Damn it. If it wasn't for bloody Sharon Aura, he wouldn't be in this position. Wouldn't have to be. He'd wish Aura dead, Zeb thought, were it not for the fact that her prices would automatically soar. As it was, he felt a clench of loathing almost more painful than Fuchsia's clawing at his genitals.

As he steeled himself to kiss her, Zeb saw Fuchsia's Botox-hard features soften with the wonder all women displayed at being up close to such a handsome face. It was, he knew, really very useful being as good-looking as he was. It got you a long way. It had probably got him all the way, artistic talent or no artistic talent. Good-looking, and good in bed too. That, in a nutshell – and shells were how his nuts felt at this moment – was why he was here.

He forced himself to smile adoringly, knowing how the expression suited him, whilst at the same time tenderly stroking the hairspray-stiffened carapace of Fuchsia's big blond hair.

Fuchsia was panting and gasping her way to yet another climax when a sudden commotion outside stopped her in her tracks.

The high-pitched, excited, yelling voices Zeb recognised as being those of Fuchsia's twin daughters by her hugely – and mysteriously – rich husband Herman Klumpp. A man who, judging from the panicked way Fuchsia was running about, naked apart from the shoes, scrabbling for her clothes, would not live happily with the knowledge of his wife's infidelity. Even if it was with a titan of contemporary art.

'I'd better go see what's going on.' Fuchsia dashed for the door. 'I can't have them coming in here.'

As she departed, Zeb squeezed himself back into his jeans and edged with the stealth of a cat to the office door, peering through the keyhole. The view was of the landing just below that of Fuchsia's office. Here two girls with ribboned plaits, white dresses, white ankle socks and white T-bar sandals were running up and down the stairs. They were shrieking with excitement and tossing a brightly coloured inflatable to each other. A young woman in a pale brown dress and white apron – their nanny, Zeb guessed – was trying to control them.

'Stop them!' shrieked Fuchsia, joining the chase down the stairs. '*Stop them!*' she screamed to the woman in brown. 'Can't you see what they're doing?'

'I'm so sorry, Mrs Klumpp,' the nanny gasped. 'I keep telling them. The stairs are very dangerous for small children.'

'I don't give a freak about the *stairs*,' Fuchsia bawled. 'That's my Jeff Koons they've got there!'

Chapter 27

After his uplifting visit to the National Portrait Gallery, Dan decided to drop in to another favourite haunt from student days, the British Museum. Somehow or other, however, he had got lost in thought and emerged from his reverie to find he had taken a wrong turn west and was now in Silver Street, one of the oldest and grandest of the city's shopping thoroughfares. It was an area unashamedly, indeed triumphantly, dedicated to luxury: the bow-fronted and stuccoed Georgian buildings, carefully preserved and charmingly idiosyncratic, were home to some of the most thrusting and famous names in fashion, jewellery, perfume, precious metals, luxury stationery and high-end leatherware.

Dan walked slowly along, taking in the impeccable appearance of everything. Even the ball-shaped bay trees flanking doorways looked as if all their leaves had been individually polished. Halfway down the street, a gap in the shops gave way to a Georgian arcade with top-hatted guards and classically inspired ceilings curved like chest lids, their scenes of goddesses and nymphs picked out in shades of rose and creamy orange.

It was a part of London Dan knew well from his days at the Royal Academy on Piccadilly, a mere toss of a paintbrush from where he now stood. He sighed, remembering the promise he had shown then, the prizes he had won, the excitement that he had felt, and that others had felt about him. Everything had seemed possible. His life had widened out before him, as exciting and full of promise as a newly prepared canvas.

He looked into the thickly glassed jewellers' windows with their dazzling displays of tear-shaped emeralds, rubies like blobs of jam, sapphires like flashes of sea or sky and diamonds like white fire. Diamonds seemed the most popular of all the stones, lying indolently on white velvet in the form of dazzling collars, improbable earrings and even tiaras. Dan found himself staring at stratospherically expensive watches whose faces, flanked by shining crocodile straps or set in the middle of jewelled bracelets, stared smugly back, seeming to say, 'You can't afford me. You can *never* afford me.'

Dan, walking on, knew that he didn't care. He didn't want them. None of them. But not wanting them was a separate thing from not wanting to be able to afford them. Seeing all this massy, sparkling material wealth was a reminder of how far he had *not* come since leaving London. How *un*successful he had been. As a student, lauded and laurelled and with all his career before him, he had felt able to laugh about Silver Street. Now, a couple of years down the line, a failed artist living in a rented cottage in Suffolk with reality biting hard, it seemed Silver Street was laughing at him.

And not only Silver Street. Parallel to it, as Dan knew well, was Gold Street, home of British contemporary art. But home only in the sense that the work of the most famous and notorious artists was sold here. Gold Street was galleries, expensive galleries. Nothing was created here. Nothing was created in contemporary art full stop. Apart, of course, from obscene amounts of money.

Standing at the street's end, Dan found his feet strangely reluctant to go further. He pushed them on with a savage sense of inevitability. He was here now. He may as well go and look. It was, he persuaded himself, due diligence. Every artist, whatever his persuasion, needed to familiarise himself with the current market.

Consisting of two rows of Georgian buildings facing each other across a narrow road, Gold Street had an unmistakable atmosphere of money, exacerbated by the sports cars and Rolls-

Royces drawn up to the kerb. The ground floor of every building had been converted into a gallery, all of which, from a distance, looked broadly similar. Shiny yellowish beechwood floors, greenish perspex display boxes on white plinths, spotlights and white walls, including false walls which rose up in the middle of the floor to create more display space. Each gallery had a desk close to the front which invariably contained an attractive assistant, a flat-screen monitor and, opposite the desk, two tubular steel chairs arranged to look as if the gallery's last customers had just got up and left, some considerable millions lighter. All had big front windows with the name of the gallery painted above in black letters against white. They had unattractive, aggressive names like Dystopia and Rabid, Dan noted. Or strange hybrid ones like Miroslaw Butterworth and Cornelius Sump.

The Sump Gallery, the nearest to where Dan stood, had two items in the window. One was a large white unframed canvas to which various items had been attached. The other was a small black trolley containing a lower shelf in the middle of which was what looked like a video recorder. On top of the trolley were two small black televisions, one on top of the other. Some hard squinting enabled Zeb to make out that both televisions were showing the same film, one some minutes behind the other.

The subject was an old man with an extremely large penis taking his clothes off and replacing them before removing them once again. Dan came right up to the window. The piece was titled *Old Cock*.

The objects stuck to the canvas, meanwhile, did not appear to have a name at all. They seemed to comprise a battered Maltesers box, a ragged Mars Bar wrapper and what looked like pieces of levered-up chewing gum stuck in a circle? Written on the gallery window in large red capitals was *SHARON AURA: WHAT THE EYE SEES AND THE HAND FINDS. NEW WORKS IN FILM AND FOUND OBJECT.*

Dan vaguely remembered the name Sharon Aura. Someone of that name had been a talented draughtswoman a couple of years below him at the Royal Academy. An artist especially gifted at faces, he recalled. Was this really what she was doing now? What a waste.

Directly across the road was a gallery called OneSquared, its front window dominated by what looked like a gold-sprayed hospital bed. *NEW WORKS BY ZEB SPAW*, declared the lettering on the glass.

So this was Spaw's gallery. Dan felt his lip curl of its own accord. He walked closer, up to the window, and stared in. *The Right Hand of the Father II*, declared a sign by the bed. *POA*. Price on application, Dan translated.

The sudden, crazy urge to do just that seized him. He pushed at the gallery door; realising it was locked, he rang the small brass bell to one side.

After the second ring, the girl at the front desk, who was playing Patience on the computer in full view of any passer-by, glanced up and saw him. With obvious reluctance she raised herself from her seat. After some minutes' frowning and scrabbling at the door, which evidently had a very complex security system, she let him in.

'I just wanted to find out how much that is,' Dan said, pointing at the gold bed.

For a second, as she looked him doubtfully up and down, Dan expected her to refuse, to tell him that there was no point as he obviously couldn't afford it. But instead she returned to the computer, clicked her mouse and tapped some buttons on the keyboard. There was about her, Dan felt, the detachment of the air hostess. She was an air hostess of art.

She looked up. 'Four hundred thousand pounds.'

Dan knew he should not be surprised, but he felt the room spinning round him nonetheless. *Four hundred thousand pounds?* For a gold-sprayed *bed*?

A wave of loathing for Spaw, Sharon Aura, Gold Street and all they stood for swept through him, closely followed by one of despair.

Then the girl gasped. 'Oh, silly me,' she exclaimed, giggling. Dan grinned. 'I thought it must be wrong,' he said, feeling his vertical hold right itself again.

'I just quoted you the gallery commission.' She looked up, her face crimson with mirth. 'The actual artwork is priced at four million.'

Curled in the zebra-skin armchair in her office upstairs, Angelica looked out of the window at the young man walking quickly – very quickly – out of her gallery below.

Resplendent in a beige fringed suede skirt and leather waistcoat, she noticed his charity-shop clothes and felt a wave of contempt. What the hell had he been doing, coming in? It wasn't as if he could afford anything in her gallery. And it wasn't good for business if people walked past and saw someone so obviously poor standing inside. Art buyers were aspirational.

Angelica tried to concentrate on the fact that Penelope from Diamond Snail was sitting opposite and they were supposed to be having a meeting about the party. It was, however, hard. Her thoughts kept jumping about in nervous excitement, as they had ever since Zeb Spaw had left Sump and come over to her.

'Such a shame, Cornelius,' she had purred with satisfaction the first time she ran into her defeated rival on the party circuit. 'But I know you've done all you can for Zeb. Someone else has to take him to the next level.'

Rather to her surprise, Cornelius had merely smiled back serenely. 'The next level down, you mean? Spaw's over. Totally sub-prime. No one's going to be buying stuff like that any more, least of all at those prices.'

Of course, he was only jealous, Angelica told herself firmly. He would say that. She averted her eyes from the display in the window opposite. Sharon Aura was *not* a bigger star than Zeb Spaw.

'We really need to make some canapé solution decisions,' Penelope from Diamond Snail was saying. Open on her wrap-dressed knee was a large, leatherbound ringbinder; threaded between the rings were plastic-sleeved photographs of enlarged and very elaborate finger food.

'This one,' she began, turning the binder so the photograph faced Angelica, 'is Diamond Snail's trademark canapé. Our hit record, if you like. Shaved fennel with truffle oil accompanied by lobster bisque in a test tube.'

It all sounded rather gynaecological, Angelica thought. All that shaving and test tubes. She looked at her fingernails absently. 'What are the other galleries doing?'

Penelope tucked her hair behind her ear and scrolled down her BlackBerry. 'Rabid is having a pata negra ham being sliced to order so guests can see the theatre.'

Angelica looked up in panic. 'What theatre?' she yelped. 'You mean to say they're building a bloody theatre in the back of that gallery as well?'

'The theatre of the ham being *carved*,' Penelope explained. 'It's an art form.'

'Is that so?' Angelica narrowed her eyes. She would be the judge of what was an art form, thank you very much. Was it not her job? Was it not how she had managed to land the big fish of Zeb Spaw?

She tried to drag her mind back to lobster bisque test tubes and ham theatres but found it simply sliding away again. For some reason she could not concentrate. She was triumphant at the moment, but also jittery. A dangerous condition, she knew. Jitters meant bad decisions. She briefly considered calling Natasha, her gallery assistant, upstairs to bounce some canapé ideas off her, before remembering that one didn't bounce ideas off Natasha. Any ideas aimed in her direction sank in and disappeared without trace, like pebbles in particularly thick, deep mud.

Chapter 28

Released by Fuchsia, his duty done, Zeb was free. The surge of relief he felt upon leaving her mansion lasted just as long as it took to listen to the messages on his mobile.

Dirk Finkelstein had called again. A leading luxury interiors company had requested that Zeb design the piece of furniture of his dreams. Zeb listened to his manager droningly explaining that a female film star had designed a luxury chihuahua kennel complete with platinum food bowls and a music system her pets could operate with their feet. Perhaps Zeb could do something similar?

Zeb pressed the off button impatiently. Did he want to design pointless pieces of crap like that? No he bloody well didn't. He didn't know what he wanted to do. Apart from finding an outlet of some kind for the enormous frustration he felt. Having so recently been Fuchsia's plaything, crushed by her phenomenal power, made him want to assert himself in every way possible.

He decided to drop in on OneSquared – kick ass, crack the whip. He could transfer his own feelings of humiliation by making someone else feel small. And one never knew; perhaps seeing what Angelica was doing with his work really would make him feel better. She might even have sold *The Right Hand of the Father II*.

He roared up Gold Street in his Lotus and, with a tearing screech of tyres, came to a halt outside OneSquared. He swung the long red driver's door open and casually got out.

As he walked towards his new gallery, Zeb threw a casual glance across the street in the direction of his old one. Did he care if Cornelius was standing there in his Prince of Wales check cashmere, glowering through his lenseless glasses? The hell he did. He could not have cared less that Sump had taken on Sharon Aura.

His eye, nonetheless, could not resist flicking sideways to the window of his erstwhile representatives. It was fuller than he had expected. There was a television there – two tellies, in fact, piled on top of each other. Some old bloke taking off his underpants. Zeb stared. And what was stuck to that canvas? Looked like a bloody Maltesers box. *SHARON AURA: WHAT THE EYE SEES AND THE HAND FINDS. NEW WORKS IN FILM AND FOUND OBJECT.*

Zeb stared, hot-eyed. His mind teemed, maggot-like, with questions. How come Aura was doing video and found objects all of a sudden? It had been vomit on paving stones last time he looked, or rugs like the one Fuchsia had. Some people would do anything to be fashionable.

Furiously he turned away and stomped towards OneSquared. He scowled through the door at Natasha, the assistant, clacking towards it to open up. Her beam was bright and welcoming. She did not, Zeb realised, seem to have registered his mood at all.

Jesus, she was good looking. He looked her up and down as he passed, taking care to move close enough to brush her breasts as he stomped into the gallery, the rubber soles of his trainers squeaking on the wooden floor. Something surged within him as he felt the breasts spring back without the presence of any restraining underwear.

'Hey, babe,' he growled, tossing his shining black hair over his muscular shoulders and putting his hands on his narrow, tight-black-jeaned hips.

'Good morning, Mr Spaw,' Natasha lisped toothily.

He nodded at *The Right Hand of the Father II*. 'Sold that yet?'

Natasha shook her glossy swirl of black hair. 'No, but we had an enquiry just now.'

'A collector?' Zeb demanded.

Natasha looked thoughtful. 'Might have been.'

Zeb felt impatient. These girls should have pictures of all the richest and most influential patrons taped to their bloody bedroom walls; he certainly had, when starting out. 'What did he look like?'

'Thin. Glasses.'

Not Saatchi, then. 'Bill Gates?' Zeb pursued.

Natasha looked helplessly back at him.

Zeb tried to suppress his irritation. Thick she may be, but gorgeous all the same and, frankly, a spot of light relief would not come amiss. As an antidote to the encounter with Fuchsia, for one thing. Natasha's girlish floral perfume floated into his nostrils as he smiled wolfishly and glanced around. Angelica did not appear to be in residence.

'Cat away?' he murmured, turning to Natasha, who giggled and swung her long hair.

'We don't have a cat, actually.'

He rolled his eyes. 'Angelica?'

Natasha did not seem to make the connection between that and the cat reference. 'Actually, Miss Devon's having a meeting upstairs with Diamond Snail.'

'Who the hell is that?' Zeb barked. Suspicion flared within him. Another happening new artist, one he had not heard of?

'They're party planners, actually.' Natasha smiled. 'I'll just get her—'

'*No!*' Zeb hissed quickly, reaching out and enclosing the slim white wrist with his large brown fist. 'No need to disturb her,' he added to the big, beautiful eyes now staring in surprise. 'I can wait. Well – for her, that is.' Otherwise, his situation demanded immediate relief. The way this girl was shaking her hair over her face made him feel his trouser zip was about to burst.

Natasha looked back at him blankly. She really was spectacularly stupid, Zeb realised glumly. He hadn't thought he would have to work this hard. It crossed his mind that she was double-bluffing, but he rejected it. He prepared to gird his straining loins and try again.

'Maybe,' he suggested to the dark-haired beauty, 'you could make me . . . a cup of tea or something. In the back room, if you've got one?'

'We have got a back room,' Natasha confirmed brightly. 'But we haven't got any tea.'

'Well,' Zeb purred, pulling the wrist he held towards him. 'Why don't we go in the back and see what you *have* got?'

'Miss Devon doesn't touch caffeine. Only alcohol . . .' Natasha was saying as they walked away.

'Of course, the invitations went out some weeks ago?' Penelope was enquiring upstairs.

Angelica raised an eyebrow. If this was Penelope's roundabout way of trying to get her to share that most private of assets, her all-important, top-secret guest list, she had another think coming.

'*Months* ago,' she corrected. 'Gold envelopes and all. All hand-calligraphed, obviously.'

'Obviously.' Penelope nodded. 'I'm only asking because I was at Elle Macpherson's the other day helping plan her son's birthday party and I couldn't see a OneSquared invitation among all the Gold Street ones on her mantelpiece.'

'It would have been there somewhere,' Angelica insisted comfortably. 'Natasha sent them out.' But even as she spoke, she was conscious of an odd flicker of doubt. Within seconds, it seemed, a swift, sick surge was swirling round her insides. Of *course* Natasha had sent them. Hadn't she?

Angelica, now she came to think of it, could not remember checking. But surely, not even Natasha, dim as she was, could possibly have failed to take them to the post office at the end of that long day when Angelica had painstakingly checked every card and envelope for spelling mistakes when the written invitations and addressed envelopes had returned from the calligrapher. No. It was impossible. Not even Natasha . . .

Angelica's eyes flicked towards a distant corner of her office, to the grey filing cabinet in which the cards had been placed after she had checked them, ready for Natasha to take to the post office. Even Penelope had stopped talking, as if realising that something else far more weighty was occupying her client. A heavy and horrible silence hung in the room as Angelica got to her feet and stumbled over the wooden floor towards the cabinet. With trembling fingers she seized the edge of the top drawer and yanked it. The drawer opened with a screech of protest.

Looking up at her was a pile of thick gold envelopes, their addresses carefully written in purple copperplate.

Angelica gasped and staggered backwards. She collided with the side of an occasional table, knocked it over and was herself hit on the head by a lamp. She crashed to the ground, temporarily stunned.

'Are you OK?' Penelope gasped, concerned.

Angelica scrambled to her feet. 'Natasha . . . the invitations . . .' She was gibbering, her eyes as wild as her hair as she staggered across the room to the circular hole in the centre of the floor which formed the entry point into the office for anyone coming up the spiral staircase from the passage below. She shot down the stairs and into the gallery. No one was there. Hysterical, she ran into the passage, shouting Natasha's name and crashing open the doors to the various rooms. It was by this means that, in fairly short order, she discovered her errant assistant on the floor beneath the gallery's panting new star artist, the veins standing out on his neck with the effort as he pumped furiously between her thighs.

She stood on the threshold, seething but helpless. They were both making too much noise and effort to notice her. Besides, interrupting them might have unpredictable consequences, which Penelope, upstairs and no doubt straining her ears to listen, would have round the rest of Gold Street in seconds. No, discretion was the better part of valour. Reaching for the handle, the tight-faced gallery owner closed the door. She would, she decided ominously, deal with Natasha later. Deal with her hard and conclusively.

Dealing with Zeb was trickier; he was crucial to the future success of OneSquared. She could hardly complain even if he was having his wicked way with her assistant.

Angelica walked angrily back across the floor of her gallery. A movement outside caught her eye; looking up, she was pleased to see, through the window, on the other side of the gold-sprayed NHS bed, a particularly vengeful-looking traffic warden writing out a ticket and placing it with evident satisfaction on the windscreen of Zeb's parked Lotus.

Chapter 29

Was it the shock about Albertine? Alice wondered. Something about events earlier that day seemed to have galvanised her finally to action. Since she could obviously be waiting for ever for Adam's permission to begin the development plan, she had decided she would just begin it anyway. It wasn't as if there was much else to do in the gallery these days; it would keep her usefully occupied.

She had fetched down from Adam's messy office the mailing list as it currently stood. She had taken out the empty cigarette packets – long-extinct brands in most cases – and the envelopes on which names and addresses were scribbled, and had spent most of the afternoon sitting at the desk at the back, copying them out into a coherent alphabetical list for checking.

While squinting at the illegible writing tired her eyes, Alice felt happier and more positive than she had for some time. Taking her fate into her own hands and doing something about it gave her the illusion of control; the time, in addition, seemed to go much faster. Occasionally, she even hummed.

She was frowning over a name that could either have been Monty or Minty Fortescue when she heard the entrance bell ping. Surprised, she jumped to her feet and hurried to greet the unexpected customer. She was fairly sure that it would not be Adam.

It was not. A tall, dark-haired young man was looking round, walking from table to table and rack to rack in soft-soled shoes that made no sound on the floorboards.

He was, Alice thought, interesting-looking. He wore a white shirt, pale baggy trousers with turn-ups, a matching jacket that looked too big for him, and tennis shoes worn with white socks. A funny mix of thrift shop and sports shop, she thought. And yet, somehow, it worked. She watched as he picked up a small Burne-Jones pencil sketch. He really looked at things, she noticed.

Not handsome, she thought, but interesting, sensitive, his eyes long and dark beneath the black-framed glasses he wore. He had a delicate nose and cheekbones, a long, humorous mouth and floppy jet-black hair that had a clean sort of flash about it.

Dan had been coming from Gold Street, on his way to the British Museum, when he had spotted the Palladio Gallery. By the looks of it, it had been here for years but he couldn't recall seeing it before. Perhaps he had always approached the museum a different way.

He was immediately attracted to the gallery; it was so unassuming, so unshouty compared to those he had left behind him in Gold Street. He pushed open the door, feeling a wave of joyful relief at the sight of all the pictures hanging in traditional fashion from the picture rails, the unframed mounts stacked against the chair backs, the battered reference books lined up on the mantelpiece. There seemed not one single square inch of this place that was not covered in paintings, etchings, sketches or prints of some sort. It was a gallery that breathed passion and enthusiasm, spontaneity and eccentricity. It was obvious it would have no truck with contemporary minimalism, with gold-sprayed beds and video installations.

As such, he had expected to find some tweedy old buffer lurking at the back, or a matron in bifocals. Not a red-headed bombshell with lively, curious eyes. He took in her pale face and wide red mouth. Her body was slim and lithe in a black poloneck jumper and black Capri pants. She reminded him of someone but he could not think who.

'Like it?' Alice asked him, brightly. He was looking intently at an Augustus John sketch of a woman's head.

'It's great,' he said, putting it regretfully back. 'But I'm afraid I can't afford it. I'm not really in the picture-buying league. I have a hard enough time selling my own, to be honest.'

'You're a dealer?' Alice asked, suddenly suspicious.

'Not a dealer. An artist.'

'What sort of artist?' Alice was curious.

'Portraits. Just old-fashioned portraits. Of people.' There was something almost apologetic about the way he said it, Alice noticed.

'But that's great.' She smiled.

He shot her a quizzical look. 'Think so? I'm beginning to wonder.'

'Why?' Alice asked. 'It's a wonderful thing to be.'

Dan smiled. A warm feeling was spreading through his insides. He remembered the triumph he had felt in the National Portrait Gallery, before he had gone to Gold Street. This girl was right. Sod Kevin Swift, Zeb Spaw and the rest of them. It *was* a wonderful thing to be.

'I'm Dan,' he said.

'Alice.'

'You work here?'

Alice nodded. 'You sound surprised.'

Dan shrugged. 'It's just that . . .' He paused, wondering what he meant to say, exactly.

'Just that what?' Alice pressed. She could guess exactly what – the place was clearly on its knees. But now that she was working on the solution, the problem no longer upset her as it had. 'Just that I don't look as if I'm the sort of girl who would work here?' she demanded of Dan, eyes dancing. 'That I'm more the Gold Street sort?'

He reddened. 'Something like that. I'm sorry,' he added,

imagining he had offended her. 'I always say the wrong thing,' he admitted.

She smiled. 'It doesn't matter. Everyone says that. But actually, I don't want to work in Gold Street. I don't like that sort of art.'

'Me neither,' Dan said eagerly.

Alice laughed. 'Well there you are, then. And I can imagine what you're thinking about this place.' She waved a hand around the crammed and dusty walls, shelves and chairs. 'But I've got a plan to get it back on its feet.'

'Good for you,' Dan said warmly. Relieved she was not cross, he shook his flop of hair back from his glasses.

Alice noticed how his fingers seemed to twitch, as if he longed to reach for his paintbrush. She was sure he must be good at what he did. His old-fashioned portraits. She remembered how bringing in exciting new work – done to old-fashioned standards of excellence – was one of her development objectives. 'I'd like to see some of your paintings,' she said. 'Perhaps we could sell them here.'

Dan reddened with joy. A London gallery was offering to represent him! Admittedly, this ramshackle and decidedly eccentric place was not what he had imagined. But it was a start. A platform. He beamed at Alice.

Now the doorbell pinged and Adam came in.

'Hello,' Adam said, looking Dan up and down with his bright brown eyes.

'Hello,' Dan replied genially.

'Good afternoon, Beatrix.' He was speaking fast and excitably; he was, Alice guessed, several gins to the good. Her heart sank. Fortunately, he didn't – or possibly couldn't – say anything more, just headed for the stairs leading to his office. They listened as he stumbled noisily up them, opened the upstairs door with a crash and then, amid a series of shattering bangs, entered the office.

'That your boss?' Dan was looking at her doubtfully, Alice saw.

She nodded glumly. It was obvious he was having second

thoughts about selling his work through an establishment run by such a person.

'But he called you Beatrix.' Dan's tone was curious. 'Aren't you called Alice?'

She nodded; her red hair, he saw, shimmered and glowed in the light. 'He thinks I look like Lizzie Siddal.' She took a deep, resigned breath to explain.

Dan cut in excitedly. '*Beata Beatrix.* He thinks you look like that Rossetti painting.' He nodded. 'He's bang on there. I *knew* you reminded me of someone.'

Chapter 30

Later that evening, at the Federation of Portrait Painters' dinner, Dan's renewed confidence in his profession had long since seeped away. His buoyant mood at the Palladio Gallery seemed a very long time ago as he sat at a long, polished rectangular table in the panelled dining room of a St James's club. The walls were hung with large portraits whose frames seemed to exhibit a higher degree of skill, liveliness and artistic commitment than the pictures they contained. Blurred, flat and expressionless of face, the subjects of these portraits gazed out, each one more bored than his predecessor.

There were at least forty attendees at the dinner, Dan counted, if you included partners as well. He had not realised that wives were invited; on the other hand, he had no one to ask but Birgit, and clubland London – well, this type of club, anyway – was hardly her scene.

Was it his, for that matter? It was evident already that his hopes of gaining useful information and contacts from his fellow FPP members were doomed to disappointment. Far from being a celebration of the art of portrait-painting, the gathering seemed more about reading the last rites over it.

The evening began with a speech in which the President of the Federation, a lean, weary-looking man with grey hair and dandruffed shoulders, lamented the unfashionability of portraiture. 'There is an unprecedented lack of demand for our particular skills,' he intoned in a dolorous fashion that made Dan's heart sink into his boots. With such a man representing their interests, it seemed unlikely that matters would improve. He looked around at the huge frames on the walls – bad, certainly, but equally certainly from the golden age of portrait-painting – and felt rather that they were mocking him.

Over the dinner of rubber chicken and what seemed to Dan to be rough red wine despite the smartly labelled bottles, the painters around him lamented their lack of success. 'Don't you hate Young British Artists?' Dan's neighbour, a man with alarming eyebrows, demanded.

Dan smiled. 'Well, I suppose I am one, really.'

His neighbour snorted rudely. 'Oh yeah?'

'By which I mean I'm young and I'm British and I'm an artist,' Dan pointed out, slightly defensively.

'But you're not *successful*, are you?' the eyebrows remarked witheringly.

'Er . . .'

'No, you're not. None of us is.' He thumped the table, making the cutlery jump and the glasses chink nervously. 'I'm talking about the successful ones.' *Thump*. 'The ones who make money.' *Thump*.

'I see,' said Dan, crushed.

'All they care about is being famous,' his neighbour ranted. 'It's I want to be famous first and then I want to be a famous artist second, and ooh, shall I work in shit or shall I work in sick or shall I work in rubbish. And then someone buys it and sells it for a fortune. *Pah*,' he added, stabbing his rubber chicken as if it were Tracey Emin's naked breast.

'You don't want to be famous, then?' Dan asked mildly.

The bushy-eyebrowed man, now taking a swig of red wine, choked into his glass and threw Dan a glare.

On Dan's other side, a heavily bearded man in paint-spattered glasses was tearing into Lucien Freud.

'Yeah, of course he's done some works of genius, but you know, that was a while ago, and his late stuff, well, frankly, I wouldn't hang it in my downstairs loo.'

'I would,' said Dan immediately. 'It's worth millions, isn't it?'

The beard turned to him, his eyes baleful behind his glasses, which were flecked with paint. Rose madder, Dan spotted. Prussian blue.

'In money, yes,' the man said heavily. 'But artistic merit, well, that's another thing.'

Dan frowned. 'Yes, but how do you judge it? *Who* judges it? Is it the artist, the sitter, the establishment, posterity?' He raked a hand through his glossy black flop of hair. 'I mean, I've just painted what I think is the best portrait of my life. But when I showed it to the sitter, he . . . well . . .' He shook his head.

'Typical,' spat the man with the eyebrows, who was leaning in to listen. 'There's no autonomy in portrait-painting any more. They don't give a toss about how well it's painted, they just want to look good. *Bastards*.'

As the beard now started to boast about painting the Queen, Dan decided he had had enough. He rose to his feet.

'I'm sorry,' he muttered. 'I have to go.'

No one took the slightest notice.

'Her Majesty's the most amazing mimic,' the beard was asserting smugly to a rapt audience as, unnoticed, Dan left the room. 'Her Ken Livingstone impression is quite impossible to tell from the real thing . . .'

Dan walked swiftly to the nearest tube station. Hopefully, if the tube was behaving itself, he would get to Liverpool Street in time for the last train home. He would be cutting it fine, certainly, and the rush would be stressful. But he could not afford to stay in London, and so there was no choice.

Maddeningly, Piccadilly Circus station was closed for some reason, and so Dan crossed the road and dived into Soho. He hurried along the dark pavements, running over the evening's events. The company he had kept seemed a miserable confirmation of how far portrait-painting had fallen in the public esteem, as well as in terms of interesting members. Past ones included Joshua Reynolds, Thomas Lawrence and William Hogarth. It was tempting, he mused, to speculate what the famous satirist would have made of the unintentionally comic bunch he had just quit.

Dan felt he recognised where he was, that he had been here recently, and he realised now that the Bloomsbury side street up which he was hurrying was the one on which the Palladio Gallery was located. Yes, there it was up ahead – the one property in the street without a single light in its window. There remained, however, the memory of the comfort he had felt there earlier. He paused by the shopfront and squinted into the shadows. As he did so, something moved in the dark and deep-set doorway beside him and made him jump.

Alarmed, Dan backed into the street and appraised from afar the slumped form. A tramp, he thought at first. But then two things happened: the form groaned, and at the same time moved a hand on which a signet ring glinted in the soft orange light of the street lamp. Whoever it was sounded ill, Dan realised. And he was obviously not a tramp; tramps did not wear signet rings.

Of course, signet ring or not, it was the ill aspect that mattered. Dan approached the man – he was pretty sure it was a man – on the floor and bent over him. In the limited light he could see he was wearing a suit, tweed it looked like. And a tie and shirt. By the time Dan noticed the glasses, the feeling that, somehow, he knew this person, had seen him before, was becoming too strong to ignore. Then, as he gently removed the arm covering most of the rest of his face, he remembered where. This was the man he had seen earlier in the day, coming into Palladio and going upstairs. The gallery owner, who called Alice Beatrix, after the Rossetti.

Dan looked at his watch. Ten minutes to his train. On the other hand, he felt a sense of responsibility to the prone form before him as well as to Alice, who had been so friendly – even offering to sell his works. It was unthinkable that he turn on his heel and leave. But what, on the other hand, should he do?

Dan was no doctor, but it was obvious even to him that the owner of Palladio was in a bad way, and getting worse by the second. In the few minutes he had been there, the man's groans had started to become punctuated by a dreadful rasping sound.

Had he had a stroke? Dan tried to roll him on his back to look at his face. He tried to remember the checks you could do for stroke: if the face sagged and the arms were floppy and the speech was slurred. But this poor man was some distance beyond speech. And his face had been saggy to begin with, from what Dan remembered.

Dan whipped out his mobile and called 999. It took only a few minutes before the siren of an ambulance could be heard wailing towards them over the general West End evening noise. He stood protectively beside the body as the narrow street was suddenly filled with shattering noise and revolving blue lights.

While he was now certain of missing the one to Suffolk, his suspicion was growing that the man on the pavement beside him had got his own particular last train home.

Chapter 31

The discovery of the unsent invitations had been one of the worst moments of Angelica's entire life. Natasha's witterings, as she was bundled out of the gallery door, about there having been a long-running postal strike at the time had proved little compensation.

There was nothing much she could do about finding her assistant and star artist in flagrante. Obviously, no blame for what had happened could be attached to Zeb, even though it was more than likely he had initiated it. Natasha was far too dim to have tried to seduce him. That sort of fast and fancy footwork had been Angelica's own speciality in her groupie days. How else had she snared Nick Devon, one of the richest rock stars of his generation, but also the most stoned and drunk? To this day she was fairly certain he had had no idea who had been standing beside him at the register office.

Nick had been so out of it that she had literally had to move his pen-holding fingers across the page to help him sign. But it had been worth it – his money had helped her realise her long-held dream of being a powerful mover and shaker in the art world, a dream that would last as long as his fortune did. And that, thanks to a canny accountant and the fact that teenagers in China and Eastern Europe still bought his music, showed no sign of running out yet.

Now that Nick no longer drank or took drugs, he was also

capable of making the occasional highly lucrative festival appearance, although Angelica was careful not to push him too far. His seat on the wagon of sobriety had not been achieved easily. Years of therapy had seen him in and out of clinics everywhere from Roehampton to Arizona, undergoing treatment for everything from paranoid schizophrenia to addictions ranging from sex to drugs and most things in between. One of the institutions, which had an organic garden, had made the clinical breakthrough and found that what Nick enjoyed most was getting his hands dirty. This had been mixed good and bad news for Angelica. Had all the expense and annoyance of the therapy years been worth it, when the eventual solution was sending Nick down the bottom of the garden with a hoe?

Still, he had been clean for some years now, and if that meant there was a permanent surplus of carrots in the house, a vegetable Angelica particularly hated, it was a small price to pay. Or at least, a smaller one than had been paid for any previous form of treatment.

Even so, Nick had been hard work and Angelica often thought that had she had her time over again, she might have turned to the art world to find a husband. Art was almost as good as showbiz for finding rich men. Celebrities and oligarchs came in and out of Gold Street all the time, and some of the girls from the other galleries had struck lucky. Yet Angelica doubted Natasha had harboured ambitions of this nature, or ambitions of any nature for that matter. Had she been Natasha, she would without question have tried to entangle a rich and powerful man like Zeb Spaw in her toils, albeit in a more subtle fashion than allowing herself to be caught in the office with her skirt over her head.

But the fact that Natasha was nothing like her had been one of the reasons Angelica had employed her in the first place. She had thought, then, that she didn't want anyone with more than one brain cell. The post incident had radically altered this view, as had the girls she had interviewed so far. Natasha, admittedly, had been far from brilliant, but even she hadn't thought Leonardo da Vinci starred in *Titanic* with Kate Winslet.

The assistant she was now looking for, Angelica decided, needed to be sufficiently without guile as to be trustworthy. But also with enough brains so as to be useful, and, given Zeb's recent activities, slightly less drop-dead gorgeous whilst still being decorative. But where, Angelica wondered, was such a paragon to be found?

She slumped in her zebra-skin chair and stared out of the window, as she frequently did these days. The naked old man flickering on the screen across the road at Sump had a strange claim on her attention. Had she missed a trick by taking on Spaw instead of Aura? Had she allowed delight at beating a rival obscure her usual lynx-eyed business vision?

Spaw's behaviour had been a disappointment, to put it mildly. Of course contemporary artists should behave in a rock-and-roll way; it was good for business, essential to the image. But the sight of Zeb and Natasha at it like rabbits in the back room had been rather too much rock and definitely too much roll.

She had lost money already by taking him on, because Ganymede Steam, objecting to Spaw on artistic grounds, had taken his frozen urine sculptures down the street to Sell Out. This constituted a loss of face; the fact that the faces in question were made of iced wee was beside the point.

Angelica pulled herself together with a will. Getting Zeb was a triumph, there were no two ways about it. Aura might yet prove to be a flash in the pan. She took some deep, advanced-Pilates breaths and tried to still the rising feeling of panic. Yet for all her efforts to forget it, Cornelius's description of Zeb as sub-prime kept returning. And it was a fact – she could see it from her own window even now – that more people were going into Sump's to see Sharon Aura's installations than were coming to hers to see the gold bed. Perhaps it was time for Zeb to come up with something new – newer even than these *Sponge* pictures he'd mentioned, possibly.

The telephone suddenly rang and jerked her out of her reflections. After automatically waiting for someone else to answer it, and then realising there was no one else apart from her, she seized it in panic.

'Hello?' she drawled in an elaborately relaxed manner. It was crucial, in Gold Street, to seem in control at all times.

It was not Zeb. Angelica was not immediately sure who it was. The voice was high-pitched and speaking very rapidly in an excited foreign accent. After some moments, and having caught several key words, Angelica eventually recognised Mercedes, her Filipino housekeeper.

'What is it, Mercedes?' She cut irritably into the incomprehensible torrent.

'Meester Nick, he go boom,' Mercedes exclaimed in reply.

'Boom?' repeated Angelica, panic clawing at her concave belly beneath her wide and ornate belt.

'He come in kitchen and go shoutycrackers,' Mercedes reported breathlessly. 'He take off all his clothes.'

'Where is he now?' Angelica shrieked.

'I no know. He ran out kitchen and ran street waving big carrot.'

'Big carrot?' Angelica clutched her poodle fringe of hair in despair. Her worst fears had been realised. On top of all her other problems, as if she didn't have enough to cope with, Nick had now, by the sound of it, fallen spectacularly off the wagon.

'I call police, Mees Angelica?'

'No, I mean, yes, oh God, I don't know!' Angelica yelled. What exactly was the correct course of action when one learned that one's husband was running unclothed down the Queen's highway brandishing a large vegetable? 'Just wait there,' she said, trying to sound decisive. 'I'll be straight back.'

Just as Angelica, with shaking fingers, was locking the gallery, her Hermès bag began to ring. Hurling it to the ground and rummaging in it for her mobile, Angelica prayed as fervently as a non-believer could that it wasn't Zeb Spaw on the other end.

'Angelica? It's Caroline here. Caroline Ramage, from the BBC?' Distractedly, Angelica tried to think, then remembered the rather forceful woman with the bob who had arrived and taken a great many notes some weeks ago.

'Remember we were talking about a documentary about Gold Street?'

'Oh . . . yes,' Angelica said. 'Yes,' she added, with more enthusiasm. 'Absolutely. Yes.'

'Well it looks as if we've got the green light. Also, I think we might focus on OneSquared as our main gallery. We'll follow you through the preparation for the street party, the run-up, that sort of thing.'

'Oh,' said Angelica, absorbing this information. Suddenly, the morning did not seem so bad after all. An entire BBC documentary devoted to OneSquared! The publicity would be fabulous. If that didn't satisfy Zeb Spaw, she could not think what would.

'We need to meet,' Caroline said crisply. 'Will you be free this afternoon? Four, at your gallery?'

Angelica calculated the likely length of time it would take to get home, deal with Nick and return to OneSquared. If it was another sectioning, like last time, it could be a few hours. 'I'll do my best,' she said. 'But I'm without an assistant at the moment, so I'm a bit stretched. But yeah, four should be OK.'

In accordance with her usual drill on such occasions, Angelica immediately picked up the phone and ordered sumptuous flower arrangements for everyone in the street who may have seen her unclothed husband – she wanted no trace of the incident appearing in the press. Then, and only then, she called Nick's doctor and demanded a psychiatrist be sent round to deal with the patient.

By the time Angelica reached the large house in Twickenham she shared with her troubled husband, a semblance of order had been restored. Nick, his long, straggly hair sticking to his pale and sweating brow, was in the sitting room, lying on the chaise longue. His skinny naked form was covered with a sheet and his eyes were wide, crazed and rolling wildly around their sockets.

'He thinks he's the victim of a conspiracy between MI5 and the world's biggest art collectors,' explained the specialist psychiatric doctor, to whom Angelica had taken an instant dislike despite his smooth good looks. There was a relentless seriousness, not to mention an improbable name, about Dr Love. Was he for real? He seemed impervious to Angelica's charms and would not, she sensed, be the pushover that Nick's previous doctors had been.

'Oh fuck,' said Angelica, instantly grasping that her husband had gone considerably further beyond the bounds of sanity than on any previous occasion. Was it all her fault? Had she been talking about the gallery too much? On the rare nights when she was home and not out at some art party, he was always interested to hear the latest, just as he expected her to be interested in the progress of his beetroot.

Nick's pupils, she noticed, had shrunk to pinheads. Nonetheless, they seemed to be focused on her. She flinched as one of his skinny hands suddenly shot out and grabbed her arm. 'They're beaming through the walls at me,' he shouted suddenly and without warning, his voice terrifyingly loud in the silence of the sitting room. 'There was a dead cat on the porch and I've been followed by cars with foreign licence plates.'

'Very far gone indeed,' murmured Dr Love, shaking his head. 'A very serious case, I'm afraid.'

Angelica looked at her husband in fury. Trust Nick to be a serious case when she had a meeting with the BBC at four o'clock. The sooner she had someone she could trust in the gallery again, the better.

Chapter 32

Adam's death was a profound shock to Alice, although not, it seemed, to the doctor who performed the autopsy. His view had been that Adam's liver was so enlarged it was a miracle not only that there was still room for his lungs but that he had survived as long as he had.

The end had, thankfully, been quick. This and the liver information had come courtesy, if that was the word, of Adam's nephew.

Alice, blissfully unaware of events overnight, had opened up the gallery as usual. She had been unsurprised when, also as usual, her employer had not arrived. The day had been uneventful, with few customers and fewer sales, but she had persevered with her mailing list in the knowledge that she was helping to improve matters.

At closing time, and after checking Adam's office to make sure he was not there, she had gone home. She was puzzled as to Adam's whereabouts, and the fact he had not been in touch, but not seriously worried.

The next morning, all was revealed. A fat young man with narrow eyes and a snout-like nose was waiting for her at the gallery. He introduced himself – brusquely – as Nigel Clasp, the son of Adam's sister. He then moved with amazing speed to assert his rights over the property that had apparently been left to him in its entirety. Nigel Clasp, it turned out, was Adam's sole heir.

Even allowing for the unpleasant circumstances, Alice thought, Nigel Clasp seemed a profoundly uncharismatic individual. Adam's eccentric charm had evidently not been passed on through his sister.

'Seems he'd been to the pub, overdone it and had a stroke,' Clasp summed up briskly. His thinning hair was the main point of resemblance to his uncle, Alice thought. That and the graph-paper shirt and corduroy trousers. Nigel Clasp, it turned out, had not known his uncle well; Adam had been estranged from his sister, who had apparently regarded him as a madman and his profession as lunacy.

Throughout his meeting with Alice, Clasp's eyes flicked about. 'Suppose the only good thing about it was that someone spotted him and called an ambulance. Otherwise,' Clasp sniffed matter-of-factly, 'he would have croaked in his own shop doorway.'

Alice swallowed and her eyes pricked. She would not cry in front of the ghastly Clasp, but the urge was very strong. Adam's had been a desolate end. But not lonely, at least; someone had been there with him for his final hours. Whoever they had been, they had exhibited more human kindness towards him than this alleged blood relation was doing.

'Mind you,' added the nephew lightly, 'that might have been what he wanted.'

'I don't think so,' Alice exclaimed indignantly.

Clasp glanced at her. His eyes were small and mean, with no echo of Adam's warm amber ones. Alice blinked hard and bit her lip.

'I don't know anything about art,' Nigel Clasp announced, not greatly to Alice's surprise. 'So I'm relying on you to show me the good stuff.'

Alice nodded, eager to demonstrate her worth. Clasp's remark seemed to confirm her hopes that he would want to keep Palladio open and ask her to run it. Should he be the one to give her the chance she had always wanted, Alice thought, she was more than ready to overlook his shortcomings in the charm department.

Breathlessly she dashed about the gallery, picking up a picture here, an etching there, and adding a lithograph and an oil painting to the collection. 'That's probably the best we have,' she announced proudly.

'How much is this lot worth?' Clasp demanded.

Alice told him, keen to show her knowledge. Clasp sniffed. 'Of course,' he said in his nasal tones, 'I'll be shutting the shop with immediate effect.'

'It's not a shop, it's a gallery,' Alice said before she could stop herself. 'You're *shutting* it?' she added immediately, appalled, eyes widening as the main information sank in. '*No*. You can't.'

'Can't I?' Clasp smiled; not a nice smile, Alice noticed. 'Try me,' he added, thrusting his hands into his pockets and rocking back and forth on his fat little feet.

'But I've got a development plan,' Alice protested. 'I've got plenty of ideas about how to increase trade and raise profits. We've got a mailing list . . .'

But Clasp was twisting his big head from left to right on top of his fat, bristly neck. 'I have to say,' he remarked crushingly, 'that the phrase too little, too late comes to mind.'

Alice struggled to control herself. 'But what about Adam?' she demanded. 'This business was his life. Don't you think you owe it to him to carry it on?'

Clasp raised a fat hand, whose wrist bore a heavy, rather vulgar watch, and gave her a mirthless, contemptuous smile. 'My uncle, it seems, wasn't a very good businessman. I see no virtue in carrying on his mistakes. I'll be liquidating everything.'

'Selling it . . . *all*?' Alice whispered.

'You heard me.' Clasp looked up at the ceiling and sniffed. 'The shop will go, obviously. I'll be selling the freehold of the building. Got a few agents interested already, I'm happy to say. Luxury flats, serviced offices. The potential's endless.'

'But there are some – a few, anyway – important works in

here,' Alice said faintly, looking around at the crowded surfaces and trying to imagine them as serviced offices, whatever those were.

'No need to concern yourself.' Clasp looked at her coldly. 'I'm taking advice from a specialist, thanks all the same.'

A *specialist*. The word hit Alice like a flying knife, as no doubt it was intended to. What was she, who had worked here for so long, if not a specialist?

'Of course, that makes you redundant. You're dismissed with immediate effect.' Nigel Clasp now stuck out a short arm with an envelope at the end of it. 'A cheque to cover your salary up until the end of the month. A generous gesture, as I am sure you appreciate.'

Alice took the envelope without a word. Stunned, she turned and walked out of Palladio for the last time. She did not look back.

She raised her head and set her jaw, determined once again to force back the tears that threatened. But there was something about the way the sun was beating down so cheerfully on the often-gloomy little Bloomsbury lane that was suddenly impossible to bear.

She pulled out her mobile and looked at it. Could she call David? Suki had, after all. David had not criticised her for it, either. Following all the drama, he had returned from Notting Hill very late but with the news that Albertine, as he had all along suspected, was suffering only from a slight rash.

Alice pressed the keys and lifted the mobile to her ear. To her surprise, David answered instantly.

'Hi.' His voice was warm, welcoming, even, Alice noticed with relief.

'I've lost my job,' she said baldly.

'*What?*'

'Adam's died. The gallery's being closed.' Alice forced back a sob.

'What?' David repeated, now sounding shocked. 'Alice? Is this *you*?'

'Of course it's bloody me,' Alice snapped impatiently. Her vision was misting and something hard and painful was rising in her throat. Adam had died in the deep shadows of his Georgian shop doorway, like one of the more maudlin illustrations from his own collection.

And then horrid, *horrid* Nigel Clasp. Dashing her hopes. Closing the gallery . . .

'Oh, David.' She reined in the tears with huge effort. David hated women crying; presumably he saw enough of that sort of thing at work.

'Poor you,' he soothed gingerly from the other end. He sounded, she thought, distinctly uncomfortable. 'Look, we'll talk about it later. Don't worry. Look, I've got to go . . .'

'You won't be late home?' Alice demanded.

'No. No, of course not.' He sounded utterly distracted. 'Well, perhaps a bit,' he confessed.

'*David!*' Tonight of all nights. Did he not realise her career was at an end? She needed tea and sympathy, or perhaps curry and beer at the Indian round the corner, *their* Indian, the one with the polite waiters and the low, flickering tea lights that always seemed such a comfort, as well as romantic.

'Sorry. *Sorry*. You know what it's like. We get emergencies here and . . . look, I'm sorry about your job.' He sounded defensive, she thought. Then there was a buzz and a click, and nothing.

Alice felt suddenly, utterly desperate. Her throat ached and the inside of her stomach was a knotted screw. She wanted to throw herself on to the pavement and burst into racking sobs. She could almost feel the hot concrete against her cheek, smell the dust in her nostrils.

The phone in her pocket rang again. Alice pulled it out – David again? Thinking better of the short shrift he had given her?

'Hello?' she croaked, her voice crackly with hope.

'Hel-*lo*.' The voice, easy and confident, wasn't one she immediately recognised. 'Caroline Ramage here. From the BBC. We met at Suki and Rafael's, if you remember.'

'Oh . . . yes.' Alice fought a swooping, sickening disappointment, followed by a sense of impotent rage with David that it had not been him calling back.

'How *are* you?'

'Oh . . . you know.' Alice took a deep breath. 'Fine.'

'I just wondered . . .' Caroline's voice was smooth and speculative. 'I know we talked about jobs before, and I know you're absolutely wedded to that gallery of yours, but—'

'Not so wedded, as it happens,' Alice broke in bitterly. 'In fact, I've just been fired.'

There was an exclamation of surprise from the other end. 'But that's great news!'

'Is it?'

'Couldn't be better!' Caroline exulted. 'Your timing is immaculate. There's a gallery owner I know in Gold Street who'd *kill* for someone like you.'

'Gold Street? But I don't know anything about contemporary art . . .' Alice began.

'So learn,' came Caroline's no-nonsense reply. 'Read up on it. Bluff your way through. Do you want a job, or don't you?'

Yes. Of course. But did she want one in the contemporary art world?

'I need to know now,' Caroline warned. 'There are plenty of girls who will want this job if you don't.'

Alice thought quickly. What did she have to lose? Gold Street, if nothing else, would be good experience. She would learn a lot. Marketing plans, mailing lists, promotion, PR; the galleries there had no doubt raised them all to an art form. More of an art form than what they were selling, very possibly.

'Thank you,' she said humbly. 'It was good of you to ring me.'

'You're welcome. It's all entirely self-interested, of course.' Caroline laughed.

'How do you mean?' Alice asked indignantly.

'Well, you know I'm making this documentary about Britart?

It'll be a damned sight easier if I have a gallery assistant on side. My own fifth columnist, if you like.'

'Oh . . . yes.' Alice could see that made sense. 'Well I'll do my best to help. If I get the job.'

'You will, don't worry.'

Alice wished she had a quarter of Caroline's self-assurance. Failure simply did not seem to enter into her equations.

'By the way,' Caroline asked casually, 'seen Suki lately?'

Alice groaned. 'I spoke to her a couple of days ago. Isn't it awful about Albertine?'

'Albertine?' Caroline said sharply. 'What about Albertine?'

'She's ill,' Alice said, thinking it strange that Caroline was unaware of the drama.

'I don't know anything about it,' Caroline sounded surprised and concerned. 'How awful. I'd better ring Suki.'

'Well hopefully the worst is over,' Alice reassured. 'Suki probably didn't want to worry you.'

'Yes,' Caroline said thoughtfully. 'I'm sure that must be it.'

Chapter 33

Siobhan, on the ground below, was oblivious to the noisy helicopter thrashing above her. For one thing, she was plugged into her iPod. And for another, she was absorbed completely in her drawing, sketching out the picture that glowed in her head. She wanted, with an almost desperate urgency, to get down on paper the bright grass and the dazzling sky that stretched above her. It would be no masterpiece, she knew – only the first hesitant steps on the path that would, she hoped, lead her back to where she had paused ten years ago.

It was extraordinary how peaceful she felt when she was sketching. She had forgotten what it was like. Engaged in her work, all her frustrations and resentments disappeared. Now she had connected with her pencil, paints and pad again, she felt energised. Like a plug that had been pushed back into the circuit, having lain for many years disconnected on the floor.

How had she borne not doing it for so long? she wondered as her pencil whispered over the cartridge paper. She sketched on joyously, smiling as she worked.

She felt grateful to Dan, who had encouraged her to draw and paint again. He had told her it was never too late, and so it had proved. She wished she could tell him what his encouragement had meant, but to her regret, their paths had never crossed since.

More than once she had walked down to the Manor entrance in case he might be passing. He never was, however. She had wondered about going to his cottage, at the unsmart end of Aldeham. But she was not entirely sure where the unsmart end was; looking for it, meanwhile, she would run the gauntlet of the scrutiny of the entire village. As it was, her appearances at the drive end had attracted the attention of Toni Swift, whose repeated invitation to pop in for some Dom Perignon Siobhan had eventually been unable to avoid.

'We're so excited to have a celebrity in the village,' Toni had gushed, her tan astonishingly dark against one of the many huge yellow sofas in her sitting room. Siobhan had taken in the decor with amazement. The interior design of Toni's house was unbelievable. It made Maeve Kandinsky-O'Halloran look like Robert Adam.

'Boyfriend was my favourite band. And your husband was my favourite singer.'

Siobhan had smiled politely and sipped the Dom Perignon which Toni sloshed into huge black glasses. After what Siobhan estimated to be her third refill, Toni leaned forward, fixed her with an eye that seemed less than focused and launched into a bitter diatribe about her husband.

Siobhan, while looking as if she was listening, soon tuned out. Her attention had been caught by a truly magnificent painting over the fireplace. It shone out like a beacon: one pure, true, lovely thing among all the questionable and downright bad taste that surrounded it.

Dan's picture, Siobhan guessed, with a joy that surprised her. The one he had been about to deliver when they met. The bottom of its frame was almost invisible thanks to a forest of scented candles – thankfully not lit – but the quality of the work, the subtlety of light and shade, the sensitivity and skill with which the artist had rendered the image, were exceptional. All the more exceptional given that the subject was so ugly.

Toni shifted her leather bottom on the sofa and took another slug of champagne. 'That's my hubby,' she announced sourly, pointing at the portrait and knocking back the rest of the glass.

'Yes, I'd guessed. Who painted it?' Siobhan knew, of course, but she was interested in Toni's reply.

The tanned shoulders, exposed in the small leather dress, shrugged. 'Just some bloke from the village,' Toni said dismissively. 'We gave him a lot of help, let me tell you.'

'Really?' Siobhan was intrigued. 'Financial help, you mean?'

'Well that, yes, obviously. He was desperate for the work,' Toni said with a touch of contempt. 'But we had a lot of artistic input too.'

'You did?'

Toni tossed her much-streaked hair. 'His first attempt was rubbish. But then Kev told him what to do and he went next door and redid the whole thing.'

Siobhan felt, if she ever saw Dan again, that she would like his side of the story.

In order to make a landing pad for his helicopter, Kevin Swift had levelled a copse of ancient oaks and an eighteenth-century rose arbour in the garden of the Dower House. He was relaxed about any planning regulations such action may have flouted. Regulations were for little people. And there was nothing little about Kevin Swift.

Now, as his pilot descended towards it, Kevin, with a grunt, bent his stout form further over to take in the bird's-eye view of Aldeham Manor. He noted with satisfaction that Ciaran O'Sullivan had not yet built a helipad of his own. Kevin experienced an inward glow at this evidence that, while his house was only the second largest in the village, he might nonetheless be its richest inhabitant. Richer even than the famous – well, once-famous – pop star who had just moved in next door.

His small, sharp eyes passed beyond the boundaries of the Manor and up the low rise of hill behind it. There was a figure, he saw as the helicopter juddered closer. It looked like a woman down there, a young, slim woman with brown hair. She wore jeans and a white T-shirt and had something in her hand.

Something square and white. A book? Some paper?

Kevin felt a swell of excitement. The helicopter was close enough now to allow, if she would only look up, the frankly gorgeous Siobhan O'Sullivan to see him descending from the heavens in his expensive machine.

Toni had, after many attempts, finally managed to get their celebrity neighbour round to the Dower House, although not for the dinner with her husband that Kevin would have preferred. Face-to-face encounters were, he had discovered over the years, the best way of making enquiries into people's wealth; no one could ever resist boasting about how rich they were. Toni, needless to say, had found out nothing on this front, nor had she even told him Siobhan was coming round. He had arrived unexpectedly as their little get-together was ending.

She wasn't looking up; was she drawing? Kevin wondered, squinting crossly to see. She'd mentioned she was an artist when he had shown her the portrait of himself; she'd been very impressed by it. Kevin wished he'd bloody known. It wasn't bad, the portrait by Dan whatever-his-name-was, not now he'd made the adjustments, anyway. But no one had ever heard of him, or ever would.

Siobhan's thoughts, as she sketched, had turned to her husband. Now she had found a way to fill her time, she now felt almost grateful for Ciaran's precipitate action in bringing her here. But Ciaran himself seemed less than happy about her new hobby. He hadn't said it in so many words, but there had been looks and veiled references.

Siobhan paused now, biting the end of her pencil. Why was he so discouraging? He was reviving his boy band career; why should she not do the same with her artistic one? It wasn't as if Ciaran was even here much; his days were taken up with seemingly endless trips to London to see managers, producers and promoters for the reunion album and tour.

Siobhan pushed these reflections aside to concentrate on the beauty of the scene around her. One happy consequence of her rediscovered passion for drawing was looking at Suffolk in a whole new light.

She was not even afraid of her garden any more. It might be big, but it was beautiful. There were pictures everywhere you looked, possible paintings everywhere you turned. The challenge of the garden now, Siobhan felt, was not so much Bert and Dean, but the fact that she wanted to capture it all, in colour, on canvas. Even though she had not painted for years, had no idea whether she still could.

But the possibilities pulled at her. Like the double row of yew hedges, getting on for two centuries old now and commanding a height which ensured nothing between them could be seen from the house unless one was actually on the roof. The intimacy and secrecy of the yew walk was one reason why it was one of Siobhan's favourite parts of the garden. But she loved the sheer simplicity of it too, the bold graphic statement made by the hedges as they ran from one end of the huge garden to the other. What a painting that would make. But no – she should not rush herself. Better stick to drawing for the moment.

Her eyes flicked from the Manor in front of her, back to the countryside round about. Now, in high summer, the small hill on which she sat was covered in thick green grass, plucked to a ripple by windy fingers. In winter, she imagined, it would be bare apart from low-lying bushes. The few bent, twisted trees would hang with diamonds, frozen puddles would flash in the sun and snow would stipple the curving grassland. She was almost sure she could capture it in oils . . .

Why not? She knew exactly which packing case her brushes were in, in which spare-room wardrobe. The thought of them sitting down there in the Manor, along with her charcoals, sketchbooks, paintboxes and a couple of stretched blank canvases sent a surge of excitement through her.

Could she paint out here, as well as sketch? She had expected it to take some time to get her hand and eye back in. Yet it all seemed to have returned amazingly quickly. That connection, almost like a wire between eye and hand and page, moving smoothly together. When it worked, as it seemed to be now, there was no feeling like it in the world.

Even so, Siobhan felt nervous. *Could* she set up her easel out here? But . . . alone in the wide landscape, trying out her rusty painting skills again after so many years? It would be reassuring to have some encouragement. Some teaching, even. Was there, she suddenly thought, an art class in the area?

Chapter 34

Alice was on her way to meet Angelica Devon in Gold Street. Caroline had variously described Angelica as 'legendary', 'powerful', 'determined' and 'doesn't suffer fools gladly', which didn't suggest the cosiest of personalities.

It was difficult to know quite how to dress for such a person. Last night, in the Nutthouse, she had spread out the contents of her wardrobe on the bed and tried to decide.

'Black,' David had suggested ironically, when she had called him in from the sitting room for his opinion. 'Or white.'

Alice had grimaced. As it happened, her clothes *were* almost entirely monochrome, but she had hoped David might be a little more constructive. He was, however, even more distracted than usual at the moment: some staffing crisis at the hospital was involving still later nights at work. Last night, it had been past ten when he had finally come through the Nutthouse door.

'Well, what about this?' Alice had asked, snatching up a fitted black shirt and tight black skirt and waving them at him. 'With these shoes?' she'd added, digging out a pair of black stilettos from the back of the wardrobe.

David had looked at them vaguely, his mind obviously elsewhere.

'Oh, never mind,' Alice had snapped, exasperated. 'I'll just ring Suki. Ask her what she thinks.'

'I wouldn't,' David had said quickly, unexpectedly. Looking at him, Alice had realised that she now had his full attention.

'Why not? I *should* ring her,' Alice had gone on. 'She promised she'd let me know how Albertine was, but I haven't heard from her for days.'

'Albertine's fine,' David had assured her.

Alice had blinked. 'How do you know?'

'Suki told me.'

'You went to see her?' Still holding the stilettos, Alice had looked at him in surprise.

He'd met her gaze, irritation puckering his swarthily handsome face. 'Well of course I did. I always check up on my patients.'

She had nodded. 'It's just that you never said.'

'I've been busy, I forgot, OK?' He'd smiled at her and shaken his head apologetically. 'Sorry. It's been a hell of a week already, and it's only Tuesday.'

For the interview, Alice had stuck with the black shirt, skirt and shoes. The sharp high heels, which she was unused to wearing, made her stumble slightly in the cracks of the pavement. She made her precarious way up Silver Street, hoping she wouldn't topple over in front of all these haughty, expensive shops.

She had, in the past, made the occasional Christmas trip here; on her last visit, after she had plucked up the courage to enter an exclusive stationery store, a ruthlessly glossy sales assistant had effortlessly converted her original intention to buy a few smart correspondence cards into the purchase of an overpriced black wallet. David, who prided himself on not having expensive tastes, had been slightly bemused to be given it for Christmas.

Alice was passing the designer shoeshops now, their gilt-framed windows filled with footwear displayed like jewels in silk-padded boxes. She looked at the gleaming stiletto, the ingeniously engineered ankle boot and felt a dim stir of desire. That was the problem with streets like this: they made you want things you didn't know you wanted, things you never knew existed, in some cases.

Smart chocolates in rose and violet flavours, for instance, in round gilt-edged boxes with royal warrants on. In the designer clothes shops, burly security guards stood foursquare in the entrance while across the polished floor, haughty blonde sales assistants arranged piles of pastel cashmere jumpers. Alice wondered about their relationships: whether the guards ever fell in love with the aristocratic-looking assistants, or whether, vice versa, the assistants ever fancied a bit of rough. If distance prevailed, was it icy or indifferent? It would make a good play, she thought. If she were a playwright. But, she reminded herself, squaring her shoulders, she was not; she was an out-of-work gallery assistant hoping to become an in-work one again.

But would she fit in? Everyone round here seemed so sleek. The very air was perfumed. Alice caught whiffs of delicious scent as glamorous, skinny, long-legged creatures with flowing hair clacked past on high heels. They clutched expensive-looking handbags in one hand and expensively suited men in the other while exclaiming into mobile phones squeezed between elegant shoulder and shapely cheekbone.

Alice turned the corner into Gold Street – and instantly the light was blocked out. Simultaneously she felt the impact of a powerful collision and then found herself reeling backwards. Her trajectory abruptly arrested by some black iron railings, Alice, slumped and slightly stunned, began the process of collecting her scattered wits and working out what on earth had happened.

'I'm so sorry!' exclaimed a voice. A man's voice. 'Are you all right?'

Alice, seeking equilibrium on her wobbly high heels, looked up into two concerned blue-grey eyes set in a pleasant, clean-shaven face. Then she felt a large, strong hand clasp hers and pull her fully upright. The other person, however, seemed to go on unfolding.

He was enormously tall, wore a suit, a pale blue shirt and tie and over it a sandy wool coat which emphasised broad shoulders and swung open in deference to the mild weather.

'I'm so sorry,' the man repeated, staring down from at least a foot above her. Yet for all the advantage of his height and breadth, he looked rather anguished, Alice saw. He glanced ruefully at something in his hand: a small, silver, state-of-the-art mobile. 'I was talking on this.' He shook it. 'Just wasn't looking where I was going. My fault entirely. I should never try to walk and talk at the same time.' He shot her a sheepish sideways grin.

'It doesn't matter,' Alice muttered, surprised that he had admitted being the guilty party. People striding around on mobiles normally seemed to expect the world to accommodate them, not accept they had responsibilities too. She felt suddenly self-conscious, and pulled down her skirt in the realisation that, sprawled all over the pavement as she had been, he would have been able to see her knickers. Had he been looking. She examined the sleeves of her black shirt where they had been in contact with the pavement; dust was, thankfully, the only damage they had suffered.

'Are your clothes all right?' the man asked. He had a kind voice, she registered. He sounded genuinely concerned. 'Oh dear, you *are* a bit dusty. I hope you weren't going anywhere special.'

'Only an interview,' Alice muttered.

'An interview!' He sounded shocked. 'I'm so sorry. Please, as it's all my fault, could I possibly . . .' He waved a helpless hand in the direction of the nearest emporium. 'Buy you something to change into?'

She smiled at him in astonishment. Was he serious? Anything from the shops round here – even a plastic bag, probably – would be the wrong side of a hundred pounds. And a skirt or shirt easily double. 'It's OK,' she assured him, wiping the dust off her skirt. 'It's very kind of you, but you really don't need to.'

She could hear, in the back of her mind, Suki's exclamations of horror. 'Darling! A man's offering to buy you a little designer something and you're saying *no*?' Suki, of course, would not have hesitated.

'You don't need to,' Alice repeated, as her assailant/rescuer continued to press his offer. 'I'm fine, honestly.'

He gave up and smiled. 'Well perhaps, in that case, you might allow me to take you out for a drink. If you get the job.'

Alice's eyes narrowed with suspicion. She wondered if this had been his intention all along: did he routinely knock over women in heels and then try to date them? He might be notorious for this sort of thing in Gold Street. He was tall, evidently prosperous, and, if not handsome exactly, certainly presentable. No doubt he appealed to a certain kind of woman, although he was, Alice decided, a bit stuffy and City-ish for her taste.

'That's very kind of you,' she said, slightly stiffly. 'But you don't have to, really.'

He nodded vigorously. She noticed that he had reddened slightly. 'Well, good luck with the interview anyway,' he said.

He made no effort to move, Alice saw. 'Thanks,' she said, turning gingerly on the treacherous heels and stepping off the pavement to cross the road to OneSquared.

Things were going from bad to worse in Twickenham. Nick's latest bout of lunacy was, Angelica had to admit, showing every sign of being a real humdinger.

'Can't we just stick him in the Priory again?' she demanded of Dr Love, who had attended daily since the breakdown. He looked doubtful, raking an uncertain hand through his side-parted Robert Redford blond hair.

'I'm not altogether sure that's what he wants,' he remarked, to Angelica's dismay. Her fears about Dr Love had been well founded. As she had suspected, he placed a disturbing and quite unnecessary emphasis on what was best for his patient rather than most convenient for her.

They were standing in the state-of-the-art red kitchen, which always heightened Angelica's angry moods. 'Why not?' she demanded. 'He's been there before. Frankly, he's been to them all before.'

'That's exactly what concerns me,' Dr Love remarked mildly. 'I rather feel we need to try something new.'

'What sort of new?' Angelica was instantly suspicious.

Dr Love tapped his manicured brown hand on the kitchen surface. He didn't wear a wedding ring, Angelica noticed. Then again, neither did she – in the conventional sense. Nick's wedding-day love token had taken a more unusual form – a necklace in the shape of a small silver willy that stood to attention at the press of a button. It was not a button Angelica pressed often, on either the necklace or its human inspiration. Since taking up full-time gardening, Nick had rather gone off sex, much to the relief of Angelica, for whom it had always been a means to an end.

'Something more precisely tailored to the nature of his concerns,' Dr Love said.

'More precisely tailored?' Angelica queried ironically. According to Dr Love, the trigger for Nick's breakdown had been the discovery of root fly on his carrots. Something precisely tailored to concerns like that was difficult to imagine. Perhaps a job in a pesticide factory.

'Yes. For example, he's mentioned a spiritual retreat in India he wants to visit.'

Angelica felt her fury mount. Not that bloody retreat crap again. She'd refused to discuss it apart from to say that her idea of a retreat was the sort where you had your own butler and horizon pool and Kate Moss was in the next beach hut. She had hoped Nick had forgotten about it, but evidently she had hoped in vain.

'He seems to think that living apart from the material world for a while will do him some good. Actually, I tend to agree with him,' the doctor said.

Angelica's pupils dilated with horror. Her poodle fringe shook from side to side in denial. 'Definitely not. No way Jose. He can't go alone, not in this state. He'll get on the wrong plane . . . he'll end up God knows where.'

A speculative gleam now appeared in her eye. Actually, come to think of it, perhaps there was an up side to this. Nick disappearing off the face of the earth would be a weight off her mind, no question. But only, of course, if he could be persuaded to sign over the whole of his fortune to her before he went. The gleam in her eye died away. There was less than no chance of that.

It was a running sore in Angelica's marriage – her whole life, in fact – that she had no financial independence. Nick's accountant, since his first flush of fame, had always stood squarely in the way of his client handing over his fortune to his wife, bouts of madness notwithstanding.

This had resulted in a situation where, while Angelica enjoyed a generous allowance to keep herself and OneSquared in the manner to which they had both become accustomed, the allowance very much depended on Nick being around to authorise it. His accountant, Angelica knew, would lose no time in pulling the plug should Nick disappear. Or if he decided for any reason that he no longer wished to be married to her.

'I wasn't suggesting he should go alone,' said Dr Love. 'You'd go with him, obviously.'

Angelica stared at him in disgust. 'I can't do that,' she burst out. 'I've got a *gallery* to run. I've got a *party* coming up.' Her eyes bulged. 'And I've just signed an important new artist who needs some serious attention.'

The doctor shrugged. 'Your husband needs some serious attention too.' He placed the tips of his fingers together and looked intently at her over them. 'Perhaps some time away together would be just what he needs.'

'But it's not what *I* need,' Angelica snapped, grabbing a fur bag from the top of one of the fire-engine-red kitchen units and startling Dr Love, who had until then assumed it was a cat.

How dare he suggest that she reschedule appointments and stay at home? She simply could not – *could not* – spend any more time with Nick. Too bad if, as Dr Love claimed, her husband resented the time she spent at work. Her schedule today was crazy. It included, among other things, a crucial meeting with Penelope to discuss the possibility of underlit Perspex canapé trays. Nick would just have to rehabilitate without her; he had before, and he sure as hell could again.

'You're going to have to come up with another idea,' she informed Dr Love as, head high, she clacked past him out of the kitchen. 'I've got to go to my office now.'

'You're not going to say goodbye to your husband?' Dr Love enquired.

Angelica glared at him. 'I haven't time,' she said icily. 'I've got back-to-back meetings today.'

'This might be the most crucial of them all, though,' he called, even though Angelica had swept down the black-painted hall and was halfway out of the door.

Dr Love looked after her and shook his head slightly. His eye caught that of Mercedes in the shadow of the hall. She was gazing at him dreamily.

'Interesting lady,' observed the doctor with a sardonic lift of his eyebrow.

'You're right. Is complete cow,' agreed Mercedes.

Chapter 35

Outside, and unaware of this insurrection, Angelica shoved on her sunglasses and hurried down the stairs to the chauffeur-driven blacked-out four-wheel-drive that waited for her every morning, irrespective of the double yellow lines on the road, and the obstruction that the vast, wide, bull-barred vehicle presented to anything trying to pass on the other side.

There was also the fact that Sebastian, hired from a funky Westbourne Park firm called Crucial Chauffeurs, was a dim public schoolboy. While he looked good in a cap, he had a very vague grasp of London's geography, despite having grown up in the city. As a result, the time it took to get to work could vary wildly. His indifference to traffic lights had also made Angelica wonder, on more than one nerve-racking occasion, whether Sebastian was colour blind.

She settled herself in the back, whipped her BlackBerry out of her bag and, as Sebastian shot through red lights and narrowly avoided small children, was soon absorbed in the list of meetings. She saw Alice on her schedule. Alice? Who was Alice?

Then she remembered. Of course, the girl that Caroline, the documentary-maker from the BBC, had recommended so highly. Behind her huge black lenses, Angelica rolled her eyes. Waste of bloody time; she'd only agreed to see her to please Caroline, who had very nearly promised to focus on her gallery alone for the BBC documentary. That the girl would be no use Angelica had no doubt. Who was she, for a start? All her previous assistants had been the daughters of famous people, wealthy clients or aristocrats. Or otherwise connected to celebrated artists in a way that could be exploited.

But this Alice person fitted into none of these categories. She sounded unconnected, unaristocratic and hopelessly unwealthy. On the other hand, Angelica thought, given the publicity potentially at stake, if Caroline asked her to interview Osama bin Laden for the job, she would. Actually, that wasn't a bad idea. Bin Laden's grasp of the contemporary art market might not be all it could be, but neither was that of Natasha or any of her predecessors. And having the world's most wanted man behind the desk would definitely attract attention to OneSquared.

Her BlackBerry beeped sharply. Her daily horoscope had just been texted, she saw as she checked the message. She squinted at the screen through her sunglasses. *Beware of unscrupulous people trying to take advantage of your generous and giving nature* . . .

That bastard doctor, Angelica thought savagely.

Alice carefully picked her way down Gold Street. Her first impression was that the art in the gallery windows was worse than she had imagined. One gallery proudly displayed a large mould in the shape of a moustache filled with oil. In another, a child's plastic doll had been stuck all over with fake jewels.

What did it all mean? Her researches on the internet over the weekend had failed to shed much light on the question. On the contrary: after looking for many hours at pictures of wax seeping out of buildings, mythical animals performing sex acts and life-sized models of people dead in swimming pools, Alice felt her grasp of such things was less firm even than before.

On the other hand, she now had a battery of fashionable artists' names and some impressive-sounding phrases. 'Principle of bisymmetrical reason', 'conceptually united', 'site-specific installation', 'enclosing narrative', 'posing fundamental questions' and 'network of motivations' had cropped up frequently in relation to the works she had viewed on screen.

The galleries, it seemed to Alice, appeared in no great hurry to open up. Most of them looked as if they were closed, including OneSquared. Alice rang the bell hard. There was no one visible in the gallery space beyond the glass.

What *was* in the gallery space, however, sent her heart spiralling downwards. *ZEB SPAW*, read the huge red capital letters on the plate-glass expanse. Behind it stood what looked exactly like a hospital bed sprayed gold. Angelica's gallery, Alice realised, were Zeb Spaw's dealers.

For a second, she teetered on the brink of giving the whole idea up. Gold Street, yes, but Zeb Spaw? Spaw was the cause of all her problems. Had the twenty-million-pound prosthetic limb sale not provoked a crisis of confidence in Adam, she might be working at Palladio yet. Possibly anything could have provoked the crisis, given Adam's obvious instability. But in as much as the limbs had, the blame for her situation lay squarely at Spaw's door. Which was this one. Could she actually bring herself to sell his work?

On the other hand, did she have a choice? She needed a job, and jobs in art galleries – her only area of experience – were by no means easy to get. Lack of work would, in addition, mean goodbye to the Nutthouse; discovering her painting was worthless had done little for Mrs Nutt's temper, and Alice's every encounter in the lift with her since had been distinctly uncomfortable. There would be no quarter over the rent from the landlady.

Angelica's continuing failure to materialise meant that Alice had plenty of time to ponder her situation and familiarise herself further with the Spaw oeuvre. The interior of the OneSquared Gallery consisted of a large, halogen-lit, wooden-floored, white-painted exhibition space lit by a window whose glass filled the whole of the front wall. The gold bed dominated the window; looking about her, Alice could see no other works on display. This seemed puzzling. The OneSquared website had listed a great many artists. Where were they all?

The more she stared at the gold-sprayed bed, however, the more difficult it became to reach a conclusion about it. Was it so bad that it was actually good? Who was to say? On the other hand, she could imagine David saying rather a lot about such a waste of a hospital facility.

Alice glanced across the road. The gallery opposite had *CORNELIUS SUMP* painted above it in neat black capitals, and *SHARON AURA: WHAT THE EYE SEES AND THE HAND FINDS. NEW WORKS IN FILM AND FOUND OBJECT* running across the glass of the window in vast red ones.

Cornelius Sump rang a bell for some reason. After some seconds' brain-racking, Alice remembered Suki saying this was the name of her next-door neighbour. The one building a home spa in his vast basement. He was obviously hugely wealthy; this, presumably, was how the huge wealth was made.

Alice was about to cross the road to examine Sharon Aura's work more closely, when the slam of a car door behind brought her whirling round. A woman in vast black sunglasses was emerging from a huge shiny black four-wheel-drive. She was very thin and had long, dark-blond hair in scrunchy curls. She wore a beige suede jacket covered in fringes and buckles and a strange black skirt full of zips and with an unfinished asymmetric hemline from which threads hung messily down. Her tanned legs were bare and ended in enormous and rather aggressive motorcycle boots.

'Angelica Devon?' Alice asked brightly, as the large black car slid off. She received in reply a curt nod. 'I've come about the job. I think Caroline mentioned me?'

It was difficult to see the reaction to this behind the black glasses.

'Did Caroline say how the documentary was going?' Angelica demanded.

As it happened, Caroline hadn't, but Alice sensed it would be impolitic to say so. 'Brilliantly, so far as I know,' she said brightly.

Angelica nodded. 'What do you think of that?' she rapped

suddenly, throwing out a brown wrist jangling with bracelets at the bed in the window.

Alice searched for the exact phrase. It took a while. 'Very interesting,' she managed, eventually.

Angelica now pushed up the sunglasses. Her bright hazel eyes glared out through thick rings of mascara and eyeliner. '*Interesting?*' she snarled. 'It's *groundbreaking*.'

Alice gave herself an inward shake. More was obviously expected. Hastily she summoned her mental list of phrases. 'When I say "interesting",' she began, 'I refer of course to the manner in which it conforms to the principle of bisymmetrical reason. It's astonishingly conceptually united. The site-specific installation enables the enclosing narrative to pose fundamental questions concerning the network of motivations, both the artist's and our own.'

As Angelica did a double-take, Alice stopped, embarrassed. She waited, half expecting the other woman to burst out laughing.

Angelica was, in fact, amazed. What the girl had said sounded edgy, educated. Even Zeb hadn't come up with that interpretation of his work. His only comment, in fact, had been to insist she got no less than four million for it.

She looked at Alice with an interest she had not expected to feel, reminding herself simultaneously that there were no other candidates for the job on the horizon.

'That's better,' she conceded. 'Know about art, do you?'

'A bit. Well, quite a lot, really.' Understated modesty, Alice realised, wasn't going to get her very far here. 'As a matter of fact, I've got a degree in it. And I've got art gallery experience. I was deputy manager of one.'

'*Which* one?' Angelica demanded.

'Um, Palladio.'

'Never heard of it.'

Angelica, Alice saw, was looking at her disdainfully and flaring her nostrils in a world-weary kind of way. Her heart sank.

'But I *have* got a vacancy for an assistant,' Angelica drawled eventually.

Alice waited.

'And I suppose you'll do,' she added with a sniff, after raking Alice up and down with her eyes for some seconds. 'You're reasonably thin and you'll probably scrub up well. Come in and we'll talk about it.'

Chapter 36

Bo was the first to arrive at the art class and began to strip off in her usual businesslike fashion. An organised sort, she liked to be ready when the students came. She was, Dan thought, diverting his eyes from the vicinity of her large exposed breasts, arresting tattoos and the bright pink underwear she was currently removing, shaping up to be an excellent model.

She displayed at all times a most impressive sangfroid, as well as an impressive everything else. For instance, she hadn't made the smallest fuss when she had arrived early enough one session to see that the reason Dan threw an old white sheet over the chaise longue wasn't only for 'texture', but also to cover up the frayed holes made by a nest of mice. This evidence of the rodents, long evicted though they were, had been enough to send one former model running hysterically out of the hall, never to return. But not Bo, thank goodness.

The hiring of the pagan council-worker for his art class was, Dan felt, his only success of any sort in the past few weeks. Which was just as well. After the blow of Kevin Swift and the painting and the disappointment of the portrait dinner culminating in the death of the gallery owner in the doorway, he needed something to feel good about.

The Palladio business had, at least, put the Swift one in perspective. It had been shocking and saddening. Dan had accompanied the poor man to the hospital, even though it was virtually certain, according to the paramedics, that he was already dead.

This had, however, resulted in his missing the train and spending the night in the waiting room.

He had tried, when he finally got back to Suffolk, to contact Alice to explain what had happened. But the phone had been answered by someone male, rude and pompous, and when Dan had called back later, hoping to bypass whoever this was, it was to be told by the operator that the line had been disconnected.

Now, Dan took a final glance round the art class to make sure everything was ready. Aldeham's village hall was a small, strip-lit space with a raised stage at one end, a shiny pale wooden floor and a row of windows down one side over which, during the life classes, the curtains were pulled to preserve the modesty of the model. For Bo, however, modesty did not seem an issue. She had not exaggerated, Dan was finding out, when she had described at the interview how she revelled in her femininity. Some of the poses she struck were bordering on the provocative, and more than once he had had to discreetly intervene and arrange her in a more seemly fashion.

He glanced at her now. She had draped herself over the chaise longue in a Monet-esque manner, one arm thrown back, the other placed with splayed fingers on her thigh. The great globes of her breasts rose like mountains, but at least her legs were together.

'By God, woman, there's a sight for sore eyes!' The appreciative roar had come from the doorway, where a familiar straggle-haired figure in a broad-brimmed black hat and scarf was making his entrance.

'Sod off, Roger,' Bo said good-humouredly.

Roger cackled and rattled his drawing materials in their plastic supermarket shopping bag. As he walked slowly past Bo and chose the nearest seat to where she had arranged herself, the librarians came in, murmured their hellos and scuttled to the pair of seats Dan had placed close together with them in mind. They were a pair of quiet, respectable ladies in their mid fifties who dressed in unassuming pastels and peered anxiously over their half-moon spectacles. Dan was relieved they had not overheard the last exchange.

Three teenagers entered, art students from the local college, self-conscious in black jeans and black eyeliner. They were followed by a middle-aged woman. She was broadly built and wore a blue and white matelot top, white trousers and an extravagantly largely brimmed sunhat. Although he could not see her face, Dan recognised Mrs de Goldsmith.

He could tell by the perfume, for one thing. Mrs de Goldsmith was invariably very thoroughly scented, with something eyewateringly powerful which always spread through the hall with the rapidity of poison gas.

'Bloody hell,' Roger was saying, taking off his hat and waving it about. 'What's that stink?'

'Hello, Mrs de Goldsmith,' Dan said genially.

Mrs de Goldsmith was taking off her hat. Her hair – a chin-length bob of blazing blondness that Dan suspected might be a wig – was dishevelled above her red face. She turned a majestic beam in his direction.

'*Dear* boy,' she said fondly. She twitched her lips, which were thick and painted with some pearlised pinky stuff. 'I've got something to show you.'

Dan watched as she rummaged in a large blue and white striped bag with a gold anchor on the front and white rope handles. Mrs de Goldsmith always dressed, accessorised and acted as if she were holidaying at Cap Ferrat and not the survivor of an apparently bitter divorce living in a Suffolk village where the usual weather was less than sunny. On the other hand, Dan thought, feeling a sudden wave of sympathy, what was wrong with her delusions? Delusions were what got you through. He had delusions of his own, after all, not least that he had a future in art.

'My first foray into sculpture!' Mrs de Goldsmith announced.

Dan stared at the small and unidentifiable lump of Plasticine being held proudly out towards him. He tried to ignore Roger snorting derisively in the corner.

'Sculpture!' He did his best to sound encouraging. 'How interesting.'

'Well of course,' Mrs de Goldsmith trilled, sweeping a brown, gold-ringed hand around the hall with its easels and sketchbooks, 'I realise I possess *considerable* drawing talent. But I prefer not to be pigeonholed.'

'Not on the first date, at least,' Roger cackled, causing the students to snigger and the librarians to give him twin looks of disgust.

'What's it of?' Dan asked, gazing at the lump. It could have been anything, from what he could tell. Animal, vegetable or mineral.

'An animal,' Mrs de Goldsmith elucidated.

That narrowed it down, at least. 'Um . . . which animal?'

'I'm planning a series of four,' said Mrs de Goldsmith grandly. 'This one's Lying Dog, but I'm working on three others. Snake in the Grass, Slimy Toad and Old Goat.'

'Interesting names,' said Dan.

'All inspired by my ex-husband.' Beaming, Mrs de Goldsmith sailed across the hall and chose a seat as far away from Roger as possible.

Dan inserted the first CD of the evening – Vivaldi's *Four Seasons*, to inject a bit of energy into things – and the class got under way to the strains of Spring. All that could be heard – apart from Nigel Kennedy – was the scratch of charcoal on paper and the occasional grunt as Bo shifted position.

Dan paced softly about the class to monitor progress. 'That's very interesting,' he told the older librarian, peering at a sketch so uncertainly rendered it was doubtful which part of Bo it represented. But it was essential to be encouraging. 'You've given her a really, um, monumental quality.'

The older librarian beamed. 'I'm very inspired by ancient forms,' she told him.

A peal of laughter came from Mrs de Goldsmith's direction. 'Well you're in the right place for those, dear.' She looked meaningfully at Roger.

Roger seemed about to retaliate, but then Dan saw the outrage fade from his face. He was staring, as at a vision, at the entrance to the hall. Dan looked too.

It was Siobhan.

Dan was completely unprepared for the impact of seeing her again. Through the front door of the village hall, open behind her, poured rich golden rays of evening sun. Siobhan, her hair blazing with light, the outline of her body clear through her simple white summer dress, appeared like a goddess. Dan, staring helplessly at her, realised with awe the extent to which she had, since their meeting, dominated his every subconscious thought as well as his every conscious one.

Siobhan was surprised – but pleasantly. Very pleasantly. She had not expected to see Dan here; she had, in fact, rather given up hope of seeing him anywhere. She had found out about the life class online, through the local council website, and had noted it was run by a D. Hart. But it did not occur to her that this was Dan.

'You've come to the class?' Dan gasped, finally grasping what was going on.

'You said it was never too late, remember.'

Dan's mouth opened and closed like a goldfish's. 'Never too late, no, never. Absolutely. Great. Erm. Wow. Come and sit down.'

His feet felt as though they had suddenly tripled in size, and his hands quadrupled. As he stumbled about finding a chair for Siobhan, his route seemed impossibly impeded with more chairs, easels and people's bags, all of which, of their own accord, seemed to catch at him as he passed.

'I didn't realise you ran this class,' Siobhan, following him, remarked. He was acting rather strangely, and the way everyone was staring made her feel abashed. 'But of course it makes sense.

You being an artist and everything. That picture you did of Kevin Swift is wonderful.'

'You . . . you . . . saw it?' he stammered, struggling to disconnect one chair from another. They separated with a mighty crash.

She jumped back, startled. 'Toni asked me round. I saw your picture over the fireplace. I gather it required a few, um, adjustments.'

He looked at her dejectedly; was she mocking him? Her eyes were sparkling, he saw.

'Toni said you went into another room and spent hours repainting it.'

Sheer indignation now helped Dan, finally, to gather himself. 'I did go into another room. But I didn't actually do anything. They just thought I did.'

She clapped her hands and laughed. 'Good for you!'

'Erm, excuse me, Dan old chap.' It was Roger Pryap who had spoken. 'But aren't you going to introduce us to this, um, friend of yours?'

Dan looked distractedly into the eyes twinkling beneath the big black hat brim. 'Um, sorry, yes, everyone. This is, um, Siobhan. She's just moved into the village and . . .' And what? he suddenly asked himself. And I've fallen madly in love with her? And, guess what, she's married?

Fortunately Siobhan came to his rescue.

'Where do you want me to sit?'

'Sit?' Dan repeated, hoping she had not noticed the suggestive guffaw that the question had provoked from Roger.

'Sit down.'

'Yes. Oh, yes,' Dan said fervently. He was dimly aware that the *Four Seasons* CD, which was of a temperamental disposition and prone to sudden bouts of non-compliance, had switched itself off. In the ensuing ringing silence, the class was listening hard to the exchange.

'Siobhan, um, used to go to art school,' Dan explained nervously to the gathering.

Siobhan nodded. 'I wanted to get my hand back in.'

There was a clearing of a throat, a cackle and the sound of a hand slapping wood. 'Come and sit here, dear,' Roger invited. 'You can get your hand back in anywhere you like.'

Blushing furiously, Dan rushed over to the CD player and wrenched Vivaldi out.

'I enjoyed that *so* much. Handel *is* marvellous, isn't he?' declared Mrs de Goldsmith. 'By the way,' she went on in her fruity tones, 'does everyone know we've got a celebrity in the village?'

'You mean that bastard Spaw?' fulminated Roger. 'We all know *that*,' he added disdainfully. 'Although he hasn't been seen around much lately, thank God.'

'Ciaran O'Sullivan,' Mrs de Goldsmith said loudly, over him.

Roger looked blank. 'Who?'

'Oh yeah.' One of the art students had raised his black dyed, backcombed head. 'That guy who used to be in Boyfriend. He's gorgeous. Even though he's ancient. Nearly forty.'

Roger bristled. 'Nearly forty . . . ancient?'

'What's Boyfriend?' asked Dan. It rang a vague bell, but too vague to identify. Names were never Dan's forte.

'A boy band of the nineties,' answered one of the librarians, rather to Dan's surprise. Then again, librarians probably had to have a working knowledge of many subjects.

'Can't stand boy bands,' Dan remarked. He smiled at Siobhan as the rest of the class continued to debate the news. As she had not evinced the slightest interest, presumably she felt the same. He remembered, not without pain, that her husband was a classical musician.

Siobhan looked up. Her big green eyes rested on his. 'I don't know what to say,' she said. 'You see, Ciaran O'Sullivan's my husband.'

Chapter 37

David, who was on call from the hospital, had taken some persuading to accompany Alice to the fashionable east London farmers' market. But he had the day off – an increasingly rare occurrence – and she was determined to celebrate being back in employment. She planned to treat them both, buy some of the food the market was famous for, for a special supper.

Celebration, however, seemed far from David's thoughts as he wandered scowling among the stalls full of Parma Hampstead – cured ham after the ancient Italian model but made in north London rather than northern Italy. Alice noticed the way his fingers played constantly at his belt loops, where his hospital beeper was clipped. She was beginning to wish she had never suggested they come here. David was utterly preoccupied, his mind obviously elsewhere. Resentment began to rise in her: could he not share, if not her joy about the job exactly, then at least her relief? Her career might not be as important or useful as his, but did that mean he had to ignore it altogether?

As David grumbled on at her side, Alice looked, hot-eyed and angry, round the market. Beneath the Victorian wrought-iron roof, the stalls stretched away, every one, it seemed, a magnet for well-heeled, well-turned-out, happy-looking couples straight out of Sunday supplements.

Take those two over there, Alice thought, her attention on the rear view of a blonde woman in a slim, well-cut blue dress that reached almost to her silver Birkenstocks. Next to her, also with his back to Alice, was a man in jeans and a pink shirt which perfectly suited his tawny skin and thick black hair. As they stood before a stall offering a bewildering array of different types of rocket, they looked, Alice thought, the epitome of the wealthy, fashionable couple. They positively radiated satisfaction with life and their lot.

Their purchase completed, the woman turned to the man, and Alice gasped. It was Suki. Suki and Rafael.

'Hey!' she exclaimed, bounding over to them. 'Out of your manor, aren't you? Not your neck of the woods, this.'

'You know me,' Rafael grinned, brandishing the rocket. 'I'll cross continents for the latest fashionable salad leaf.'

'Rocket's not fashionable,' Suki corrected him irritably. 'It's completely ten minutes ago. It's all about matsui now. Or wild-gathered.'

Rafael rolled his eyes. 'Calm down, darling. I was joking.' He grinned at Alice. 'Where's David?'

'Over there,' Suki said shrilly. 'By the artisanal breads.'

Rafael ambled off.

'What's the matter?' Alice asked. Her friend seemed very tense.

Suki, who was marginally taller than Alice, swooped close, attended by a swirl of light, herby perfume. 'Darling,' she hissed hotly in Alice's ear, 'I just wanted to ask you not to mention the Albertine business in front of Rafa. He was away and he doesn't know she was ill . . .'

'Doesn't *know*!' Alice exclaimed, before Suki pressed a long, cool white finger to her lips and shook her shining blond hair, caught loosely up in its pencil.

'He was busy on some big deal. I didn't want to worry him. Especially once I'd spoken to David and knew it was all OK.'

She glanced behind her at Rafael, but he was talking and, from time to time, letting out his genial boom.

'But how could you not tell him?' Alice could hardly believe it. It might not be her business, but it was not, she was sure, the way she would have done things. Surely Rafael, as Suki's husband, was the person she was closest to in the world. How could she withhold information so essential?

Perhaps some of this showed in her eyes, because Suki now flared her nostrils and threw a look at Rafael markedly different from the usual affection-filled glance. Then she looked at Alice with a hard, blue, assessing gaze, as if, Alice thought, wondering whether to tell her something.

'What's the matter?' Alice asked anxiously.

Suki looked away. 'He's been having an affair,' she muttered.

'No!' Alice exclaimed immediately. 'No. It's impossible.'

'All too possible, I'm afraid,' Suki replied lightly.

Alice was shaking her head. 'What? *Rafa?* But he *adores* you. He'd *never* . . . I mean . . .'

But Suki was looking at her with narrowed eyes. 'Believe me. He *has*. I found out the same day that Albertine fell ill.' She passed a hand over her eyes. 'My daughter sick and my husband unfaithful.'

Alice swallowed. Poor Suki. Her life was not gilded after all. She was not immune to misery.

'That's why David was so long at my house that night,' Suki sniffed, looking at Alice with suddenly wet eyes. 'He was the first person I told.'

Alice gasped. David had never said a word about this to her.

'I made him swear not to tell you,' Suki explained, when Alice had stuttered this out. 'And I can see that he didn't. You're so lucky.' She sniffed. 'He's a man of such principle. So . . . upright.'

Alice squeezed her eyes tightly shut. It didn't make sense. *Why* hadn't David told her? She would have told him, without hesitation.

'And that's not all,' Suki went on, blinking her large blue eyes as if to force back tears. 'The Other Woman . . .' she pronounced the words with contempt, 'is someone I know. One of my closest friends.'

'Who? *Who?*' There was something in the way Suki was

looking at her . . . but *no*. No. It was crazy, impossible. Suki could not possibly suspect . . .

'It's Caroline,' Suki said levelly.

'Caroline!' Alice gasped, receiving her third mighty shock in as many minutes. '*BBC* Caroline?' The Caroline who just got me a job in Gold Street, she was about to blurt, but did not.

Awareness of her difficult situation now dawned. Would Suki demand she resigned before she started, out of loyalty? Had Caroline's motives for getting her the job been less about the documentary, and more about shoring up support among Suki's friends? And if Alice did not mention the Caroline connection, did that make her part of the deceit too, in the same way as not mentioning Albertine to Rafael compromised her? She stared helplessly at Suki. 'I can't believe it.'

'Believe it,' Suki said bitterly.

'What are you girls nattering about?' Rafael's genial tones interrupted proceedings. The boys had suddenly joined them, David looking at her shocked face questioningly.

Alice found herself dragged off for a coffee.

Over cappuccino, macchiato and a plateful of cantucci biscuits apparently made in Clapham, she tried to behave as if all was normal. Most surprising was that Suki especially seemed determined to pretend everything was just as it should be. And if Rafa knew that Suki knew, Alice thought, he was covering that up well too.

With the chattering of Suki and the interjections of Rafael in his good-humoured bass, it could have been any Saturday, any meeting of the four of them over the last six years. David's attitude to Suki was utterly normal too: ignoring her completely, as usual. It was as if, Alice thought, his interventions with Albertine had never happened. As if he was not also the keeper of a secret about Suki's husband.

'Alice told you her news?' David asked the other two, aiming his question mainly at Rafael.

'No!' Suki jumped in. 'Pregnant, are we?' she asked, looking teasingly at Alice.

Alice gave her a warning look; in the circumstances, it was a joke too far. Suki just stared innocently back, however.

Alice broke the news about OneSquared, not mentioning Caroline and hoping that Suki would not make the connection.

She did not – or did not seem to. She clapped her hands. 'Fantastic. I always wondered why you were wasting your time in that deadbeat gallery.'

'Hey, Sukes,' drawled David sarcastically. 'Don't beat about the bush, will you?'

Suki tossed her head.

'Well,' Rafael said grinning, 'I hope this means party invitations.'

Alice could not help staring at him. Knowing all he knew, Rafa was talking about *parties*? Or was he, as his wife evidently was too, just very good at compartmentalising?

'What party?' asked David innocently. He had, Alice noted with exasperation, taken in precisely nothing of what she had told him about her new job.

Suki gave him a shove. 'The Gold Street party, of course!' she said excitedly. '*Only* the biggest party of the London summer season. Every gallery in the street opens up and has champagne and live bands and artists and celebrities and crazy things happening. It's amazing, but it's incredibly exclusive.'

A disdainful expression crossed David's face at this; Alice, catching it, felt both insulted and confused. Gold Street and its party might be ridiculous, but it was also her new job; could he not be more supportive? And why be so sneery to Suki, when he was faithfully keeping such a great secret about her marriage?

She contained her annoyance until they got back to the Nutthouse. 'Why didn't you tell me about Suki and Rafael?' she thundered.

David replied, with icy calm, that he had been sworn to secrecy and he had stuck to his word.

'But it was Suki!' Alice yelled. 'You don't even *like* Suki.'

'No,' David admitted. 'But that's not the point. It's the principle.'

He refused to discuss any other aspect of the situation, claiming it was none of his or her business. He simply went into the kitchen, made a cup of coffee, then shut himself up in the small spare room with his work. An hour or so later he departed for the hospital, claiming it was an emergency.

Chapter 38

Amid the purple excesses of her Aldeham Manor bathroom, Siobhan was soaking after a long day's sketching. Contemplating the leaded window panes, open to admit the soft summer air and the rays of the evening sun, she felt calm and contented despite the strawberry-hued claw-footed tub in which she soaked. Even the ridiculous black glass chandelier and hot pink towels no longer held their former power to annoy. Since rediscovering her métier, Siobhan felt liberated, although, she thought with a sudden smile, probably not quite so liberated as the model in Dan's life class. Probably no one anywhere was quite so liberated as Bo, and yet, according to Dan, who had walked her home after the class, her day job was the epitome of restraint: in the planning department of the local council.

Siobhan thought about the life class and how much she had enjoyed it. The people were funny and friendly. Especially Dan. She smiled at the thought of his kind, encouraging face behind its glasses, his dark eyes and shining flop of hair. He had been so embarrassed when he found out about Ciaran. For some reason Dan had imagined her husband was a classical musician; Siobhan, however, had thought better of mentioning the orchestra supposedly backing Boyfriend on their reunion tour.

If the tour happened, that was. Ciaran, Siobhan knew, was having a great deal of difficulty tracking down the last band member. He was in London at the moment, continuing the search. Declan had been found working as an osteopath and Padraig managing a garden centre called The Flowerpot Men. Both had jumped at the chance to get back into Boyfriend. With three of the original four on board, rehearsals had begun and schedules been planned in the expectation the fourth would be found any minute. But Michael seemed to have disappeared off the face of the earth. He was last heard of in America, so far as anyone knew.

Siobhan slipped her shoulders under the water, savouring the delicious warmth, and thought again of Dan. She was grateful for his encouragement at the art class. 'You've got real talent,' he had told her. 'An instinctive feel for form and colour.'

The ever-lascivious Roger Pryap had sniggered. 'I'll give you an instinctive feel, love,' he had rasped.

'Shut up, Roger, you lecherous old bugger,' Bo had intervened from her model's podium.

Siobhan closed her eyes, so Dan's face swam before her. Sweet, easy-going, kind and gentle. Fond of music and art. She liked in particular his baggy, obviously second-hand clothes. They reminded her of the students she had known at art college. Herself at art college, come to that. She liked his modesty, his lack of vanity, his wonderful talent. That portrait . . .

'What are *you* thinking about?'

Siobhan opened her eyes and gasped slightly to find Ciaran sitting on the edge of her bathtub, a mere few feet away. She had not heard him enter; he must have crept in like a mouse, on purpose to surprise her.

'Ciaran! I thought you were in London!'

'Just back.' He grinned. He looked down and pushed her just-removed clothes along the floor with his foot. A pencil dropped out of a pocket and rolled across the pink tiles.

'Been out drawing again, have you?' She stiffened at the words, but his voice was easy. Encouraging, even. She took this to mean he was finally coming to terms with it, and felt relieved.

'Yes,' she answered. 'That art class was really fun, really got things flowing again.'

'Good,' Ciaran said lightly. 'Good. Just make sure you don't get too into it, though.'

Siobhan frowned. 'Why not?'

'Because there's only room for one artist in our marriage, remember.' Ciaran was grinning, as if he were joking, but there was an expression in his eyes which hinted otherwise.

Not knowing what to say to this, Siobhan pretended to look for the soap, sloshing the water about vigorously.

'Oh, by the way, I've found Michael,' Ciaran said casually. His thickly lashed eyes were crinkled with satisfaction.

Siobhan stared at the whirling waters. The reunion was complete. She lifted her face.

'Where? Where'd you find him?'

'Grabbed him just before he went into the jungle.'

'Jungle?'

Ciaran narrowed his eyes. 'You really need to get with the programme, Siobhan,' he said sarcastically. '*I'm A Celebrity, Get Me Out Of Here*. Heard of it? It's a TV celebrity survival contest.'

'Of course I've heard of it. You mean he was on it?'

'He'd been asked. An agent friend of mine tipped me off. He was considering it pretty seriously, apparently.' Ciaran twisted his mouth contemptuously.

'Er . . . how is he?' Siobhan asked.

'He's gone prematurely grey and his dye job's bloody awful,' Ciaran said with obvious satisfaction. 'He's out of condition as well. I've told him he has to lose it if we're going to be ripping off our shirts.'

'Ripping off . . . your shirts?'

Ciaran turned level, amused eyes on her. 'It was our trademark moment. Always got the most screams in any Boyfriend show.'

Siobhan absorbed this. Of course, such male sexual preening was part and parcel of what boy bands did. Nonetheless – was it what married men did? Men married to *her*, moreover?

Ciaran stood up, and Siobhan noticed that his shirt was open. There was something different about his torso – but what?

Then she realised. The undulating planes of smooth, muscled skin rippling before her were clear of the merest hint of hair. 'You've waxed your chest,' she said, surprised.

He glanced at himself in the mirror and struck an attitude. 'Yeah. It was fucking painful, frankly.' He was making rhythmic movements in the mirror, flexing his biceps. 'Yeah,' he repeated softly to himself. 'This used to drive the girls wild. They used to throw their knickers and everything.'

Siobhan felt a stir of indignation. 'You're obviously looking forward to that bit.'

'It's unbelievable,' Ciaran was saying softly to his reflection. 'That moment when you come on stage and millions of fans just start screaming. It's the *best.*'

Better than what? Siobhan wondered. Better than *me*?

Ciaran turned and bent over the bath. His eyes looked intently into hers. 'Look, Siobhan. You are pleased about all this? The reunion? You want it too?'

It was part of Ciaran's method, Siobhan knew, never to ask open questions. Rather, to make assumptions with question marks at the end. His eyes continued to search hers, obviously trying to read her thoughts. *His* thoughts, on the other hand, were obvious enough. He expected her to support him. He earned the money, she enjoyed the enviable lifestyle. Or so he supposed.

'Get out of the bath,' he said softly. 'I've got a surprise for you.'

He watched as, self-consciously, she rose from the water and grabbed a towel from the pink metal rail.

In the bedroom, the low, wide black bed was covered in gleaming bags. Prada, Dior, Versace, Chanel. Siobhan made herself smile and look pleased, but she knew that everything within would be smart, tight, dark and minimal, the sort of thing that screamed money. The sort of thing Ciaran liked her to wear.

She opened the Chanel bag and drew out the predictable tight-fitting dress. It was difficult, increasingly difficult, to remember how such presents had once excited her. How thrilling it had been, as a penniless twenty-year-old art student, to be swept off her feet by a rich, famous, young and charming pop star.

'Pleased? You like them?'

His tone was insistent. He was pulling at her towel. It fell away; she felt his hands clamp her breasts. A thrill went through her as his mouth found hers; even now, he could make her melt. He pushed her roughly backwards on to the carrier bags. Panting, he pulled himself up on her, and their varnished exteriors stuck to her wet back; as he entered and began to thrust, their sharp corners dug into her flesh.

'You like them?' he repeated, from between what sounded like clenched teeth.

'Yes,' Siobhan gasped, eyes wide with the pain both inside and out. 'Ye-es.'

Chapter 39

On Alice's first day at OneSquared, the tube was in more uproar even than usual and the delays forced her to sprint from Piccadilly Circus station to Gold Street. She arrived, hot and with a thumping heart, just in time. Angelica's massive black four-wheel-drive screeched to a halt outside the gallery mere seconds afterwards.

As Angelica emerged, Alice saw that despite the warmth of the day, she was wearing ripped fishnet tights under a very tight black dress and a big black sheepskin flying jacket. 'Here,' she snapped, hurling a bunch of keys in Alice's direction and hardly looking at her. 'The security code's SPAW1.'

As Alice fumbled at the super-reinforced entrance with the triple locks and state-of-the-art alarm system, Angelica continued to take several deep breaths. Not only had Sebastian gone spectacularly off-piste on the route front – they had been heading towards the M4 before Angelica finally noticed – his making up for lost time had involved contravening several one-way streets and almost annihilating a gang laying water mains.

Added to which, her texted daily horoscope had seemed ominous. *Your patient, giving and optimistic nature will be more than usually tested today . . .*

Alice's interview with Angelica, such as it was, had taken place in the front of the gallery. Now Angelica stomped across to a door at the back and threw it open. She beckoned to Alice, standing nervously by Zeb Spaw's bed, to follow. Like the gallery, the passage was wood-floored, halogen-lit and white-painted. It contained three white doors, two of which Angelica threw open. Behind one was a small, smart new kitchen with granite units and brushed-steel appliances; behind the other, a small white bathroom with a green glass basin, a cupboard crammed with make-up and a pull-out magnifying mirror Alice recognised as the type that made every pore look as if you could pothole down it. The mirror and cupboard contents seemed to suggest that this was a room in which Angelica spent a great deal of time.

The third door remained closed. But as they passed the spiral staircase, Angelica pointed upwards. 'My private office. Go up there only when I ask you to. There,' she added, leading her back to the main gallery, 'that's the tour. You sit over there.' She pointed to the middle of the room, where a white desk with a phone and a flat-screen monitor on it stood next to four fluffy white beanbags arranged in a conversational square. The state-of-the-art black cordless phone was shaped rather like a penis.

'I'm going up to my office now,' Angelica announced.

Alice started to walk across the acres of polished beech towards the desk. Something, she felt, was not quite right, and not only the stool, which, as she pulled it out, proved to have a triangular seat. She looked back over at the gallery owner, who was disappearing through the passage door. 'Aren't you – I mean – shouldn't I know something about the, um, *artists*?'

Adam, for all his faults, had made sure she was fully appraised on everything Palladio sold, however small and obscure. In fact, it was the smallest, most obscure ones he particularly liked.

Angelica turned with a mighty rattle of buckles and bracelets. Through her poodle fringe, her kohl-rimmed eyes were wide with surprise. 'You want to know about the artists?'

'Yes.' Alice wondered why Angelica seemed so surprised.

Angelica was, in fact, amazed. None of her previous assistants had ever evinced the slightest interest in OneSquared's artists. Not in their art, anyway. She thought of Natasha and twisted her pale frosted lips. 'You'd better follow me,' she said curtly.

Opening the closed door in the passage that Alice had noticed previously, Angelica ushered her into a large storeroom. She flicked on the lights.

'There's a few artworks here,' she remarked. 'Left over from recent exhibitions mostly. We never display more than one artist at a time in the gallery, for obvious reasons.'

The reasons were not obvious to Alice. Everything had been displayed at the same time at Palladio. To the extent that you could hardly see anything. Now, in the echoing, austere minimalism of OneSquared, she felt a searing nostalgia for the crowded old gallery.

In the centre of the room was a table on which stood four constructions. They were all about three feet tall and apparently made from loo rolls, possibly with a dash of eggbox, held together with papier mâché, which gave an unpleasant crusting effect to the exterior. They were daubed, deliberately badly – or perhaps just badly – with white paint.

'Hero Octagon,' Angelica said, waving a thin, careless and heavily beringed hand at them. 'Her *Phallusy* series asks fundamental questions about our macho sensibilities in what is in effect an investigation of gender stereotypes.'

Alice now realised that the white things were supposed to be penises. Well, they didn't look like any penis of her acquaintance. None she had seen had been three feet long and the width of the centre of a loo roll. What they did look very much like, on the other hand, were the sort of things she had made in primary school. Of course, she had never made actual penises in primary school. Willies weren't the sort of thing you could come running out of class with at the day's end, waving at admiring parents.

Angelica, at the back of the room, beckoned Alice over.

'This is Balthazar Ponce,' she told her, waving a pebble with strands of hair stuck all over it. 'Remember – pronounced Pon-Kay. And this is Koo-Jeong Cuckoo.' Alice looked at what appeared to be a hideously misshapen carrot.

She was beginning to wish she had never asked to see any of it, but there was no stopping Angelica now. 'This is *Tit Gnome*,' she supplied next, her skinny fingers lingering on the head of what looked like an ordinary garden gnome covered in red rubber nipples. 'It's by Empathy Collective and subverts the twin British traditions of Page Three girls and horticulture.'

Alice nodded.

'Brian Sewell called it "a travesty",' Angelica added proudly.

Walking over to the wall, she turned round a large rectangle to reveal a confusing jumble of images, amongst which Alice could make out a pair of naked, open female legs, a woman with freakishly large breasts, and a cartoon mouse.

'This is a Cruz Backhausen,' Angelica revealed. 'It's a psycho-sexual take on the fairy tale.'

'Which fairy tale?' Alice asked, eyeing the breasts and the open legs and thinking that it didn't look like any she was familiar with.

Angelica's kohl-rimmed eyes flashed indignantly under her frazzled fringe. 'Isn't it obvious? Cinderella, of course.'

'*That's* Cinderella?'

'Backhausen uses snippets from lads' mags to create the figurative element of his artworks. It's an *hommage* to feminism.'

Alice bit back an enquiry as to how snippets from lads' mags could constitute a homage to feminism. The question clearly was not relevant. She contented herself with observing that the mouse in the picture had a strangely shaped nose.

'A penis nose,' Angelica said briskly. 'It represents the prince's fear of impotence in the face of the fairy godmother, who represents the sapphic alternative. The mouse has a penis nose, but that penis is floppy. The mouse is not having sex with Cinderella, nor is the pumpkin. Together they represent the patriarchy defeated. The whole thing's a monarcho-psycho-socio-sexual metaphor. OK?'

'Er, OK,' Alice muttered.

'Right. Now let's get on with some work.'

As Angelica stomped back to the gallery, bracelets rattling, the mobile rang in the depths of her Burberry tote. Her heart sank as, pulling it out, she saw that the number on the screen was Dr Love's. Damn that smooth, interfering medic.

'I'm afraid you're going to have to come back,' he said in his trademark relaxed style.

'Can't,' snapped Angelica, striding across the polished gallery floor, the buckles on her flying jacket jingling. Did he have any idea what her day was like? She flicked the ball on her BlackBerry to remind herself. Ah yes. How could she have forgotten? This lunchtime, the most ultra-conceptual of her stable of artists, Evelyn Legg, was arriving with what promised to be a cutting-edge piece of sculpture. Angelica, fired by Evelyn's assurances that it was wildly exciting, completely original and would set new artistic standards, was hoping that it might attract the crowds that the gold bed had failed to and take Sharon Aura on at her own game.

After Legg, there was another canapé meeting with Penelope; underlit Perspex platters had now been ruled out and tray-integral DVDs were once again under consideration. The devil was in the detail, Angelica knew. Maybe – and hey, this was a thought – she should put the devil in the trays on the DVDs.

Then there was a call with Caroline about the BBC art documentary. *Then* there was Advanced Power Pilates, followed by a party at the home of an important collector. Come *back*? she thought scornfully. Was Dr Love joking?

He wasn't, as it turned out. 'There may be a very high price to pay if you don't,' the doctor warned lightly. 'Mr Devon is talking about divorce.'

Angelica screeched to a halt. '*What?*' she gasped.

Divorce! Being cut off from the unstoppable golden stream of Nick's wealth! The wealth that financed OneSquared and made her such a powerful figure in this most arcane and privileged of worlds! The thought was – well – unthinkable. Especially as she had just got Zeb Spaw and was determined to justify the decision. Plus pull off the most triumphant party the street had ever seen.

Angelica looked furiously out through the window. Damn it, Sebastian had just gone. 'Give me half an hour,' she snarled at Dr Love, before dismissing him abruptly into the ether and pumping frantically at the keys of her BlackBerry, searching for her Crucial Chauffeurs Premium Client number.

She had entirely forgotten about Alice, who was staring at her employer in concern. Angelica had gone purple in the face and was emitting strange gasping noises, as if she were about to have some sort of seizure.

'Are you all right?' Alice ventured.

Angelica's eyes were wild as she stared at Alice. 'I've got to go out,' she muttered savagely. 'You're in charge. OK?'

Alice nodded. 'Any instructions?' she asked.

Something about Perspex platters and concept art flashed through Angelica's panicking mind, but just as quickly it was gone. The mere mention of divorce had blown her cognitive capacities right out of the water. 'God . . . I mean, I don't know . . . can't think.'

She clutched her hair. 'Just don't do anything stupid, OK? Like leave the gallery. Like, *ever*.'

Before Alice could reply, the gallery door had slammed behind her boss. She saw the skinny black-clad figure hobble furiously past the window. Then the large black four-wheel-drive she had seen earlier appeared, hurtling towards Angelica at a speed, Alice was quite sure, that was completely illegal for central London. She saw Angelica shout something at the person behind the wheel, who had his cap shoved rakishly back on his head and blond hair hanging down over his eyes. As the car set off again, Alice wondered how he could see.

With Angelica gone, the place seemed very silent. Alice took a deep breath. She was alone on her first day. Alone with a gold-sprayed bed, a hairy pebble, a mutant carrot, some eggbox willies, a nipple-covered gnome and a monarcho-psycho-socio-sexual metaphor. And strict instructions not to leave them – ever.

Chapter 40

Alice went to the window and stared at Cornelius Sump, *Old Cock* and the Maltesers box. It was difficult to imagine the latter especially hanging up in one's house and being a source of pleasure and admiration.

As she continued to stare at it, the Maltesers box slowly peeled off, hung drunkenly by its lid for a couple of moments and then fell to the bottom of the window.

Almost immediately, a girl appeared behind the glass, climbing in from the gallery behind. Presumably she had heard the box fall. She was young and very pretty, with a curtain of very black, very shiny hair, very black, very tight and very shiny PVC leggings and very high heels. She bent with difficulty to retrieve the box, then, straightening and looking swiftly behind her to make sure no one was passing, which they weren't, she whipped out a Pritt Stick, smeared glue liberally over the base of the Maltesers box and pressed it back on to the canvas.

Alice must have moved, or done something to attract attention, because suddenly the girl glanced across the road straight at her. Alice found herself looking into a pair of laughing eyes, one of which closed in a big, audacious wink. The girl then put her finger confidingly to her lips and flashed a huge and irresistible smile before turning, climbing out of the window and disappearing into the shadows of Sump.

The telephone began to ring. 'Hey, gorgeous,' said a growly, self-assured male voice as Alice picked it up. 'Free for some fun at lunchtime? Artistic genius seeks somewhere to put his brush?' There followed a filthy cackle.

'Bugger off!' Alice laughed, assuming it was David, and this a first-day-in-a-new-job joke. She felt a wave of relief; relations between them had been strained since the meeting with Suki and Rafael and the subsequent row. Her heart leapt at the thought that he had recovered his sense of fun enough to make a prank call.

'Who is this?' demanded the other end indignantly. Not, Alice realised, David after all. She felt disappointed, but even more amazed. Was the lascivious invitation, then, a genuine one?

'Who are *you*?' she demanded,

'This isn't Natasha?' growled the voice, answering her question with another.

'No. She's left.'

Alice's tone was stern. Whatever extracurricular services Natasha had offered as gallery assistant, they had been discontinued.

She went into the kitchen to make tea, and instead made the unhelpful discovery that there were no supplies of milk or tea bags. The fridge contained nothing but champagne and white wine.

Someone rang the doorbell, and she hurried out again.

A tall, sandy-haired man in a pale blue shirt and tie stood peering uncertainly in from the other side. With a pang of annoyed surprise, Alice recognised him as the man with whom she had collided on the day of her interview. He was clearly not giving up in pursuit of a drinks date.

She frowned at him discouragingly. To her surprise, the two wide blue-grey eyes grew wider still. Either he genuinely hadn't recognised her before, Alice thought, or he was a very good actor.

'May I come in?' he mouthed.

Alice hesitated. She was alone, and she didn't entirely trust him. On the other hand, if he was a customer, and he complained to Angelica . . .

Reluctantly, she undid the locks. She would stay within sight of the window, where she could summon help if necessary.

He walked in, large feet in shiny shoes on the slender herringbone pattern of the floor. She caught a suggestion, no more, of subtly expensive cedary aftershave. He stopped and turned to her, with a wide but uneasy smile. 'Sorry. I didn't realise you worked here.'

'Did you want to buy something?' Alice returned, with as much poise as she could muster. The sooner he was out of here, the better.

'Possibly.' As, perhaps to cover awkwardness, he pushed his sandy hair back from his wide forehead, she caught a flash of a smart but unostentatious watch. 'But I was also here to do some research.'

He did not sound threatening, or like a mad person. His voice, as she remembered it being before, was low, warm and eminently reasonable-sounding.

She wondered what he meant by research. Was he a student? she wondered. He didn't look like one. Nor a dealer, come to that; he had none of the sharp-eyed, ingratiating ways of those jackdaws who had come in regularly to plunder Adam's best pieces. He looked, on the contrary, like someone from an altogether more solid and prosperous profession. 'Research?' she asked.

'I run a business. I've – ah – made a bit of money recently.' She was intrigued to see that he coloured slightly, looked down modestly, as if the fact was somehow embarrassing. 'I'm, um, thinking of investing in art.'

Alice's doubts were increasing – about her own suspicions. If this was merely a chat-up, it was a very elaborate one. Was it likely that someone like this – presentable, intelligent, charming, possibly successful – would go to such lengths, and for her?

'That's what I was doing here the other day,' he added, as if reading her mind. 'Checking out the galleries, seeing what appealed.'

Alice finally decided to believe him. Everything he said made sense. Apart, that was, from wanting to invest in art in Gold Street. Who in their right mind would do that?

He was looking at her speculatively. 'I was hoping for some advice,' he said. 'From someone like yourself.'

Alice swallowed. The tables had been thoroughly turned. She had felt indignant and suspicious; she now felt defensive. Expert on contemporary art? Her? When her only definite view was how bad it was?

'I'm good in my own area,' he was saying. 'But when I'm dealing with something I don't know about, I always take expert advice.' He smiled and held out his hand. 'Jasper Bright,' he said warmly. 'I didn't introduce myself before. Sorry.'

'Alice,' she muttered, as her own hand disappeared into his large, warm, dry one. It felt comforting and familiar. Of course, she remembered. He had helped her up when she fell over.

Jasper was looking round the gallery. 'Zeb Spaw,' he mused, apparently to himself, his tall frame bent as he studied the label for *The Right Hand of the Father II*. He glanced questioningly round at Alice. 'He's the guy who sold those false gold legs for twenty million pounds, am I right?'

'Dead right,' Alice confirmed.

Jasper straightened up. Up, and up, Alice thought, watching the tall body restack itself. 'Was that any good?' he asked.

'Sorry?'

'That prosthetic leg thing. Was it any good? Was it a work of art?'

'Er . . .' Alice stammered. What sort of a question was *that*, especially in Spaw's own gallery? 'Well, someone paid twenty million pounds for it, so . . .'

'Yes, but does that make it *good*?' Jasper pressed. 'People pay huge sums of money for all sorts of rubbish.'

She gazed at him. They did indeed. Nowhere more so than in

the case of *Prostheseus Bound.* She tried to find the right phrase, but it eluded her.

'Hard to say, I can see,' he remarked lightly. He extended a cufflinked wrist in the direction of *The Right Hand of the Father II*. 'OK, well what about this one? Same artist, I can see. Is *this* any good?'

Alice felt panicky. Was Spaw's bed any good? Well of course it wasn't.

She opened her mouth to tell him the truth, then shut it again. A clammy feeling of horror swept over her. What was she thinking of? Giving her genuine opinion about the gallery's star artist would be career suicide. She opened her mouth again, about to spout the rote list of cod-art phrases that had so impressed Angelica. But then she saw the serious, attentive expression on Jasper's face. She knew that, for whatever reason, he trusted her, and suddenly she felt unable to betray that trust.

She took a deep breath and smiled.

'I suppose it's a difficult question,' Jasper prompted gently.

Alice's grin was becoming rictus. 'It's a perfectly valid question,' she replied. 'And it depends,' she went on carefully, 'whether you like this kind of thing. If you do, it's the kind of thing you'll like.'

Jasper looked surprised. 'You know, I wasn't expecting you to say that. I imagined you'd say everything in your gallery was marvellous and that I should certainly buy it.'

He was looking around consideringly. He had a good profile, Alice found herself thinking. And she liked his fair, open face, his frequent smiles. 'With art of this nature, it's rather in the eye of the beholder,' he finished.

'Yes, *exactly*.'

'Great.' Jasper rewarded her with a broad smile. 'That helps a lot. Thanks.'

She watched him move towards the door, and realised that she had wondered if he was going to ask her for a drink again. She had, she also realised, planned to say yes. Of course, she was with

David; a drink was all it would be. But now that she worked at OneSquared, client entertainment was no doubt part of the job description.

'Bye,' said Jasper, raising a hand as he exited. He did not look back at her; neither did he repeat his offer.

Alone again in the gallery, feeling vaguely regretful, she resumed her seat behind the desk. The triangular stool was no doubt the *dernier cri* amongst avant-garde designers. But Alice already had cause to wonder whether it was doing much for her back. She twiddled the mouse and tapped the computer keyboard, but nothing seemed to happen on the screen. It was obviously a very expensive computer, far more expensive than the one she had at home. It was probably better to wait for Angelica to show her how to use it.

A noise made her look at the window. A large van was heaving itself up on to the pavement outside and parking, its hazards flashing. A grizzled-looking man in blue overalls jumped out of the van and began to ring wildly at the bell.

Alice hurried over and pulled open the heavy door.

'Delivery for Angelica Devon.' He shoved a large brown paper carrier bag at her.

'She's not here,' Alice said, noting with the alert senses of the hungry that the bag contained food. A delicious savoury-sweet smell was emanating from it.

'Can you sign for it then?' The man proffered a black electronic pad on whose screen Alice was required to write her name to acknowledge receipt.

After he had gone, Alice peered into the bag and saw she was right. It was food. Chinese food, she guessed from the smell and from the characteristic stack of silver cartons with white cardboard tops. The topmost carton was slightly open, and she caught a glimpse of thick, shiny red sauce that hinted strongly at sweet and sour pork. Her stomach gave a loud growl. What would she not give for sweet and sour pork right this minute? Sinful, sticky and calorie-loaded as it was, Chinese takeaway was one of her most favourite treats. Angelica's too, it seemed, as this was obviously her lunch. Or perhaps her supper, if she was coming back to the gallery later.

Alice tried to ignore the growling in her own stomach. She was, in any case, sure of eating well tonight, when she and David were going to the local tandoori for his birthday. Hopefully the hot food and intimate glow of the tea lights might bring about a thaw in relations. Surely, Alice thought, even David's famously Arctic bad moods could not withstand being told about Angelica, the gold bed, the mutant carrot, *Tit Gnome* and the psycho-sexual Cinderella.

Chapter 41

Dirk Finkelstein called just as Zeb was parking alongside the railed enclave of the Klumpps' white stucco mansion on the outskirts of Regent's Park. He had an appointment with Fuchsia, and he was not looking forward to it.

'Hey, Zeb.'

'Hello, Dirk.'

'We've had a great offer for you.'

A shock of hope went through Zeb. Could this be the National Gallery show he was secretly craving? He had been trying to persuade Fuchsia to lend her collection of his work to the National; public institutions normally jumped at contemporary art, as it gave them crowd-pulling exhibitions for nothing whilst buttering up the collector for donations of work in the future. The return favour – that a show at a respected public gallery bestowed credibility on a contemporary artist and sent his prices skywards – didn't exactly harm things either.

'What offer?' Zeb said excitedly.

'Artist in residence.'

'That all?' Zeb snapped. But then caution intervened. Artist in residence. While unwelcome in as much as it required him to work, there were possibilities depending on where it was. The White House. The Pentagon. Buckingham Palace, even. 'Artist in residence where?'

'On *The Graham Norton Show*,' Dirk said.

'What? *Whaaaatttt?*'

'Hey, calm down, man. It's a big show. Audience of millions.' Dirk reeled off some statistics.

'But why do they want an artist in bloody residence?'

'Well, Richard and Judy had one, remember. It's all about art for the masses. Accessibility. As well as being kind of avant-garde, if you think about it.'

'Avant-garde?' sneered Zeb, aware that Dirk Finkelstein didn't know his avant-garde from his elbow. He knew bugger all about art full stop. When they had met, he had cheerfully confused Matisse and Magritte, referring to the former as 'That guy who did the pipe, right? Or was it the banana?'

'And they pay well,' Dirk said, hurriedly scuttling back to the area in which he *was* expert.

'I don't care,' Zeb snapped, shoving his manager back into his pocket and striding up to Fuchsia's front door.

The hall had had a makeover since his last visit. The formerly cool and understated space was now lacquered red, and the dome that formed the centrepiece of the classical interior had been lined inside with gold leaf. The decorators had sure as hell been busy; it was less than a week since he had last been there.

'It's meant to suggest a temple to art,' Fuchsia drawled, floating down the great central staircase to meet him. That had changed too, Zeb saw. The fawn runner which had been on the wooden stairs before had been replaced by a leopardskin-patterned carpet.

'Temple of art! That makes you its high priestess!' Zeb forced himself to remark, right on cue.

Was it a temple, though? he asked himself. Or more of a warehouse? Fuchsia's latest purchases, after all, were displayed for all to see over the hall area. The flashing breasts were on the wall, the pink neon outline endlessly jumping from flat nipples to hat pegs. A set of three irregular rectangles of murky brown with rough black scrawls must be the triptych, Zeb guessed. He could not see the goat dung tent for which Fuchsia had fought to the death with Bigsky, but – Jesus, who was that?

Standing at the bottom of the stairs, next to the newel post, was a teenage Goth, dressed from head to foot in black leather. It looked male and its face, dead white with thick black eye make-up, scowled horribly from underneath black and neon-green dreadlocks. Zeb stared. It could not be one of Fuchsia's children, surely. They were no more than five, last time he looked. And girls, into the bargain.

'Like it?' Fuchsia trilled, striding over and slapping the Goth hard on his leather bottom. It was resin, Zeb realised.

'It's my new sculpture. It's by an alternative Finnish collective; I forget the name.'

'It's all right,' Zeb allowed. 'I didn't realise you'd been to any more art fairs.'

'I haven't. I decided to pass on Art Falklands after all. But you know me!' Fuchsia rolled her eyes. 'Art addict or what!' She tweaked one of the Goth's facial piercings. 'I call him Asterix.'

'Asterix?'

'Because he's a Goth, silly.'

Zeb stared. 'But Asterix was a Gaul.'

'Whatever.' Fuchsia waved a casual, diamond-flashing hand. 'I got him from Dystopia. And picked up the darlingest Ganymede Steam at the same time.'

'Ganymede *Steam*?' Zeb was outraged. 'You mean you bought one of those heads made of frozen pee?'

'Correction. One of those challenges to conventional concepts of the cerebral and the cloacal.'

'What?'

'In answer to your original question, yes, I did.'

Zeb's brow darkened. He wasn't going to argue about frozen bloody wee. The point was that Fuchsia had been shopping in Gold Street. Waving her fat chequebook just feet from his gold-sprayed bed. 'Did you go into OneSquared?' he demanded.

'Sweetie, I was dying to. But I just ran out of time. I was late for lunch with Julia Peyton-Jones as it was.'

'Why don't you buy *The Right Hand of the Father II*?' Zeb demanded, deciding to stop beating around the bush.

'I haven't got room,' Fuchsia insisted. She was, he noticed, avoiding his gaze.

'But you've got fourteen houses.'

'Yes, but they're all full of my other artworks. I should really,' she declared, 'open a contemporary art museum. Nicky – Serota – is always telling me so. It would be a great benefit to the nation – my adopted nation,' she added complacently. 'Anyway,' she added, stepping close to Zeb and looking round as if to check that none of her army of retainers was listening. 'Upstairs now, lover boy. I want you to screw my brains out.'

She meant it too, Zeb saw with a sinking heart. Out of sight of the butler, up the fourth and fifth staircases, Fuchsia went like the Grand National. She barely waited for him to get through the office door before she tore at his clothes. 'I need you,' she growled, clawing at his zip whilst simultaneously shrugging off the fitted black dress she wore. By Victoria Beckham, he noticed, seeing the label just before it crumpled, with the rest of the dress, to the polished floor.

'Hey, slow down,' he protested, trying to disguise how he was panting slightly from the ascent.

Fuchsia, stepping out of a pair of white crocodile Hermès boots, gave him a pitying smile.

Sex was frenetic, violent, but by no means a quickie. On the contrary, it seemed to take longer than ever. 'God, that was good. I was just so tense,' groaned Fuchsia, eyes closed.

'Why?' What had Fuchsia to be tense about? Zeb asked himself crossly. Stinking rich, and with the whole art world at her pedicured feet.

The eyes beneath him flicked open. 'Ha ha,' Fuchsia drawled sardonically.

'Ha ha what?' Zeb was genuinely baffled.

'Very funny. Pretending you'd forgotten my party tonight.'

Zeb gulped. Fuchsia's annual bash for the art world was an

event that almost rivalled the Gold Street party. He'd known it was in the offing, but had not realised it was so soon. How could he have forgotten?

He stared at the floor for a second, trying to collect himself. What was the matter with him these days? He remembered getting the invitation; no doubt his PR woman had uploaded it on to his BlackBerry. No doubt, if he switched his BlackBerry on, it would explode into rings and bleeps to remind him that the great day had dawned. But he hadn't switched it on for some time now, knowing that nothing it had to say would interest him.

Fuchsia's party. Zeb's heart sank at the thought. He hated meeting other artists at the best of times, and seeing Fuchsia preening herself in the midst of a sea of fawning painters on the make was enough to make him feel sick. 'So that's why you've done the house up,' he said, to give himself time to invent an excuse.

'Cor-rection. Maeve Kandinsky-O'Halloran's done the house up,' Fuchsia said serenely as she stepped into her Agent Provocateur.

Who? Zeb was about to ask, but then thought better of it. It wasn't as if he cared.

'You'll be there, of course,' Fuchsia added, flashing him a look. 'We might be able to get together in one of the cloakrooms.' Zeb, buckling his jeans, felt a ripple of dismay beneath his taut stomach.

'You're joking. In the middle of all those people?'

She licked her lips. 'Sure. That'll make it more fun. You know how parties make me tense.'

'I can't think why.' Zeb pulled his black T-shirt over his head. 'All you have to do is stand there and let everyone lick your ass.'

She gave a suggestive, throaty laugh. 'I'd prefer you to lick me in some other places.'

Zeb ignored this. 'Won't Herman be there?' he objected.

Fuchsia curled her lip. 'Yeah. But he never notices anything.'

Zeb raised his eyebrows, acknowledging the truth of this.

Herman Klumpp seemed to glide along in a state of vague bonhomie, although he was said to be a savage in the boardroom. Zeb suspected that all he cared about was work, and that he was happy to have his demanding wife occupied in whatever fashion she pleased, so long as no one talked. Perhaps surprisingly, no one had, not about herself and him, but Fuchsia was a powerful woman and could finish careers as well as start them.

Fuchsia was now hooking up her bra, the movement causing her Tiffany diamond necklace to ripple and catch the light. 'So when can I expect you?'

'I'm not sure,' Zeb hedged, strapping on his watch.

'Not sure, huh?' She regarded him archly from the office sofa, where she was now engaged in slipping on her stockings.

'I'm pretty busy with work, actually,' he said. Time to remind her, he decided, that he was, after all, the artist and she just a customer. An important customer, admittedly. But the artistic wellspring, the person who would be remembered by posterity, was himself. Especially now that he had a new gallery, although admittedly Angelica hadn't sold anything yet.

'Doing some new stuff?' Fuchsia drawled.

'You know I am,' he replied curtly, deciding to go back to treating her mean and keeping her keen. She had found that irresistible when first they had met. '*Sponge*,' he added casually, whilst watching her carefully from underneath his brows. Fuchsia's reaction to *Sponge* was important. He was banking – quite literally – on her buying a great many of them, a set for every one of the many houses she owned around the world, ideally. But so far she had evinced little interest in them.

Fuchsia looked back at him expressionlessly, but there was nothing new in that. Zeb had never been sure whether it was just Botox or a full-on facelift that gave her that very smooth, stretched expression. He sometimes wondered, in fact, whether Fuchsia had had an entire body-lift; the thin figure now being eased back into the black dress was that of someone half her age, or even half of that.

Quite suddenly and unexpectedly, the urge to paint Fuchsia, the rich man's wife, the powerful patron of the arts, just as she stood there in all her bought and surgically enhanced glory, came over him.

He forced the crazy thought instantly away. He hadn't wanted to paint a person in years. He didn't do portraits. Never had done, not since his earliest days at art school. He had quickly realised that that was not where the money was. Not if you weren't Lucien Freud.

'Speaking of new work,' Fuchsia said lightly, presenting her back so he could zip up her dress, 'I've just picked a new piece up myself.'

Zeb shook his hair back with the most noncommittal air he could manage. He had, however, splayed his hands on his knees to stop them shaking. 'What piece?' His voice was meant to be unconcerned, but it emerged as a tense growl.

'Great piece I saw in Sump. An installation in mixed media.'

'Who by?' Zeb asked quickly.

'It's called *Old Cock*.' Fuchsia smiled at her reflection in a compact, then took a lipstick out of a nearby bag and started to adjust it.

Zeb's stomach muscles clenched. He felt he knew what was coming next. Mixed media, Fuchsia had said. Could one of the media be video, by any chance? 'That piece by Sharon Aura?'

'That's the one.' Fuchsia stretched her lips into the mirror. 'Great, I thought. I'd been waiting for Sharon to move into video.'

Panic clutched Zeb. The urge to paint Fuchsia had suddenly been replaced by the urge to scream.

Fuchsia stood up, pulling the short jacket down over her dress's fitted skirt, and gave him a dazzling smile. 'So will I see you tonight? At the party?'

'I'll be there,' Zeb growled. After that speech, what choice did he have?

'Good,' said Fuchsia, regarding him coolly from the doorway as she slipped out of the room. 'I thought you might. Hey,' she added, sticking her thin face back round the door.

Zeb shot her a resentful look under his eyebrows. 'What?'

'The dress code,' she smirked, 'is Daring!'

Chapter 42

'David, are you listening to me?' Alice asked anxiously across the table.

Had the tandoori been a good choice? She was beginning to doubt it, even though the evening had started well. David had not, in the event, been all that late home at all and had walked in the door at the precise moment that the bottle of chilled champagne Alice had splashed out on had reached drinkable temperature.

He had received with every appearance of pleasure the bottle of Chanel Pour Monsieur aftershave. David was a traditionalist when it came to male scent. Or so he had always claimed. For some reason Alice thought he had smelled slightly different recently, but no doubt she was imagining it. Or it was hospital soap, possibly.

They had then walked hand in hand downstairs. In the restaurant, the waiter had been glad to see them and given them their favourite table in the corner. All in all, things had gone better than Alice had expected.

Until now, that was.

'What . . . oh, yes. Sorry.' He looked up, his handsome features, drooping with tiredness, flickering in the light from the food warmer.

Alice silently ground her teeth. She had spent the last ten minutes telling him, with great liveliness and embellishment, about the back-room art collection at OneSquared. But David had not reacted. She had expected incredulous laughter but had instead got preoccupation.

'What did I just say?' she tested him, forcing a smile. The words Balthazar Ponce or psycho-sexual Cinderella were all she was asking for. Surely, even if he was only half listening, even a quarter listening, such arresting phrases as those could not have failed to sink in.

He looked at her helplessly, then shook his head. 'Sorry, I was miles away. Work . . . you know.' He made an apologetic gesture with his hands.

She noticed now the way that he was sitting; his broad-shouldered body bent over the table, positively rigid with tension. Like an animal about to spring, Alice found herself thinking. His fingers were constantly on his on-call belt beeper, tapping in a way that made her nervous.

With a great effort, she decided to avoid recrimination, move on, and try again at conversation. They were both now examining the menu and she leaned over towards him. 'I think I'll have the chicken tikka and the vegetable curry for a change.' This was a joke; she always had the chicken tikka and the vegetable curry.

David, however, failed to smile. After they had both given their orders, Alice stared desolately at the painting of a serene-faced Hindu god hanging opposite her. Its calmness only increased the worry inside her, unease sizzling away just as loud and hard as the sizzling dishes of chicken and king prawns that arrived at the table at the very moment that David finally got the call from the hospital he had evidently been waiting for.

He ripped the pager off his belt and ran outside with his mobile. Two minutes later he was back in and grabbing his bag. Before, Alice thought later, you could say 'cycle clips', he was out of the door, heading towards his bike in the block's communal cycle store. His last, hissed words, 'I'm sorry' and 'I'll make it up to you', hung, along with the food smells, in the air between their table and the exit. Alice stared down at the food, from his full, untouched plate to hers. She was horribly aware of the stares from other tables, whose concerned gazes and whispered exchanges made obvious their assumption that she and David had had a row resulting in his abrupt departure. The awful thing, Alice thought, was that she almost felt that they had.

Chapter 43

The situation, Dr Love had told Angelica, was this. Nick wanted to divorce her. The only possibility of salvaging the marriage was for her to go with him as soon as possible to an Indian spiritual retreat of his choice. Here they would renounce all material and professional concerns in order to rediscover what had brought them together in the first place, work on their relationship and find a way to go forward.

Angelica had received the news with fury. She had met Dr Love's mild gaze with one of white-hot loathing. She could see she had no choice. Damn Nick and his spiritual retreat. Damn it to hell.

That had been yesterday. Angelica, now panting on the Power-Plate in her Twickenham bathroom, hoped Nick had had a change of heart in the night. Or even just a heart attack – especially if he had had no time to change his will.

Failing that, that she had just dreamed it all. Or, more precisely, nightmared it all. The entire conversation with Dr Love was nothing more than a figment of her overheated, overworked, overworried imagination.

Beep!

She leapt off the machine and stumbled to her BlackBerry. Today's texted horoscope had more than even the usual significance for her.

You're in transition. Change is afoot. Embrace and explore the challenges that are even now coming your way.

'Fuck off,' Angelica muttered, snapping the message away. There was only one sort of embrace she felt like doing with regard to the changes now afoot – her hands, ever tighter, around Dr Love's smooth, tanned neck. And then round Nick's and then his accountant's.

She stomped into her dressing room, threw open the black louvred doors of her walk-in wardrobe and bad-temperedly swept back the dresses on the rails. The jangle and swish of the agitated clothes matched her mood exactly. She pulled out a Vivienne Westwood suit with a tightly cinched waist, and was just breathing in to button it up when what sounded like a knock on the door of the bedroom beyond caught her ear.

'What is it?' Angelica snapped, panting and red-faced from the effort of hurrying across a large bedroom in tight clothes only to find it was the person she least wished to see.

Dr Love, dressed, shaved and smoothly in control even at this time of the morning, gave her a relaxed smile. 'I just wanted to let you know you're leaving in an hour, Mrs Devon.'

'Leaving?' Angelica shouted. 'You bet I'm leaving, buster. I'm leaving for my gallery. Sebastian's due any time. I've got to get there early; I've got some serious time to make up.' She glared at the doctor in such a way as to make it absolutely clear that this was his fault. But Dr Love's smile shone serenely on.

'I'm afraid that's impossible, Mrs Devon. You see, two places have come up at the retreat in India and—'

'What? All of a sudden?' Angelica exploded. 'There was no mention of this last night. When the hell was this booked?'

'No, but as I explained, my dear Mrs Devon—'

'I'm *not* your dear Mrs Devon,' Angelica roared.

'The retreat that your husband is interested in does not take bookings, as such,' an unruffled Dr Love went on, adding, with an ironic smile, 'It's not the sort of place with white sand, gourmet cuisine, cocktails and spa treatments.'

'No,' Angelica retorted. 'No such effing luck.'

Dr Love chose to ignore this outburst. 'People arrive and leave as the Master sees fit.'

'The Master?' demanded Angelica derisively.

Dr Love looked at her almost pityingly. 'The spiritual head of the retreat, Mrs Devon. A man of great wisdom, holiness, learning, spirituality, compassion, modesty, simplicity, poverty, austerity . . .'

'Stop, stop!' Angelica bellowed, both hands on her ears. Anyone worse qualified to manage the sort of place she wanted to stay in could not be imagined.

'Last night,' Dr Love continued after a pause, 'in the middle of the night, I received intimation from the Master that he had two places available and he would be happy to welcome you.'

'Bugger the Master!' Angelica shouted in panic. 'Bugger his places. I don't want to go. I *can't* go. I've got to get to the gallery. I've got to brief my assistant. She's new, she doesn't know—'

Dr Love held up his hand. 'I'm sorry, Mrs Devon. When the Master calls, he must be obeyed immediately. It is non-negotiable. Otherwise the places will be withdrawn and all plans cancelled.'

'Fine!' Angelica stormed. 'Cancel!'

Dr Love folded both white-coated arms and looked at her chidingly. 'And cancel your marriage as well?' he asked lightly.

Angelica met his cool, strangely light eyes with her own hot hazel ones. Fury coursed within her. He had her over a barrel, and what was more, he obviously knew it.

'If you and Mr Devon are unable to go to this retreat he so particularly wished to visit,' the doctor went on, 'I'm sure you can see where that will leave you.'

Angelica wanted to strangle him. She had been outwitted, a new and unpleasant feeling.

She had, however, one last card up her sleeve. Or, rather, her BlackBerry. Even if she was unable to physically go to OneSquared, she could keep in touch via e-mail and telephone. Even Skype. Always assuming the Master was within reach of a mobile phone mast, which he must be. Presumably he had contacted Dr Love by means other than telepathy?

'May I suggest you go and pack, Mrs Devon?' the doctor said smoothly, pulling his hand away from the door frame to let her know the conversation was ended. 'Nothing elaborate or designer, though,' he added, looking her up and down critically. 'Only the very simplest clothes for the journey there and back. At the retreat, the Master supplies everything you need.'

Angelica gasped in horror. 'Some smelly old yogi decides what I wear?'

'On the days when you actually wear clothes, yes.' Dr Love smiled. His light eyes, through their very clean rimless glasses, dropped to the BlackBerry she was clutching in her hand. 'Oh, and no telephones, e-mails or anything like that. No technology whatsoever. One of the points of the retreat is that there is no contact with the outside world. No contact with anything that could interfere with the process of healing, forgiveness and rebuilding under the supervision and guidance of the Master.'

'No technology!' A red mist burned before Angelica's eyes. 'You've got to be joking! That's out of the bloody question. I've got a gallery to run. A major party coming up. Another party to go to tonight . . .' She clasped her hair in anguish as Dr Love looked on, a pitying smile playing about his handsome lips. '*Grrrr!*' Angelica finished, with a roar of pure frustration.

Dr Love shrugged. 'Your assistant will have to do it for you. I'm sure she'll be more than capable. You can ring her on the way to the airport.'

Defeated, Angelica looked at him in anguish. 'How long will this bloody retreat last?' she howled.

Dr Love cocked his head. 'For as long as it takes, my dear Mrs Devon,' he said simply. 'For as long as it takes for the Master's healing process to work.'

Angelica was not at the gallery when Alice arrived. Nor had she been there at any stage during the evening before. As Alice opened the fridge to put in the half-pint of milk she had bought on the way, along with a box of tea bags, she saw that the Chinese takeaway was still there. Angelica had not returned for her supper.

The phone in the gallery rang. 'I won't be in today,' Angelica announced, through what sounded like gritted teeth. 'I'm ill at home.'

Not for anything was she going to admit that she was being dragged off to some subcontinental hellhole in order to save her marriage.

'Don't worry,' Alice assured her confidently. 'I'm used to being in charge.'

'Well if you are,' Angelica said disbelievingly, 'you'd be the first of my assistants who was.'

'I used to run my old gallery,' Alice pointed out indignantly. 'I—'

'Look,' Angelica cut in. 'I need you to go somewhere for me tonight.'

'Tonight?'

'Tonight, yes,' Angelica said crisply. 'Is that a problem?' It was clear from her tone that it had better not be.

Alice blinked. She had intended, after the curtailed birthday dinner, to have another attempt tonight. Albeit at a different restaurant; the tandoori, she felt, was somewhere to avoid for a while. 'Er . . .'

'It's a condition of your employment that you are available in the evenings,' Angelica snapped. 'The art world is very sociable. Going to parties is part of the job – especially *this* party.'

'It's a party?'

'The Klumpp party.'

'The . . . ?'

There was a tsk of impatience from the other end. 'The *Klumpp* party. Don't tell me you haven't heard of the Klumpps?'

'Er . . .' Alice tried to sound as if she had and it had just briefly slipped her mind.

'Fuchsia Klumpp is one of the most important collectors in London,' Angelica snapped. 'When the Klumpps have a party, the whole art world goes. So *you'll* have to represent OneSquared.'

'I'd love to, but you see, the thing is—'

'Fuck whatever the thing is,' Angelica shouted. 'This is the thing. The thing is that you are going to that party. You'll find the invitation with the address upstairs in my office. On my desk probably.'

Alice groaned. Refusing to attend would clearly have consequences. Such as her first week in her new job being her last.

'So that's OK, is it?' Angelica demanded. 'You'll go?'

'Fine,' Alice said grimly.

'Make sure you do your face. There's make-up in the loo. The dress code for the party is Daring.'

'Daring?'

'Yes,' Angelica snapped. 'Daring. So if what you were wearing yesterday's anything to go by, you'd probably better borrow something of mine. There's a wardrobe in my office. Go up the spiral stairs. Remember – *Daring*. As much flesh as you can. We want your picture *everywhere*.'

'*Picture?*'

The other end drew an angry breath. 'Well of course! The party will be crawling with paps. That's why you're going, to get publicity for the gallery. Oh, and one more thing.'

Alice suppressed a groan. 'Yes?'

'Evelyn Legg's new work should come in today. In fact, it might have arrived yesterday after I left.'

'Nothing came yesterday,' Alice assured her.

'Did you leave the gallery?' Angelica demanded suspiciously.

'Absolutely not.'

'Because you know that leaving OneSquared during working hours is absolutely forbidden?'

'Er, right.'

'You never know when a billionaire starting an art collection might come past.'

'I suppose not.'

'Well in that case, if you didn't leave, you couldn't have missed

Evelyn. About sixty, has purple hair and wears a tutu and ballet shoes.'

'A sixty-year-old woman with purple hair who wears a tutu and ballet shoes?'

'No. Evelyn's a sixty-year-old *man* with purple hair, a tutu and ballet shoes.'

Alice was able to say with perfect certainty that no one even remotely answering that description had come into the gallery.

'And just tell anyone who calls that I'll be back later,' Angelica barked over what, Alice now thought, sounded strangely like an airport announcement. But of course it couldn't be. Angelica was ill, at home.

Alice texted David the bad news.

Hv to go to work party. Prob back late. Sorry. Axxx

It made a change, she thought, to be the late one. Perhaps that was why his reply, when it came, was understanding.

Dnt worry. Stay as long as u hv to. Dxxx

One or two people came in to look at the Spaw, but no one seemed in any danger of buying it. Jasper, to Alice's regret, did not make a return visit.

A fashionable-looking woman with an even more fashionable child came in to ask if OneSquared could restore her Banksy. 'Milo was playing football in the sitting room and the ball hit a glass of Coke that went all over it.'

Alice glanced at the child, who wore a designer motorbike jacket.

'That's not so good, Milo,' she couldn't help remarking.

'Actually, this isn't Milo,' the woman said sternly. 'This is Arlo. Milo's his father. Well, his stepfather.'

By the time lunchtime approached, Alice, whose breakfast had been skimpy, was more than aware of it. She pictured the hungry afternoon stretching ahead. As she'd been instructed not to leave the gallery, ever, going out for a sandwich was obviously out of the question. The billionaire starting an art collection might be passing at that exact moment.

To distract herself from the growls already building in her stomach, she walked to the window and looked longingly over the gold-sprayed sheets at the sunny street outside. Her gaze dropping to the bed, she spotted a few places where Zeb Spaw had missed a bit, grey metal patches in between some of the rails. But no doubt that was deeply significant too. Some metaphor for the incompleteness of the government vision for health. Some pithy comment on the lack of joined-up thinking.

The hunger pains were getting worse. Perhaps, if she had been busy, it would have been less noticeable But there was nothing to do. No one had been in since the Banksy woman left. OneSquared, Alice felt, was rather less popular than she had imagined such a cutting-edge gallery would be. And yet across the road, a constant stream of people seemed to be going into Sump to see the Maltesers box stuck on the canvas. The old man on the televisions, thankfully, had gone. Was it possible someone had bought it? Alice hoped desperately that that someone was not Jasper.

Her stomach surged once more. She could not, she thought, looking out at the sunny street in despair, go all afternoon like this.

Suddenly, with a spark of joy, she remembered the Chinese food in the fridge. Angelica would obviously not be coming to get it now. There was no point leaving it to go mouldy and rot. And there was a microwave in the kitchen . . .

Alice slammed the food in to heat up while she found a plate – they all seemed to be square and black – and cutlery. Some minutes later, she set to with a will, closing her eyes to relish the noodles both crisp and golden; special fried rice generously endowed with egg and prawn; spare ribs spicy, sticky and sweet; the outside of the pork crunchy and the inside deliciously chewy. It was the Chinese food of her dreams. Having cleared all the noodles and a great deal of the sweet and sour pork, she felt her fading strength ebb back. She could face anything now. Even the Klumpp party; dress code Daring.

Chapter 44

Dan, in the studio bedroom of the cottage, was finding it hard to concentrate. For one thing, the weather outside was close and hot, making the near-unventilated small room positively furnace-like. For another, Birgit, naked as usual, was bounding about downstairs to some pounding heavy rock which was seriously compromising *La Bohème* on Radio 3.

Dan reached for the off switch. He had been wondering for some minutes anyway whether the romantic anguish of Mimi and Rodolfo was appropriate background music for his current commission. This was a portrait of the unromantic Marjorie Trout, a friend of Kevin Swift. The very friend, in fact, who had encouraged him to find fault with Dan's portrait at the party where it was first unveiled. She was, to all intents and purposes, a female version of Kevin: large, red-faced, unpleasant and somewhat bristly.

Dan rootled about in the battered cardboard box on the floor which contained his collection of CDs, their cases either split or missing altogether. Mozart's *Requiem* seemed best to sum up the fact that his career was, if not deceased entirely, then certainly in its final throes. He stuffed the disc – a flash of silver in the close shadows of the room – into the elderly paint-spattered ghetto-blaster which squatted on the floor among the dust, flattened paint tubes and screwed-up bits of dirty rag. As the music began, he pressed the fast-forward button to a section that was loud, pounding and dramatic enough to drown out Birgit and demonstrate that there was nothing about heavy metal that Mozart didn't know, either.

Confutatis, maledictis
Flammis acribus addictis

This, dinning ominously in his ears, made him feel glorious in defeat. Restored somewhat, he turned back to where Marjorie Trout glowered out at him from the easel. He had done the preliminary sittings and started the final picture. All that remained was to work it up.

His task had not been made any easier by the fact that Marjorie, whose short, dog's-coat hair had been black to start with, had dyed it blond halfway through the sittings. There was also the fact that whenever he started blocking out the shape on the canvas, Marjorie's fleshy features contracted into a long, slim oval, her small piggy eyes became wide and green and her chemically treated hair changed colour to a rich auburn.

He was, of course, painting Siobhan; it was Siobhan's lovely face that floated before him night and day now, and particularly when he was trying to render a reasonably faithful likeness of Marjorie. It was as if his brush and his paints were interested only in painting one woman – one woman, moreover, he seemed eternally fated to make a fool of himself in front of. But how, Dan asked himself for the thousandth time, was *he* to know that when Siobhan had said she was married to a musician, she had meant a singer in a boy band?

As he painted wodges of blotchy Majorie flesh over the creamy Siobhan cheekbones, his mind, if not his brush, could not help returning to the subject which filled his mind, his heart, his days and his nights.

Siobhan, fortunately, seemed to have forgiven him. She had, at least, come back for another life class. During which, Dan miserably suspected, he had mooned over her in such a way that it was only a matter of time before everyone realised.

Perhaps they had already realised. Roger, who sat next to Siobhan, had clearly wondered about Dan's sudden interest in his sketches. Only Mrs de Goldsmith could be counted on to notice nothing, being, at all times, exclusively occupied with Mrs de Goldsmith.

What Siobhan must think was anyone's guess. Probably that he was mad. As indeed he was, in the sense that infatuation made him behave in ways he could not control. He blushed whenever she spoke to him, whenever she looked at him. It would have helped had she not been so talented; as it was, he got hopelessly tongue-tied trying to praise her, or even suggesting small improvements. He was in love, hopelessly in love, and he could hardly have chosen a less suitable recipient of his passions.

Siobhan was married. And not only married, married to someone who, however doubtful his musical credentials, was indisputably rich, famous and handsome.

The dust motes sparkled and danced in the rays of the sun as Dan began to shape Marjorie's mean, downturned mouth. His mind soon slid back to his favourite subject. There was a mystery there, he was sure. Perhaps it was the hypersensitivity of unsuitable passion, but he sensed, for all Siobhan's beauty, wealth and fame-by-association, that she was not happy.

But what could she be sad about? Well, listening to Boyfriend possibly. Dan had looked them up on the internet – much to Birgit's amusement – and been appalled at the syrupy lyrics, the derivative melodies, the general desperate unoriginality. Could Siobhan possibly be a fan?

He had been painting automatically for the past few minutes and now noticed that the mean mouth he had started to paint had spread itself out and was pink and full. Siobhan's again. It was hopeless, Dan decided, resignedly wiping his brush and packing it in for the day.

He longed, for all the barriers between them, to capture Siobhan's attention. Do just one thing that would make her admire him. She had been generous about his portrait of Swift, admittedly, but she was obviously just being kind.

He switched off the *Requiem* and went down the gritty and uncarpeted stairs with a feeling of absolute failure in his gut. He would never do anything to capture *anyone*'s attention or make *anyone* admire him. Having opted for the least successful branch of art, he was set on a downward path.

There was one pinprick of light in the general gloom: the cottage was finally silent. Birgit had gone out. Dressed, Dan hoped. He went to the fridge, hoping for a beer, only to find she had drunk the last one.

He drooped against the kitchen units and looked out. A feeling of surprise, of awe, awoke within him.

Spreading across the sky like a showgirl on a chaise longue was a sunset of extraordinary, almost sensual intensity. Squinting at it through a dusty window was, Dan suddenly felt, all wrong. This was a sunset to admire at leisure, with full concentration. It occurred to him that sitting on his front step and losing himself in the splendour might distract him from both his pervading sense of failure and his utter beerlessness.

He opened the front door and sat down on the warm, if unswept stone step. He leaned his elbows on his knees and his head on his hands and lost himself in the show in the sky.

The Artist of the Universe had got this one off pat, he thought admiringly. Just the right shade of mellow, yellow, almost liquid-looking gold. His brush had been everywhere; the clouds were framed with blazing gilt; gold rods slanted across the fields, picking out every stone, every hedge and giving it a halo. Gold was thickly plastered across the backs and bottoms of the sheep and across the sheds, shacks, tractors and hay bales that made up the sprawl of the nearby farm.

Dan sighed. It was a sight to bring a certain perspective to things. No earthly painter, no matter how wonderful, could create anything approaching the magnificence of that blaze of molten gold and copper.

Another heavy sigh – more of a groan, really. But Dan suddenly realised it was not his own. He was not alone out here on Milkmaid's Walk. He looked around, away from the sunset.

Next door, Tadeusz was sitting on his own step, ostensibly admiring the evening sky as well. He wore shorts, and his heavy white legs, lit orange by the sinking sun, were wide apart. His meaty forearms leaned on his massive knees. Dangling in one huge red hand, and reflecting the show in the sky, was a whisky glass containing clear liquid. Vodka.

Dan eyed it for a moment. He swallowed, imagining the strong spirit ripping through him. Then, as Tadeusz's eyes met his, he looked hurriedly away. Since the stopcock incident, there had not been so much as a hello between the two men. Dan had every reason to think Tadeusz despised him as much as Stamina did.

As he returned his gaze to the dipping sun, Dan heard something like a grunt. Not an unfriendly grunt, however. He looked back round and saw the grizzled and habitually stern face of Tadeusz transformed with the first smile from that direction Dan had ever seen. What was more, Tadeusz was waving his glass, seemingly by way of an invitation. 'Wodka?' he grunted.

Dan's eyes widened. He nodded eagerly – and then felt scared. 'Stamina?' he asked nervously.

'Is go out,' Tadeusz assured him cheerily. 'To gym.'

A terrfying vision of Stamina, huge thighs pumping an exercise machine, flashed through Dan's mind, and for a moment or two he felt faint.

Tadeusz, on the other hand, seemed on unusually expansive form. From somewhere down by his side he produced a large vodka bottle and waved it. 'Got glass have?'

'Oh yes. Yes. Hang on.' Dan scrambled to his feet and rushed back into the house. In the undusted depths of the kitchen cupboard he unearthed a small tumbler that had once held a scented candle. He hurried back outside to Tadeusz, and watched gratefully as the Lithuanian poured in a measure of vodka.

A very big measure. The glass that Dan eventually took back to his own step was brimming with alcohol. He took a long, grateful sip, and as the liquid burned a path of fire through him in just the way he had imagined, he felt immediately much better.

Tadeusz was looking at him, his brow corrugated beneath his thick, low hairline. The expression on his heavy features was not easy to read; it seemed to Dan poised between humour and melancholy. Then Tadeusz sighed, raised his eyebrows and jerked his brawny forearm, the one holding the glass, upwards. 'Women,' he said gloomily.

Dan nodded ruefully. 'Women!' he affirmed, raising his own hand. Tadeusz, he saw, had knocked his entire glassful back for the toast; politeness, Dan felt, required he do the same. After he had swallowed it, finished coughing and his eyes had stopped streaming, Tadeusz stood up and came over to refill his tumbler. To the top.

'Is good wodka,' Tadeusz mumbled thickly. 'Is best in world.'

Dan gathered from Tadeusz's miming that the next toast was his.

'Art!' he said without hesitation, jerking his arm into the air.

'You are artist, yes?' Tadeusz nodded.

'Yes.'

'Stamina say you are piss artist.'

'Yes, I rather suspected she held that view,' Dan said resignedly. Then he grinned and knocked back the second tumblerful.

Something amazing was happening to him. The liquid was expanding and warming within him and the sensation he now felt was of his body expanding and growing hugely. He felt suddenly big and strong and ready to take on the world. The blaze building within him felt like his own burning talent. It raced around his veins like liquid fire, and as it did, he felt his sinews stiffen with an absolute self-belief. The confidence that had seeped from him over the past few weeks – since the ghastly unveiling of the Swift portrait, in fact – came rushing back in an overpowering wave. He suddenly felt that he could take on the world. What was more – that he must.

He would not hide his talent under a bushel. He would not stay in this obscure village and paint Marjorie Trout. Not without trying to do something else first. He would not give up. He would not descend into bitter envy like all the other members of the Federation of Portrait Painters. No. He would fight. He would show the world what he could do.

Tomorrow, Dan vowed, he would go to London and try his luck. He would show everyone what he was capable of. He would get some big gallery interested.

And if that didn't impress Siobhan, he didn't know what would. Siobhan loved art, and whatever else Ciaran O'Sullivan could do, however sexy, rich and famous he was, he couldn't draw. Or paint.

Chapter 45

The boots Alice found in Angelica's wardrobe were black, shiny, thigh-length and spike-heeled. Teamed with the leopard-print minidress, they certainly fitted the Daring bill, although the dress was actually the most discreet and unshowy of all the items in the cupboard in the upstairs office. Some of the other clothes – black PVC leggings with rips in them, fishnet stockings, a dress made of transparent plastic bags – were enough to make Alice wonder what sort of parties Angelica was in the habit of going to. Or giving.

Aided by the enormous resources of the gallery bathroom, she had bundled up her hair in as near an approximation of a glamorous chignon as she could manage, and, after a few initial more restrained attempts, had thrown caution to the winds and put on industrial quantities of make-up. There was no point having a subtle face when one was wearing clothes and boots like Angelica's.

Finished, she grinned at her reflection. It was unrecognisable. The long-legged, wild-haired, smokily eyelined creature in the bathroom mirror neither looked nor felt like herself. Her breasts, thrust upwards by the cantilevering beneath the leopardskin, almost touched the bottom of her chin. Her hemline, no matter how hard she tugged it downwards, remained skimming her crotch. Frankly, the invitation was bigger than her dress.

Was this, she wondered, head consideringly on one side, her

inner rock chick? It was quite fun, playing a part, dressing up. Liberating, in a way. Empowering.

Or was it, on the other hand, just grubby and tasteless? Alice gave way to a sideswipe of doubt as she looked again at her breasts and hemline. The opposite of empowering, in fact. Degrading.

The doubt swiftly became fully fledged anxiety. At least David was not around to see her. But what would people think of her at the party? Would she actually get there, given that she had to venture on to the tube like this? On to the pavement outside, even. Alone, unprotected and apparently asking for everything she got.

Alice's heart began to hammer. She wondered if she would actually prefer to appear naked on the street than in this outfit, which was practically naked anyway. The thought of going outside would have made her toes curl, had the cripplingly high boots left sensation enough in her feet to make this possible. The thought of travelling on public transport was unendurable.

Squeezed into the minuscule yet curiously restrictive dress, swaying on the high heels, Alice stood worrying at the window, bending the stiff engraved invitation in her sweating hands, wondering what to do. She had to go to the Klumpps'. Angelica had made that quite clear. Otherwise she would be sacked. The alternative to going out looking like a stripper was to be stripped of employment and future prospects. Between a rock chick and a hard place, Alice mused. Was discretion really the better party of valour?

No, it was not. She had to do it. Taking a deep, steadying breath, she turned all her silent inner forces of persuasion on convincing herself to view the coming horror as an adventure. As a mere act, an impersonation. A departure from the normal, yes. But one that represented self-preservation rather than self-betrayal, expediency rather than exploitation. Even so, she felt as wobbly inside as she was out by the time she opened the door of the gallery and launched herself into the close evening heat of the outside world.

'Hello!' The voice was low, friendly. Alice twisted around with difficulty in the dress and heels to find Jasper's friendly wide eyes smiling into hers. 'Alice, isn't it? I thought it was.'

If he was at all surprised to see her looking like a particularly flamboyant sex worker, Jasper did not show it. Had she been dressed in a high collar, pleated skirt and double row of pearls, Alice thought, he could not have treated her more courteously.

Her immediate impulse, nonetheless, was to run away, but the boots put paid to this. She found herself reeling back across the pavement in horror and was already steeling herself for the thud of skull against stone when, just in time, he caught her. 'Steady on!'

Alice now found herself for the third time in as many encounters in receipt of Jasper's strong, cool hand. Her flight instinct thwarted, she looked at him defensively. 'This isn't my usual evening-out gear, in case you're wondering.'

'No,' Jasper said, sounding uncertain. Alice then remembered that during both their former encounters she had been wearing a small skirt and big heels. 'I usually wear jeans,' she added, forcibly.

He nodded, apparently keen to agree. 'Right.'

Alice swept a hand down her mostly exposed front. 'I'm dressed like this,' she said heavily, 'because my boss is making me go to a party. The dress code is Daring. Basically, if I don't go, I'll get sacked.'

'Nice boss,' Jasper observed.

'Well, yes. But we are where we are, as they say.'

'If you say so.' He was, Alice saw, studiously trying not to look her up and down. She felt a pang of gratitude for this display of chivalry, which she doubted would be repeated after she had left him. Fresh images of the impending hell of the underground rushed her imagination, bringing a wave of fear and nausea in their wake.

'Are you . . .' Jasper was looking down at her, his face more concerned now than bemused. 'Are you, um, waiting for someone?' His voice was doubtful. 'Here, I mean.' He waved an arm at the sunny evening street along which glared the shining fronts of the galleries.

Alice shook her backcombed and pinned-up head.

'You're going *alone*?'

She nodded.

'You're sure?' he said tentatively, trying but failing not to look at her outfit. His eyes fixed eventually on her boots. 'In a taxi, by yourself?'

'In the underground by myself,' Alice corrected.

Knowing how inflating her lungs pushed her breasts up all the more, Alice had been trying not to sigh, to breathe, even. But now, at this, she could not resist one deep, regretful intake of breath.

Jasper raked a hand through his fair hair and gave an uncertain smile. 'Look, er, I know you don't know me very well, but I'd be happy to give you a lift. You know, to wherever the party is . . .' He paused and added doubtfully, 'It's just that, you know, it might be a bit easier for you.'

Alice could have hugged him. 'A lot easier,' she agreed, grinning foolishly with relief.

'This way then. Oh,' Jasper added as, attempting to move off, she almost toppled in the attempt. 'Let me.'

Gently but firmly he took her arm and steered her down the pavement. Despite her vertiginous heels, she was, Alice saw, still nowhere near impacting on his height, which seemed positively tree-like, although reassuringly so. A sheltering tree.

She had calmed down enough now to notice what he was wearing: suit trousers of a soft brown, no jacket or tie, white shirt-sleeves rolled up to the elbow. She could detect, as they moved, a faint slipstream of cedar aftershave.

'What's the address?' Jasper asked. She passed him the invitation and watched his sandy eyebrows go up. 'Fuchsia Klumpp. That's quite a name.'

Alice giggled. 'One you're probably going to get to know quite well.'

'How do you mean?'

'Mrs Klumpp is an important collector of contemporary art. Very, very rich, apparently.'

Jasper grinned. 'I doubt if I'm in her league. I'm not sure whether I'm collecting it yet anyway.'

'Good,' Alice said, before she could stop herself.

There was a surprised jerk on her arm. The grey-blue eyes above looked curiously into hers. 'Why do you say that? You're one of the Gold Street gallery girls.'

Alice grimaced. 'Not by choice,' she was about to say. Then, as caution kicked in, she smiled and shrugged. His eyes lingered on hers for a moment, as if he intended to pursue the subject further. Then, to her relief, he let it drop, rummaged in his pocket and pulled out a bunch of car keys.

They had walked down Gold Street and round the corner to Silver Street, where a row of expensive cars, parked at the meters, glinted in the evening sunlight. Jasper led her to one in the middle: blue, open-topped, a Mercedes, Alice saw from the badge on the grille. A vintage one, she guessed, noticing the burr-walnut dashboard, white-walled tyres, chrome door fittings and seamed red-leather seats that looked shiny with use.

'The love of my life.' Jasper smiled.

'What?' Alice exclaimed, looking round as if to spot some passing woman.

'This.' He had reddened, she saw as he bent to open the passenger door.

'Oh.' She found herself colouring too, but managed to hide it in the delicate contortions that inserting herself into such a low seat required.

They set off, Alice hanging on to her hem in the face of an insistent breeze around the footwell. They were not going fast, but what wind there was made it hard to talk. Alice contented herself with watching the life on the passing pavements, intrigued to think that those looking back would imagine that she and Jasper were a couple. A strange thought, but not an unpleasant one. If she were free . . . she found herself thinking.

Except that Jasper was very different. She was used to charismatic, opinionated men, men with dark good looks and hot tempers. Men who were possibly a bit selfish and unreasonable, even. Jasper was eminently reasonable. He was cool and pleasant. It was difficult to imagine him raising his voice. Very straight, Alice concluded. Not her type at all. The only non-straight thing about him was his interest in contemporary art; but then that wasn't her type either.

She found that her eyes were on his arms and hands, tensed and strong as they moved the walnut steering wheel, the forearms attractively muscled, the plain face of the low-key watch contrasting with a slight but definite tan. She glanced up to his face; he was looking back at her, his expression faintly puzzled. Alice, wrenching her eyes to the front, stared out at the pavement again.

Shortly afterwards, they drew up outside a pair of imposing square white pillars with black iron gates between. Gas flames were rippling from torchères atop the posts. 'Poor trees,' Jasper remarked, observing the surrounding scorched fir branches. 'They've even got sentries,' he added, astonished, as a burly figure with a clipboard in one hand, a receiver fixed to his ear and a walkie-talkie strapped across his chest emerged from behind one of the gate pillars and glared suspiciously at them.

'Enjoy the party,' Jasper said.

'Thanks. I will.' Alice was determined to say nothing else that could be interpreted as ironic or ambiguous.

She climbed carefully out, hanging on to the car door until she found her equilibrium in the heels.

'Who'll be there? Do you know?' Jasper asked as she tried taking an unsteady step forward, swaying dangerously as she did so.

'Art people, I suppose,' Alice groaned, abandoning the attempt to sound upbeat. Hearing the music and loud laughter coming from the direction of the party, she felt ill with nerves at the thought of entering such a gathering alone. A gathering where she would know no one – although frankly, given her clothes, maybe that was a good thing. That she was embarrassingly dressed and under orders to get herself all over the papers remained, however, definite bad things.

Then, in this moment of desperation, an idea struck her. She looked at Jasper, her formerly gloomy features now alight with speculation. Should she? Would he? But how better to reward him for his kindness?

'Look,' she said eagerly, waving the by now rather curled invitation almost in his face. 'I've got a plus one on this. You could come too, if—'

But he was shaking his big sandy head already, smiling. 'Sorry. I'd love to, but . . .'

'Oh do come,' Alice begged, impetuously clutching his arm. 'Anyone who's anyone's going to be there. In the art world, that is. There'll be lots of artists. Famous contemporary artists.' She knew she was gabbling but pressed on anyway. 'People like . . .' She tried to think. 'Hero Octagon. Um, Ganymede Steam.' Oh, and who was the hairy pebble one? The psycho-sexual Cinderella? 'Cruz Backhausen. Balthazar Ponce. I mean, of course,' she corrected herself immediately, 'Pon-kay.'

He was looking at her incredulously. '*Who?*'

'He does pebbles with hair on them.'

'Ah.' She saw his long mouth twist slightly. 'And the other? Crooth . . . ?'

'Backhausen,' Alice supplied. 'He does psycho-sexual Cinderellas.'

'What?' Jasper's shoulders were shaking now.

'Both leading practitioners of the principle of bisymmetrical reason,' Alice told him, straight-faced. 'Their work is astonishingly conceptually united. Their site-specific installations enable the enclosing narrative to pose fundamental questions concerning the network of motivations, both the artist's and our own . . .' She ended the sentence with a squeal, unable to carry on. Jasper's laugh was infectious, and he was bent over in the driver's seat, hooting almost.

Finally he looked up, his pale face flushed and his eyes wet with mirth. 'You paint such a wonderful picture,' he gasped. 'As it were. But the thing is . . .' His expression became rueful.

'Zeb Spaw?' Alice put in quickly, sensing another refusal. 'He'll be there too.'

Jasper was shaking his head regretfully. 'I wish I could come, I really do. But I have to work, I'm afraid. Have fun with the in-crowd.' He looked at her expectantly.

Alice realised she was still clutching his arm. Rather hard, in fact. Hurriedly, she detached her fingers.

Jasper smiled and drove off.

Standing on the pavement, watching the small blue car round the corner, Alice reflected briefly that she had no idea what work he did and had completely missed the opportunity to ask him about it. And now, most probably, she would not get the chance again. She took a deep breath, clutched her invitation and prepared to enter the party.

Chapter 46

After the revelation that Fuchsia had bought Sharon Aura's *Old Cock*, Zeb was tempted – very tempted – to avoid her party altogether.

She was mad if she thought she could treat him like that. On the other hand, he realised, his walking away and leaving the field to Sharon Aura would be even more insane. Fuchsia *could* treat him like that, anyway. As she knew only too well, she could treat him any way she damn well liked.

So, a little after the stated party start time Zeb walked through the red lacquered hall and under the gold-leaf dome. He headed straight for his hostess, shook his long black hair forward over his high-cheekboned face, narrowed his eyes and prepared for battle.

'Zeb!' Fuchsia detached herself from a crowd of people and hurried towards him, arms outstretched. She had had a restyle, he saw; the upwhoosh of big blond hair now had marmalade tints and was cut slightly choppily round the edges.

Zeb clashed the tanned and scented sides of his face with her powdered skeletal cheekbones, blinked in the blaze of her diamonds and almost choked on her expensive scent.

'You look good,' he told her. And – for a walking wallet – she did. She wore a long flowing white dress, vaguely seventies, with an embroidered panel on the front, huge diamond earrings and a collar thick with the same precious stones. 'Great dress.'

Fuchsia tossed her head, seemingly unmoved by the compliment. '*You* could have made more of an effort, though.' She waved a glittering hand at his skintight black jeans and unlaced trainers. 'The dress code's Daring. Not Usual Boring Crap.'

'I'm an artist, baby,' Zeb flipped back. 'Artists don't do dress codes. We keep our daring for our work.'

'Yeah?' Fuchsia replied archly, moving away to greet some newcomers. 'Charles! Nigella!' he heard her exclaiming behind him. 'So lovely to see you. You both look *fabulous*!'

Zeb shook his hair even further over his face and scowled under it as he grabbed a glass of Veuve Clicquot from a passing tray being proffered by a punk in full spike-haired and pierced-nose regalia. Zeb hardly favoured him with a second glance. Unusually dressed waiters had long been the USP of Fuchsia's parties. Last year, the drinks had been handed out by boys in Eton uniform, some of whom, given Fuchsia's intense snobbery, were very probably studying there.

There was something odd about his drink, he noticed, holding it up. Was the glass dirty?

'Fuchsia's not having the usual Krug because of the recession,' he heard someone say behind him. 'She's serving Veuve Clicquot as a gesture of solidarity. But with gold flakes in.'

Zeb passed on down the hallway. Just before it opened out into the dining room, he became aware of a strange, strong smell about his nose. In an alcove to one side was a unsteady erection made of some very dirty, rough-looking cloth. He realised he had hit upon the location of the dung tent from Art Timbuctu.

In the dining room, people were pressing in at him from every side.

'Zeb!'

'Hi, Zeb, great to see you.'

'Can I have a word, Zeb?'

Journalists, young artists, gallery owners. He ignored most of them, although gave the ghost of a smile to the more important ones. A few flashbulbs went off, Zeb frowning into them. Part of him appreciated the interest; it was gratifying to see that even walking through a room, holding a glass of wine, he was still news. Still one of the biggest players on the British contemporary art scene.

Even so, a bigger part of him than he had expected shrank from it all. For the first time, he even felt a flicker of fear. He felt, for all the interest in him, very alone. Vulnerable, even. It would be so much easier to walk into these gatherings with someone. Someone who genuinely cared about him, for whom he was more than a name and a wallet. A supporter and a friend as well as a lover.

He put the thought aside to concentrate on his surroundings. He hadn't seen this room for some time – he rarely saw any of Fuchsia's house these days apart from the hallway and her sex room – sorry, office. The drawing room was vast, stretching from the back of the house to the front, and seemed to be filled entirely with strong-smelling white lilies. Perhaps to counteract the smell from the dung tent.

He looked about for some pieces of his work. In theory they should be everywhere; Fuchsia had bought enough over the years to fill several homes. And there had been plenty on display the last time he had been in here.

He looked at the mantelpiece, over which one of his early works, a gilded tap, had once hung. Fuchsia had mentioned *en passant* that the mantelpiece had had to be doubled in size to accommodate the invitations she received daily. But she had said nothing about removing his piece.

Even so, it was no longer there. In its place, on the mantelpiece, holding back the tide of invitations, was a row of plastic dolls with teddy-bear heads. All the dolls held machine guns, and on each teddy-bear head sat a teddy-bear-head-sized SS cap.

The long white sofas were covered in people Zeb wearily recognised. Artists, collectors, a few curators, gallery owners, all with their accompanying crowds of nobodies and hangers-on. He nodded at the important ones, wondering why Angelica Devon was not among them. He wanted to know what the hell was going on with *The Right Hand of the Father II*. Had she sold it yet?

On a table in the centre of the room was a head made of yellow ice. It was rapidly melting, and people were holding their glasses beneath it to catch the drips. 'So typical of Fuchsia, to have a whole new twist on party ice sculptures,' a woman in a see-through body-stocking twittered to her companion in a transparent plastic dress. 'This cocktail is marvellous. A really unusual yet distinctive taste.'

Zeb was still looking around for evidence of his work. There had been another of his pieces, a giant gilt-sprayed crisp called *Golden Wonder*, on a table on the far side of the room behind where Jake and Dinos Chapman were currently standing. As they moved away, it was to expose another new sculpture. This one was a clenched fist made of flowers, its middle digit thrust upwards in the universal sign of contempt. Zeb had no idea who the sculptor was, but it was hard not to take the message personally.

Something flickering caught his eye; looking to a corner, he angrily recognised *Old Cock*, removing his underpants to an audience of appreciative elderly ladies. Zeb wondered crossly who they were and what they were doing there before recognising them as distinguished actresses, at least two of them dames. Fuchsia's celebrity acquaintance evidently did not confine itself to the art world. 'He'd make a marvellous Lear, don't you think?' one was observing admiringly to another.

Zeb, who now realised he had not eaten all day, swiped angrily at a lobster canapé as it passed him on an underlit tray. He could see Herman Klumpp across the room, expensively dark-suited, thick white shirt open at the collar. He was looking tanned, prosperous but stressed as he spoke to a black-haired woman in a rubber dress who Zeb recognised as Miranda Whiplash, a posh but edgy poet. She was being pretty edgy now, he could see, on the edge of the Klumpps' prized piece of Egyptiana, no less. Herman was evidently working up to asking her to detach her rubber derrière from the fourth-century sarcophagus on whose lid she had perched herself, her food and her wine.

Having braved the security sentry at the entrance gate and brandished her invitation, Alice, missing very much Jasper's anchoring arm, swayed and tottered up a drive flanked with more flaming torches.

It being summer, it was still daylight but nonetheless the house before her blazed with light. It was a magnificent white stucco mansion of the early nineteenth century. A pair of double doors as black and shiny as Alice's boots stood open to reveal a red interior reminiscent of a mouth. A queue of people was sprawling out of it, like a multicoloured tongue.

Alice, tottering up with her breasts mere millimetres below her chin, noticed nervously that no one else looked particularly Daring. The men before her all seemed to be in suits, the women in little black dresses. If this was Daring, she wondered crossly, what did they normally wear? Burkhas? Suits of armour?

But then she spotted, with relief, through the gap, a man at the front completely naked apart from a strategically placed posy.

A tremendous thumping roar now sounded from behind. Or was it above? Alice looked up, but could see nothing unusual in the sky above the trees. Perhaps the noise was in her own head, the roar of her panic. She decided she would get away as quickly as humanly possible. After she had shown her face, greeted the hosts, been photographed if possible, she would then disappear into the night. Hopefully without breaking any of her limbs.

She could see more of the entrance hall from here. Red walls, a gold dome. A house, she thought, to put Suki and Rafael's in the shade. But then Suki and Rafael's entire lives were in the shade at the moment, the sun completely gone. Poor Suki. Horrid, betraying Rafa. Whoever would have thought it?

Alice remembered the strange afternoon at the fashionable farmers' market, when Suki had broken the news about Rafael and Caroline and afterwards acted as if nothing was at all wrong. Only last weekend that had been; it seemed an age ago already. What was happening with Suki and Rafa now?

She was interrupted by an exclamation from behind. 'Hello! I know you, don't I?'

Alice turned, looked into merry black eyes and immediately recognised the girl from the gallery opposite. The one she had seen in Sump's front window sticking the chocolate box back on the canvas.

'Yes.' She grinned. 'You were sticking—'

'Shh!' The girl waved her hands, laughing. 'Sharon'll kill me.'

'Sharon?'

'Sharon Aura,' the girl hissed. 'Our gallery's star artist. She's behind us somewhere. She just got here – in a motorcade of Harley Davidsons. Didn't you hear them?'

Alice remembered the ear-splitting roar. She now found herself, in her high heels, struggling to keep her balance as a small, compact female with crew-cut peroxide-white hair, leather trousers, biker boots and arms full of tattoos shoved aggressively past her to the front of the queue. Alice saw the security guard extend a hand in restraint and the spiky-haired woman throw it angrily off.

'Gerroff me, ya bastard,' she snapped in a northern accent. 'Do you know who the fuck I am?'

'You wouldn't believe she's a convent girl from Surrey, would you?' the girl from the Sump Gallery whispered.

Alice's heels, at least, gave her a grandstand view over the heads in front. She could see Sharon Aura picking something up in the hall. A clear plastic mat, the sort spread over flooring to protect it.

'Hey,' the security guard objected. 'What do you think you're doing with that?'

'Making sure *you* don't try anything,' the artist snarled.

The guard looked confused. 'What am I gonna try with a plastic doormat?'

The artist glared at him. 'People'll pay anything for work by Sharon Aura. Even something I've wiped me *feet* on.'

There was a ripple of laughter from the waiting queue and even a scattering of sycophantic applause. 'Wow,' the girl from the Sump Gallery breathed into Alice's ear. 'Say what you like about Sharon, she's pure showbiz.'

'I'm not having you flogging it after I've gone,' Sharon snapped at the security guard.

'I wasn't going to,' he riposted indignantly.

The artist eyed him contemptuously. 'More fool you then,' she snarled, and stalked on into the party.

Alice saw now that the girl from Sump was looking her up and down with interest. 'What's your name? Mine's Portia.' She had a breathless, excited, exclamatory way of talking. 'You look great. Sex on a stick.'

Alice smiled, accepting that this was meant as a compliment. She was feeling marginally more relaxed. Portia, at least, had taken the dress code seriously. She was, if anything, more revealingly attired than Alice. A truly magnificent cleavage was barely contained by the red lace basque she wore above the tiniest of black satin miniskirts.

'Do you like my tights? They're *trompe l'oeil*!' Portia extended a shapely leg in Alice's direction. 'Glass of poo?' she asked as they finally reached the threshold, where Alice was surprised to see punk rockers with neon spiked hair and safety pins through their noses proffering, somewhat incongruously, trays of champagne.

'Punk parties.' Portia sniffed. 'Trust Fuchsia to get there first.'

'What?' Alice asked.

'Those waiters. They come from Punk Parties. It's an events company. All the waiters look like old-school punk rockers. They're quite hip. I was thinking of hiring them for our gallery party.' Then she clasped her hand to her mouth and regarded Alice with alarmed eyes. 'Oh God. That's classified information.'

Alice was only half listening. She wasn't interested in Sump's gallery party, at least not as much as she was in the condition of her champagne. Something seemed to be floating in it. She hoped the punks hadn't taken their duties too literally and spat in it.

'What's Angelica doing for her party?' Portia asked.

Alice looked up. 'What party?'

Portia widened her huge dark eyes. 'You know. The OneSquared bash. That you'll have as part of the street fest.'

'Oh yes.' Alice had caught up now. The famous Gold Street party.

'Who's your featured artist?' Portia asked.

'Featured artist?'

The other girl was looking at her in amazement. 'Don't you know? Every gallery picks its most high-profile artist and gives them the front window. It's incredibly prestigious, as the whole art world sees them. Artists fight tooth and nail to get the window,' she added with relish. 'Violence is not unknown.'

Alice frowned. Angelica had mentioned nothing about featured artists. She hoped it wasn't Hero Octagon, or the hairy pebble. Or, God forbid, the psycho-sexual Cinderella.

'It'll probably be Zeb Spaw,' Portia said confidently. 'He'll certainly expect to be the window, anyway. We'll have Sharon Aura in ours, of course. What's your theme, anyway?'

'Er . . . theme?'

'You know. What's your party about? Ours was going to be a barbie on the beach, but everyone found out about it – we still don't know how. So now we're doing Glitter. Glitter cocktails, glitter make-up and on the day a truck's going to come and pour half a ton of glitter through the door.'

Alice absorbed this. 'I don't know what Angelica's doing,' she admitted. 'She hasn't told me, and I haven't seen her today.'

Portia took another sip of champagne. Alice watched whatever was in it whirl crazily round in the bubbles. 'Dirty, debauched and decadent,' Portia announced.

'Who?' Looking around, Alice felt the description could have fitted any number of people.

'Your party, silly. That's the theme. Or so Penelope from Diamond Snail's been telling everyone.'

'What does *that* mean?'

Portia grinned. 'You'll be dressed up in a dirty, debauched and decadent way. Gold hotpants, I heard.'

Alice stared. This had to be a joke, surely. Portia was teasing. She might, for her career's sake, be in black dominatrix boots now. But no way, *no bloody way*, was she going to wear gold hotpants. Not even if her future depended on it.

Chapter 47

'Excuse me? Mr Spaw?' Zeb turned to find himself looking into a pair of bold brown eyes. The woman was short, black, dressed in black and propped up on a pair of dizzying heels. She seemed very self-confident.

'Yes?' He regarded her coldly.

Smiling broadly, she pushed her hand into his and shook it. 'I'm Jess Knight. Personal assistant to Mr Steven Bull.'

Steven Bull, as Zeb well knew, was the chief celebrity judge on the current national obsession, the Saturday-night talent show *Brilliant Britain*.

'I wondered whether you might be interested in some work?' Jess asked, her beam undimmed.

'If you mean am I going to sit there covered in spray tan being nasty about fat girls from Berkhamsted singing Celine Dion, the answer's no,' Zeb snapped. 'I'm an artist. I don't do telly.'

'I *know* you're an artist. That's what I want you to do – some art.'

Some art. *Some art!*

'It's Steven's birthday soon, and a hundred of his closest friends in showbiz want to throw a major surprise party for him.'

'You want me to jump out of the cake?' Zeb snarled.

'Ha! No. I want you to draw, live on stage, at the party.'

Zeb's eyes bulged. 'What? Like Rolf bloody Harris? Can you see what it is yet?' he mocked in a cod-Australian accent.

Jess giggled. 'Steven's a big fan of your work. We thought you could draw something in five minutes and then give it to him. That would be his present.'

Zeb felt a wave of despair. Was this what art was reduced to? Was that all he was, a performing dog? 'Sorry,' he said in strangled tones. 'If you want a party entertainer, try that bloke over there.'

Jess glanced over at the nearby famous singer and then looked back. 'Actually, we had him at last year's major surprise party organised by Steven's hundred closest friends in showbiz. Flying in pop stars is all a bit five minutes ago. Art's the new black. You really not interested?'

Zeb folded his arms in their black silk shirt. 'Nope.'

'Shame.' Jess shook her head sadly. 'Steven's hundred closest friends in showbiz will be *so* disappointed.'

Zeb shrugged and drained his champagne glass.

'Oh well,' Jess added, cheerfully gathering up her bag. 'Sharon Aura's just come in. She might be interested. Steven's just started collecting her stuff . . .'

A jolt of horror ran through Zeb. 'Er, now just hang on a minute,' he said quickly.

'What does your boyfriend do?' Portia was three glasses of champagne to the good already. Her head was tipped back against the wall and her eyes were starting to roll.

'Doctor,' Alice said, taking a sip of her own drink. She had only just found out what the foreign bodies were and so had remained entirely sober.

'Doctor. *That's* a new one.' Portia lolled her head consideringly on one side. 'Doctor. *Sweet.*'

'What do you mean, that's a new one?' Alice asked sharply.

Portia looked back at her with wide, innocent eyes. 'Most gallery girls start with a banker or a hedge funder. Then they trade up.'

'Trade *up*?'

'Don't sound so shocked.' Portia eyed her laughingly over her champagne. 'What else are you working in Gold Street for?'

'Not to get a husband, if that's what you mean,' Alice spluttered indignantly.

Portia looked her up and down and grinned. 'You could have fooled me, in that outfit.'

Alice looked angrily into her cleavage. She did not have to look far. It was impossible to deny that Portia had a point. 'I was forced to wear this!' she exclaimed.

'Of course you were, darling,' Portia assured her with wickedly sparkling eyes.

'Angelica told me I'd be sacked if I didn't.'

Portia was busy draining her glass and not listening. She licked her lips, on which flecks of gold leaf still lingered. 'One Gold Street girl,' she said dreamily, 'married a viscount she met in the gallery. Another married a Hollywood producer she met the same way. Aristocrats and celebrities are in and out of Gold Street all the time. And you meet some simply adorable unattached oligarchs . . .'

Was there anything, Zeb wondered, more tedious than other artists? He'd had half an idea about bedding this one; she'd seemed young and keen. But then, fatally, he had asked her about her work, which was a bit like asking people about their health. And now he was having to endure the consequences.

'. . . at the moment,' she was droning relentlessly on, 'I am engaged on a small series of works inspired by my poem *Worm*, which is a question to the worm about whether its simple life is better than my more complicated one . . .'

Zeb had thought he was too drunk to be this bored. He should have left ages ago; he had, after all, had as much face time with Fuchsia as she had seemed prepared to give. He had exchanged a few curt words with some collectors and curators. The photographers from the magazine and newspaper diary sections had all duly captured his trademark brooding. He'd done his job, in other words.

And yet somehow he didn't quite want to leave, to make his solitary way back to the luxurious yet lonely riverside flat. It was uninviting, ironically enough given the hundreds of invitations that crowded its grey concrete mantelpiece. There was a lot of concrete, as well as brickwork; the flat had been bought during the height of the loft living craze, and its now-outdated feel was one of the reasons Zeb disliked it. An outmoded flat made him feel outmoded himself.

He flicked a glance from beneath his eyebrows at Worm Woman. Was she really too boring to one-night-stand with?

'. . . exploring themes of time and space, music and maths, science and life . . .' she was continuing.

Zeb looked wearily around him. The room was full of yabber: artists yabbering to collectors, curators yabbering to each other. Hangers-on, meanwhile, were hanging on to anything they could, especially the drink. Was there any business as crammed with yabberers and hangers-on as the art one? he wondered disdainfully.

'Look, I gotta go,' he interrupted Worm Woman, turning and diving unsteadily into the room behind him.

'I am too Latin to live anywhere than a Latin country; it's the rhythm and light of Paris that inspires my creativity,' Worm Woman yelled after him.

Portia might not be the most determined feminist around, but she was, Alice was discovering, a good person to be with at a party. Especially this party. She knew who everyone was, and more.

'See that girl over there?' she giggled, leaning confidingly over. 'She's going out with . . .' She cupped her hand over Alice's ear and whispered the name of an extremely famous artist into it.

Alice was amazed. 'But she's about a quarter of his age.'

'Gerontophile, darling. Just can't get enough of old men. *Old Cock* – that Sharon Aura installation we've got – now *he* would be her idea of heaven. Ooh, and look. There's Evelyn Legg. He's a conceptual artist . . . oh, silly me. He's with OneSquared, you must have met him?'

Alice eyed the old man with purple hair in the tutu and pointe shoes. He looked even more incredible than Angelica's description had suggested.

'And that's Grizel Sidebottom,' Portia hissed as a very pale, tense-looking woman with scraped-back red hair and bulging blue eyes stalked past. 'She does waxworks of Disney characters in the electric chair. Oh, and that's Balthazar Ponce.'

'I thought it was Pon-Kay,' Alice corrected.

'Oh, is it? Anyway, that's him with the mod parka and the eyepatch.'

Alice regarded with interest the genius behind the hairy pebble.

'There's Elton John,' Portia said, screwing up her eyes concentratedly.

Alice grinned. 'Yes, I just about recognised him, thanks. Who's he talking to?'

An almost impossibly handsome dark-haired man in a baggy white shirt and silver trousers was in conversation with the veteran star.

Portia peered, and then gasped. 'Oh my God, it's Ciaran O'Sullivan. You know, out of Boyfriend.'

The name rang a vague bell with Alice. 'That boy band from ages ago? Didn't they split up?'

'Yes, but they're re-forming, apparently,' Portia said excitedly.

Moving slightly away from Alice in the direction of the two stars, she shimmied her hips and hummed something Alice did not recognise.

But Ciaran O'Sullivan evidently did. Turning slightly from Sir Elton, he looked straight in Portia's direction and stared piercingly at her with what even Alice had to admit were a pair of truly killer eyes.

'Oh my,' gasped Portia, once Ciaran had turned back to Sir Elton. 'Did you see that?' She flopped against the wall, closed her eyes and crooned. '*Baby, without you I'm just one big zero. Baby, without you, I'm no kind of hero . . .*'

'What on earth was that?' Alice snorted, unimpressed.

Portia's eyes flew open. Their expression was wide and hurt. 'Their big hit. "Without You". Don't you remember it?'

'No.'

Portia squealed and clutched Alice's arm. 'Oh my God, he just looked at me again. Did you see? Shit, shit, he's coming over!' She began to jump up and down with excitement.

A warm hand now descended lightly on Alice's bare shoulder. Indignant at the familiarity of the gesture, Alice turned crossly to find herself looking into the self-assured gaze of Ciaran O'Sullivan.

'So. Boyfriend fan, are ya?' he said in a low, rumbling Irish accent.

'No,' Alice said flatly, shaking her shoulders to remove his hand and trying to look as dignified as possible over the wobbling this provoked in her breasts.

'Not you,' the pop star snapped, his eyes narrowing to sharp, angry splinters. 'Your friend. She was humming "Without You".'

Alice turned the other way. Portia, she saw, was openly ogling Ciaran O'Sullivan. Time to tactfully withdraw.

'Just going to find the loo,' she muttered.

'Good idea,' said O'Sullivan coldly.

'If you find a gold one, don't use it,' Portia called laughingly after her. 'It's a Zeb Spaw original.'

Alice moved hurriedly away, narrowly avoided a punk bearing sushi and found herself almost colliding with Evelyn Legg. He stared at her twitchily.

'Do I know you? Have we met?' he demanded in fractious tones.

Now she was up close to him, she felt there was something rather tragic about Evelyn's slumped and withered shoulders, the way his back bent into the stiff satin bodice.

The hair on his head was severely cropped and somewhat inexpertly dyed. There were holes in his tights revealing expanses of leg – or perhaps Legg – and his pink satin shoes were grubby.

'We haven't met, no,' Alice said warmly. 'But I'm glad we are doing. I'm the new assistant at OneSquared.'

'Natasha gone already? Tut tut,' Evelyn said. 'They never last. Well, I'm pleased to meet you . . .'

'Alice.'

He frowned and cupped his ear.

'Alice.'

'Alice. Yes, well I'm pleased to meet you. I hope to come into the gallery tomorrow to supervise the installation of my new work. I meant to come in today, but . . .' he waved the wand down his front, 'you know how long it takes us girls to get ready.' He bared yellow teeth in a hideously skittish smile and fluttered his eyelids in a parody of flirtatiousness.

'When is it coming in?' Alice asked.

'When is what coming in?' Evelyn stopped fluttering.

'Your new work.'

Evelyn frowned, provoking millions of cross-hatched creases across his powdery forehead. 'I can't think what you mean. It was delivered yesterday by the art couriers.'

'What did it look like?' Alice was puzzled. After all, Angelica had claimed it had been delivered as well. She wondered if somehow she *could* have missed it. If, for example, it had arrived when she was in the loo. If it was very tiny, say, it might still be outside, leaning against the wall. Her heart hammered at the thought.

Evelyn's wrinkled and inaccurately carmined lips were pursed. He was looking Alice disapprovingly up and down. 'You surely remember taking delivery of it. It's a groundbreaking piece,' he complained. 'Completely original. A visual metaphor for the decline of a once-great culture.'

'Yes. Of course. But what did it look like exactly?'

'Impossible to say – exactly. The point is that it's mutable.' He narrowed his wrinkled eyes at her. 'You know what mutable means, I take it?'

'You mean that it changes.' Apart from knowing what mutable

meant, Alice was utterly confused. Nothing – nothing at all – had been delivered to the gallery yesterday, let alone a mutable piece of conceptual art. The only thing that had come was the food for Angelica.

'It's a work in progress, changes all the time,' Evelyn declared. 'It's been designed to slowly decompose, to go mouldy and rot. To symbolise the gradual death of traditional Oriental culture and of all the great cultures of the world.'

'Yes, but what does it *look* like?' Alice pressed. The feeling was strong within her that if only she could establish this one point, everything else would fall into place.

The artist looked at her in disgust. 'Oh well, if I really *must* reduce it to its simplest,' he said dismissively, 'I suppose you *could* say it looks like a Chinese takeaway.'

Chapter 48

Zeb had been all over Fuchsia's house now – in the public areas anyway – and had been unable to find a Spaw original anywhere.

A cold, creeping feeling of horror was taking possession of his body. It was obvious that his former patron had removed all his works – works of which she had once been so proud – from display. Presumably they were gathered together somewhere. For what? Why?

Then, with a swoop of relief, he realised. Of course. It was obvious.

His National Gallery show. Had to be. Fuchsia was lending them an entire exhibition. Possibly as a surprise for him; his fortieth birthday was on the horizon. And what better gift could there be for such a landmark date?

Everything was all right after all. How could he have doubted her?

Nevertheless, a scintilla of doubt remained. He had to be sure. After all, he had not checked the private areas of the house; if Spaws remained there, it might confound his theory.

Was *Flash in the Pan* still *in situ*, for example? And that rather more intimate piece of art he had created to go above Fuchsia's bed? He decided to check. The gold lavatory had been installed upstairs, in Fuchsia's private bathroom. It was not a room he had seen a lot of recently.

He took the back route upstairs from the kitchens, the grand main flight would have been too conspicuous. Herman Klumpp might be studiedly unaware of the relationship Zeb had with his wife, but even he could not fail to recognise the significance of the man the whole art world knew was his wife's lover going upstairs to the bedrooms.

Herman would tolerate anything, Zeb guessed, apart from direct embarrassment and direct confrontation with the truth. And it was certainly not in his interests – not now, anyway, with a possible National show in the offing – to present him with that truth.

The upstairs landing featured more from Fuchsia's latest art shopping trolley. An oversized champagne glass with a large stuffed rat in it was fixed to the main display wall. Fuchsia had caught up with the taxidermy trend, though she'd gone, as it were, a bit overkill, he thought, spotting elsewhere on the landing a parrot on a telephone receiver and, above his head, a stuffed black and white cat wedged in a contemporary glass chandelier. He cast it another, more doubtful glance. *Was* the cat stuffed? Or just stuck? But no, it had to be stuffed. Fuchsia hated small animals clawing at her designer clothes. It was one reason she hardly ever saw her children.

The door to Fuchsia's personal suite was shut. He opened it and strode through the small inner hall into the bedroom. It had not changed much. It was still gallery-like, with white walls and a wooden floor; the furniture – though Fuchsia called it sculpture – the same transparent Plexiglas. The transparent headboard of the bed still featured – Zeb bent to check – the mixed pubic hair of the sculptor and his wife. The only thing that had changed in the entire bedroom, in fact, was the artwork above the bed.

The giant gold-sprayed dildo he had presented Fuchsia with had gone, Zeb saw. In its place, slap bang above the centre of the headboard, was a vast black plastic crucifix with a grubby thong nailed to the centre.

There was no doubt, not the slightest, that the piece of work he was looking at was by Sharon Aura. Zeb contemplated it with delight. He felt no threat, only that his hunch had been proved right. The Aura was only there to fill a hole. While his dildo was being displayed at the country's most famous gallery.

He walked over to the white door that led to Fuchsia's private bathroom. Of course, he no longer expected to see *Flash in the Pan* there, but he was interested in what might have replaced it. As he approached the door, he heard the sound of someone laughing. Fuchsia's assured, wealthy cackle.

Zeb ceased to breathe. Time stood still. Silently he dropped to his knees, his eye to the small keyhole below the handle.

Fuchsia was sitting on the lavatory seat, her eyes closed, gasping in a way Zeb instantly recognised. Her dress was pushed up around her thighs, which were wide apart and had the back of a platinum-blond crew-cut head between them. It was a head Zeb had no difficulty recognising either. The woman was naked from the waist up; waist down, she wore leather motorbike trousers and heavy boots. There was a pot of something silver beside her. Caviar, Zeb recognised.

He watched as Sharon Aura dug in her black-tipped fingers, scooped up a glistening heap of caviar and smeared it on the insides of Fuchsia's thighs. He watched as she licked it off, Fuchsia shuddering and moaning in ecstasy.

The edges of Zeb's own vision were shuddering too. His teeth were chattering wildly, his chest agonisingly compressed, and despite the heat, his body shook with the cold of complete and utter shock.

He had been replaced. There was no doubt about it now. Wherever his art was, whatever Fuchsia intended to do with it, Zeb now knew with a sudden, deadening finality that it was not destined for any exhibition in the National Gallery.

He stood before the bathroom door for a few seconds, then threw it open. He remained in the doorway just long enough for Fuchsia to see him. Her eyes, meeting his over the top of Sharon Aura's busy head, widened in horror.

Sharon, however, seemed oblivious to his presence. She continued to lick the fish eggs off Fuchsia. 'I love this stuff!' she growled. 'Know what it tastes like?'

Fuchsia did not reply. Her attention was on Zeb. Her mouth was opening and shutting like a goldfish's and he guessed she was searching for something to say.

If he moved his head slightly to the side, Zeb found, he could see Sharon's profile. Her lips were drawn back over teeth flecked black with caviar.

'*It tastes like money!*' she roared.

Zeb felt a sense of something shattering. There was a flash and flood of light inside his head as if the electrical circuits had exploded. The tightness in his chest suddenly gave way. His muscles released; he almost fell over. As he walked away, he felt as if he were stepping out of a space in which he had long been confined.

'Zeb!' he heard Fuchsia yell from behind him.

He did not pause. Swiftly – or as swiftly as he could in his unanchored sports footwear – he crossed the landing. By chance, Herman Klumpp was coming up the main staircase. He stared at Zeb, smooth, tanned face puckered with surprise.

'You've got to help Fuchsia,' Zeb informed him urgently. 'She's in her bathroom. She's in a bad way.'

Alice's one aim had been to escape from Evelyn with all speed. Before he could work out that not only had she taken delivery of his conceptual masterpiece after all, but that she had eaten it into the bargain.

At least she had kept the containers. She had by now calculated that if she could leave the party quickly enough and pick up another takeaway on the way home, she could put that in the boxes Evelyn had sent. No one need ever know.

It was a miracle that Angelica was away. But there was still the possibility that she would arrive early at the gallery tomorrow and discover what had happened. Alice would, she accepted reluctantly, have to be there at the crack of dawn.

Fortunately, new supplies were relatively easily secured. There were plenty of Chinese restaurants near the Nutthouse. It was simply a case of remembering what the original dishes had been. Sweet and sour pork, she was pretty sure about that. And spare ribs, definitely. But had it been Peking duck or chow mein? No doubt, in the context of conceptual art, there was a big difference, affecting the entire tone and meaning of the work.

In the wide passage linking the ground-floor rooms, a photographer with long hair was capturing Balthazar Ponce for posterity. The sight reminded Alice that she had not, as yet, fulfilled her original brief, her entire reason for coming. No one, as yet, had taken a picture of her.

She was slinking past when, without warning, the photographer turned on her and began snapping furiously. The violent brightness of the flash was unexpected, and for some seconds Alice felt quite blinded. As she blinked and the room returned around her, she saw the photographer, who had a foxy expression, looking at her with his pen poised. 'Name?' he demanded.

Alice gave it.

'You an artist?'

For a second she was almost tempted to say yes. She was, after all, about to create a conceptual artwork with the help of whatever Chinese takeaway she found open first. Or perhaps, given the circumstances, that made her a fraudster.

What she actually said was that she was from the OneSquared Gallery, and Angelica Devon's new assistant.

As he wrote it down, stifling a yawn, Alice realised with relief that her mission was accomplished. She had been photographed. She could go home – and get the takeaway. She looked at her watch; given the time it would take her to hobble there, she should just about make it if she left now.

If she could find her way out. She soon realised that she was lost. The house was more enormous even than it looked. She had imagined she was heading for the red-painted entrance hall, but somehow she had taken a wrong turn. She was in one of the enormous reception rooms, but it was difficult to say which, because the people all looked different from when she had last passed through. And the orchids weren't much of an aid to orientation; they were everywhere.

The air was thick with heat, perfume and the sound of excited, drunken voices. Alice tottered through the crowds with difficulty. The party had clearly reached a stage where everyone had availed themselves fully of the hospitality on offer, and the volume was as high as the heat. Everyone seemed to be shouting to each other.

Someone very drunk was teetering back and forth diagonally, crashing into groups of people and cursing them volubly.

'He's absolutely paralytic,' Alice heard someone observe.

'No he's not,' answered someone else. 'He's a Slovenian neo-avant-garde artist highlighting the random nature of encounter. Or so I've been told.'

Passing behind a sofa writhing with people, Alice was relieved to see that a pair of large French windows were open on to the garden. Perhaps there would be a path, a gate or something, and she could make her escape the back way.

The night was warm and scented with flowers. The Klumpps' garden was obviously very big and very beautiful; white blooms on huge bushes glimmered in the gloom and from somewhere there was the tinkle of water, as from a fountain or stream. Alice picked her way across the dark grass quickly to prevent her heels sinking into the turf. It was darker here than was usual for London, no doubt because of the proximity to the park. Having found a piece of solid path to stand on, she paused and looked back across the lawn at the house, white and graceful in its setting of trees and bushes. The French window she had gone out through was a great yellow rectangle from which the tinkle of conversation and laughter floated out into the balmy night air. What had been raucous close up sounded glamorous and even romantic from out here, she thought.

There was, all the same, no time to hang around. The Chinese must be got to, the takeaway secured. As Alice hurried, as best she could, down the path, she heard a distant giggle, which even on this short acquaintance she instantly recognised as Portia's. There was some movement in the bushes to her left, a flash of white and silver and some suppressed laughter which sounded male. Alice felt sorry for the absent Mrs O'Sullivan, whoever and wherever she might be.

The way out of the garden, Alice saw, involved practically stepping over the spot where her fellow gallery assistant was enjoying enthusiastic congress with the pop star. So uninhibited was their union that they were practically out of the bush now; there was, Alice saw, no mistaking the moving, heaving flash of Portia's red basque.

Chapter 49

'So, Siobhan. What's your take on the band getting back together?'

Siobhan dropped her eyes to the floor. 'Er, well, obviously Ciaran's very keen on it, so of course I support him.'

The journalist looked at her closely. While friendly she had shaken hands warmly with a breezy 'Hi, I'm Sarah' – she was obviously nobody's fool. 'But Siobhan, it can hardly be easy. I mean, waving your husband off to soak up the adulation of millions of adoring women?'

Siobhan's face retained its fixed grin, but inside, her heart had sunk. 'Of course women find him attractive,' she admitted eventually. 'But I, um, trust him completely.'

Sarah nodded again. 'You've got one of the most enduring marriages in showbiz.'

It was all Siobhan could do not to raise her eyebrows. If theirs was among the strongest marriages in showbiz, the weakest ones did not bear thinking about.

Ciaran had arrived back from London that morning, having promised he would be back the night before. His excuse had been that his meetings with various promoters had gone on longer than expected and had continued over dinner, after which it had been too late to return. The reason he had not responded to her increasingly frantic calls on his mobile was because the dinner had been in the type of restaurant that required all clientele, no matter how rich, famous or otherwise distinguished, to turn their phones off.

As always, Ciaran had had an answer to everything, and as always, Siobhan had had to accept it.

And now Ciaran was in the bath, and had been for the past half-hour, despite the fact that Sarah, who was from a leading celebrity magazine, was here to interview him. Siobhan had had to accept that as well; as, in point of fact, had Sarah.

Siobhan had answered Sarah's questions as best she could, all the time worried about what Ciaran would think of her answers and also that she was not looking her best. She had on no make-up, tracksuit bottoms and a T-shirt, and her hair was stuffed back into a ponytail under a baseball cap. The telephone shrilled, and Siobhan wanted to scream along with it. She was the most hospitable of women, but even her hospitality could not extend to taking personal calls in front of the celebrity press.

It rang and rang. Siobhan had hoped – *expected* – that Julie, the housekeeper, would answer the one in the hall, but this had so far not happened. Possibly because Julie was in the utility room with Jeremy Vine turned up full blast. The answerphone for some reason was not on. The ringing was shrilling inside Siobhan's brain.

'You want to get that?' Sarah nodded towards the handset on the big wooden kitchen table.

Siobhan nodded dumbly, snatched it up, and then, flashing Sarah an apologetic look, scuttled from the room.

In the hall, she connected to the caller. Hopefully it was something and nothing. Or one of Ciaran's managers. What it actually was was agitated, high-pitched and with a strong German accent.

'Ees Florian Fritz here. Chief Guest Conductor with the Berliner Sinfonia.'

Siobhan's surprise deepened to amazement. She had several compact discs featuring this highly regarded maestro. But why was he calling Aldeham Manor?

'Ees about zees boyzgroup!' announced the other end in forcible tones.

'Boys' group?'

'Zees pop band.' Florian Fritz sounded withering.

'You mean Boyfriend?' Siobhan frowned. She would not have had Fritz down as a fan.

'Ja. Zees concert I help on . . .'

Siobhan suddenly understood. Florian Fritz – *Florian Fritz* – was conducting Boyfriend's supporting orchestra. The news struck her as little short of incredible. The disloyal thought flitted through her mind that either Fritz was very short of money or Boyfriend were a better pop band than she had imagined. She forbade herself to speculate on the likely answer to that.

There was, however, no denying that getting Fritz was impressive. He would add weight to any project, boy bands not excepted. And with him on board, Ciaran's claims to musicianship would finally have validity. While sales had never been a problem, Siobhan had gathered that the critical acclaim for Boyfriend that her husband evidently longed for had been rather harder to come by.

Darting a worried glance towards the kitchen, where Sarah waited, Siobhan leapt the stairs two at a time and burst through the bedroom. Ciaran had locked the bathroom door. There was the thunder of water from the other side. Siobhan banged on it.

'Look, I'm busy,' Ciaran yelled, his voice muffled by the roar from the taps. 'She's got to wait. We always kept the press waiting in Boyfriend. Sometimes up to an hour.'

'You can't do that!' Siobhan yelled, panic-stricken. The thought of enduring Sarah's cunning questions for an hour was horrendous. But she would have no choice. Sarah's publication was aimed squarely at Ciaran's potential fans and supporters. Offending her was inadvisable.

But that, of course, was not the only issue. 'It's Herr Fritz. Your conductor. On the phone,' Siobhan yelled.

'Only losers turn up on time,' Ciaran yelled back, having

obviously misheard her last sentence. 'Treat 'em mean, keep 'em keen.'

Groaning, Siobhan returned to the telephone. 'I'm so sorry, Maestro,' she said reverently. 'I can't find my husband. May I take a message?'

'Ja. Tell 'eem zat I no longer wan' conduct orchestra for zees boyzband.'

'I'm sorry?' Siobhan gasped, horribly aware that she was in the hall and the journalist was only on the other side of the kitchen door. Admittedly it was a very thick oak kitchen door. But Sarah had looked the type who could hear through anything.

''Ees music ees sheet and 'ee theenk 'ee ees Brahms.'

'Er . . . I'll certainly pass that on.'

'I 'ave worked weez finest players in world. Some of greatest divas. And nevair 'ave I met anyone as harrogant has Queerun . . .'

'Ciaran,' Siobhan corrected.

'Hmm. Well whatever 'ee ees called, I no want to conduct any more.' And with that, the line went dead.

Siobhan returned to the kitchen, trying to look relaxed and not as if she was the bearer of a piece of news that, when he heard it, would cause her husband to bite the carpet with fury. But not immediately, Siobhan vowed. Ciaran was the type to shoot the messenger, and neither the shooting nor the message was something Siobhan wanted a high-circulation magazine to print.

From her seat at the kitchen table, Sarah looked at her closely. 'Everything OK?'

'Fine.' Even to her own ears Siobhan 's voice sounded high and strained. She wished Ciaran would come down and start the interview.

Sarah shook her blunt-cut blond fringe and recommenced her smiling interrogation. 'Good news about the *Brilliant Britain* slot,' she remarked.

Siobhan nodded. The news, a few days ago, that Boyfriend were to be given a spot on *Brilliant Britain*, the TV talent show holding the nation in thrall every Saturday night, had certainly been good for Ciaran. It had sent him into ecstasies of self-congratulation.

Siobhan was not so sure. While the exposure was second to none, not everyone came out of it well. The band had been apart for a decade, after all. But Ciaran had been withering about her concerns. 'God, Siobhan. Can't you see the bright side of fucking *anything*?'

But if she had been uncertain about it then, now, with the conductor of the orchestra walking out . . .

Siobhan swallowed and felt a wave of pure dread.

'Does your relationship with Ciaran ever come under . . . pressure?' Sarah asked, right on cue.

Siobhan took a deep breath. 'Well,' she answered brightly, 'you have to work at it, obviously. But you have to work at all relationships. Don't you?' She gave an appealing smile.

'You tell me,' Sarah replied, turning the question round without batting an eyelid. After Siobhan did not take up this invitation, she continued, 'I'm interested in yours because you're both so . . . *creative*. That surely leads to . . .' she raised her eyebrows smilingly, 'clashes?'

'Not at all.' Siobhan smiled. 'Ciaran's the artistic one.'

'But so are *you*, surely?' Sarah jumped in. 'You trained as an artist. According to the cuts I've read, anyway.'

'You've been doing your homework,' Siobhan said nervously.

'What sort of thing did you do?' Sarah pressed.

'Abstract. Kind of colourful abstract.' Siobhan reddened.

'Sounds like you should have been at the Klumpp party last night instead of your husband.'

'Klumpp party?' The words meant nothing to Siobhan at all.

The other woman looked surprised. 'Fuchsia Klumpp? The famous art collector?'

Siobhan shook her head. 'Sorry.'

Sarah leaned forward, her eyes fixed on Siobhan's face. 'The Klumpps hold a full-on party once a year for their favourite artists. The whole art world is there, and loads of celebrities. Ciaran was there . . .'

'Ciaran?' Siobhan frowned. 'But he couldn't have been. He was in a restaurant all night. Having a meeting . . .' Her voice trailed away.

Sarah had been rummaging in the baggy brown leather holdall before her on the kitchen table and was now pulling out a newspaper. 'Here,' she announced, brandishing it triumphantly at Siobhan.

Siobhan found herself looking at a large photograph of her husband, wearing silver trousers and talking to Elton John. Beside him – very close beside him – was a woman whose face could not be seen for long dark hair, but the red basque she wore was visible enough. As were her breasts, spilling over like cream.

Siobhan gripped the newspaper, unwilling to lift her head lest Sarah see her face was on fire.

Sarah, it seemed, sensed it anyway. 'You didn't know?'

Siobhan breathed in. It was only a party, she told herself, not the end of the world. And the girl in the basque was probably just passing him on the way to the loo or the canapés or something.

'Ciaran's a famous man,' she breezed eventually. 'He gets asked to places. He doesn't tell me everything and I don't keep a collar and lead on him.'

Her mind raced with questions. The Klumpp party? A celebrity gathering thrown by contemporary art collectors? What had Ciaran, of all people, who had no understanding whatsoever of art, been doing there? And why had he lied about it – or, at the very least, neglected to mention it?

Just then, Ciaran himself walked in. He entered with a bounce in his step, exactly as if he was striding onstage. Siobhan, still processing what Sarah had just told her, found herself wondering whether they were both expected to applaud.

Broodingly, she watched him approach. He had a large, shiny guitar round his neck, which he wrenched off and tossed on the end of the long kitchen table as if he had just bounced backstage after a sell-out concert. He was dressed casually, even slouchily, although as always with Ciaran it was expensive, well-thought-out slouch. Siobhan recognised the long, black, thick-knit Martin Margiela cardigan she had bought him for his birthday, worn over a white Louis Vuitton shirt and leather trousers of dark moss-green.

She made no attempt to hide the newspaper in her hands as Ciaran stalked up to them both, his shining hair bouncing in the light from the Jacobean windows. She saw him spot it, saw the slight reflex in his eye and experienced a sensation which felt like falling.

Then his handsome face split into its customary easy grin, and he bent over Siobhan and looked at the picture. 'God, those trousers,' he said in the creamy Irish burr he used, Siobhan knew, when he particularly wanted to charm. 'What an eejit I look, sure to God.'

'Good party, was it?' Sarah asked lightly.

'Ah, it was, to be sure it was,' Ciaran answered, raking a hand through his hair as if in rueful recollection. 'You know, I'd almost forgotten I went there. Just popped in, you know.' He grinned at Siobhan, as if in explanation. 'Before that dinner I told you about.'

She opened her mouth to say something, but he got there first.

'My new PR makes me go to every party. She's very keen on me getting out and about. Probably a bit too keen. Silver trousers!' He shook his shining head. 'But the dress code was Daring, you see.'

Siobhan wasn't sure she did see. She was busy trying to reconcile the claim that this was a pre-dinner diversion with the fact that Ciaran's Patek Philippe in the picture clearly said half past eleven.

Yet as he flashed his brilliant smile at them both and crinkled his eyes, Siobhan could feel herself, yet again, willing to be convinced. Wanting to believe him. She saw him as Sarah must see him. As a good-looking man. Really, a *stunningly* handsome man. Clear, tanned skin like gold; clean, manicured nails; soft, shining hair. He looked, she thought, like an angel. Not the tallest of angels, but an angel nonetheless.

'You must be Sarah,' Ciaran said warmly to the journalist, turning on his full-wattage killer smile.

Sarah, however, seemed to be managing admirably to keep her cool. 'Your wife,' she announced to Ciaran, 'was just telling me about her art career.'

'Is that so?' Ciaran answered, rather flatly. He looked coldly at Siobhan.

Swallowing, she met his glare with the hint of a challenge. Even if he didn't like her work, could she not even *mention* it? Especially as he had just been to an artistic gathering and not even told her.

Ciaran snatched his eyes away and favoured Sarah with another killer beam. She looked steadily back at him. 'Ready?' she asked.

He inclined his head, smiling dazzlingly.

'So what makes you think,' Sarah asked, 'that Boyfriend can imitate the very successful comebacks by bands like Boyzone and Take That?'

Ciaran's smile disappeared instantly. 'We have a lot of fans,' he asserted stonily. His eyes narrowed slightly as he looked at her.

'I see that your world tour includes Tokyo,' Sarah remarked next. 'Isn't that a bit brave, given what happened last time Boyfriend were there as a band?' She waited a few beats for Ciaran to respond; he didn't.

'The infamous clothes-down-the-toilet incident and Declan's defection?' Sarah prompted.

Ciaran's beam did not now quite reach his eyes. 'No comment,' he said.

Sarah shuffled in her seat and smiled. 'I'm told you're going to start your tour with a slot on *Brilliant Britain*,' she said. 'You must be thrilled about that.'

'Delighted,' Ciaran confirmed bullishly. 'The judges are all huge fans of ours, I'm told,' he added complacently.

Sarah eyed him. 'So you're not concerned that it could backfire? Big acts don't always do well, as you know.'

Ciaran smiled. 'I think we can be fairly confident. We've got some tricks up our sleeves, after all.'

'Ah, yes. How *are* things going with the symphony orchestra?' Sarah asked.

Siobhan kept her eyes on the floor as her cheeks flooded vermilion. She hoped neither of them would look at her, but thankfully all Ciaran's attention was on Sarah.

'I'm incredibly pleased.' He smiled at the journalist. 'The conductor's amazed how similar some of my arrangements are to Brahms.'

'Really? That *is* amazing.'

'Not really,' Ciaran corrected smoothly. 'In fact, it gets better. He actually said some of the chorus hooks reminded him of Mozart. He's really enjoying working with us.'

Siobhan stood up, burdened with the knowledge to the contrary. And suspicion: what had Ciaran *really* been doing in London last night? She felt beset with fear, doubt and distrust.

She longed to leave the room, to escape from the worries that seemed concentrated within it. Outside it was a beautiful clear day, and her sketchbook and colours were sitting under the lid of the chest in the entrance hall, along with her iPod. What was more, there was a painting that had been in her mind for days. She had prepared a canvas, had sketched out the main idea. That was in the chest too, wrapped in an old pashmina.

'I'll leave you to it,' she said to her husband and the journalist with a quick, nervous smile.

'Just how excited are you?' Sarah was asking Ciaran as she left.

'Very. I can't *wait*. That moment you come onstage and see millions of screaming fans. Man, it's just *the best*.'

Chapter 50

Alice opened her eyes. There was a drilling pain in her head and a sour, burning sensation in her mouth. A hangover. She had drunk more at the Klumpps' than she had thought. Perhaps it was the gold flakes that had done it.

Her arm fell on a warm heap in the bed beside her. David. He was back after all, and had returned even later than she had. Alice felt, through her nausea, a wave of relief.

The trip home from the party had been horrible. She had endured a much-delayed tube full of villainous types staring at her thighs, followed by a long wait in the takeaway with yet more villainous stares. And then she had gone home to an empty flat. A cold and messy flat, into the bargain. David had left after her that morning, and without tidying up.

But she'd done it. Saved the day, or Legg's artwork. Spare ribs, sweet and sour pork, chow mein; she'd got it all. It was sitting in the fridge even now, and needed, with all speed, to be transferred to the fridge in the gallery before Angelica found out what had happened.

Alice heaved herself out of bed to the shower. As she had anticipated, David had taken all the hot water on his return in the middle of the night. But this was almost an advantage: the freezing water, while not easing her pain, at least moved the focus of it elsewhere. And when, clad in her damp towel, she opened the wardrobe door, it was to find – oh joy – that the clean clothes fairy had been at work: on a hanger right at the back of the wardrobe were a pair of black cigarette pants and a fitted white shirt.

Together with her newish zebra-striped pumps, this constituted a positively chic outfit and one in which, Alice felt, she could face most things, even the secret early-morning substitution of one piece of conceptual art with another.

As she went into the kitchen to make a cup of tea, she had even started to hum.

The humming stopped abruptly. She froze in the doorway. Scattered all over the kitchen table were silver foil containers, their white cardboard lids nearby. The containers were empty apart from a dribble of sauce in the bottom of each one. A scrunched brown paper carrier bag lay drunkenly on the floor, having evidently been tossed inexpertly in the direction of the bin. Alice raised her hands to her head and howled.

Thuds from the bedroom. 'Whazzup? Whattimeizzit? Whazzamatter?' David, blundering into the kitchen, unshaven, and swollen-eyed from lack of sleep. It was a look that in normal circumstances Alice loved, but which only increased her fury now. 'You ate my bloody takeaway,' she raged.

A pair of surprised, bright, rather bloodshot brown eyes stared at her. 'I thought you'd bought it for me.'

'Bought it for you?' Alice's heart was pumping. The banging in her head had returned.

'I found it in the fridge when I got back,' David whined. 'It was still warm. I thought you'd got it for me to have when I came home, honestly, Alice, I did.'

Alice was doing some swift, panicked calculations, and the answer already coming back was that there was no chance, no chance at all, of her getting another substitute before the gallery opened. No one, not even in London, sold Chinese takeaways at half past six in the morning. She was sunk.

'It's just the kind of lovely thing you'd do,' David added ingratiatingly.

Alice was rattling her way among the empty cartons. She had been hoping for a hank of chow mein, a few spare ribs, but David had made a clean sweep. 'I hadn't eaten all day,' he moaned, assuming a pathetic expression.

'It's a disaster,' Alice wailed. She was thinking furiously. Could Legg be persuaded that empty takeaway cartons were an even more poignant comment on the decline of world culture?

David shook his head, bewildered. 'But I don't get it. Since when did you eat Chinese takeaway for breakfast?'

She looked at him with burning eyes. 'It's not for my bloody breakfast. It's for the gallery. It's a work of cutting-edge conceptual art.'

'What?' David gave a shout of laughter. 'That – *that*' – he picked up one of the cartons – 'was a work of art?'

'Yes, and believe it or not, my job depends on it.'

'Your job depends on a Chinese takeaway?' he said hilariously. 'Oh come on, Alice. You can't be serious.'

'That's right. Laugh,' Alice snapped, striding into the hall and flinging on her coat. 'But as it happens, I'm *entirely* serious.'

Chapter 51

Dan, weighed down with a horrible vodka hangover and the heavy portfolio of his best work under his arm, was making his slow and painful way to the station to catch the train to London. Whatever his physical state, he was going to seek his artistic fortune.

This was the overwhelming imperative that had driven him, earlier that morning, head throbbing, upwards from the pillow and out of bed into the peeling bathroom, telling him all the while that if he stayed at home today, he was missing a chance.

He had resisted the imperative as it drove him towards the station, however. He felt too sick, as yet, to face the forward pull of what would almost certainly be a hot and smelly carriage. He decided first to take some air on the hill at the top of the village, on the hill above Aldeham Manor. Perhaps just to be near Siobhan, in sight of her house, might make him feel, if only ever so slightly, better.

This being Suffolk, the hill was neither high nor steep, but feeling as Dan did, and with a heavy portfolio to boot, it was challenge enough. Now, however, he was here, and below him was the Manor, and in it, presumably, Siobhan.

But he wasn't feeling better, not at all. Rather, he felt worse. Both sick and sheepish. What, exactly, did he hope to achieve in London?

He had no appointments, knew no galleries, had no contacts.

Where would he go? There were galleries all over the city: edgy in the East End; sleeker and more mainstream in the West End. Probably it was best to try the West End, on the whole, although he would be careful to avoid Gold Street, of course. No one there would be interested in representing a portrait artist with a degree in drawing and painting.

Would anyone, anywhere, be interested, though? With the excitement and courage of the vodka long gone, Dan felt he understood the word 'dispirited' in every possible sense.

He screwed his eyes up and briefly considered going straight back home and putting himself to bed. What was the point of struggling down to London in a hot train on a day of what was already promising to be stifling heat? What was he expecting when he got there?

As the larks rose about him into the brightening air, he put his head in his hands and groaned. No, he *was* going. And that was that. The inside of a train would be hot and messy, but not as hot and messy as the inside of his cottage. And at least, in the train, there would not be a crazy Dutch woman dancing about naked to heavy rock music.

It was past mid-morning, but the remains of a sticky mist still tickled the air as Siobhan set up her easel. She had chosen the highest point of the hill behind the Manor. As far a point as possible from where Ciaran and Sarah were conducting their interview.

Determinedly, she put them from her mind. Perhaps, today, she would really start the painting. Put oil to brush and brush to canvas for the first time in years. She felt nervous and excited as she snapped the easel legs into place, then straightened and looked at the view.

The early fog was clearing and the sun was just starting to burn through. In the milky light, the rolling land appeared ethereal and mysterious. The grass close to her sparkled with a thousand drops of dew; the fairies had scattered and left their diamonds, she thought. The sky was pale, a blaze of silver around the sun.

Siobhan removed her box of oils from her backpack and set the canvas on the easel. She stared at it for a while, frowning at the pencil lines she had sketched in the day before as guides for the colour. She bit her lip, superimposing the mental image of the work she intended. Would it all work out as she planned? Possibly not, but there was virtue in that as well. A slip of the hand could turn out a happy accident.

She had always been inclined to the abstract; had, in the past, started to develop her own style. After her long fallow period she had been pleased to discover that the intervening decade had not strangled her abilities stone dead, as she had feared. On the contrary, after an initial stiffness, ideas and the means to execute them had flowed freely, in spate, indeed, at times. It was as if a tap long turned off had suddenly been turned on again.

This painting was to be the essence of the view before her when the day was at high noon. Not the detail of every bush, field, tree and leaf, but rather how they felt, the glow of them, the heat, the sound of the birds, the scented air in her nostrils, the light breeze lifting her hair.

She picked out the tube of green oil paint, pinching its plumpness beneath the thin metal, and unscrewed the small black cap. She began to think of Dan; he liked her figure drawings, but what would he think of her paintings? There was an abstract portrait based on her sketches of Bo taking shape in one of the Aldeham outhouses, a former saddle room to judge by the wall pegs, and the only one light enough to use as a studio. She had not exactly concealed from Ciaran the fact that she was painting there, but nor had she exactly advertised it.

How long she would be able to use the room was another matter, however. Ciaran had plans to convert the entire range of Elizabethan service buildings into a studio complex. The brick-floored washhouse would go, the shadowy potting shed, the narrow stairs up to the servants' attics, her own saddle-room studio, with the open fireplace so suggestive of the days when stable staff lounged by it, gossiping about the great folks across at the Manor.

'Of course there won't be any problems over planning permission,' Ciaran had said scornfully when Siobhan had voiced this possibility. 'I'm a celebrity, yeah? I'm a local asset.'

Determinedly Siobhan pushed her thoughts back to her work. What would Dan think of the picture she was planning? Of course he would never see it. He would be certain to condemn it as an example of the contemporary art he so despised.

They had had various conversations on the subject in the life classes. Their talks had been brief but sufficient nonetheless for Siobhan to know that Dan considered most contemporary work ugly and lacking depth.

He was wrong, she thought. There was much beauty in contemporary art. It could be strong, relevant, important even. Dan might claim – and did – that the great age of painting was dead and gone, but Siobhan knew that this would never happen. There would always be people who wanted to look at paintings, and for this reason there would always be portraits too. Dan need not fear for the future so much.

Dan had been an almost constant presence in her thoughts recently, but perhaps that was natural enough as she thought almost constantly about painting. And Dan was, in effect, her art teacher.

And . . .

She pushed the thought away, but it came back.

And . . .

She looked up from her canvas, pushed the end of the brush between her teeth and smiled. She had suspected from the first that Dan was a little in love with her. And while that wasn't ideal, given Ciaran, it was certainly flattering.

Especially flattering, given Ciaran. He was so snappy, so tense in general, and he made her feel the same. Was it guilt? Had he lied to her? Had he claimed to be at dinner with promoters when he had really been out with lissom girls in PVC?

Oh no. Better not to think about it. She took a deep breath and slipped on her iPod. As the familiar notes of the first Brandenburg Concerto filled her ears, she felt a sense of immense well-being. Calmer, she loaded her brush with colour.

This, she thought, was the perfect moment. Everything was in line, in readiness. Her eye, her hand and her brush. Her ears, even. The picture in her head. The weather, the view. Even the air was still, as if watching and waiting for her to make the first stroke.

Her hand moved towards the canvas – and stopped. Someone was behind her, looking over her shoulder. She turned round, surprised and rather fearful.

The face was one she knew. Siobhan removed her earphones.

The new arrival beamed, raised its arms aloft and declared, in a fruity voice, 'The Majesty of Nature!'

Mrs de Goldsmith was red and beaming beneath a wide-brimmed straw hat upon which a white silk scarf had been somewhat fancifully arranged. As well as a blue and white striped top on which the word 'Cannes' was stitched in gold letters, she wore wide white trousers and a pair of gold sandals quite unsuitable for the business of climbing up hills. Matching the gold sandals was a large quilted gilt bag with gold chain handles.

Siobhan nodded guardedly. 'It is a nice morning, isn't it?'

'*Nice?*' Mrs de Goldsmith demanded. 'More than nice, my dear. I feel as if I've stepped into another dimension. Somewhere soothing and wonderful for the spirit. Oooh,' she shrieked suddenly, clamping a hand to her head as a gust threatened to snatch her hat.

'You're here very early,' Siobhan said, after a pause in which she had hoped her interlocutor might take the hint and go away. Then she remembered from the art classes that Mrs de Goldsmith had the hide of a rhinoceros.

'The morning called me,' Emmeline de Goldsmith declaimed, one hand on her capacious bosom. 'I could not resist it. Some people don't *understand* us artists, do they? They don't understand how art *drives* one, how it *demands*, how you just *have* to keep at something until you get it right. No matter *how* long it takes.'

She was standing almost on tiptoe, reddened nose raised in the air, eyes closed in ecstasy, large hands clasped rapturously to her chest. Then she dropped the hands, opened the eyes and beamed at Siobhan. 'I really feel like going home and getting my own easel, to keep you company,' she declared.

Alarm seized Siobhan. She did not want to paint in company. Least of all in this company. Emmeline de Goldsmith was very garrulous, very curious, and she talked a lot, and bitterly, about her former husband. Just at the moment, Siobhan felt, she had no desire to swap anecdotes about marriage.

'Carrying on the great *plein air* tradition,' Emmeline was declaring, 'following in the footsteps of all those great nineteenth-century masters like Turner. All those magnificent, muscular men in floaty robes.'

Siobhan frowned. 'Did Turner do men in floaty robes?'

Mrs de Goldsmith looked puzzled. 'Who do I mean, then?'

'Titian?'

'Of course!' Her expression became curious. 'Is *that* how you pronounce it? I thought it was Titti-an.'

Siobhan picked up her brush again and hoped the other woman would take the hint.

But Mrs de Goldsmith was gazing upwards. 'The clouds look just like cotton wool, don't you think?'

'Look,' said Siobhan, wondering how many more banal observations she must endure. 'I've really got to get on with some work.'

'Of course!' exclaimed Mrs de Goldsmith. 'I *completely* understand. We artists . . .' she reached out and tweaked – actually *tweaked* – Siobhan's cheek, 'we need our solitude.'

Siobhan nodded, hoping that now, finally, Mrs de Goldsmith would leave. She did not, however. Siobhan looked up resignedly to find her staring, one plump hand over her eyes to shade them, down into the garden of Kevin Swift.

'What's that?' she demanded, pointing at the expanse of the Swift lawn with the great white-painted H on it.

'His helicopter pad.'

'Yes, yes, I can see *that*. It's what's next to it, I mean.'

Siobhan peered. 'I can't see anything.'

Mrs de Goldsmith crossed her large, freckled forearms. 'It looks as if he's cut down a considerable number of very old trees.' There was a quiver of outrage in her voice. 'Did he have planning permission for that?'

Chapter 52

Dan had been on the hill for some time. Fresh air had made no difference. He felt dreadful, still. He had never had a head for alcohol, but the first drink always made him forget this was the case.

Nonetheless, if he intended to make the trip, he had better get on with it. He took a final deep breath and walked across the top of the hill, intending to descend the other side from the one he had come up.

To his amazement, he now found himself approaching, from the front, a large easel with someone sitting behind it. Who? He could see only jeans and tennis shoes beneath the back of the stretched canvas.

Jeans and tennis shoes didn't suggest Roger, Mrs de Goldsmith or one of the librarians.

The hideous thought that it could be Zeb Spaw vanished as soon as it arrived. Spaw, as everyone knew, had not touched a canvas with a brush for years. Brushes weren't things he tended to use; Dan had heard strange stories recently concerning a room full of swinging sponges.

Gaining on the seated painter, Dan now spotted a slender arm in a white shirtsleeve. A lock of dark hair rippled out.

Dan paused. The pain in his head and the nausea in his stomach seemed to have suddenly, miraculously, gone. He was holding his breath very hard and feeling completely off balance. He clutched his portfolio with all his might.

She must have sensed something; she turned.

She found herself thinking that, even with his glasses, he looked like a romantic poet in his flowing white shirt and over-long linen trousers, the sun blazing a halo around his black hair. There were dark shadows beneath his narrowed eyes. His lips looked swollen. She felt a pulse of excitement.

She looked pleased to see him, he saw with relief. He was close enough now to see the downy hairs on her forearms. He swallowed.

'Is that your portfolio?' she asked.

Dan nodded. 'I'm just going to London to, um . . . Well I know it sounds a bit silly, but . . .' He stared at the grass in embarrassment.

'But what?' she pressed.

He tried to sound insouciant. 'Well, um, find myself a gallery, actually. I, um, decided it was now or never.'

Light flared in her eyes. 'Fantastic!' she said warmly.

He smiled at her, gratified.

'Which gallery? Where?'

'Erm, considering a few options. What are *you* doing, anyway?' He was desperate to move the subject on from himself.

'Don't look!' She was trying to cover her work with her arms. She looked up at him with fearful eyes the exact colour of the grass.

'Why not?' Gently, curiously, he was pushing the arms away. Her skin felt as soft as water. He looked at the canvas before him. Her work was breathtaking. Full of light and warmth.

'Don't say it,' groaned Siobhan. She had put her head in her hands and was rocking to and fro. 'You hate it.'

'No . . . no. This is . . . great.'

'I thought you hated modern art,' she accused.

'Yes, but this is . . . different.' He searched for more words. 'Simple. Colourful.'

She looked up. Her eyes were huge and frightened. 'But it's . . . *modern*. Contemporary. Sort of.'

He nodded, eager to reassure. 'Yes. Yes it is. Sort of.'

Siobhan's painting was not finished, but he could see where it was going. It was abstract, in harmonious colours meant to look abrupt and spontaneous shapes that were, in fact, very carefully arranged. It was airy, glowing, beautiful. He knew instantly, though without quite knowing how, that it was the view from the hill.

'There's the church,' he said, his finger hovering above a patch of grey in the midst of greens and pinks.

'Yes, yes! You could tell?' Her face was a confused picture of excitement and anxiety.

He nodded.

Was it her or was it the picture? Whatever it was, he felt a new sense of well-being, a freshness, as if he had slept well and not touched alcohol for the past year at least.

He narrowed his eyes at the work. It was assured and confident; one could imagine nothing else in place of any of the individual colours and shapes. And yet for all its perfection of composition, it was not flat. It had an experimental boldness to it.

'It's wonderful, Siobhan,' he said sincerely. 'You're very talented.'

'Thank you.' She gave him a bright, uneasy smile. 'Your turn now.'

'My turn?'

'Your portfolio.' She gestured to where the battered rectangular object lay askew on the grass; he had put it there while he inspected her painting.

'Oh yes. That.' He felt immediately uncomfortable. Among the pictures he had blearily selected that morning was a certain watercolour, recently completed from memory, of a beautiful woman with dark hair and serene green eyes.

'Er, actually, I'd better be going . . .'

It was too late. She had untied the black cotton strings which held the two flaps together. She flipped one of the battered maroon cardboard sides over and started, with infinite gentleness, to remove the work within, gazing reverently at the paintings, the sketches, the finished drawings before placing them down on the inside of the flap. He was anxious, but the way her long, beautiful fingers stroked the paper made his heart race.

'These are wonderful,' she said, meeting his nervous gaze with her own steady green one.

Horror seized him as he watched the fingers now pull out the work he least wanted her to see. 'No . . .' he started to say, but it was too late. She had turned the watercolour over and was gazing into her own face.

In an agony of embarrassment he stood there, not knowing whether the burning he felt was his own shame or the heat of the increasingly strong sun.

She turned her face towards him. The eyes that now searched his were red and wet, and her mouth trembled with the clear effort not to cry.

'Is it *that* bad?' Dan asked, awkwardly jovial to cover his panic.

'Oh, it's not the picture.' Siobhan sniffed. 'That's . . . that's *beautiful*.'

'What, then?' Dan asked, puzzled.

She shook her head agitatedly; the dark glossy locks shot light in all directions. 'I can't . . . it's so boring . .' Yet there was an appeal in her eyes; she wanted, he sensed, to unburden herself.

'Not boring at all,' he assured her early. 'I mean,' he added shyly, 'you can tell me about it. If you like. Of course,' he went on hurriedly, reddening, as she continued to look at him, 'it's none of my business or anything. But . . . you know . . . if you feel you can tell me . . .'

He was making a mess of this, he felt. Gabbling stupidly. What must she think?

'Have you got time?' Siobhan asked, her voice low.

'Yes.'

'But you said you were going to London . . .'

'London,' Dan said grandly, tying up his portfolio, taking off his jacket and spreading it out beside him for her to sit on the grass, 'can wait.'

After a moment or two's hesitation, Siobhan walked over, bent her slender legs under her and sat down beside him. A faint grassy scent, very fresh, swirled into his nostrils.

'Now what's the matter?' he asked, trying to sound brisk. 'You're not worried about your paintings, I hope. Because I can tell you now, they're exceptional . . .'

He stopped. Siobhan's hair was now hanging over her hands; her face, meanwhile, was buried in them. Her slender shoulders were shaking beneath their white shirt. Dan stared helplessly; another bout of weeping was the last thing he'd intended to unleash. Hopefully she would recover herself in a minute. He looked uncomfortably away at the sunny landscape, then returned his gaze to the still-sobbing Siobhan.

He extended an arm gingerly towards her, then, terrified at his presumption, hurriedly withdrew it. After a few seconds he tried again, and this time his moving limb must have caught her attention, because suddenly, and he was not quite sure how, her face was very close to his.

There was a green sparkle of eye, a flutter of lashes, a soft pink gasp, and then there she was, in his arms. His heart felt as if it would stop. Or else race until the beats became indistinguishable, one long, uninterrupted current of excited life. He could smell sun and perfume in her hair. While he held her as carefully as a piece of eggshell-thin porcelain, he could still feel her heat, the softness of her breasts against him . . .

He swallowed. He could not remember the last time he had held a woman like this. Recently, it had been the women doing the holding. Gripping, in Birgit's case. But the feeling welling within him now was a mixture of wonder and desire. He laid his cheek against her warm shining hair and closed his eyes.

Siobhan pulled herself away, but only slightly. Anxiously he tipped her red-rimmed gaze upwards.

'What is it, Siobhan?'

She shook her head and looked away. 'My husband,' she said, blinking rather a lot. 'I think he's having an affair.'

'An affair?' Dan gasped. The jolt of surprise could not have been greater if he had been plugged straight into the National Grid. An *affair*? Was Ciaran O'Sullivan insane?

He listened, speechless, to Siobhan adding sadly that her husband was no longer interested in her. That he felt he deserved more: namely another crack at international celebrity, and a bigger slice of it this time. He was more interested in that than in his marriage.

Dan held her close, rocking her slightly as one might a baby. It was so bloody unfair. Why did the wrong people always get the breaks? Ciaran had fame, wealth, the devotion of a beautiful, talented woman. How could he not appreciate his luck? What could Siobhan see in such a dolt?

Yet her delicate face, as she spoke, was utterly dejected, her eyes downcast. 'I don't know what I'd do if I found out . . . you know . . . he'd been . . .' she said wearily.

Dan was about to reply, but it came out as a splutter. The splutter became a choke and suddenly Siobhan was no longer sighing languorously in his arms but banging him forcibly on the back.

'Thanks,' he said as his proper respiratory functions resumed, aware that his own eyes were now as red and streaming as hers.

'I was just trying to say,' he added, 'that I can't believe it.' Siobhan looked more animated now, he saw. Her successful intervention during his difficulty seemed to have restored in her some spirit.

A flop of black hair now chose this moment to slide down over Dan's glasses and obscure his vision. As he tossed the flop back, perhaps more violently than was necessary, his glasses flew completely off.

'About your husband,' he went valiantly on as he felt for his spectacles in the grass. 'I can't believe that anyone lucky enough to be married to you could possibly think of even looking at anyone else.' The fact that he could not really see who he was delivering this outburst to made it easier, somehow.

'You think my husband is lucky?' Siobhan asked softly.

'Lucky?' exclaimed Dan incredulously. 'He's more than lucky. He's blessed. Of all the men in the whole world . . .'

'You're sweet. You're so kind.' She looked at him with something like longing in her eyes.

'I'm not being *kind*,' Dan cried. Instinctively, encouraged by that glance, and before inhibition or any other check could stop him, he had reached for her again and pulled her close. His mouth was on hers, at first softly, experimentally, then, as he felt her warm lips part, more assuredly, more deeply. A sudden certainty that she wanted this, had been willing him to do it, rose within him. And she was kissing him back. It was a miracle. He was dreaming it. A dream he never wanted to end.

She was pulling him down towards her now; he had rolled off his jacket completely. He did not feel the green grass juice soaking through his pale trousers. That his glasses had disappeared was immaterial. The entire world had shrunk, or perhaps infinitely expanded. It contained now only Siobhan's kiss, her slender body beneath his and her shining hair spread about them on the sunny morning grass.

Chapter 53

Zeb had not waited around at the party to witness the fallout once Herman Klumpp got upstairs. He was not interested in what happened to Fuchsia now. That part of his life, his career, was over.

His instinct was to drive due north, as far away as possible from London and the metropolitan art world. Something rather more sensible than instinct, however, told him he was far too drunk, would certainly die in a car crash and should wait until the morning. It wasn't so much that he wanted to survive himself, Zeb decided, but it seemed unfair to kill anyone else.

Feeling the need to purge himself, to get everything out of his system, he had drunk a lot of water. Pints and pints. Perhaps this was one reason why sleep, among the black linen sheets in the bare-walled bedroom of his now-unfashionable riverside loft, had been fitful. In spite of the water, closing his eyes plunged him into a whirling pit of nausea. He had spent much of the night wide awake, musing on the wrong direction he had taken – in art, in life, in every possible respect – and the number of years he had spent taking it.

Why exactly had he begun to spray things gold? Or to get roomfuls of fashionable Japanese people to fling paint-soaked sponges at canvases? So unaccustomed was he to the habit of self-examination that it was at first hard to remember.

Slowly, between the whirl and the nausea, it came. He was a child of six. There had been a party. The boy whose party it was had lived in a big house – much bigger than Zeb's – and the presents he had received had been numerous and expensive. Placing his own gift on the pile – a gift that by his standards had been exciting and generous – Zeb had felt ashamed. His clothes, he had realised, were not as smart as those of the other children.

Zeb, in the riverside apartment, was suddenly whirled back in time to his thirty-four-years-ago self, sitting out the party, humiliated, longing for his mother to come and rescue him. Afterwards he had vowed that he would never feel like that again. He would set his sights on being rich, famous, successful.

It was fourteen years later. He was taking a painting and drawing degree at art college. A new tutor flounced into the studio where Zeb was working and told him that representational art was irrelevant. Over. Dead. Concept was all. Why bother trying to capture likenesses when you could just drip wax on glass?

Why bother indeed? Zeb groaned and rubbed his eyes. Then the circus had begun. The parties, the magazine features, the money, the parties, the magazine features . . .

Then the rocket blast, the Cape Canaveral moment, when his career went into orbit; the moment when Fuchsia swept into his studio and bought up everything – even the mug he drank his tea from and the paint-spattered CD player that had supplied the musical background he worked to. This had been, for the most part, booming stadium rock; he listened to only the most successful bands. Since he had, as he saw it, been in the business of painting money, he had decided that he should listen to money too. It would be an inspiration.

But now all that had ended. And strangely enough, for all he had feared this moment he always knew was coming, Zeb felt no terror or regret. He knew what Fuchsia would do next, but felt no fear about that either. What he actually felt was relief.

Dawn had come. Zeb got up, feeling a little better. Lighter, somehow.

He stood for a while beneath the great silver plate of his

oversized power-shower head, and after that felt better still. He had dressed – rootling, head thumping, in his wardrobe for anything that was not black and not skin-tight. Only a maroon velour tracksuit, never before worn, fitted the bill; he revelled in the wonderful comfort of an elasticated waistband after so many years of restricting black denim.

His days of unlaced high-top black trainers were, he decided, over. Rootling further in the apartment's capacious closets, he found, still in their original packet, a pair of simple black flip-flops. Walking across the apartment, toes firmly anchored in rubber, he was struck at the ease with which he now moved.

Only his hair, hot, itchy and falling over his face as usual, remained a problem. Its silky length had been tended for years by the most expensive stylists in town, but not one of them had ever succeeded in making it comfortable. He vowed to get it cut at the first opportunity.

Zeb found that he longed above all else for a bacon sandwich, an indulgence he had routinely denied himself on account of his previously restrictive waistband. But now the world was his oyster, not to mention his fish and chips, his hamburger, his hot dog.

The apartment fridge, however, was empty. The neighbouring cupboards, meanwhile, contained only depressing items such as miso soup – low in calories, low in excitement, Zeb felt.

Where could he get the warm, savoury comestible of his dreams? Not downstairs, that was for sure. While modish delis and restaurants abounded in the apartment block's immediate vicinity, Zeb suspected that the type of honest-to-goodness greasy-spoon caff, producing the exact sought-after humble-yet-majestic soft-white-bread-sizzling-pink-bacon-and-mushy-fried-tomato combination he craved, would be some distance away.

So he would drive. He would seek this holy grail and he would find it. His mouth was watering at the thought of the bacon especially; that incomparable smell, the rose-pink meat seared here and there with brown, the crisp, crimped edges. He felt, rather like Richard III and his horse, that he would give his kingdom – of money, fame and especially artworks – for the perfect bacon sandwich.

In a rage of lust stronger than anything he had ever felt before – for Fuchsia, certainly; for money, even – Zeb slammed the flat door and rode, jiggling impatiently, the transparent-sided lift into the depths of the apartment block car park. The piped music dinned in his hungry ears as he threw himself into his Lotus and screeched off.

As he snaked through the east London back streets, he had anticipated, without much pleasure, that a car like his would cause a considerable stir outside an unsuspecting and unpretentious café. Drawing up alongside the street-facing window of Ken's Kaff, he found himself, for the first time, wishing he drove a less ostentatious vehicle.

He need not have worried, however. Within minutes of getting inside, he gathered from the proprietor that performance cars were by no means unknown in the area, indeed, outside the Kaff, thanks to the many wealthy artists, members' club owners, property developers, fashion and film people whose personal and professional stamping ground this was.

As his bacon was frying, Zeb learned that Ken's Kaff itself had made at least four film appearances and was currently auditioning for a television series. And that Ken, despite being balding, diminutive, middle-aged and plump, was taking acting lessons and had worked as an authenticity consultant on the few productions that had not featured his establishment in the flesh. Zeb did not ask what an authenticity consultant was. He could imagine all too well.

''Ere,' Ken said, looking at Zeb closely as he handed him his change. 'You're that Zeb Spaw bloke, aintcha? The artist wot got twenty million for them false legs?'

The customers sitting at the tables looked up from their plates. The place was so silent you could have heard a fried egg drop.

Zeb shrugged his shoulders. 'Yes.' He looked round, his chin raised defensively. Let them make of that what they would. Let him who was without sin cast the first sausage. And actually, he would not blame them if they did.

But there was no censure in their eyes, only admiration. They weren't ordinary working men, Zeb noted now; they were young and trendily dressed, with spiked or otherwise fashionable hair. Very probably they worked in fashion or film themselves, or even art.

'Good on yer, mate,' Ken said, banging down his grill pan for emphasis. 'Good call that.'

Zeb did not respond. It had seemed like a good call at the time, certainly. But now he looked back, what it had actually been was the beginning of the end.

'Gonna be turned into a work of art meself, I am,' Ken was saying proudly.

Zeb, on his way to the door, turned. 'A work of art?'

'That's right,' Ken confirmed, beaming cheerfully. 'You ever 'eard of Sharon Aura?'

Zeb, suppressing a groan, nodded.

'Used to 'ave a studio round 'ere, she did. Before she made it big. But she ain't forgotten 'er roots, she ain't.'

I bet, Zeb thought. He said nothing, however. He knew exactly what was coming.

'She's gonna enter my bacon sarnie for the Turner Prize,' Ken announced triumphantly. 'Just it, on its own, in one of them see-through boxes. How about that, then?'

Zeb raised his fine black eyebrows. 'Great.'

What else was there to say? When he was Sharon Aura's exact equivalent, he would have done the same thing – except, of course, that he would have sprayed the sandwich gold. In five years' time, no doubt, Sharon would be in the position he was in, dumped by Fuchsia, her career in smoking ruins. He should not envy her; nor did he, Zeb thought. Sharon should gather her rosebuds – and her bacon sarnies – while she may. And good luck to her.

The image of Sharon's peroxide head between Fuchsia's fish-egg-smeared inner thighs rushed suddenly back to him, followed by a swell of unexpected sympathy. At least, Zeb thought, he had never had to do that. Cunnilingus was one thing, but caviar quite another. He had never been able to stand the stuff.

Nonetheless, as he walked out with the bacon sandwich in its greaseproof paper wrapping, he felt a surge of dislike. Not for the sandwich itself, which seemed admirable in all respects, but for the artistic culture it would shortly represent. A culture so shallow it was almost profound. A celebrity-obsessed, money-driven artistic culture to which he had not only contributed, but which he had actually helped form.

Slamming himself back into the Lotus, he felt ill with self-disgust. What had he done, when plebeian foodstuffs entered fine art prizes and every East End sandwich bar owner thought themselves a cross between Robert de Niro and Michelangelo? What had happened was a crime against reason, against society and, of course, against art. He, Zeb Spaw, was a criminal.

And as such, he wanted to escape the scene of the crime. He had no idea where. Just somewhere.

Up through north London. By the time he reached the bottom of the M1, the tightness in his gut had relaxed. He had not, after all, touched the sandwich, but he was feeling better already. Things in his head were starting to clear. Plans were starting to form.

After an hour or so, he pulled in at a service station. He wanted a hamburger and some coffee and to make a phone call. Passing Hemel Hempstead, he had made a tremendous decision. He would call the OneSquared Gallery and announce that he was withdrawing his work.

Fuchsia's next move would, he knew, be to dump him. Not only as a lover – she'd effectively done that already. But in the commercially more direct sense of dumping her collection of his work on the market. As this vengeful act would send his value plummeting and effectively ruin his career, he wanted to jump before he was pushed.

Chapter 54

Alice rushed breathlessly up Gold Street, a plastic bag in each hand. One contained the borrowed attire of the night before and the other some Chinese ready-meals.

The twenty-four-hour supermarket culture had its good points, especially when one had a cutting-edge piece of conceptual art to restore to its former glory.

Elbowing her way through the morning commuters musing over lunchtime chicken wraps and sushi, Alice had stormed the store's Oriental section and, after pawing the ground in the checkout queue like an impatient horse, finally fled with her prize. Never had the tube journey seemed so slow. Her one chance of success, of non-detection, was to get to the gallery before Angelica did, fill the empty tubs with food and hope for the best. There seemed little risk of Evelyn beating her to it – he had looked distinctly drunk as she had tottered past him out of the party. His wings were bent and his wand had developed a noticeable droop.

Angelica was not there, thankfully. OneSquared was dark – or as dark as an entirely white-painted interior whose main exhibit was a gold bed could be. Fumbling with the keys, stabbing at the security code pad, Alice let herself in. Over at her white desk in the corner, the phone was shrilling.

It was Angelica. Her line seemed very crackly and her voice muffled.

'Hello,' Alice sang, trying to sound completely normal.

Angelica was speaking agitatedly, but not a word could be understood. She sounded, Alice thought, as if she were calling from under a duvet.

'What did you say?' Alice shouted.

'I won't be in for a few days,' came Angelica's faint voice. There was a delay before she spoke, in which Alice could hear the echo of her own voice. It sounded as if Angelica was thousands of miles away, which of course was impossible.

What mattered was the fact that she was not coming in. Alice felt almost weak with relief. 'When will you be back?' She tried to sound regretful.

'Well it all depends on the fucking Master . . . I mean, I'm not sure yet.' Even on the bad line, Angelica sounded angry. 'Anyway, you're in charge,' Alice heard next. 'Or you're *responsible*, I should say,' Angelica corrected herself.

Her next words Alice could not quite make out, but they sounded to be something about a party. The Gold Street party, Alice guessed. And OneSquared's contribution to it. What had Portia said? Debauched and something. And gold hotpants.

'It's all arranged,' came the faint voice. 'Zeb's in the window, Diamond Snail's doing the catering, the theme's Debauched, Dirty and Decadent.'

'When is it?' Alice shouted.

'Sorry?' she yelled, moments later. It was the bad line, obviously, but what Angelica had just said sounded like . . . next week.

'I did say next week,' came the faint squeak from the other end.

'But . . .' A whole huge party? All by *herself*? In a mere few days' time?

The line flickered briefly into audibility at this point. 'Look, all you've got to do is welcome the fucking guests,' Angelica snapped, her voice suddenly terrifyingly loud in Alice's ear. 'Diamond Snail are providing the waitresses, all that stuff. So it's easy. Wear neon fishnets. Just don't do anything stupid, OK?'

The connection went altogether at this point and Alice, having taken a deep, stiffening breath, went into the kitchen. She tried to push the party to the back of her mind. There was enough to worry about at the moment. Angelica might well change her mind and come back. During her limited exposure to her new boss, Alice had not formed the view that she was an especially reliable or stable person.

Transferring the supermarket Chinese to the cartons was a messy business. At last she pressed the stained white cardboard lids down and, as there had been no instructions from Angelica or Evelyn as to how to display them, transferred the pile of boxes back into the fridge.

The phone was ringing again as she returned to the gallery. Alice grabbed it. Angelica again, no doubt.

'It's Zeb.'

Alice was struck by how normal he sounded.

She had glimpsed Zeb at the party last night and he had looked terrifying – brooding and unapproachable. She had not dared go near him. Better to wait until they were formally introduced by Angelica.

'Hi, Zeb,' she said brightly. 'Enjoy the party last night?'

He made a noise like a savage snort. '*Enjoy* it?'

'Well, erm, weren't there lots of people you knew there?' Alice hazarded.

'Oh *yes*,' Zeb said with savage irony. 'Anyone who was bloody anyone was there. The whole mendacious, exploitative, greedy, snobbish, shit-filled circus of the contemporary art world.'

Alice's mouth dropped open. This was, of course, more or less her own view, but Zeb Spaw, contemporary artist supreme, was the last person she had expected to share it.

She searched for something to say, but then Zeb spoke and saved her the trouble.

'I'm not calling about the party anyway,' he growled. 'I'm calling about my bed.'

'Ah,' said Alice nervously. She had gathered from Angelica that the unsold status of *The Right Hand of the Father II* was a source of some friction between the gallery and its most prestigious artist. 'Well there has been some interest,' she hedged, 'but no concrete offers, as such . . .'

Her fingers were crossed behind her back. It was starting to appear, taking the Chinese food into account as well, that at least part of the business of running a contemporary art gallery involved routinely lying to the artists. This had never been the case at Palladio, where the artists were all dead anyway. But even if they hadn't been, Alice could not imagine Adam telling them anything but the truth.

'Good,' said Zeb. 'I'm sending a van for it,' Zeb said.

'You're taking it away?'

'Yes. And I'm taking myself away too. I'm leaving OneSquared.'

'Leaving?' Alice repeated, incredulous.

'Leaving.'

Was he going somewhere else? But he couldn't. The party. He was the gallery's top artist. Angelica would go spare. She would be sacked.

'Please,' she begged, her mouth dry with nerves. 'We've all been trying our best with the bed.'

'It won't work,' Zeb said. His voice was not angry, just quiet and categorical.

'But it will, it *will* . . .' Spurred on by the prospect of Angelica's rage, Alice set about convincing him.

'Look, if you give OneSquared another chance . . .' she pleaded.

'It won't work,' Zeb said patiently.

'Just let us *try*. We'll—'

'It won't work,' he said forcibly over her, 'because Fuchsia Klumpp is about to dump all my work on the market. My selling price will go down to about five quid per piece. If you're lucky.' There was, in his voice, none of the rage one might have expected. He spoke with a certain quiet relish, even.

His mobile cut off then. As she put the telephone down, Alice felt sick.

Angelica had left her with no instructions in the event of such a catastrophe; which of the gallery's artists, for instance, would be the obvious replacement for Zeb? Who was heir apparent? The decision was bound to be political; even in only a very few days she had picked up that much.

She groaned and sank on to the stool behind the front desk. Why had she chosen a career in art? Why hadn't she gone into banking? Property? Party planning, even? At least with the latter she would have known how to cope with one of the many problems she currently faced. As it was, she was absolutely clueless. Was the maker of the penises more important than the psycho-sexual Cinderella, or even the Chinese in the fridge? Where did the hairy pebble come into it?

And what on earth was she going to tell Angelica?

Chapter 55

Zeb, ending the call with Alice, felt, by contrast, almost joyous. Rarely, in fact, had he felt so positive after talking to his gallery. Ironic, given that he had called them to announce a withdrawal of his work before any of it could be sold. It had, in professional terms, been an admission of complete failure.

Even so, he felt lighter and happier than after any of the many conversations he had had over the years with galleries that had sold his work for record-breaking prices. Feelings of competition and paranoia had always diluted any pleasure. Had there been any real pleasure anyway? Only now, he felt, was he starting to realise how little joy the fabulous sums realised for his work had brought him. It was possible that they had even made him miserable.

There was no time to dwell on the negatives, however. He was on a journey. And before he could continue it, he had to make two more phone calls. The first, to GIT, Global International Talent.

'Dirk?'

'Hey! Zeb! How's it hanging?'

'If you're referring to my work,' Zeb said levelly, 'there's not much of it hanging anywhere. Not any more.'

'What are you saying? I'm not sure I'm hearing you right.'

Zeb decided not to beat about the bush. 'Fuchsia Klumpp's about to dump all the stuff she has of mine on the market. I'll be finished as an artist. I'm just giving you the heads-up,' he said, with a faintly sardonic emphasis on the last two words. His manager was very fond of such jargon.

Dirk seemed lost for words. Zeb decided to help him out. 'So I won't need you any more,' he said gently.

'So I guess you're not interested in designing an album cover for Cheryl Cole? Her management company called and—'

'Tell them to try Sharon Aura,' Zeb said wearily, and clicked Dirk into the ether.

Immediately he pressed another number on his speed-dial.

'Josh?'

'Hello, Mr Spaw.' His Director of Production sounded nervous. It flashed through Zeb's mind that Josh probably regarded him in the same way Bob Cratchit had regarded Ebenezer Scrooge. Before his transformation. Certainly he had never paid him particularly well. Did Josh have a crippled son, though? Zeb had no idea; it occurred to him now that he knew nothing about Josh's personal circumstances. He had never been interested enough to ask.

'I want you . . .' Zeb barked, in his usual authoritarian way, before clearing his throat suddenly and adding, with unusual gentleness, 'to stop doing the *Sponge* paintings, please, Josh.'

There was silence from Josh's end.

'Are you there, Josh?' Zeb asked, concerned.

Josh was there. He was wondering whether he had heard properly. Could Zeb Spaw – Zeb Spaw – really have said . . . *please*? Never, in all the time he had known his demanding, irascible boss, had Josh ever known him use the magic word.

'Er, stop them, right. OK,' Josh agreed readily. Zeb noticed that he asked no questions, and wondered why, before guessing, with a stab of guilt, that Josh, ground down by years of bullying, probably did not dare.

'Yeah, stop. It's all . . .' *A load of crap*, Zeb was going to say, before remembering that it was a project on which Josh and his team had spent a good deal of time. Such a description, however true, would be hurtful. 'On hold,' he finished awkwardly.

It felt odd, having to consider other people's feelings. But not unpleasant. Not unpleasant at all.

In the car park of the service station, Zeb approached his red Lotus, noticing, as he had in the apartment car park, what a truly preposterous car it was. As he edged out of the service station, he wished with all his heart that he was driving something less flaunting and ostentatious. The glances passing drivers cast at it – some sneeringly envious, some even pitying – embarrassed him. He could not now imagine what pleasure he had ever gained from the car. The sort of savage triumph he had felt in the past when driving it, that sense of being so much richer and more successful than everyone else, was now gone.

At the exit, Zeb wondered vaguely where he was going. He had no real idea. Should he come off the motorway at the next opportunity and return to London? The thought filled him with horror. London, for all it had been the theatre of his great success, seemed now to represent everything he disliked most about his life.

The alternative, then, was to keep driving north. Zeb found that he did not mind this; on the contrary. North wasn't somewhere he knew well, or even at all. But that was all to the good. Exploring places which were new to him, where he was a stranger, felt suddenly important.

Beyond this, however, he did not want to think about anything. To prevent his head filling with unwelcome thoughts, he stretched out and activated the car's music system. As pounding rock filled the air around him, he winced at the assault on his eardrums. It sounded so violent, so harsh. He wondered that it could have been the soundtrack in his studio all these years.

Changing the CD in the fast lane of the motorway was obviously not a good idea. Nor, for that matter, was changing it in the slow lane, where Zeb had chosen to drive. If people in the middle lane wanted to come alongside him, staring and jeering at the sight of a performance car barely managing to hit sixty miles an hour, well that was their business. Zeb did not care. He had, he decided, been in the fast lane of life for long enough. Now it was time to go slow.

Flicking the radio button with his forefinger, he waited for the digital search facility to alight on something amenable to his mood. The swirl of violins that came out of the station first chosen sent a bolt of horror through him – he had never liked classical music. He knew nothing about it. But as the piece continued, soothing, gentle, melodic, he found himself settling into it, and a sense of peace stealing round him. When it ended, he found himself making a mental note of the title and the composer. Classical music probably wouldn't be his cup of tea all the time. But he could certainly imagine listening to it every now and then.

Otherwise, he thought about little, avoiding the yawning question of the future by pondering the immediate. He would, he had decided, buy up all he could of the work that Fuchsia put on the market. It wasn't that he particularly wanted it, but he didn't want anyone else to have it either, at least not in the humiliating circumstances in which they would acquire it.

What would he do with it then, though? He was hardly going to exhibit it, even given the unlikely possibility, in the future, of his time coming again and his art becoming newly fashionable. The pieces he had done were no longer pieces of art to him anyway. Perhaps they never had been. Perhaps they had never been anything more than counters in Fuchsia's power games, just as he had been himself. As she had been in his, if he were honest. Rather to his surprise, he found that he no longer felt any rancour towards her. They had served each other's purpose. In a way, it had been a perfectly fair exchange.

But none of this made any of his work art. All it made was money.

Perhaps he could stick the stuff in various rooms in the Suffolk house. That, at last, would give Blackwood some sort of purpose. Some use.

After another hour or so on the grey stretch of motorway,

driving to the calming strains of Radio 3, Zeb spotted signs for Nottingham.

Nottingham. The name seemed to answer something within him. He had never been there, which was a definite plus point in the city's favour. Another was that it was a place strongly associated with Robin Hood, who had been one of his favourite heroes as a child. Zeb had thrilled to his adventures against Guy of Gisborne and that favourite medieval bogeyman the Sheriff of Nottingham.

Robin and his Merry Men had robbed from the rich and given to the poor; Zeb wondered how he compared to this himself. He had robbed from the rich, certainly; perhaps, in a way, they had robbed from him too. But he had never given anything to the poor. Nor did he know any Merry Men; he certainly wasn't one himself.

He drove into Nottingham. He was expecting something cutesy and half-timbered, but it turned out to be low, run-down suburbs – boarded-up pubs, disused shops – leading to a town centre full of boxy concrete buildings, as well as an Eye.

The great white metal wheel of the Nottingham Eye, dangling with smoked-plastic cabins, loomed disproportionately massive, like some cycle wheel of the gods, above what otherwise seemed to be a handsome main square bordered by elegant Victorian buildings. Zeb wondered why cities felt bound to have Eyes at all; presumably the people charged with attracting tourists to a borough thought they were a good thing, but they seemed to him to confer an ugly and depressing sameness on noble and interesting historical centres.

He wondered what Robin Hood would have made of the Eye; presumably the famous outlaw would have had other matters on his mind than aesthetics. Yet Zeb felt that lumbering the city skyline with such a monstrosity was robbing from the people all the same. It impoverished their view and degraded their surroundings.

He looked about him for traces of Robin Hood. His heart leapt when he spotted brown heritage signs to the castle. He walked quickly through the shopping centre, across a vast and noisy ring road and then up between some elegant, if neglected, seventeenth-century townhouses to where a great solid wall, unmistakably medieval, spread down the hill. To the right, a towered, portcullised gatehouse with a coat of arms above the arched entrance announced that he had indeed found the place he sought.

Zeb crossed another busy road eagerly, and strode up the winding path between the flower beds to the great gate. Here, entering the ticket kiosk, its interior colourful with the heraldic devices of the past, he discovered that the castle was actually Nottingham's art gallery.

For a moment his heart sank. Looking at pictures and sculptures – other people's pictures and sculptures, moreover – was the very last thing he felt like doing at the moment. On the other hand, he could really use a sandwich and a hot cuppa, and the gallery was sure to have a café. He didn't need to look at any of the art; on the contrary.

He bought his ticket and entered the castle bailey. According to the leaflet he was given with his ticket, the gallery and café were in the mansion rising before him, on the site of the original keep. The strong, cold gusts that blasted across the hill as Zeb walked doggedly up the pathway almost knocked him clean over. His toes froze in his flip-flops and his hair whipped painfully round his face, lashing him in the eyes and across the lips. Damn the stuff. He would get it cut off; like his silly trainers and skin-tight jeans, it was part of his old life. And like them, it was nothing but uncomfortable and inconvenient.

Breathless at the top with the wind and the effort, he lingered for a minute or two at the terrace edge, which offered a stupendous view of the valley below. Not of the city centre or the Eye, thank goodness, but of the older, smaller industrial buildings that crowded about the river, and then beyond to the horizon. Zeb stared at it, noting the unexpectedly ethereal effect of the winding waterway, and the old chimneys making delicate strokes upward into the air. It would make a good picture, he thought.

Already he felt his resolve not to look at any of the art in the gallery weakening. He opened the heavy entrance doors and dashed up the wide staircase, looking for signs to the café. He felt mildly panicked to find himself in a well-lit white-walled room containing various low-key, modern-ish bits and pieces, although none of his, thank God. But this was enough. No more art. Where was the blasted caff?

That way? He pushed through a pair of large glass doors with brass handles and found himself standing in a huge, long, light gallery, with a thickly varnished floor which creaked as he moved. He wanted to push himself forward, on to the end and out; he tried to pull his eyes away from the walls and back to the glossy floor. But it was too late.

Slowly, holding his breath, Zeb walked to the picture that had caught his attention. It was an industrial landscape, yet idealised and made beautiful, rendered in pastel pinks, blues and greys, with a great deal of white. The chimneys, rising delicately upwards, were painted like the columns of Greek temples, and the well-spaced buildings were ranged gracefully about a hill which rose like Mount Olympus into a pale, clear sky. The suggestion was that this was the realm of gods and goddesses, not down-trodden factory hands. It reminded Zeb of the view outside, of the similar vision that had momentarily sparked in his own mind. Who had shared this vision, had beaten him to it, in fact? He bent to read the name. L.S. Lowry. He grinned. Well, that was good company to be in.

Another painting across the room now beckoned to him. A sunny garden giving on to a field. Zeb gazed at it, lost in the scented flower beds, imagining lying on the bright, warm lawn at the edge of the sparkling pond. He wondered why it had never occurred to him to paint his own lovely gardens at Blackwood. What a missed opportunity. Stanley Spencer, whose work this was, had obviously not hesitated.

Nearby was a beautiful painting of purple-red peonies. Zeb

stared at it, drinking in the deep, seductive colour, the glossy layered petals, the near-detectable scent. He peered at the label. Stanley Spencer again. This was no mean collection.

He straightened up and inhaled deeply. He felt alive and awake, in a way he had not for some time. Excited, even.

A vast Victorian painting in a great flat, wide gold frame now caught his eye. He hurried across the shining floor in his flip-flops. It was a mountain landscape by John Brett, painted from above. As if, Zeb thought, the artist had balanced with his palette on the wing of an aeroplane passing over, and for several solid months, to judge from the painstaking, near-photographic detail. But of course planes were decades off; Brett had obviously endured the elements to achieve the dramatic effect he sought. Crannies, crevasses, clouds, plunging chasms, trees thrusting out of cliffside cracks at right angles . . .

Zeb felt a wave of self-disgust. He knew little about John Brett, but it seemed likely he had put more vision and honest effort into one day painting this picture than Zeb himself had in the whole of his career.

The painting was glazed, and such was the position of the striplights in the gallery that their reflection made the work difficult to see properly. Zeb ducked and moved his head, trying to see more of the detail.

'Excuse me.'

The voice behind him was soft and unobtrusive. Zeb whirled suspiciously round to find himself looking at the room guard, an old man of hesitant, gentle appearance.

Zeb met his eye defensively. Had he been recognised? Was it his hair? He *would* get the damn stuff cut off, and at the first opportunity.

The old man's expression, however, was calm and kind. There was no suggestion of excitement, Zeb realised, at the proximity of contemporary art's most terrible *enfant terrible*. Rather, in his regulation dark blue guard's uniform, the old man had an air more of patient concern.

'If you stand just here, you can see it perfectly,' he said, tapping the shining floor with his shoe at a point some three feet from Zeb.

Zeb frowned. 'See what?'

'The Brett,' the old man replied politely. 'It can be hard. Because of the lights.'

Zeb stood in the place indicated. The guard was right. Free of the reflected glare of the overhead lights, it was as if the glass did not exist, and the mountain ranges, their snow, shadows, crevasses and boulders, could be seen in every last, exhilarating detail. Zeb took a deep breath, imagining the sharp chill in his lungs as he inhaled a great gulp of that sharp, cold, bright air.

After a few minutes, he turned to the guard. 'Thanks.'

The old man nodded. Zeb noted his hair: grey and comb-parted, possibly with Brylcreem, over his faintly yellow scalp.

'I've been in this gallery for thirty years,' the old man told him, his voice warm with pride. 'I've worked out where to stand to see the best of every painting.'

Zeb regarded him in awe. 'Thirty years,' he said. 'Don't you get bored?'

The old man's pale blue eyes registered surprise. 'Never. I still get surprises, every day. Look over here.'

Zeb followed his guide over the creaking floor to stand in front of a large wedding scene.

'Just look at that.' The old man pointed to a figure in the left-hand corner, a musician in striped tights, playing a lute. 'His shoe's so worn the sole's coming off. He wouldn't have wanted you to see it, especially at such a smart event. But the artist has noticed it. It's very personal. It gives it soul, I suppose.'

'Sole,' Zeb quipped instantly.

The old man grinned. 'Yes. I suppose so.' He shook his head wonderingly. 'You know, I'd seen this picture a thousand times, but I'd never noticed that shoe until yesterday. You never get tired of looking at great art. There's always something new to see.'

Chapter 56

Alice knew it was against the rules to lock the gallery. But she urgently required lunch, and if she stayed put, there was a strong risk that she might eat the second Chinese takeaway. Besides, Angelica was not coming back for a week. If she called, Alice could pretend she had been with a potential client. Although what she was to say if Angelica asked whether that client was interested in Zeb Spaw, she had not yet decided.

Zeb had not said what time his van was coming to pick up the bed. Alice hurried back from the sandwich shop, half expecting to see a large vehicle, hazards flashing, drawn up on the kerb. There was no van on the kerb, although there was, she saw, a woman.

The woman was standing in the sunshine and waving excitedly as she saw Alice approaching. It was Caroline.

Alice stopped still in alarm. She was still to get to the bottom of what was happening with Suki and Rafael. Her efforts to phone Suki – both landline and mobile – had met with answerphones, and Alice had concluded that she must have gone away somewhere to lick her wounds. David, when questioned, had not heard from her either. He seemed to resent her asking, which struck Alice as particularly unsympathetic. David might not be fond of Suki, but she was Alice's friend, and in trouble.

And Suki's trouble was all to do with this woman. Caroline. She was in the middle of it all. The femme fatale. The husband-stealer. The preening, self-satisfied spider at the centre of the web.

And she did indeed look very self-satisfied. Even from the distance of the other side of the sunny road, Caroline's face radiated feline contentedness. What the hell, Alice wondered, the anger rising within her, did *she* have to be so pleased about?

Alice strode across the road, clutching her tuna sandwich. 'What are you doing here?' she demanded.

Surprise flashed across Caroline's face. 'Researching my documentary, of course. I've been talking to galleries. Now I'm coming to talk to you. Saving the best till last.' She grinned, then, as Alice's face failed to relax, she added, evidently puzzled, 'Why? What's the matter?'

Alice had no intention of holding a conversation with this woman, this woman who had deceived her best friend. Walking quickly across the road, she whipped out the keys to OneSquared and tried to unlock the door.

'What's the matter?' Caroline moved quickly and grabbed Alice's arm.

She shook it off angrily. 'What the hell do you think you're doing?'

'Calm down, can't you?' Caroline's voice sounded, even to Alice, less guilty than exasperatedly bemused. Her eyes were dark with concern. 'Look, what's the matter? Why are you so cross with me? Has something gone wrong at OneSquared or something?'

This apparent reminder that despite everything, she actually had to be grateful to Caroline for getting her a job only increased Alice's annoyance. 'You know bloody well what's gone wrong,' she spat.

Caroline stared. She was a good actress, Alice had to acknowledge. But of course she was. That had been a command performance at the party as well; sailing about the place, chatting to Rafael and Suki as if nothing could be more natural.

Alice had by now managed to open the door. Caroline followed her in.

'No, I don't know what's gone wrong. I really don't. Tell me.'

Alice turned to face her, trembling with a sudden resolve. 'Suki told me,' she began, in a voice shaking with anger. 'Suki told me . . . told me,' she blurted, 'that you're having an affair with . . . with . . . Rafael.'

Having delivered her grenade, she folded her arms and waited.

Caroline's face was perfectly blank. 'I see,' she said, after a pause of some seconds.

Alice had not expected her to react so composedly. Obviously she was even more brazen than previously imagined.

Minutes passed. Caroline breathed in. Then she turned her eyes fully and unwaveringly on Alice. 'First of all, I am not having an affair with Rafa—'

'But Suki told me . . .' Alice interrupted hotly.

Caroline held a pale palm up. 'She was lying, I'm afraid.'

'*Lying?*' gasped Alice. 'Of course she wasn't.' *You're the one that's lying*, she was about to add, in furious defence of her friend. But something about Caroline's level gaze caused the words to fade on her lips. Besides, for Suki to be economical with the *actualité* was not entirely unknown. 'But . . . . but . . . why would she?' she muttered eventually. '*Why?*'

'A smokescreen?' Caroline suggested, almost wearily. 'To distract someone from the real scent? To stop them finding out what's really happening?'

Impatience filled Alice. 'Oh, come on, Caroline. Distract *who*? Stop who finding out *what*?'

Caroline regarded her silently for a few moments before saying, in a low voice, 'You.'

'Me? *Me?*'

'To stop you realising that she's sleeping with your boyfriend.'

For a moment, Alice experienced the stillness of absolute shock. Then the world began to spin giddily. She started to shiver and her teeth to chatter. 'That's not true,' she heard a voice quite unlike hers saying. 'That's not true,' it added hysterically. '*You're lying.*'

'I wish I was,' Caroline said quietly.

Alice stared out through the front window. Gold Street looked the same as usual, with the orderly gallery fronts stretching away in the sun. People were walking past. Everything looked perfectly normal.

She looked back to Caroline, frowning and shaking her head. 'Look, you've got the wrong end of the stick,' she said, trying to sound reasonable. 'David's . . . he's . . . been spending time with her because of *Albertine*. Albertine's been ill—'

'Yes. I was worried about that too,' Caroline interrupted. 'Until,' she added crisply, 'I spoke to Rafa and found out that she's been perfectly fine all along.'

Alice had been trying to suppress a rising feeling of panic. But at this, the lid blew off. The implication was too awful to be borne.

'Are you saying,' she began, 'that Suki *pretended* Albertine was ill? Just to . . . just to . . .' She found that she could not finish the sentence.

'Rafa had no idea that David had been at his house. He still doesn't,' Caroline said gently. 'I wasn't going to tell him. That's Suki's job.'

There was a horrible silence.

'But . . . but . . . Suki and David . . . they didn't like each other,' Alice whispered.

'Well, that obviously changed,' Caroline said shortly. 'But if you don't believe me,' she added, 'ask David. Or, if you really want to put the cat among the pigeons, Rafa.'

Alice felt her way to the stool, slumped on to it and flung her head into her arms on the desk. She wished Caroline would go. Then she could begin to try and make sense of it all. There had to be a logical explanation.

There were no retreating footsteps, however. Caroline had not moved.

'Look,' she said, sounding contrite. 'I'm *really* sorry about all this. I wish I hadn't been the one to tell you.'

Alice screwed up her eyes in the semi-darkness and said nothing. She heard Caroline sigh.

'OK. I'll go. But I *am* sorry, really. And if there's anything I can ever do – to help you, or whatever – let me know, OK? Here's my card.'

She tiptoed over to Alice, who had changed position slightly and had her forehead down on the edge of her desk, staring under it. Caroline placed the small piece of card at the extreme edge, as if feeding a dangerous beast. Alice, watching the floor, saw her skimpy red sandals retreating hurriedly across the beechwood.

'Goodbye, then,' Caroline said, from the door.

When she was certain she had gone, Alice raised her head. She felt dizzy. Caroline's words seemed to echo in the silent air, bounce from one white wall to another. But they could not be true. It was impossible. David didn't just dislike Suki, he *hated* her . . .

It was all a horrible misunderstanding. It had to be. Caroline was lying. David would never be unfaithful. And Suki was her friend; she would never betray her.

With trembling fingers, Alice texted David. *Call me. Urgent.* The sooner he called and denied everything, the better.

For a few moments Alice stared at the white walls of the gallery, conscious of nothing but the horrible buzz in her head and her longing for David to call and deny it all.

Then, with a great jump of her heart, she heard her mobile ringing, and picked it up with shaking hands. The number, thank God, was David's. She felt every hair in her ear, every muscle and bone, prime itself to hear his disbelief, his outrage, his horror.

'Oh *David*!' She was, Alice found, almost sobbing. 'That horrible Caroline – you remember, from Suki's party? Well, she's just been in, and you'll never guess what she said. That you and *Suki* . . .' She tried to inject a laugh here, anticipating how ridiculous he would say it was.

'Alice. Stop.'

Through her rushing ears, above her thundering heart, she recognised that the voice on the other end was quieter, less familiar than David's.

'David?'

Was it a wrong number? She checked it again. But no. Definitely David's.

'It's Rafael.'

'Rafa! But this . . . this . . .'

'Is David's mobile. Yes. He left it here. Last night.'

'Last night?'

'About nine o'clock,' Rafael said in measured tones.

Nine o'clock. Alice forced her reeling mind to do the calculations.

She would have still been at the Klumpps' at nine o'clock.

'That's when I came back. A bit earlier than Suki was expecting,' Rafael told her drily. 'That's how *I* found out.'

Alice's hand was in her mouth. She was chewing her nails and whimpering. She felt utterly sick.

'I'm afraid, Alice,' Rafael said, almost gently, 'that that horrible Caroline was telling the truth.'

Chapter 57

Dan had hardly dreamed it possible. And were it not for the green grass stains on his trousers, he would have doubted it had ever happened. He and Siobhan. Rolling round on the ground. Locked in a passionate embrace.

Until, that was, she had pulled away, sat back on her heels and looked at him with horror.

'Oh God,' she had said, into the heel of the hand pressed tightly to her mouth. 'I'm no better than he is.'

Dan, confused, had propped himself up on his elbow – more grass stains. 'No better? No better than who? What do you mean?' He had found his glasses now and put them on. Seeing everything in sharp focus again brought an unwelcome sense of returning reality, of waking from a dream.

She was on her feet now, buttoning her shirt, her hair tumbling over her face. 'No better than Ciaran. Worse, in fact. I've got no actual proof that he's seeing someone else, after all. But look at me!' Her voice was harsh with self-disgust. 'And you!' she added, flinging him an accusing green glance.

Dan stared at the grass, not knowing what to say. The tables had turned so suddenly and so completely he felt winded. One moment they had been kissing passionately; the next he was practically being blamed for leading her astray.

But how much of what had just happened had been his fault?

Yes, he had made the first move. But she had hardly pushed him away. Far from it; she had seemed to enjoy it. He recalled the encouraging expression in her eyes.

She was frowning as she packed up her painting things. He could see she was angry, which made his heart ache miserably. His head ached too; the hangover was returning with a vengeance.

'Will I see you again?' he called weakly, as she stalked off down the hillside, her hair billowing in the wind.

Siobhan did not turn, nor did she answer. After she'd gone, Dan sat for a while. Then he remembered that, what seemed like years ago, he had been intending to go to London to seek his artistic fortune.

In the train, Dan felt utterly wretched. His thoughts dwelt bitterly on how he had, in one moment of madness, one crazed impulse of lust, ruined everything. Siobhan would certainly never want to see him again after this, let alone come to his life classes. It was all ruined.

He fell asleep with his face against the train window, dreaming of her. He awoke with his cheek stuck to the glass and every part of him she had touched burning with a mysterious fire. More real to him by far than the people in the carriage were his memories of how her panting, parted lips looked up close, the faintly mint scent of her breath and her luminous skin, so smooth as to seem poreless. Her eyes – wide, green and wet.

Dan groaned as a feeling of utter, helpless yearning possessed him, followed by a feeling of utter, helpless foolishness. What had he been thinking of? He was only her art teacher, after all. And teachers getting involved with students never ended well.

As the train drew into the station, he reflected what a pointless exercise now lay before him. The original spur for the gallery visits had been the desire to impress Siobhan. But now she clearly never wanted to see him again, why bother? Why did he simply not turn round and get on the first train back?

*

Following Rafael's bombshell, Alice sat alone in OneSquared. She kept her mind as blank as the white wall in front of her. Her eyeballs were fixed, still, and staring hard, straight ahead. She did not move.

She would not believe that David was unfaithful. Still. Even though Caroline and Rafael had both insisted that he was. It was a mistake. Something had got twisted. Rafael had to be lying, or mad. Or spectacularly confused, somehow.

She contemplated calling David at the hospital, on the landline as Rafa had somehow got hold of his mobile. But was this a good idea? He would be irritated, it would be rushed, and besides, this of all things was something to be discussed face to face. She needed, Alice felt, to see the whites of his eyes

So she called the only other person she could.

Suki was incredulous. 'No! Oh, you poor darling. She told you *what?*'

Hesitantly, Alice repeated everything Caroline had said. To her immense relief, Suki exploded. '*Bitch.* I can't bloody believe it. Except that I can. It's exactly the cover story I'd expect. She's always been a fantasist,' she added wildly. 'And now she's trying to cover her not inconsiderable arse. You can see that, surely?'

'Yes,' Alice agreed, wanting very much to see it. Then she told Suki about Rafael's call.

'Well he would say that, wouldn't he?' Suki said bitterly. 'He's covering his own tracks as well. He and Caroline have cooked this whole thing up between them. Can you believe it?'

'No,' Alice said stoutly, feeling as if an immense weight had been lifted from her shoulders.

'It's just so ridiculous,' Suki went on agitatedly. 'I mean, OK, David helped when Albertine was ill, but . . .'

A prick of doubt entered Alice's mind at this. But of course, she swiftly reminded herself, Caroline *would* say that Albertine never had been ill. It was all part of her counteroffensive. The web of lies was beginning to appear much more obviously now.

Then a thought occurred to her. 'How *did* Rafael get hold of David's mobile, though?'

There was a moment's pause before an ear-splitting noise.

'I can't believe it,' Suki shrieked. 'My daughter's been ill, my husband's having an affair and now my best friend doesn't believe me.'

'Of course I believe you,' Alice gasped. 'No, Sukes, please. Calm down. That's not what I'm saying. I just wondered, that was all . . .'

There was a dreadful, racking sobbing from the other end of the phone. 'You can't believe how awful it's been,' Suki gasped. 'I want to kill myself. I just feel that there's no one I can trust, no one who believes me . . .'

'Oh please, Suki. I believe you,' Alice said desperately. 'Look, I'll come round. Straight after work. Sooner, if I can get away.'

'You don't need to.' Suki sounded calmer. 'I'll be OK. Honestly. You've got a job to hold down. I don't want to be a burden. I'm just so boring about it, honestly.'

'But . . .'

'Oh, there's someone at the door. Got to go.' And Suki rang off.

Dan had not gone home immediately after all. His weakness, despair and sense of defeat had got him as far as the home-bound platform, but then something else – a flickering of self-respect, perhaps, of ambition possibly, of pride, even – had sent him back through the station and out into the world.

Now, however, he was regretting his decision. His time in London had been one long rejection, made up of many smaller rejections.

There had been no interest whatsoever in his work. Dim gallery assistant after dim gallery assistant had called supercilious gallery manager after supercilious gallery manager out of back rooms where, moments before, they had been heard loudly saying things like 'Tell him to hold the Giacometti' and 'D'you think she's for real about the Monet?'

Dan had imagined unfolding his work before sceptical eyes. What he had not imagined, not even for a moment, was not having the chance to unfold it. Many galleries did not even want to see his portfolio, just sent him away at the door. Of the ones that did, a tall, bespectacled man in a blue shirt and grey trousers flicked wearily through and said, 'These are very nice. Perfect over-the-mantel stuff for the upper-middle-class market. Why don't you take out an ad in the back of *Country Life* or something?'

That had been the low point. The high point had been when the most supercilious dealer of all, a chisel-featured, side-parted European-prince type in one of the Bond Street galleries, had smoothed an eyebrow with one finger and observed that as portraiture was so unfashionable at the moment, it must be about to come back. But even though that was possibly the case, Dan's work was still not quite right for his gallery.

Everyone in every gallery seemed slightly distracted; some big art news had just broken, Dan gathered. A celebrated artist was being dumped on the market. This, apparently, was a great humiliation, although it seemed to him less of a humiliation than his own position. To be dumped on the market, you had to be bought in the first place.

It took visits to three or four galleries before Dan managed to work out that the dumped artist was Zeb Spaw. A very wealthy American collector called Fuchsia Klumpp had, apparently, chosen to sell her entire Spaw series at once. 'Pieces everywhere, prices rock bottom. He's finished,' Dan heard a dealer observe with evident pleasure to an assistant in the back of one gallery. 'Sub-prime art, that's what they're saying. Luckily we never bought any. Angelica Devon's gonna be stung, though,' he had added with satisfaction.

Dan had not heard of Angelica Devon and thought he might only possibly have heard of Fuchsia Klumpp. He knew all about Zeb Spaw, of course, and was surprised not to feel even a touch of *Schadenfreude*. For all Spaw's arrogance, for all the splashing with the Lotus, what Dan felt for him was mainly sympathy. Art was a difficult business, whether you were at the bottom of it, like Dan himself was, or at the top, as Zeb was – or had been. At least, being at the bottom, he did not have far to fall, Dan supposed. Not that that was much comfort.

After the eighth supercilious gallery manager, Dan decided to call it a day. He was getting nowhere; he was flogging a dead horse. But by no means as successfully as the artist whose stuffed, full-size horse lying on its side and pierced by a stake had been a recent main exhibit at Tate Modern. Roger Pryap, spitting with fury, had told him about it.

Dan shook his head at the thought. What was beautiful and uplifting about a stuffed dead horse? A contemporary artist, dead, stuffed and with a pole through him, now you would be talking. Although from what he was hearing about Zeb Spaw, that seemed to sum up his situation nicely.

Dan now decided finally to do what good sense was urging him to: head back to the station and take the first train home. He gathered his bearings and realised to his surprise that thought and wandering had brought him to where he least intended to go. Where dealers would be even less interested than the ones he had met already – although admittedly that was hard to imagine. Where he would be the wrongest of the wrong.

In the wrong clothes, for a start. He glanced down at his long thin arms in their old, white, grass-stained cotton shirt and equally ancient, grass-streaked baggy cream trousers and tennis shoes. But the clothes were only the start. He had the wrong art, too.

He was, in other words, standing by the sign at the end of Gold Street.

Chapter 58

After talking to Suki, Alice felt a wary relief. Thank goodness she had resisted the temptation to ring David at the hospital.

Thank goodness that none of it was true after all. It was as if she had been on the edge of a yawning abyss but had been pulled back just in time. For a few dreadful minutes she had seen the horror below – David's infidelity, and with her friend too. It had been terrifying. But almost as terrifying was the fact that things had somehow got to the stage where she could, even for one second, entertain such a possibility.

A wake-up call, Alice briskly decided. Perhaps what had happened – or, thankfully, not happened – was in some ways a good thing. It emphasised the extent to which things between herself and David had been drifting. Work – his hospital schedule, her engrossing new job – had somehow got in the way. It was her fault as much as his. A reassessment of their relationship was in order. She and David needed to talk, and urgently.

David needed to make a particular effort. He was, of course, very driven and had no tolerance for those less ambitious than himself. And his hours at the hospital had always been brutally long. Nonetheless, he seemed more driven, less tolerant and working longer hours even than normal at the moment. This could not go on, Alice decided now. It was unreasonable of him to expect her to put up with it. Their relationship worked well in every respect but one. Time together was more and more scarce, and time, as everyone knew, was the oxygen which kept a relationship alive.

In the silence of the gallery, her thoughts gathered momentum and focus. Beyond spending more time together, what did the future hold for her and David?

Was he, Alice wondered, The One? Did he think that she was, for that matter? They had been together two years; how long, for example, must they continue to share the Nutthouse, with its nasty studenty bathroom and a kitchen whose long-unpainted ceiling was stained yellow and brown? Was it not time for a mortgage, a flat bought together and all that normally led to? Marriage even?

Alice blinked. Did she want to marry David? Have children, even? She had never thought this far ahead before. Whenever anyone had enquired – her mother, for example, or Suki – she had shrugged the subject off. David, on the other hand, had never even mentioned it. But perhaps now, after the recent drama, all this was relevant.

Well, perhaps not marriage. But more time together was certainly a priority. As was moving out of the Nutthouse, as soon as possible. David might be content being the eternal student, but she, Alice decided, most certainly was not. When she saw David later, those would be the items on her agenda. She could not imagine him objecting; they were eminently reasonable.

Yes, on balance she was almost grateful for Caroline and Rafa's interventions. They had done none of the damage intended; on the contrary, they had been a reminder – a much-needed reminder – to repair matters between David and herself. Things would be better from now on.

Having decided this, Alice felt calmer, more positive and more in control. She took a deep breath. Then another. After another, she felt almost ready to face all the other problems besetting her.

The fact that Angelica was away and the gallery had gone into meltdown, for a start. Zeb Spaw had left, his work was about to follow him and she had no idea – *no idea* – with whom to replace him. And there was a crucial party next week, whose centrepiece was supposed to be the gallery's most high-profile artist.

But who? Alice chewed her lip, frowning. There was no one to whom she could turn for advice. Angelica was completely out of touch; she had tried every number. It was if she had disappeared into space.

Portia from the Sump Gallery might have had suggestions. She obviously knew the ways of Gold Street. But after the scene in the shrubbery with Ciaran O'Sullivan, Alice was disinclined to confide in her. She was, too, profoundly sorry for poor absent, betrayed Mrs O'Sullivan, whoever and wherever she was. The world seemed full of wronged wives at the moment.

Someone now rang the bell. Hard and repeatedly.

Alice, jerked abruptly from her thoughts, skittered across the wooden floor.

'We've come for the bed, love.' Two grizzled visages stood at the door. Revving on the kerb was a vast white van.

'The bed?' Alice stared blankly back at them.

'That one.' A hand with dirty fingernails and tape wrapped around the palm stabbed in the direction of *The Right Hand of the Father II*.

'Oh, I see. You've been sent by Mr Spaw.'

The white van, Alice realised soberly, was the hearse that had come to fetch Zeb's career.

And here were the undertakers. She stepped back as two men in jeans and T-shirts seized the formerly most expensive gold-sprayed NHS bed in human history. But now worth – what?

There was, Dan saw, a large van parked outside the Gold Street gallery into which he had gone on his last visit. He remembered how he had asked – and been told – the price of the gold Spaw bed. The van had both its back doors open, and what looked remarkably like the very same bed was being loaded into the back of it.

The actual Spaw bed, Dan realised in surprise. The asking price, he recalled, had been four million. Had somebody actually bought it? There were a great many other gold objects in the back of the van, he saw as he crossed the road. A gold wheelchair – and what appeared to be a gold loo. Shoved in, by the looks of it, most unceremoniously.

He realised that no one had bought any of them. That he was, in fact, looking at the after-effects of Zeb's work being dumped on the market by his former patroness. Here, before him, was the Spaw oeuvre. The end of an oeuvre, in fact.

Instinctively Dan bowed his head, a mark of respect from one artist to another. Even if Spaw's art had been strictly limited to self-promotion, well, that was one skill more than he had himself.

He saw that the gallery, while empty of Spaw, was not empty of people. The gallery assistant was watching the removal from the other side of the big front window. Her pretty face was sober, and, Dan felt instantly, familiar.

He knew her, he was sure. That hair; he would know it anywhere. So full, so luscious, so Pre-Raphaelite. It was the girl from the Bloomsbury gallery whose owner had called her Beatrix and who he had seen into the ambulance that terrible night.

Dan felt a shot of excitement. He wondered what had happened, whether the poor chap had recovered despite the gloomy prognostications of the hospital. Beatrix – dammit, he was hopeless with names; he couldn't remember her real one – was obviously no longer working for him, in any case.

Dan remembered the girl's friendliness that day in the old gallery. He also recalled, with a wave of gratitude, her suggestion that they sell some of his work. Well, obviously there was no chance of the offer being repeated here in Gold Street; this gallery, OneSquared, was completely different. Contemporary. Which was odd, really; he also remembered her saying she disliked contemporary art.

He realised he was hot and thirsty, and it now occurred to him that whatever else she might not be able to help him with, she would hopefully be good for a cup of tea. Perhaps she would even have some biscuits.

Alice watched the white van drive away and returned to worrying about the party. What was she going to put in the gallery? With the bed gone, OneSquared seemed an infinitely huge and empty space. Whatever one thought about Zeb Spaw's work, it took up lots of room at least.

She looked up as the bell rang. The sun was pouring down into the street outside and the figure at the door was just a black shape against the brightness. Alice could not see who it was. She could, however, see that it was holding something big and rectangular with strings hanging from it. A portfolio?

Was this an artist? One of Angelica's artists, whom she had not met before? Perhaps, within the confines of that portfolio, there was something she could put in the window for the party. Perhaps here was the answer to her prayers.

'Hi!'

Dan grinned back at the girl's enthusiastic face. He watched as the excited smile drew into a twitchy frown of puzzlement, then spread out again into surprised recognition. 'Oh,' Alice said. It was the young man who had come into Palladio just before Adam died. She could not remember his name. The portrait artist. She felt her high hopes slither away.

Dan had no difficulty reading the disappointment on her face. 'Sorry,' he said. 'You were expecting someone else.'

She looked, it had to be said, almost devastated. Strange; they had seemed to get on well at the other gallery. Another example of the corrupting influence of Gold Street, Dan thought darkly.

Alice realised how rude she must seem. She tried to pull herself together. 'Sorry. Er. Hello. We met at Palladio. I'm Alice.' She stuck out her hand, and he took it.

Alice. That was it. The name suited her, he thought. Sort of demure and punchy at the same time.

'Dan,' he said, lowering his heavy portfolio to the floor as he spoke. 'Palladio. That was your old gallery?'

She nodded. 'Until Adam – my old boss – died.'

Dan's heart sank. 'Oh dear,' he said sympathetically. 'He died then? I must say, the ambulancemen didn't hold out much hope.'

At this, her head, which had been bent slightly, flew up in a great whirl of red hair. 'It was you?' she gasped, her eyes shining. 'You went with Adam in the ambulance?'

He nodded, surprised at her excitement. 'I felt he needed someone, somehow.'

'Oh he did. He *did*. That was so kind of you,' she cried.

Seeing her eyes were wet with emotion, Dan felt a glow around his heart. Siobhan might regard him as an unprincipled bounder and general bad lot, but Alice appreciated his human qualities. 'It was nothing,' he muttered. 'Anyone would have done the same.'

'I'm not so sure of that,' Alice said grimly, thinking of the all-inheriting nephew.

It was both touching and gratifying, Dan thought, the way Alice now sought to oblige him. Nothing was too much trouble. Tea was swiftly provided, and a strangely shaped and uncomfortable stool was found for him at the desk. 'You wouldn't by any chance have any biscuits?' Dan asked, hoping he wasn't pushing his luck.

Her face fell. The red hair waved from side to side in a negative. Then her face lit up again. 'I'll go and get some!' she announced.

Before Dan could demur, she had dived into some back room, grabbed her bag and was over by the door, unlocking it. She paused and looked back at him pleadingly. 'Just don't leave the gallery, will you, while I'm out.'

Dan assured her he would not, although he wondered what she thought there was to steal. The place was completely empty.

Chapter 59

Alice had not been gone long before a figure appeared at the door and rang the bell. Dan, looking over from his seat at the desk, wondered what to do. Alice had left no instructions as to procedure if someone wanted to come in, and it was too late for him now to hide and pretend that he hadn't been seen.

He got up and slowly crossed the empty acres of wooden floor between the desk and the door. This gave him the opportunity to scrutinise the visitor; he looked, Dan thought, safe enough.

He was very tall, with sandy hair. Dan swept his face with a professional eye and found it open and honest, with wide eyes and a long mouth whose current expression was uncertain. He wore a pinstriped suit, white collar and red tie and carried a large bunch of pink peonies. It was the peonies that gave it away, plus the eager-to-please, nervous air. This had to be Alice's boyfriend.

Dan opened the door. 'Come in,' he invited.

The other man's expression became yet more uncertain.

'She's just popped out,' Dan, guessing his thoughts, informed him obligingly.

The tall man nodded. Dan was surprised to see a faint colour mount his cheeks. Why would Alice's boyfriend be embarrassed about being told her whereabouts? But the fact that he was shy was a good thing; shyness, after all, usually meant kindness and modesty too.

'Have you known her for long?' Dan pressed, ushering him in.

The colour increased in the tall man's cheeks. 'Not long, no. We've, um, only met recently, actually.' The last part of the sentence was addressed to his feet; his shoes were very shiny, Dan noted. That was good too. It implied standards. And money. His air might be modest, but it was also prosperous. Good, all good, Dan thought approvingly.

The tall man was looking around the gallery. 'The bed's gone,' he said. His voice was kind and warm, Dan noticed, his conviction increasing that with this gentle giant, Alice was in good hands. 'Did she sell it?' He sounded surprised. 'It was four million, wasn't it?'

Dan smiled at him. He was filled with the sudden urge to help Alice, to paint her as a magnificently capable creature in front of this recently acquired boyfriend. 'Yes, but if anyone can sell something for four million, Alice can. She's one hell of a girl.'

The other man looked faintly dismayed at this. 'Yes, she is,' he agreed.

'And she's told me all about you,' Dan added. 'In fact,' he enthused, now warming to his theme, 'she hardly talks about anything else.'

The tall man looked shocked. 'Me? Are you sure? All I did was give her a lift to a party.'

Dan swallowed. His eyes swept from the bunch of peonies being clutched nervously in the tall man's hand up to his face. 'You're not . . .' he said slowly, 'her boyfriend, then?'

The tall man started with surprise. 'You mean *you* aren't?'

'Me?' Dan gasped.

'I thought . . . I thought . . . when I came in . . .' The tall man swept one large hand over his brow in confusion. 'You seemed very at home, that was all.' His face was now deep purple. Dan wondered whether he had ever seen anyone look quite so uncomfortable, and part of him longed to capture the expression on canvas.

'I'm just a friend,' he said hurriedly. His insides were tight with misery. What had he done? He had only been trying to help. He glanced fearfully at the gallery window, dreading Alice's reappearance and the revelation of his embarrassing mistake. So far, however, the coast was clear.

Risking a glance at the other man, Dan was pleased to see a definite expression of relief on the open face. This man *was* interested in Alice, he was sure.

'She really talks about me?' he asked, his tone incredulous.

Dan held out his hands. 'I've got to admit that I made that bit up. But only because I thought you were – you know – and I wanted to kind of help things along. Artistic licence, I guess you'd call it. I'm an artist, you see,' he added hurriedly.

The tall man stared for a moment, then his tense face broke into a transforming grin. Dan sensed he was forgiven.

The man was looking over at the portfolio on the table. 'That yours? Can I see it?'

'Sure.' Dan went and worried at the ties. Carefully he lifted the big flap.

The tall man handled the sketches and watercolours reverently, murmuring praise as he lingered over them. He stared at the painting of Siobhan for a particularly long time. 'Very beautiful. There's real tenderness in this. Is it for sale?'

Dan shook his head, almost before he could think.

'Your wife?' the other man asked. He smiled. 'Silly me. I should have thought. Of course you don't want to part with it.'

'Not my wife,' Dan groaned. 'If only. Don't ask. But right this minute, she thinks I'm an idiot.'

The other man looked at him sympathetically. A spark of mutual understanding seemed to pass between them.

'Does Alice . . .' the tall man asked suddenly. 'Does she, you know, *have* . . . ?'

'A boyfriend?' Dan jumped in, eager to help the struggler.

The other man nodded.

'I don't know,' Dan said apologetically. 'I should think so,' he added, before he could stop himself. But it seemed unlikely to him that she didn't; he should not encourage false hopes.

'Oh,' said the other man, straightening up suddenly, clearly disappointed.

'I mean, I don't know for sure,' Dan added, worried now that he had been too discouraging. After all, if Alice *was* single, the man opposite offered distinct possibilities. Warm, modest, kind, moneyed, and obviously generous and with good taste. That bouquet, Dan thought, examining it from a distance, was not only exquisite but clearly very expensive. The peonies were huge and beautiful, in colours ranging from soft pink to deep, thrilling magenta.

'Nice flowers,' he remarked.

'These? Er . . . oh yes,' the tall man said, looking down confusedly at the contents of his fist. 'Erm, I should be going . . .'

'Do you want me to give them to her?' Dan asked kindly, extending his hand for the flowers.

'Um, yes.' The tall man marched forward and handed them hurriedly over.

'Who shall I say called?' Dan raised his voice as the other man had now reached the door. 'Any message?'

He looked round apprehensively. 'Oh, er, just Jasper. Tell her I was just, you know, wondering how the party went,' he added, before exiting hurriedly.

Alice returned shortly afterwards with a packet of custard creams, and was surprised to find her desk heaped with beautiful peonies.

'David,' she said, thrilled. Had he somehow found out about the awful twisted stories and was trying to make it up to her?

'No, they're from Jasper,' Dan said, watching her face closely.

'How sweet of him. He's very kind.' She was blushing a bit, he was sure.

'More than kind,' Dan teased. 'He's quite keen on you, you know.'

Alice's blush deepened. 'Rubbish.'

'No, he is. He asked me if you have a boyfriend.'

'He didn't!' Alice shrieked. Then she took a deep breath and composed herself. 'Well, as it happens, I have.' She opened the custard creams and bit into one.

There was a silence but for the contemplative munching of biscuits, which Dan eventually broke. 'So how,' he asked conversationally, 'did you make the move from Palladio to here? I thought you didn't like contemporary art.'

'Adam's gruesome nephew came and announced he was selling the building and the business. I was desperate for a job.' Alice pulled a face.

'You don't like it here then?'

'It's interesting, put it that way.' She smiled at him, feeling the sudden urge to tell him exactly why.

It took Dan some time to recover from the story of the Chinese takeaway. He laughed so much he almost spilled his tea.

'It's all very well for you,' Alice grumbled, sliding the packet of custard creams back across the desk towards her. 'You haven't got to find an artist out of nowhere for the gallery party next week.' Her responsibilities were beginning to crowd in on her again.

'I'm an artist,' Dan pointed out, gesturing at the portfolio on the desk.

'But you're a portrait artist, aren't you?'

'Do you want me to show you?' Dan offered eagerly, seized with sudden hope. This was a chance, after all. Here he was, in a gallery, with the ear of the de facto decision-maker. And Jasper had liked them.

Alice felt hope rising. Perhaps . . . if his portraits weren't too traditional . . . if they were very modern and startling . . . the weirder and more unpleasant-looking the better, in fact.

Carefully, she sifted through the drawings and watercolours, pausing over the different faces. Wrong genre, wrong standard, wrong place, she thought. They were far too finely wrought and wonderful to stand a chance in OneSquared. They actually looked like something. Like people. Beautiful people – that gorgeous brunette, for instance. And ugly people – those sketches of that pig-faced man in the Nehru jacket. But all of them, pretty or not, looked alive, as if they had thoughts, histories, interests.

'They're beautiful,' she said, disappointedly. 'They're really wonderful,' she sighed. 'In fact, they're no good at all.'

'I'll take that as a compliment,' Dan said, wryly.

She looked at him regretfully. 'And you're not represented by us, either.'

'I'm not represented by anyone.' He told her about his fruitless day.

Alice shook her head at the folly of it all. 'It's so bloody unfair,' she exclaimed. 'If it were my gallery, I'd take you on like that.' She snapped her fingers. 'I'd give you a whole show. But,' she added sadly, looking back at his drawings, 'it's just not what Gold Street wants, I'm afraid. People come here for dolls in Nazi uniform and eggbox penises, not work like this. The problem is, it's too straightforward.'

Dan smiled ruefully. 'I know. If I was a high-concept modern artist with a stupid name and a completely improbable body of work . . .'

'You'd be raking it in,' Alice confirmed. She shook her head. The priorities seemed all wrong.

Dan was drooping. He felt suddenly exhausted. He had walked for miles with the heavy portfolio, in the heat. All for nothing. He felt the familiar, slow pull of despair.

'I've been wasting my time,' he said dully, his eyes fixed wearily on the floor. 'I thought that talent would out and someone would see my stuff and love it. But it hasn't happened.' He paused. 'And what's more, it won't happen.'

Alice said nothing. It was true. What could she say?

'Contemporary art's all money and nothingness,' Dan added bitterly. 'And this place,' he cast an arm angrily around, 'perfectly sums it up. That hospital bed sprayed gold . . .'

Alice groaned.

'As if King Midas had been in some Primary Care Trust with the swine flu,' Dan continued angrily. 'And now the gallery is empty. Which is very Emperor's New Clothes. So why don't you,' he looked at her piercingly, 'have an exhibition about nothingness? Just show people the space and tell them to imagine the art. Tell them it's the ultimate interactive gallery experience.'

Alice was staring at Dan. There was a strange trilling in her head, which she had always in the past associated with her best ideas. Her head had not trilled for a long time, but it was trilling now, louder than she ever remembered it doing before.

'*Dan*,' she gasped. 'That's *brilliant*.'

'What is?'

He saw she was positively jumping with excitement, grinning from ear to ear. 'Come and sit down.' She gestured at the hairy white beanbags.

'Why? What's the matter?'

Alice had run through the idea quickly now, from beginning to end. It was so simple. The conditions for its execution were perfect. She was almost certain she could pull it off.

Dan was trying to sit upright on a beanbag. She lowered herself to face him. 'The point is,' she demanded, 'do you or do you not want to be a famous artist?'

'No one's interested in portraits,' Dan retorted. 'So I never will be famous.'

'I didn't say you'd be a famous portrait artist.'

Dan was confused. 'But portraits are what I do. I mean, I'm not bad at landscape, but I'm hardly Turner.'

'How about being a famous *contemporary* artist?' Alice said excitedly. 'How about being the hot new cutting-edge contemporary artist just signed by the OneSquared Gallery and about to be unveiled at the Gold Street party?'

'The Gold Street party?' He was rubbing his forehead now, completely lost.

Alice grinned. 'It's a big gallery bash and it's happening next week . . .'

'Yes, yes. I know what it is, thanks.'

'Well anyway,' Alice cut in breathlessly, 'Zeb Spaw was going to be our star attraction. But he's taken himself off, the gallery owner's disappeared and it's up to me to find some amazing, attention-grabbing artist who will get the worldwide media in a frenzy. And that,' Alice added, now almost squeaking with excitement, 'that is . . . *you*.'

Dan frowned. He blinked. He poked a finger in one ear; no, he had not been hearing things. He looked at Alice. 'Are you serious?'

'Not at all,' she enthused.

'I didn't think so,' he said.

'Because the whole thing's the most tremendous joke!' Alice's face was radiant. '*Our* joke. On the entire art establishment. Wouldn't you like to play a trick on them all?'

Dan blinked. 'But I haven't got any of that sort of work. Zeb Spaw-type stuff, I mean.'

Alice clapped a hand to her forehead so hard she almost knocked herself out. 'Dan! Don't you see? You don't *have* to! You needn't paint a stroke. Draw a line.'

'I don't?'

'No. Your show is going to be *nothing*. Like you said.'

'Nothing?'

'Invisible. Thin air.' Alice stood up, and began to whirl, red hair flying, round in the empty space. 'I can see the reviews now. *In the manner in which it conforms to the principle of bisymmetrical reason*,' she cried, '*it's astonishingly conceptually united. The site-specific installation enables the enclosing narrative to pose fundamental questions concerning the network of motivations, both the artist's and our own*.'

Dan finally understood. 'For someone who claims to be so out of step with Gold Street,' he said admiringly, 'you're actually right on top of it.'

Alice grinned. 'I'm a quick learner.' She dived over to him and pulled him to his feet. 'Come on, Zero. What do you say?'

'Zero?'

'That's your name. Don't you think? You're an enigma. A mystery.'

Dan rather liked the sound of this.

'If you do any interviews before the party, you do them behind a screen so no one can see who you are.'

'Interviews with who?'

'Oh, I don't know.' Alice said airily. 'Whoever you like. *The Sunday Times*. Jeremy Paxman.'

He shook his head. 'Come on. You're joking. How are you going to interest *them*?'

'Er . . .'

This was, Alice realised, the only weak spot in her masterplan.

Media relations. But she would find a way round it.

'We'll unveil you at the party,' she said decisively. 'You'll be naked, of course.'

'*Naked!* Now hang on a minute . . .'

She fixed him with a commanding stare. 'Referencing the Emperor's New Clothes is important. Part of the joke.'

'What if someone recognises me?' Dan objected.

'No one will. The guests are all art-world movers and shakers, celebrities and media people.'

'Thanks a *lot*.'

'Oh, you know what I mean. Come on, Dan. What have you got to lose?'

'It's not my sort of thing, though,' he grumbled.

She put her hands on her hips, exasperated. 'Aren't you missing the point? As it happens, working at OneSquared isn't my thing either. But if I'm going to get anywhere in the art world, I've got to do high-profile, attention-grabbing stuff. And so have you. If *you're* going to get anywhere in the art world you'll have to get to know the right people. And you certainly weren't going to meet them as it was.'

Even as she spoke, she remembered she had heard just these words recently, in someone else's mouth. Addressed to herself.

Behind his glasses, Dan's eyes looked big and serious. But still not entirely convinced. Alice summoned all her arts of persuasion.

'Look, it's all a joke, remember. And we both get what we want out of it. I get someone for my party. And you become a famous artist.'

'Not as me, though,' Dan said stubbornly.

'What does it matter? You'll be so famous after this stunt you could do anything. Return to portrait-painting, even.'

He brightened at that, she saw. But there was still a flash of doubt in those large Buddy Holly spectacles. This man, Alice felt, was a hard sell. An artist with scruples, with integrity. She had begun to doubt that such people existed.

She decided to appeal to his most base instincts. Although, on present form, it was doubtful that he had any.

'Oh come on, Dan. You'll be the talk of the London art world. Isn't there anyone out there you want to impress?'

He shook his head dejectedly. 'Not any more.'

Her heart sank.

'All the same,' Dan added quickly. 'I'll do it. You're right. What have I got to lose?'

'We'll call your show Nothingness,' Alice said excitedly.

'That,' Dan sighed, 'sums it up perfectly.'

Chapter 60

At Aldeham Manor, her interview with Ciaran finally over – and lunch too, which she had not expected – Sarah walked back towards the Peugeot, which she had parked at the back of the house. A tall, shifty-looking old man in a greasy cap and a younger man with a huge belly and strangely rolling eyes walked past her with a wheelbarrow. Odd gardeners for the glamorous O'Sullivans to have, Sarah thought.

Then something white caught her eye. A shirt. Ciaran O'Sullivan's shirt. He was no longer in the kitchen, where she had left him a few minutes ago. He was lounging in one of the doorways of the old row of buildings, former service buildings to the manor, Sarah guessed. It was, however, hard to concentrate on the history of architecture. Ciaran had a cat-who'd-got-the-cream smile on his face.

Sarah, to her own great surprise, felt a giant surge in her stomach. Her heart double-speeded with excitement. The look in Ciaran's eye was one she had only previously ever seen in movies.

She fought the sensation. She didn't like boy bands. Or their clean-cut, boyishly handsome singers. That was why the editor of the section had sent her. A fan, he had said, wouldn't do as good a job as a sceptic.

All the same, Sarah had felt her scepticism melting over lunch. She had refused the champagne Ciaran had proffered, but the heady effect of being under his gaze for so long was another matter altogether. Still, she had escaped with her integrity intact. She had put a number of searching questions at moments when he least expected them. His offguard answers would make brilliant copy. The editor would be delighted.

'Thanks for lunch,' she said now, hesitating by her car.

Ciaran pushed himself away from the door and walked slowly towards her. 'Hey,' he said softly, his eyes still holding hers. 'That was some interview. You know, I've been interviewed by the best in the business and you're as good as any of them.'

Sarah shrugged, whilst glowing inwardly all over. 'I was just doing my job.' But she was proud of what she had achieved. Ciaran had lost his cool more than once. And on top of that, there had been the wife business; the party. There were obviously cracks in the perfect O'Sullivan façade, and she intended to write it up as such.

He was close to her now. She looked into his eyes – those green eyes, as soft and beautiful as Irish rain on grass – and felt a sweat break out on her palms. She had a whirling sensation, as if any control she might have on events was, even now, breaking from her grasp. 'I've got to go,' she muttered.

He nodded, his soft dark hair glowing in the rich evening sunshine. 'To be sure you have,' he said in that soft Irish brogue. He paused, then added with a smile: 'Pity, though. I thought we got on rather well.'

She wanted to appear composed. But of its own accord, independent of her, a ridiculous grin had plastered itself across her face. She felt absurdly flattered.

'Mr O'Sullivan . . .' Sarah gabbled.

'Ciaran, *please*,' he purred.

'You were a dream to interview,' she heard herself gasping. 'Just fantastic. It was so exciting. I mean, I've always loved Boyfriend; I had posters of you on my wall and everything.'

What the hell, Sarah asked herself, was she saying? None of this was true. It would have been odd if it were: she had been nearly twenty at the time and out of the teen zone that such bands were aimed at. But Ciaran didn't seem to mind.

'I wondered,' he said, his voice low and intimate, his face very close to hers; he was, she realised vaguely, the same height as she was in heels, 'whether you might like to come and see where I'm planning to build my studio. It's just over there.' He waved a careless, white-clad arm behind him to the row of old buildings. His eyes, as he looked at her, twinkled as brightly as the windows in the sun.

'Er . . .' Sarah said. Too late she remembered that she who hesitates is lost.

Casting a quick glance around, Ciaran now hurried Sarah, her heels clacking on the brickwork, over to the door in the centre of the line of buildings. As he pushed it open, Sarah smelled old dust, heard scuttlings, saw a conversion in its early stages. It was a big room, with exposed brickwork and a bare wooden floor, clearly very old. Microphone stands and stools were scattered about, along with guitars. Against one crumbling plaster wall was propped a huge, beyond-life-size, blown-up photograph of Ciaran singing at some concert. The venue looked colossal; the shot was taken from behind, and he had his arms extended, Messiah-like, before a great sea of screaming female faces. She saw nothing else of the room, however, as something now obstructed her view.

It was Ciaran. With his hips he pinned her against the ancient brick wall, his hands on her breasts. She could feel their heat through the thin cotton of her blouse and the nylon cantilevering of her bra.

'You're beautiful,' he told her. 'You're the most beautiful journalist I've ever seen.'

He undid her blouse rapidly, his laughing eyes never leaving hers. 'Front fastening,' he murmured appreciatively as he reached her bra.

'But . . .' she murmured. 'But your . . . wife. She's . . .'

'What?' he muttered, his lips drawing electric impulses up and down her neck.

'She's around somewhere. Outside. I mean . . . I can't . . .'

'Can't, or don't want to?' he breathed into her neck. Sarah's resistance now crumbled. She arched her back in ecstasy, pulling her stomach in as he peeled back the bra and began to caress her breasts.

'My wife,' Ciaran mumbled into her cleavage, 'hates sex. She's happy for me to sleep with other women. Encourages it, in fact.'

Sarah's eyes flew open. 'Really?'

'Sure and she does,' Ciaran said, his breath hot on her nipple.

'We have a brother-and-sister relationship. Why do you think we don't have children?'

It was, Sarah felt through the haze of sensation, a good point. It sounded like the truth.

'She tricked me into marriage. But women have always exploited me. I've been hurt so many times.' An expression of pain crossed his smooth, elastic face.

'Really?' Sarah asked, her sympathies stirred.

'In this business,' Ciaran explained with a sorrowful shake of his handsome head, 'you get used so much. Women want you for the wrong reasons. But *you* . . .' He gave her a soft look that flipped her heart like a pancake. 'I can tell you're different.'

He drew back, extended a hand and pulled Sarah away from the wall. For a second their eyes met: his apparently intent and serious, hers puppylike and adoring.

'I want you,' he murmured. 'You were driving me crazy all through that interview. Jesus, Portia, your tits in that blouse . . .'

Sarah closed her eyes, abandoning herself to the sensation of his rubbing her nipples to aching points with the heels of his hands. She caught his scent. She gasped.

Then she remembered something. '*Portia?* I'm not called Portia. My name's Sarah.'

Ciaran took no notice. He had now unbuckled his jeans, and he grabbed her hand and pushed it urgently down inside his boxer shorts. As her fingers closed around the hardness within, Sarah fought to hold the moment, to believe she was not imagining it. Here she was, in a pop star's recording studio, with . . . well, his centre of operations hot and thick in her hand. She stared into those smiling Irish eyes. She knew she would do anything he asked her. Anything. And that he could call her what he liked.

'You're going to let me see that interview before you print it?' he murmured from somewhere deep in his throat.

Sarah gasped. Copy approval was strictly forbidden at the paper on which she worked. For good reasons; otherwise every celebrity would want to change what was written before it was run. 'Er . . .' she faltered.

'You are, aren't you? You're going to let me?' The melting eyes got closer; they blurred, she felt his lips on hers, then his tongue pushed into her mouth.

'God, I want you,' he said urgently. 'Don't you want me?'

'I, um, oh God, er . . .'

The next thing Sarah knew, she was on her back on the floor, with Ciaran, his tongue still working her mouth, tugging her skirt up. She managed to push him away just enough to gasp, 'Condom?'

He nodded, evidently irritated. She felt a rummaging, heard a tear and a snap and then suddenly her legs were being nudged apart and he was inside her, rubber-sheathed, but hard and enormous. She closed her eyes and swallowed as he began to thrust, gripping his back as she moved her hips in response.

'Well,' Ciaran remarked, rolling off her some minutes later. 'It's a good job this place is soundproofed.'

Sarah blushed violently. 'I'm sorry. Did I shout a lot?' she asked ruefully.

'Hey, I *like* girls to scream when they come. I wish my wife screamed like you do.'

The mention of Siobhan – who, really, had seemed very nice – made Sarah instantly uncomfortable again. 'Doesn't she . . . doesn't she . . . have orgasms?'

Ciaran looked affronted. 'Of course she fucking does,' he snapped, offended.

'I thought you said you didn't have sex, though.'

He looked irritated. 'Yeah, well, sometimes she wants to. After a lot of cocaine and vodka usually.'

'*Cocaine and vodka?*' Sarah was amazed. Siobhan hadn't struck her as that sort *at all.*

'Like I said,' Ciaran said lightly, 'our marriage is a sham. Anyway,' he added, his eyes suddenly flashing, 'back to the interview. You're letting me see it, yes?'

'I'm sorry, Ciaran . . . Mr O'Sullivan,' Sarah added desperately, sensing that the air had chilled slightly, 'but I'm afraid that's just impossible. More than my job's worth.'

Ciaran sighed. He looked at her with a raised eyebrow and an expression of extreme pity. 'And what job,' he asked, again in his dangerous, light voice, 'would that be? Because I rather doubt you'll have one once I've explained to your editor how you forced yourself on me.'

Sarah was aghast. 'What? You'd tell him?'

He gave her a foxy smile. 'Not that that'll be necessary, of course. I just want copy approval. And for you to make all my changes. That's all.'

She looked at him; she knew she was defeated. 'You've got me over a barrel,' she muttered sullenly.

'Now there's a thought for next time,' quipped Ciaran with a satisfied beam. 'I've never done it over a barrel.'

He walked away as she got in her car, and did not even look back. Nothing – nothing – was going to ruin his big comeback moment. Least of all some silly slut of a journalist.

Chapter 61

Alice felt wildly happy at her own ingenuity. She had not the slightest doubt that she had solved her own and Dan's problems at a stroke, not to mention those of the absent, oblivious Angelica.

And so simply, too. There were no materials required, no special lighting, no curator, no information boards. Nothing. Well, a bit of pre-publicity perhaps, but she would worry about that later.

Dan had gone home, sworn to secrecy and with orders to think himself into his new part with all the rigour of a method actor.

'Think enigma. Separateness. Mystery,' Alice had ordered, sounding even to her own ears terrifyingly convincing. 'The rest of your career depends on it.'

Dan had assured her he would, and scurried out of the gallery. He was, Alice sensed, almost entirely convinced about the idea, but nonetheless she would have liked to cage him up in the gallery kitchen and keep him there until the party. In the event, she had settled for all his telephone numbers. It turned out that there was only one number, at his cottage in Suffolk. He didn't have a mobile, even. Well, that was all about to change. She had never felt so certain about anything.

Exhausted with all the excitement, Alice was now sitting at the front desk in the gallery, turning the afternoon's extraordinary events over in her mind. As she did so, she gently stroked the petals of Jasper's peonies. She was surprised and flattered at this gift, but most of all, delighted.

After Jasper had dropped her off outside the Klumpps' party, she had not expected to see him again. She had certainly not thought that, as Dan had claimed, he was interested in her. The idea provoked a faint pang of regret. Were it not for David . . . on the other hand, things with David were most definitely now going to get better. She would tackle him head-on, this evening. The intriguing possibility that she had an admirer only served to strengthen her confidence. After tonight, and what she had to say to him, David would be sending her peonies too.

There was a ring at the doorbell. Alice looked up, heart momentarily in her mouth. The hope that it was Jasper shot across her brain before she could stop it, quickly followed by the realisation that it was a blonde woman in a wrap dress clutching a huge folder.

'Hello,' she barked in plummy tones as Alice opened the door. 'I'm Penelope, from Diamond Snail.'

'Who?'

'I've come to firm up the canapés,' she announced, sweeping in. 'Where's Angelica?' she asked, looking round with protuberant round eyes.

It was a good question, Alice thought. 'Erm, away. I'm in charge at the moment.'

Penelope turned on her kitten heels and swept Alice up and down with a look before announcing that fifty DVD-integral trays would be arriving the day before the party along with a hundred bottles of champagne. 'Plus glassware, five glitterballs, three ready-to-assemble candlelit boudoirs, one pair of gold hotpants and a rainbow wig,' she finished triumphantly.

'No,' Alice said immediately. The mention of the dreaded gold hotpants conferred new levels of courage.

'No what?' demanded Penelope. 'All these things have been ordered by Miss Devon.' She flipped open her folder officiously and consulted a list inside. 'That's it,' she added, flipping the lid back shut. 'The OneSquared Gallery. Debauched, Dirty and Decadent with glitterballs and candlelit boudoirs. As ordered by Miss Devon.'

'Who isn't here,' Alice cut in. 'I'm in charge.' And there was no way, absolutely no way, that she was going to be in charge wearing gold hotpants.

'We don't need the trimmings,' she instructed. 'It has to be completely basic.'

'Basic?' Penelope looked astounded. 'Diamond Snail doesn't do basic, I'm afraid.'

'Well basic's what we're having,' Alice said firmly.

'But . . . the DVD-integral trays . . . ?'

'We don't need them. Just the food and the champagne. What is the food, by the way?'

Penelope consulted her list again. 'Shaved fennel with truffle oil accompanied by lobster bisque in a test tube.'

It sounded, Alice thought, horrible. 'Do we have to?' she asked. 'Can't we just have sausage rolls?'

'Well, it's incredibly late to change and there'll be a fee, obviously. But . . .' Penelope ran a finger down her list. 'Foie gras rolls with basil pastry and a lobster coulis are just about a possibility within the time frame.' She looked up. 'With optional truffle salt.'

'What?'

'Truffle salt,' Penelope repeated, staring at Alice with her round bovine eyes. 'Specks of Italian black truffle mingled with Sicilian sea salt. Although we also offer clients gourmet Himalayan sea salt, which is two hundred and fifty million years old and totally free of toxins—'

'I want sausage rolls,' Alice cut in firmly.

Penelope shook her head. 'Diamond Snail has nothing like that on its menu.'

'Fine. I'll get them from M and S.'

Penelope's eyes flashed fire. 'Now just a minute. You can't do that. Sausage rolls from M and S? The whole of Gold Street would be talking.'

'Do you think so?' Alice looked at her delightedly. The more pre-publicity the better. 'That's great. Feel free to tell them anything you like.'

Once Penelope, in high dudgeon, had clacked angrily off in her kitten heels, Alice closed the gallery.

Her overwhelming urge was to go back to the Nutthouse and rest, to prepare herself to be calm and collected to face David when he got home. But conscience dictated otherwise. It dictated that she should go and see Suki.

While she shrank from the prospect of involving herself in the evident mess of Rafa and Suki's relationship, she felt impelled to. After the tense conversation of earlier and Suki's obvious anger and dejection, it was her duty as a friend. Should she give her warning? Alice wondered. But Suki might only try to put her off, insist she was a burden and a bore.

Alice sat on the tube trying to cheer herself up by thinking about Zero. Immediately her spirits soared. It was thrilling to think that everyone in the carriage, every sunken-eyed, round-shouldered commuter, would soon be talking about what only she and Dan knew now. Nothingness would be a sensation. It was so ludicrous, so audacious and so simple. For that reason, Alice felt sure, it could not possibly go wrong.

The crucial thing was to get the buzz going. Build up the anticipation in advance, so that things were at fever pitch the night Zero was unveiled. But how? That was the only difficult part of it. She could not rely on Penelope alone. Or at all, possibly.

Alice knitted her brows.

She was knitting them all the way to Notting Hill tube station, and almost missed it as a result. Climbing the stairs out, into the busy street, she turned her thoughts towards her miserable friend.

Poor Suki. As Alice walked down the white stucco streets, past the tall townhouses and along the great terraces, she relived the horror of the moment when Caroline had lied about David, and Rafa had later corroborated it. The way the floor seemed to have fallen away beneath her, the way the darkness had rushed in on her from all sides. It had turned out not to be true in her case; Suki, however, had not been so fortunate.

She turned into Suki's road and walked rapidly along it, rehearsing words of comfort and heated denunciations of Rafael and Caroline. Thinking nasty thoughts about Rafael was peculiarly difficult, however. It was even more difficult to accept that he had lied to her, even though she had heard him do so with her own ears. Rafael had always cultivated an image of breezy, bon viveur jollity, anxious to avoid being caught taking life seriously. And yet beneath this façade – at least she had thought it a façade – she had never doubted that he loved his wife and daughter deeply and that he was at heart a thoroughly good, kind man.

Alice was almost at Suki's house now, easily identifiable because of the skip servicing Cornelius Sump's home spa. The house looked smaller and less magnificent than on the night of the party. When one knew, as she did, the drama within it, it even had a tragic aspect. Alice imagined her friend weeping in one of the vast, expensive, high-ceilinged rooms. She pictured the glossy black front door slamming in anger; and yet here it was, opening.

Suki appeared. She was not alone; a pair of arms, the rest of the body unseen behind the door, were about her, pulling her back. Men's arms, they looked like. Alice watched as the hands crept up to Suki's breasts. Suki was laughing.

Delight shot through Alice. Relief followed. Suki and Rafael were back together. They had buried their differences and were starting again; the damage inflicted by the evil Caroline had not, after all, been terminal. She could go home and rest, await David and the rethinking of their relationship.

She was about to turn on her heel and go when the door of Suki's house opened further and exposed the identity of the man holding Suki.

Alice froze.

It was David.

The air was suddenly full of shouting. 'You bastards!' someone was roaring. 'How dare you do this to me!'

It was herself, Alice realised, as she paused for breath. She was shouting. Her throat was raw, her ears pounding and her chest heaving. Her fists were clenched to lash out, her nails curled with the urge to rip and tear.

'How *could* you!' she screamed.

Dimly, she was aware of other doors opening, the slide and rattle of sash windows being raised. Heads poked out. Out of the corner of her eye, she saw something slither down Suki's steps with the speed of a snake.

'For fuck's sake!' hissed Suki, appearing at the gate, her face distended with furious embarrassment. 'Just keep it down, can you? You're not in King's bloody Cross now, you know. This is Notting Hill. *Shut up!*'

So staggeringly audacious was this that Alice was sufficiently surprised to concur. But only temporarily. The pause, meanwhile, allowed an even greater gathering of sound and fury. 'I thought you were my friend!' she bellowed with all her might as Suki cowered before her. Raising her hot gaze to where David cowered on the steps, she bawled, 'And I thought *you* loved me, you lying, cheating, best-friend-shagging *bastard*!'

Chapter 62

Zeb had managed to accumulate a lot of his artwork in a very short time; it now filled the entire ground floor of Blackwood Manor. *Sponge* was there, as well as everything he had, in recent days, been able to retrieve from other sources, including Fuchsia's fire sale.

He paused by each piece, remembering who had commissioned them and why. The why was the most difficult to recall. Why would anyone have wanted any of this stuff? He could hardly believe he had anything to do with them. They already seemed part of another life.

He scratched his head – the new buzz cut could be itchy at times, but was a great improvement nonetheless. Much cooler, and no hair dangled in his eyes any more. It reinforced his sense that only now, at last, was he seeing clearly. He felt, as often he did of late, a great rush of gratitude towards the old man in Nottingham Castle art gallery. Not only had he opened Zeb's eyes to what great art really was, but he had recommended an excellent barber into the bargain.

Walking from room to room, stepping over small sculptures and around large paintings, Zeb reflected that it was like a private exhibition of his own work, for himself. And yet he didn't want to keep any of it. It was all dead to him. Dead, but not buried.

It was at this point that the thought first flashed through his mind. Dead, but not buried.

It would be good to bury it.

So why not do it?

He didn't want anyone else to have it, but he didn't want it himself either. He wanted to remove the pieces from circulation, and yet with respect, with dignity, as if they had once meant something and been worth something, which they had. The latter perhaps more definitely than the former.

Burial – yes. It made sense. The works were, after all, made from natural materials in many cases. Metal, wood, and in some instances, even paint. Materials that had come from the earth and could return to the earth. Ashes to ashes. Dust to dust.

Should there be some sort of service before the burial? Zeb wondered. A proper send-off seemed appropriate. The interment, after all, marked the end of his life as an artist, although he was increasingly beginning to suspect that it might be a beginning, too. Of being a different kind of artist.

Would a whole funeral service be out of the question?

The idea bloomed in Zeb's mind, making, for all its surface craziness, more and more sense. The art currently lying all over his ground floor was a body of work, after all. And also a body in the sense that it had meant something to him but no longer did. It was dead both physically and spiritually.

The problem was, there was a lot to bury. You would, Zeb estimated, need a couple of fields, and while that wasn't impossible, as a great many fields ringed the parkland in which Blackwood was set, it would be a big, complicated business involving commercial diggers and men in hard hats. People knowing, in other words. Whereas Zeb wanted the business to be quick, dignified and private. And over with, quickly.

How about a cremation? he thought. A funeral service, followed by a trip to the crematorium?

He had expected to be laughed at. But the local clergyman, to his surprise, was enthusiastic. 'All art is holy,' Canon Meek reassured him when Zeb had hesitantly floated his idea. 'It deserves to be treated as such.'

Zeb did not argue, even though he thought the canon was being unnecessarily generous. Was Fuchsia's dung tent holy? Dean Studio's flashing neon nipples? As for his own, Zeb doubted it. Profoundly.

Zeb expected Canon Meek to push the whole business at one of the more minor reverends in his team. On the contrary, he decided to do the whole thing himself. That the canon knew who Zeb was evidently helped. Or, perhaps, who he had been. Rather to Zeb's disappointment, news of his fall from art-world grace did not seem to have reached Suffolk.

The canon was happy to conduct an entire burial service. In Aldeham Church, Zeb's local house of prayer.

'It's a body, after all,' he agreed. 'Perhaps not a human body, but a body of work.'

The body of work being far too big to fit a normal-sized coffin, it was decided that one piece should be chosen as a symbol of the rest, to be driven in a hearse from Blackwood Park to the church. Zeb, as chief and sole mourner, would follow in a black car.

The plan was for the remaining artworks to travel to the crematorium in a series of large white vans as the service in the church was taking place. After Canon Meek's surprisingly straightforward reaction, Zeb had worried that the crematorium might be the ones to present difficulties. In fact, the chief ovens operative, with whom Zeb had a meeting, had been to art college and thought the whole concept most appropriate.

Zeb decided to leave it to Toombs, his butler, to pick the work that would go in the coffin. He did not want to be told which one; it would be like the Tomb of the Unknown Soldier. Or perhaps the Toombs of the Unknown Soldier.

It was appropriate, Zeb felt, that this honour went to the butler. Like everyone else who worked for him, Toombs had suffered long and grievously on account of his art. All the same, Zeb hoped he would not pick the gold dildo. Should the coffin be open for the service, it could be a nasty moment.

*

Siobhan was less tense. Worry about the encounter with Dan had gnawed at her; the thought that she, not Ciaran, was the guilty party in their marriage had been unbearable. Until, that was, the indication that her suspicions about her husband had had good grounds, after all.

A breathy girl called Portia had left several messages on the answerphone. Siobhan had thought immediately of the girl in the red basque in the newspaper; if ever a voice was a red-basque sort of voice, this – low, gravelly, sexy – was.

But when challenged, Ciaran had pointed out, with brutal logic, that if he was having an affair, it was unlikely the other woman would be leaving messages his wife could hear. When asked, with equal directness, who, in that case, Portia was, Ciaran had replied breezily that she worked for a London art gallery and was advising him on the purchase of certain paintings.

'Paintings?' Siobhan had gasped.

'Paintings,' Ciaran returned lightly. 'They're sound investments in an uncertain financial climate. Well, good ones are.'

He had looked at her then, a look plainly meant to imply that her own paintings were not in that category.

Siobhan had been speechless. The idea of Ciaran, who knew nothing about art, buying pictures was surprising enough. But the idea of him doing it without her, who knew so much about it, who had trained in it, who would have loved nothing more than going to London and looking round galleries; well, it was hurtful in the extreme. If he hadn't betrayed her with a woman, he had betrayed her with paintings, and it was entirely possible – though so far unprovable – that he had betrayed her with both.

Slowly, carefully, Siobhan now packed her things away. It had been another lovely day, and she had stayed out, painting, on the hill until it got too hot and she got too hungry to be able to avoid going back to the Manor any longer. Encumbered with art equipment, she walked slowly back down the hill. It was, she guessed, mid afternoon. There was a strange, measured sound coming from somewhere, a doomy boom, which suited her downcast mood.

She clenched her fingers under the half-painted canvas she carried under one arm. She would have preferred to carry it facing inward, so no one could see it, but this was impossible given that the oil paint was still wet.

Hopefully, however, not many people would see her. One of the few advantages of the Manor was that it was at the opposite end of the village to the shops. She need not run the gamut of the curious villagers in the post office and general store.

The path from the hill led down between the Manor wall and the graveyard of Aldeham Church. It was a shady route, overhung by trees from the Manor garden. Slipping out through the squeeze stile into the main street of the village, Siobhan realised what the sound was. The bell of Aldeham Church was tolling mournfully. There was a funeral going on.

There was the lead car, the hearse, with its gleaming bodywork and polished fittings, the coffin in the interior heaped high with flowers. Siobhan blinked as it slid past. One of the arrangements, displayed along the side of the coffin, read RIP YBA ZS. It made no sense to her. YBA ZS – one of those personalised number plates that were beyond interpretation. Although she was able now to recognise those on Kevin and Toni's fleet of cars: KS ACE.

YBA ZS, whoever he or she was, had few mourners, Siobhan noticed with a pang of pity. Only one black car followed the hearse out of the gate. With only one person sitting in it.

The funeral had been unexpectedly sad, Zeb thought. Mostly because he had been forced to sit there, unmoving, for forty-five minutes and think what an idiot he had been for so long. Singing 'Abide With Me' alone in an echoing church, with only Canon Meek and the organist's quavering soprano for accompaniment, had also been a sobering experience, especially when the organist, emerging at the end, turned out to be middle-aged and male.

But now that it was over, Zeb felt lighter of heart. Absolved, somehow. Shriven. He looked out of the tinted window, struck by the picture-box prettiness of the village he never recalled noticing before. Then he spotted something. 'Hey!' he yelled. 'Slow down, Toombs. I mean,' he added hurriedly and more humbly, 'would you mind slowing down, Mr Toombs?'

The black car, Siobhan saw, was slowing down alongside her. The tinted window of the passenger door slid down to reveal someone she did not recognise. He was very handsome, very tanned and had very short dark hair. He wore a dark suit and was looking at her with an expression of lively curiosity.

'You an artist?' he asked. 'Stupid question really,' he added. 'I mean, you *are* carrying all the stuff.'

It seemed to Siobhan a strange thing to stop and ask when you were part of a funeral procession. On the other hand, grief could affect people in strange and extreme ways. It was her duty to be kind and sensitive.

Loaded awkwardly as she was with easel, canvas and paintbox, she bent awkwardly down to his window. 'I'm not really a painter,' she said modestly. 'It's just a, um, hobby.'

With a flash of horror, she saw he was looking intently at her painting. She tried to swing it away. 'Hey. Let me see it,' he demanded, in a voice that sounded used to being obeyed.

Siobhan decided not to be offended at his sharp tone. Reminding herself he might be mad with loss, she obliged.

He looked at her work for some time, brutally ignoring Siobhan's agonies of embarrassment.

'It's really good,' he said soberly. 'Looks like you've had some training.'

'I did, once,' she confessed. 'But all I do now is the odd life class at the village hall.'

'Life classes, huh?' The expression in his eyes was wistful. As if, Siobhan thought, he were remembering something pleasant from a long time ago.

He asked where and when the classes were. She told him; instead of driving off, however, he lingered. He was still looking at the painting.

'Really good. Unusual colours.' He reached out, as if to touch it.

'It's still wet,' Siobhan exclaimed, drawing the canvas away. 'Well, the white is anyway.'

'You mean the others are dry and that isn't?' Siobhan was surprised at his fascinated expression.

She nodded. 'Oil paints dry at different rates. White is always the last. It can take weeks.'

'Is that so?' Amazing how interesting art was when you got down to the real basics, Zeb thought. Even the technical details. Once you took money and fame out of the equation, it was fun. Enormous fun. He'd been missing out on a lot.

He saw that the undertakers had stopped at the other end of the village street and were waiting for him. 'Well, I'd better go.'

'I'm sorry for your loss,' Siobhan said sympathetically.

'Don't be,' Zeb said shortly. 'It's actually more of a gain.' With that, his car set off in pursuit of the hearse. Siobhan looked after him, puzzled. Was he, she wondered, the beneficiary of some enormous legacy?

Chapter 63

Alice sat up in bed and looked around the strange room. She felt as though she had woken up in an interiors magazine. There was a faint scent of lavender in the air, the curtains at the window were fresh and white and the bed in which she lay had a pretty vintage cover of closely patterned rosebuds on a cream background. On top of the white-painted chest of drawers, next to the blue Toile de Jouy lamp, a blue jug painted with red roses held some great pink heads of peony.

Looking at them, Alice was reminded of a great wrong. Not David and what he had done, but the fact that she had left Jasper's beautiful flowers, that lovely, romantic gesture, languishing in the kitchen sink at OneSquared.

On the polished floorboards, a pile of fluffy white guest towels, evidently fallen from the bed, lay half unfolded. Next to them, Alice noticed, and not folded at all, were the clothes she had worn yesterday. Had it only been yesterday? It felt like years ago already. Suki hissing at her from the gate. David, shocked and humiliated under the portico.

She stared at her rumpled clothes. They seemed to her an almost nostalgic sight; she had put them on yesterday morning with no idea what would happen while she was wearing them, or that she would be taking them off later in a bedroom she had never been in before.

Caroline's. For reasons she did not entirely understand, but was in no state to question, the idea of calling Caroline had been her one coherent thought after the scene outside Suki's house.

Fortunately Caroline had answered; even more fortunately, she had seemed to understand, to realise that Alice's gasping half-sentences were one third apology for not believing her in the first place, one third confirmation of what was true and one third a cry for help.

'Here's my address,' she had said crisply. 'I'll see you there in half an hour.'

And there Alice had gone, to a smart garden flat not a great distance from Suki's house, along the same type of grand white-walled road with the W11 black nameplate. Caroline had been waiting at the white front door, and once she had pulled Alice inside and closed it behind her, she had thrust into her hand a tumbler of whisky.

Alice had looked at it in surprise. 'But I don't like whisky,' she said.

'It's not about liking it. It's about blotting out the pain,' Caroline instructed. Alice had applied herself diligently. Before long, the room had become blurred at the edges.

Nonetheless, the thoughts pressed in. Suki. How could she have? And then lied so blatantly and repeatedly? And how long had it all been going on? Since before the dinner party? . . .

As the tears ached behind her eyelids, Alice clasped the whisky in her fist. Silently, Caroline sloshed some more of the iodine-scented liquid into her glass.

Now, sitting up in bed, Alice pressed her fingers gingerly to her head. She had slept unexpectedly well. The amount of malt whisky she had consumed – she remembered at least four – hardly seemed to have affected her; there was perhaps a slight throbbing in one temple. This was surprising: strong drink, especially spirits, and Alice had never agreed. It was as if the alcohol had somehow become burnt up in the flame of her fury.

She waited for the wrecking ball to hit her again; the swingeing blow of misery. It did not, however. She waited again, summoning

David's face to mind and bracing herself. Still nothing.

She got up and went in search of a bathroom. When she returned to her room, having enjoyed a long, hot shower and warm, fluffy towels, she saw that someone had been into her room, picked up her clothes from the floor and put them on the bed along with some clean underwear.

She dressed and went off in search of her hostess. Caroline's flat was the basement floor of a roomy villa. The bedrooms and bathroom were at the front; at the back, where a large space contained sofa, dining table and, off to the side, a small kitchen, wide windows looked over a small garden. Sunshine filtered in through the leaves of a wisteria; there was the smell of coffee in the air and fresh flowers on the table. Everything was neat, clean, graceful and obviously just as Caroline wanted it. It was a bachelor-girl fantasy flat. Alice felt a powerful pang of envy.

An over-large station-style clock on the wall proclaimed it to be just past eight. Her world might be shattered, Alice saw with surprise, but she was nonetheless up early enough to take part in it. Even to go to the gallery.

Nothingness flashed swiftly across her mind, accompanied by a pulse of what she might almost have called excitement, except that it couldn't be. Not after what had happened with David. She must be too deeply hurt to feel, that was all.

Caroline popped her head out of the kitchen. She looked smooth, groomed and cheerful. 'How are you feeling?'

'Fine.' Alice nodded, expecting Caroline to exclaim in amazement at this rising from the dead. But Caroline just smiled, as if this was exactly what she had expected.

'Good,' she said, then withdrew her head into the kitchen. She re-emerged carrying a plate of toast in one hand and a cafetière in the other. Alice felt her stomach rumble and was surprised about that too. Surely women who had discovered that their boyfriends were cheating on them were supposed to be sobbing, hollow-eyed wrecks, with no appetite or reason to live?

She did not feel like that at all. She felt strangely blank about the whole thing. It was almost as if, having lived through the horror of thinking it was true before, she had no energy left to face it now it actually was.

Or perhaps – the suggestion just skimmed the surface of her mind – the discovery was in some ways a relief. Now that it was true, the worst was over. But the fact that it did not feel like a surprise was strange. Had she always suspected Suki? Alice now wondered. Had she, at some level, known all along?

Caroline had set a plate before her, along with an oversize cup of thick blue china sitting in a saucer. 'Eat up,' she urged, handing over a slice of buttered toast.

Alice bit into it. The bread was crisp, the butter fresh and salty. It seemed to her that rarely had anything tasted so good. She remembered she had had no supper the night before.

Caroline was watching her over the rim of her own thick blue cup. She wore a smart white shirt and looked businesslike and capable. Someone who looked forwards, not backwards. The sort of person, Alice felt, she wanted to be with just at the moment.

Alice groaned. 'God, I've been an idiot.'

'No more of an idiot than any other woman in love.' Caroline reached for a lump of sugar and dropped it in her cup. 'You'll move out of the place you share with him, obviously.'

Alice blinked. She had not thought that far ahead. Leave the Nutthouse? But where would she go?

'You can stay here,' Caroline offered, looking up from her stirring. 'Until you sort yourself out, that is.'

'Thank you,' Alice said gratefully. She loved Caroline's flat already. She wanted one like it. She was beginning to glimpse a life where things were ordered, pleasant and sensible and smelled nice. The scene on Suki's doorstep was already beginning to seem strangely distant and she herself detached from it.

'So.' Caroline drained her coffee cup and placed it resoundingly back on the saucer. 'Going back to work today? Of course, if you don't feel you can, you're welcome to stay here.' She waved a hand round the sitting area.

Alice's eyes lingered on the comfortable and impeccably clean white sofa. For a second she saw herself lounging there, immersed in self-pity and the daytime TV schedule. Then she shook herself. 'Thanks,' she said. 'But I'd better go in. Angelica's not here, and there's the party . . .'

Caroline was applying her lipstick. Alice watched the confident sweep of her hand and the perfect outline that resulted. Caroline seemed to have no trouble with uneven lines or wobble. She looked at Alice over the top of her compact mirror. 'Oh yes. The Gold Street party.' Her eyes gleamed. 'Quite a bash, by the sound of it. Everyone's hired a party planner.'

Alice nodded.

'Would yours be Penelope from Diamond Snail?' Caroline raised a wry eyebrow over her powder applicator.

'Yes, it would. How do you know?'

'She's doing them all. Every gallery's theme is top secret, I gather.'

Alice nodded.

'So top secret that it took her about five minutes to tell me everything about all of them. It seems,' Caroline drawled, 'that Zeb Spaw's no longer your featured artist; he's resigned from the gallery. True?'

'True.'

'And Angelica's away indefinitely and OneSquared is in the hands of the assistant who's only just started. That's you, presumably.'

Alice's eyes widened. 'So everyone knows?'

'Yes. You know how they gossip in Gold Street. I'm like a bee looking for pollen.' Caroline laughed. 'I go from gallery to gallery, picking it all up.'

Alice looked at her thoughtfully. 'What else are they saying?' she asked. 'About OneSquared?'

'That this unfortunate assistant has to find someone else high-profile and headline-grabbing to replace Zeb. And before the party, obviously, and before the gallery's other artists find out that the slot's going begging. Everyone's agreed it's going to be difficult.' She looked at Alice with something like concern. 'What are you going to do?'

Alice smiled. 'Actually, I *have* got an artist. An amazing high-concept modern artist who's completely new to the scene.'

'Is that so?' Caroline put down her compact. 'Who?' she urged.

'I can't tell you. It's top secret.'

'Oh well. If it's like *that* . . .'

'Absolutely it is,' Alice confirmed. 'I can't tell you a single thing. Without,' she added, grinning, 'being absolutely *sure* that you'll repeat it to *everyone* you meet in Gold Street.'

Caroline laughed and clapped her hands. 'It's a deal.'

'And then,' Alice went on, 'once you've told Gold Street, if you could mention it to any other powerful media people you happen to come across, I'd be grateful. I need to get a buzz going, you see.'

Caroline nodded. 'Sure. I'll do my best. Actually,' she added thoughtfully, 'I can do better than that. I need an artist for my documentary. This one sounds a distinct possibility. What's his name? Tell me all about him.'

Alice began eagerly to explain. She wondered, listening to her own excited voice, whether it was this that had absorbed her pain about David. Nothingness, after all, was the perfect vehicle for her anger and misery. It distracted her from the nothingness surrounding her heart. Zero. Nothingness. Could anything else, Alice thought bitterly, have summed up her just-ended relationship more perfectly?

'Wow,' said Caroline, when she had finished. 'That's amazing. Great idea. Great *fun*.'

'And the biggest thing ever to hit Gold Street,' Alice added grimly.

She had made an important decision in the past few minutes. Her romantic life might be an unmitigated disaster, but her professional life was going to be a success. Whatever it took. She would show David and Suki. She would show everyone.

Chapter 64

Ciaran's confidence that his celebrity would prevent the council objecting to the entirely unpermitted alteration of the Aldeham Manor service buildings had proved to be misplaced. Siobhan had been in the garden when a large young woman, whose hair was dyed the colour of red wine, had marched up the drive, announced she was from the local authority planning department and demanded to be shown 'the extent of the damage'.

Ciaran, as it happened, was in London, attending a series of meetings and rehearsals, or so he claimed. It therefore fell to Siobhan to invite the woman in for a friendly coffee and arrange a mutually convenient time for her to return. Siobhan's certainty that she recognised her from somewhere had been borne out when she realised that the planning official was none other than Bo, the model from the village hall life class.

The transformation was extraordinary. No one, Siobhan felt, looking at Bo in her sensible navy skirt and jacket and solid low heels, could imagine that under there was a pubic waterfall and all manner of other things. Perhaps it was just as well.

'I didn't recognise you with your clothes on!' she exclaimed, causing Julie, who was ironing behind her in the kitchen, to knock over a pile of sheets in consternation.

Bo grinned. 'Seen Dan at all?' she asked, with perhaps a slightly teasing emphasis. Siobhan, reddening furiously, horribly aware of Julie's proximity, shook her head violently. 'I think he went to London,' she muttered.

'Oh yes, that's right,' Bo confirmed, swigging the last of her coffee. 'Tadeusz told me when he came to fix my U-bend the other day. Is he back yet?'

Siobhan shrugged. 'How should I know?' she asked, slightly more antagonistically than she intended.

Bo looked surprised. 'No reason. Well,' she added, smacking her lips and banging the mug back on the table, 'I'd better be off. Got a lot of wind at the moment,' she explained. 'Been giving me all sorts of trouble.'

'Wind?' Siobhan repeated nervously. It didn't sound ideal, when one's other job was lying naked in a village hall.

'Wind farm applications.' Bo grinned. 'They're flying in to our department at the moment.'

'Oh, right.'

'I'll see you on Friday, then,' Bo announced at the door.

'Friday?' Siobhan repeated, confused. Had they agreed that that was when Bo was to return?

'The life class,' Bo urged. 'Of which,' she added with a twinkle, 'you're the star pupil.'

But would she go to the art class? Siobhan wondered, watching Bo bounce past the kitchen windows. Could she? After what had happened on the hill with Dan, would it not be too embarrassing?

On the other hand, she had grown to love her weekly sessions in the village hall, Roger Pryap and Mrs de Goldsmith notwithstanding. They were even part of the fun, in a way. It was all infinitely more diverting and rewarding than mouldering amid the outsize decor of Aldeham Manor.

And then there was Dan. The distance of days had allowed her to reassess events. Had she been too hard on him? Was what had happened on the hill entirely his fault? There had been no harm done, after all; it was not as if they had actually had sex. Just kissed. And when, as often happened, she replayed the scene in her mind, it was always her drawing him down to the ground. The conviction that she had perhaps over-reacted was growing.

She missed him, too, Siobhan had realised. It had been a long, lonely and worrying few days, and she longed for congenial company. For comfort in her troubles, which were many.

Matters with Ciaran were not improving. More serious by far than the planning business was the fact that there had been, on the answerphone, a message from the mysterious Portia in which she expressed, in her trademark husky tones, her excitement at the prospect of seeing Ciaran at next week's gallery party.

'What party?' Siobhan had asked.

Ciaran had pretended to be vague. 'For God's sake, woman, I'm a rock star. I get asked to hundreds of parties. You should see the invitations at the Boyfriend Reunion World Tour press office. I'm talking *stacks*.'

'But Portia hasn't come through the press office,' Siobhan pointed out.

To her suspicion about Ciaran and Portia was added suspicion that the party being referred to was another important art event. She had by now looked up the Klumpp event on the internet; it was obvious she had missed out on something significant, something she would have loved to go to. Determination not to let this happen again mingled with determination to keep an eye on Ciaran.

'I'd rather like to come,' she said brightly. 'It's ages since I went to a party.'

Ciaran had harrumphed and left the room. Shortly afterwards she had heard him roar off in his sports car. He had not returned. His temper had been worse than ever. He was so tense it seemed he might explode. Boyfriend's forthcoming high-stakes appearance on *Brilliant Britain* was giving him sleepless nights, although matters had eased slightly now another conductor had been found for the orchestra.

Siobhan had poured her frustrations into painting, and had as a consequence finished the one she had started on the hill, the abstract one of the village which the stranger at the funeral had admired. But the admiration she really wanted, Siobhan felt, was Dan's. She longed for his opinion of the finished work.

The hill incident did not matter. It was silly to take it seriously. She had been upset, that was all, and Dan had been trying to be kind. He was very kind, always. One of the kindest people Siobhan had ever met, in fact. And not just kind, either. He was practically the only friend she had in the village, and – she had to admit – a very good kisser, too.

Yes, she would go to the life class. But she did not, all the same, intend to show Dan her finished painting under those circumstances. Lots of other people would require his attention. It would be better to see him before, in private. For pure, purely art-related reasons, she instructed herself sternly. The kiss on the hill would not be repeated. Or even alluded to.

Siobhan took her painting and set off down to the other end of the village, the opposite from the smart end, as he had said at their first meeting. Somebody would be able to tell her which house.

She had taken the precaution of walking on the opposite pavement to the one with the post office on it; to her relief, no one seemed to notice her. The village was, in fact, unusually quiet; if you were, as Siobhan was, a celebrity's wife carrying something large and interesting that you didn't want anyone else to see, conditions could not have been more perfect.

She rehearsed the coming encounter. Of course, he would be surprised to see her. She would apologise for shouting at him, explain she had been overwrought and then ask him about his adventures in London. How had the galleries been? Perhaps, she now wondered with a little jump of excitement, he had been taken on immediately and was preparing his work for an exhibition.

She recalled him saying that he lived in a row of cottages at the very end of the village. Were these the ones? she wondered. There was nothing beyond them but hedges and farmland. This was the end, all right.

The cottages were small and had no gardens in front, only steps. Some were more orderly than others. The door of the cottage next to the end, for example, was battered and peeling and the front step almost invisible in the weeds that grew around it. The door next to that, in contrast, was neatly blue-painted and its step almost aggressively plucked and tidy, as if making a point to the other one.

As Siobhan looked, wondering which one of these Dan lived in, the neat door opened and a large young woman emerged. She was dressed in shorts and running vest, and had shoulder-length blonde hair and a suspicious expression on her wide red face.

She slammed the door, turning the key with amazing force. She rounded on Siobhan as she approached and looked her up and down unsmilingly.

'Hello,' Siobhan began pleasantly. 'I'm looking for Dan.'

At the mention of Dan's name, the blonde scowled.

'The artist,' Siobhan added, in case there were two Dans in the row: a nice one and a horrid one.

The blonde muttered something in a foreign language Siobhan did not recognise. But that it was uncomplimentary was obvious.

'Which cottage does he live in?' Siobhan persevered.

A large, meaty fist indicated the next door house. Without further ado, the blonde jogged off down the street. She made it look a heavy and uncomfortable business in the heat.

Shifting the canvas under her arm, Siobhan advanced to the door indicated. The peeling, battered, weed-infested one.

But her thoughts were not on the untidiness. She was conscious of a certain relief that the scary blonde was obviously not Dan's partner. Of course, his personal life, his romantic life was none of her business, but . . .

To Siobhan's surprise, loud, thumping music was coming from behind Dan's front door. Perhaps he had needed a change from classical.

She knocked, hard, on the peeling paint.

The door flew open with a crash. Standing before Siobhan in

the shabby hall was a woman, young, smiling, pretty – and completely naked.

'I'm Birgit.' She beamed. 'I leeve with Dan.'

Siobhan was so shocked, it was all she could do to stay upright.

Chapter 65

'Of course,' enthused the famous art critic on one side of the screen, 'your work is a reference to *La Condition Humaine*, the Magritte painting in which an invisible canvas is set on an easel.'

Dan, naked and crouched uncomfortably on a stool, paused, as if in thought. 'No,' he said eventually. 'It's not.'

Alice had been adamant that he must answer every question put to him in the negative, after as long a silence as he could manage. 'It makes you seem more nihilistic.'

Alice herself seemed more nihilistic too, Dan thought. She seemed, as she led him through his lines and devised ever more complex twists on his Zero persona, some distance from the lovely, enthusiastic redhead he had met in the Palladio gallery. That had been a mere few weeks ago, but it seemed like years, and in the case of Alice, it looked it too. She appeared older and more confident, certainly, but there was a zeal, a grim excitement about her that had not been there before. She claimed, with the whole Zero thing, to be sending up contemporary art, but it seemed to Dan that she was doing the opposite and taking it very seriously indeed.

He had gathered that she had ended the relationship with her boyfriend. He had been, apparently, a doctor. Not a very good one, Dan felt, judging by the physical damage he had done to Alice. Every time he looked at her, she seemed to have lost more weight, and her hair, which had been so luscious and shining, was taking on a dry, frazzled look. She was, beneath her driven façade, obviously unhappy.

Where, Dan thought ruefully, was the gentle giant with the peonies when you needed him? Here was his opportunity; the coast was clear. So what had happened to the kind, flower-bearing, genial Jasper? Had Dan discouraged him for good by speculating about Alice's boyfriend? He hoped not.

He shifted uncomfortably behind the screen. He thought it ridiculous, but Alice had insisted on it. 'Makes you more mysterious,' she claimed. It made him ludicrous, Dan felt. Here he was, answering portentous questions about the nature of art, life and the universe whilst hidden from the interviewer and sitting naked on a stool. It wasn't, for all it was summer outside, for all the gallery spotlights bearing down, all that warm, even. He was glad that the idea of Nothingness had not come up in the winter. And the way his flesh stuck to the hard surface of the stool whenever he shifted position was downright painful.

Yet Alice had insisted he should always give interviews 'in character', as she put it. But Caroline, her BBC producer friend, evidently did not realise he was in character. Alice had clearly not put her in the picture, as it were; Caroline really thought he was Zero, the mysterious modern artist. As, of course, did the interviewer, which was both funny and rather frightening at the same time.

Alice's strategy had paid off, Dan had to give her that. Speculation about his identity was apparently feverish at the moment; both Prince Harry and Ronnie Wood were suspects, Alice had told him. Dan was uncertain whether to be flattered or insulted.

He had not for one moment believed Alice when she had predicted that being Zero would make him famous. He would have been more than happy with a mild frisson. But gossip had gone round the modern art establishment like wildfire. According to Alice, no one in Gold Street was talking about anything else. The phone was ringing off the hook – well, that was true; he could hear it. It was ringing even now.

People, it seemed, had swallowed hook, line and sinker the whole idea of Zero and his chef-d'oeuvre, Nothingness. Articles had been written. Interview requests were pouring in, but Alice – with the help of Caroline – was being very selective about what she agreed to. Nonetheless, Dan had been back and forth to London almost every day. He had faced so many journalists, he was beginning to feel like Barack Obama. Except naked and on a stool behind a screen.

How he wished he had never agreed to it. Any of it. But it was too late now.

The screen, it seemed, was to be finally ripped away at the beginning of the gallery party where he was to be the star attraction. *ZERO [NOTHINGNESS]* had already been lettered in great red capitals all over the window. Naturally, there was nothing at all inside the gallery.

'Some have said your work is a comment on our tragi-comic finitude as human beings,' the interviewer said.

Dan made the obligatory pause and heard, as he did so, the whispering among the television crew on the other side of the screen. Caroline was filming this interview to be broadcast as part of the series about modern art.

As the interviewer cleared his throat, Dan realised he had not replied to the last question. What was the last question? On the other hand, it didn't matter; he knew the answer. *No.*

It was, he thought, a funny feeling, knowing the answer to everything.

The interviewer cleared his throat again. 'Some art commentators,' he said next, 'see Nothingness as the logical outcome of art. To put it another way, if contemporary art is a question, are you the answer?'

Part of Dan chuckled inside at this. To be seen as the answer to art, by an art critic – how glorious. 'No,' he said, nevertheless.

'But it's true, isn't it,' the critic asked next, 'that Fuchsia Klumpp has offered to buy all your completed pieces?'

Dan did not answer. The routine answer was irrelevant here

because, incredibly, it was true. Earlier in the day there had been a call from the celebrated collector to say that she wanted to buy up Zero's entire oeuvre, ahead of the show. The fact that there was nothing to see – nothing, in fact, to own – didn't put her off in the slightest, it seemed.

'She's offering to clear an entire floor of her house to display you,' Alice had told Dan. 'Still,' she added, 'it's probably a no-lose situation. You get the kudos of being bought by a big collector, with none of the risks.'

'How's that?' Dan said doubtfully.

'Simple. When she dumps you on the market, like she did with Zeb Spaw, how could anyone prove it? There's nothing to dump. Nothing to see.'

But the end of the madness was in sight, Dan reflected. After the unveiling at the party – a mere few days away now – he could return to Suffolk. But to do what, exactly? He hardly dared think.

Alice's breezy assurance that he could convert his celebrity as Zero into a successful career as a portrait artist clearly did not stack up in reality. On the contrary: were the truth to get out, he would probably never be taken seriously again. But it was too late now. He was on something he couldn't get off. A road to nowhere – or to Zero, anyway.

His only hope was that, when he was unveiled, people would not recognise him. Zero was not, according to Alice, a glasses-wearer, which meant, Dan hoped, that he would appear most unlike himself in the glossy magazines apparently bidding to hold the first post-unveiling photo shoot. But not being able to see properly during interviews increased his feelings of vulnerability, helplessness and general discomfort.

'Would you say that reports about the death of contemporary art are greatly exaggerated?' the art critic asked next. 'Given that Zeb Spaw has just cremated his entire body of work.'

'Really?' Dan was impressed despite himself. Spaw had destroyed his own so-called art? He felt a stir of admiration.

He opened his mouth to ask about it, but then a moving blur

appeared in his vision. Quickly, he covered up his genitals. He squinted and realised that it was Alice, furiously mouthing at him to get back on message. To stick to one-word, negative answers.

'No,' he said to the interviewer.

'Looking at your work, hanging on the walls,' the critic said next, 'I rather wonder . . .'

Dan sighed. There was no work hanging on the walls. The walls were completely empty. He knew that. Alice knew that. But neither the art critic nor, apparently, Caroline knew that, obvious though it was. He had expected to find this amusing, but it was actually depressing. He had imagined the human race a cleverer, grander affair, somehow.

'No,' he said, when the question ended.

Strangely enough, his monosyllabic answers did not seem to be annoying the critic in the least.

'And with that we must leave it,' he said cheerfully. 'Zero, art enigma and man of mystery – at least until the evening of the Gold Street party – thank you for your time.'

Dan had to sit and wait behind the screen while the interview wrapped up and the critic took fulsome leave of Caroline, who he appeared to know well. Dan could hear him booming from the other side of the gallery. 'A dream of an interview!' he declared. 'Some of these contemporary artists, they bang on at one for ever. Long, tortuous sentences, complex theories, manifestos. You can't imagine what a treat one-word answers are. Yes,' he added, consideringly. 'Zero's quite something. I personally can't wait for the party to find out who he is. Give my love to Angelica, by the way. Such a shame she's not here to see her gallery's finest hour. Funny time to go on holiday, I must say.'

Only after Caroline and the TV crew had departed was Dan allowed to peel his bottom painfully off the stool and get dressed. But still behind the screen. Alice was taking no chances. The entire TV crew and Caroline had to depart before he was finally allowed to emerge in his glasses and familiar battered clothes.

In the gallery lavatory, Dan stared into the mirror doubtfully.

Could he really be the most talked-about man in contemporary art?

'I have to go,' he announced to Alice when he returned to the gallery.

She looked up from her desk, which was heaped with newspapers, notebooks, ring-binders and diaries. 'But you can't,' she gasped. 'We have to work. Monday's jam-packed with interviews.' She proceeded to reel off a long list of media appointments. 'And there's the party at the end of it, of course.'

From sheer force of habit, Dan was looking around him for his portfolio. Then he remembered that there was no portfolio. There was no art.

'And we have to finalise the exhibition catalogue,' Alice added.

Dan groaned. He had seen the catalogue proof. It consisted of page after page with nothing on it. It struck him as a joke too far. And yet everyone else seemed to regard it with the utmost seriousness.

'Can't you stay in London?' Alice demanded. 'It's just that . . . anything might happen.'

'What, like someone getting a preview of my exhibition?' Dan asked, ironically, looking round at the empty walls. 'Or stealing it, even?'

'You know what I mean,' Alice retorted.

Dan rolled his eyes. 'Don't worry. I'll be back on Monday.'

As he left the gallery, relieved to be out in the open air and sunshine, a tearing screech of tyres attracted his attention. A silver sports car, clearly very expensive, had drawn up outside the gallery opposite OneSquared. A beautiful girl with dark tousled hair and dressed in a white T-shirt and PVC leggings was clambering, laughing, out of it. She was rattling a bunch of keys that she proceeded to use to unlock the gallery door.

Whoever was with the girl did not get out of the car. Dan narrowed his eyes. There was a lot of reflected light from the windscreen, but he could nonetheless make out a face, a very handsome face, below a mop of dark hair.

As the girl clambered back into the car and gave the man a long, lingering kiss, Dan politely looked away, not wanting to seem prurient. But then some movement in the memory, something about the man, anyway, made him glance back again.

He looked familiar somehow, as if Dan had seen him lately. But that was impossible. There were no men who looked like this in Aldeham, and there certainly hadn't been any on the train. That had been crammed with NHS middle-managers talking very loudly on mobiles about targets and spreadsheets.

And yet Dan was sure he had seen the driver before. He racked his brains. He was supposed to have a memory for faces. It was his job.

'Bye, darling,' the girl yelled, waving an expensive-looking crocodile-skin bag as she pushed open the door of Cornelius Sump. 'Can't wait until tonight!'

With a fanfare of ear-splitting horn, the driver of the sports car roared off at, Dan calculated, three times the approved speed for roads in central London.

Chapter 66

As she marched away from Milkmaid's Walk, Siobhan fiercely fought her disappointment. So what if there was a naked woman in Dan's house? It was no business of hers. She was married, even if her husband was mysteriously delayed in London and seemed to have no immediate plans to return. And as the alternative to the art class was sitting on her own in their ridiculously opulent sitting room, staring at the vast wide-screen television, what, exactly, was stopping her?

And so she gathered together her materials, looked, for a few moments, at the painting she had just finished, and then decided at the last minute to take that too. If Dan was there, he might favour her with an opinion.

She left the Manor and walked down the long, weed-strewn drive. She chose not to notice its dishevelled condition. It worried her less than it had done.

What worried her rather more, on the other hand, was Ciaran. She was ever more certain that something was going on between him and Portia. Everything – his behaviour recently; Portia's messages; Siobhan's own gut feelings – indicated it. No doubt many women in her position would have left well alone. They would tacitly accept it, find a modus vivendi, seek compensation in other areas of their comfortable lives. Clothes, travel, expensive gyms, beauty treatments, lovers. None of which appealed to Siobhan.

She was surprised to find that she was not angry. Considering the possibility of Ciaran's infidelity made her sad rather than bitter and furious. That he was having sex with someone else was hardly the point; he had betrayed her in many other, more important ways. He had imprisoned her deep in the country and abandoned her for long periods. He had openly – and repeatedly – blamed her for their lack of children. He seemed no longer interested in making love; indeed, seemed to find her generally irritating. Even to the point where he could barely stand the sight of her paintbrushes. That he still loved her seemed unlikely.

But did she, Siobhan was increasingly beginning to wonder, love him any more? He was far from being the person she had married, after all. The gentle minstrel with the soft green eyes with whom she had wandered all over America had reverted to the self-obsessed Ciaran he must have been before she knew him, waxed, buff and plainly relishing the prospect of teenagers throwing their knickers at him. That he and she had nothing in common, possibly never had, was becoming more and more yawningly obvious. Might she not be happier elsewhere? Might Ciaran, come to that?

What was the point of staying together? They had had fun in the past, had loved each other once, perhaps, but now, obviously, it was over. Without love, there was nothing but money, and Siobhan had soon tired of that and its trappings. Trappings being the operative word. Well, she wanted to escape. Start afresh, somehow. Life was short, and while art might be long, her own chances of having the artistic life she was increasingly drawn towards were necessarily limited.

Unless, she thought, she acted fast. The importance of discovering what Ciaran was doing with Portia was less about stopping him and drawing him back to her and Aldeham than it was about her own escape. A divorce? Her heart speeded up and a sudden breathlessness possessed her. It was possible. At this stage, as things were between them, it could even – just about – be amicable.

But would he let her go? That was the thing. What if he just denied everything, refused a divorce. He was not a man who liked being in the wrong. Nor would he want to hand over any money, even though that was not what she wanted. He was unlikely to let her walk away. So she would have to have absolute proof. Catch him in the act, even. But how?

'*Who's* just been?' Dan demanded, half in and half out of the door. He was devastated. He had arrived in panic from London with a mere half-hour between him and the beginning of the life class. He had hoped against hope that Siobhan might be at it, slim possibility that it seemed. And then, just as he had been rushing out of the door with his supplies of paper and charcoal, Birgit had dropped her bombshell and destroyed all his hopes.

'You said a woman with brown hair,' he accused, his voice shaking.

Birgit's naked breasts wobbled as she nodded. 'Had painting under arm. She no leave her name.'

'And she *saw* you?' The conclusion Siobhan must have leapt to was all too obvious.

'Ja.' Birgit shrugged. 'Why you worry?' A teasing look flashed across her face. 'She your girlfriend or something?'

'Of course not,' Dan growled. 'She's a married woman.'

Birgit laughed. 'I know. She Mrs Pop Star.'

Dan stared at her. 'How do you know?' Birgit rarely mixed with the locals. Or, more accurately, the locals rarely mixed with her.

Birgit tossed her blond hair back over her naked shoulder and looked knowing. 'Ciaran and I, we friends. We have fun together.' She gave an indulgent chuckle.

'Fun?' Dan repeated, in the grip of a sudden, dreadful suspicion.

'Sure, we sleep together,' she said easily. 'Ciaran, he very sexy man. I walking by Manor one day, he come out, wham, bang . . .' She slapped her palms together and grinned.

'But he's married, Birgit.' Dan was appalled.

Birgit yawned. 'Ja, but he pursue me. I no pursue him. He say wife not understand him. She not like sex. Me, I like sex. So it work.' She laughed.

'Are you still seeing him?' Dan demanded. It wasn't so much that he blamed Birgit, who was an animal when it came to sex and with much the same moral framework. But the thought of Siobhan, and her misery and humiliation when her fears about her husband were proved true . . .

Birgit shook her head. 'He have someone else now. Some girl in London. Art gallery. Gallery girl. Very posh.' She shrugged.

'Hey,' she said, a moment later, her head cocked in a puzzled attitude as she surveyed her housemate. 'What matter is?'

Dan was staring at her, open-mouthed. In a blinding flash of recollection, he had realised who it was he had seen behind the wheel of the sports car in Gold Street. Dropping off the girl at the gallery. Being kissed by her. Ciaran O'Sullivan. Of course. There was no doubt at all.

'That's fine. Ciaran, he can't keep up with me anyway.' She giggled again. 'I, too, have someone else now. Very sexy man.'

Dan hardly heard the last bit, nor did he bother to speculate who it might be. The fact that his housemate was no longer sleeping with the husband of the woman he loved was all he wanted and needed to know. That, at least, was something.

He closed the door and walked down the main street, towards the village hall. He was relieved now that Siobhan would almost certainly not be there. What would he say to her when he saw her? Would he tell her about Ciaran?

On the other hand, how could he not, when he knew she was so worried about it? She obviously needed to know. And this was no mere speculation, this was incontrovertible proof. He himself had seen them kissing.

Walking on, Dan realised that the recent discoveries had put the Zero business completely out of his head. Should he tell Siobhan about that too? But Zero and Nothingness might put him in a bad light. Siobhan took art very seriously. She might not approve of it being made fun of. Art, for her, was not a joke, any more than it was for him. Perhaps he had better not mention it, and hope that his identity was never discovered. Siobhan, at least, would not be present at the Gold Street party to witness his naked unveiling. The moment when he was exposed and – creatively speaking – crucified before the panting masses. That, at least, was something.

He should, he knew, try and relax. Enjoy these remaining few days of obscurity, which could well be his last for a while. Luxuriate in the knowledge that here, in Aldeham at least, no one had heard of Zero.

He arrived at the village hall to find the lights on and Roger Pryap, Bo and Mrs de Goldsmith already there. They were cackling together over a newspaper cutting. Dan made to join them, then recoiled in alarm as he got close enough to see what the photograph was. It was a large picture of the empty interior of OneSquared. *Zero to Hero*, read the headline.

Mrs de Goldsmith looked up excitedly. 'It says here that this Zero chap could be the most important thing in contemporary art since Sensation. He could redefine the way we look at everything.'

Dan could almost hear his heart wailing as it plummeted like a shot-down Stuka in a war film.

'Except that there's nothing to look at. It's crap,' Roger thundered.

'Apparently Zero's Jeremy Clarkson really,' replied Mrs de Goldsmith placidly. 'Although some people are saying Simon Cowell.'

'Whoever he bloody is,' Roger sneered, 'it's quite a feat to make all those crap contemporary artists look like bloody Picasso. At least you can *see* them.' He shook his head and looked, for a moment, almost sad. 'It's the bloody end, though, it really is.' Dan stared worriedly at the floor. Did he want to be the end? Was that what he wanted to be remembered for?

Roger was shaking some work out of his folder. The sketches – on big A3 sheets of paper, were of a woman. Dan felt a stab of surprise. Even given Roger's terrible drawings, it was possible to recognise Birgit.

'Beergut, she's a hell of a girl,' Roger was saying as he showed the sketches proudly to Mrs de Goldsmith. 'Woman of my bloody dreams, she is. Soulmate. Want to look?' he asked Dan.

Dan looked at the familiar shape on the page. A tiny bit of him was glad for Roger and Birgit, but the rest of him was gripped by fear. He was the omega of art. He would appear in dictionaries, on fine-art courses, even on television quiz questions, as being the full stop marking the end of a long and glorious sentence that had been written over thousands of years.

Monday night was only three days away. Three days before he appeared before the world as – what? A hilarious joker? An outrageous impostor? A cynical manipulator? Worst of all, a serious artist?

It was too late to back out now. He could not let Alice and Caroline down. Alice in particular had invested so much in the project. She'd have a breakdown, for sure. Why, wailed Dan inwardly, had he allowed himself to be talked into it?

He felt the heat and closeness of the hall suddenly pressing on him, and went outside for some fresh air. He was drinking in great gulps of it when, like a vision engendered by his frantic, worrying brain, Siobhan suddenly appeared on the village street. With a shock of joy he drank her in: the colour in her cheeks, the excitement in her clear green eyes, the way her hair flowed around her face. He knew that from the moment he had first seen her, she had not been out of his mind for one second.

She saw him, waved, crossed the car park and came towards him. She was carrying, under her arm, what looked like a finished picture.

Chapter 67

It was beautiful. Dan could see that immediately. He had seized the picture in both hands as she came near, unable to stop himself, and now his heart was beating fast as he looked at it.

He had seen it in its early stages, but it had turned out even better than he had imagined.

The colours, the composition, the sheer glow of the thing. The way in which, without depicting a single definite shape, it gave an amazingly accurate impression of the view from the top of the hill above the Manor. The green glow of grass, the bright sunny air, the grey walls, the yellow smudges of flowers, the faint mist in the rolling distance. He peered, puzzled and admiring, unable to fathom quite how she had done it.

Her eyes were sparkling. 'Do you really like it?'

'More than that,' Dan assured her. 'It's got that sense of inevitability. Once you've seen it, you can't imagine it not existing.' He blushed slightly, hoping she didn't think his speech too fulsome. Perhaps he should have sounded more casual.

She was looking at him ruefully. 'Oh Dan. I'm so pleased to see you. I'm so sorry about . . . about . . .' She looked away and bit her lip. The lip he could so clearly remember kissing, and re-kissed every night in his dreams.

'Look, it doesn't matter. It was just . . .' He paused, wondering just what, exactly. Just the best moment of his entire life? 'Just one of those things,' he finished, awkwardly pushing the bridge of his glasses upwards.

Siobhan looked at him desperately. 'I've been having such an awful time. I'm sure Ciaran's having an affair now, but I just don't know with who, and I'm so desperate to find out . . .'

Her expression of anguish was too much for Dan. Before he could think, before he could stop himself, he had told her about Birgit.

Her eyes stretched huge and wide in surprise. 'On his own doorstep!' she exclaimed angrily. 'And – oh God, I can't believe it.' She pushed an agitated hand through her hair. 'With your girlfriend! I mean, that makes it so much worse, I . . .'

'I'm . . . unattached,' he cut in hastily, blushing immediately at the risible word he had, for some reason, chosen.

'Oh. I thought . . .' She dropped her glance. But not before, in the back of her eyes, he had seen something like relief.

Siobhan was shaking her head. She seemed, he thought, more amazed than angry. 'So *that's* who it was,' she muttered. 'Birgit. And I was so sure it was Portia . . .'

'Er . . .' He might as well, Dan decided, be hung for a sheep as for a lamb. 'Well, you were on the right track,' he began, before telling her gently what he had seen outside Cornelius Sump.

Siobhan's head flew up and her eyes blazed. 'So I was right!'

Her hand had flown to her mouth. The green eyes stretched in excitement. 'Of *course*!' she exclaimed. 'Now I understand! *That* must be the party.'

'What party?' He had no idea what she was talking about.

'The Gold Street party. *That's* the invitation Portia's talking about. I've got to go,' she added, with iron resolve. 'If I can see him there – with *her* – he can't deny it after that.'

'Gold Street?' Dan said in alarm. He could not follow her train of thought, but the destination was obvious enough.

Oh no. *Oh no*. He imagined himself unveiled as Zero. Naked. A joke. In front of Siobhan. He felt sick.

'The – the silly old Gold Street party? Why bother?' he blustered in a hysterical falsetto.

Siobhan looked at him speculatively. If she told him, might he think she was unpleasantly calculating? She wanted to catch her husband red-handed, very possibly red-basqued too.

'Of course I want to be at the party,' she bluffed. 'There's this amazing new artist I keep reading about. Zero. He's going to be unveiled. It's going to be the art event of the decade. What's the matter, Dan? You've gone all . . .' She stretched her hand out to touch his face; he seized it and held it desperately to his lips.

They were standing like this, looking into each other's eyes, when an explosion of noise entered the car park. They both turned to see a battered Mini phut-phut to a halt and then collapse with a sigh in a parking space.

The door creaked open. A pair of feet in flip-flops emerged, attached to a pair of legs in grey marl sweatpants. The driver was male and wore a baggy white T-shirt with *F*** THE YBAs* emblazoned on the front. His hair was cut brutally short, and yet Dan felt sure he recognised him. Those cheekbones. That tan. That height. That T-shirt. That, of course, was the giveaway.

'It's him!' Siobhan whispered. 'The guy I saw at the funeral the other day.'

'Funeral?'

'A really odd one. At the church. He was the only mourner, so far as I could see. And he seemed really pleased about it all.'

'Hey.' Zeb Spaw grinned, striding towards them, jiggling a sketchbook under his arm. 'Am I right in thinking this is where the life-drawing classes are held?'

Chapter 68

Alice had been unable to eat breakfast. Her stomach was convulsed with nerves. Tonight was the Gold Street party; it would be a day of interviews and preparations, followed by, this evening, the unveiling of Zero. And whether that was a triumph – which seemed likely – or a disaster – which was also possible – one thing was certain. Life would never be the same again. Whether she was hailed as a curator of genius or a perpetrator of unforgivable idiocy, it would be a day to remember.

Driven by a strange impulse, she had got out of the tube at King's Cross and decided to walk her old route to Gold Street. It was a beautiful morning, and the sun shone on the sheer red-brick cliff that was the façade of the block she had formerly lived in. Instinctively she glanced up at the Nutthouse windows; being daylight, however, it was impossible to tell if David was there.

No doubt he had been at the hospital for hours. She had no idea what his routine was these days. They had not spoken since the scene outside Suki's house, although that could hardly be described as a conversation. It had had the virtue of succinctness, however. After that, what else was there to say?

David, on the other hand, seemed to want to say a lot. He had texted her, although from a new, different number. Had Rafael, Alice wondered, destroyed the old phone?

He wanted to see her; he wanted her to forgive him. It was over with Suki; it had been a moment of madness. And he had, David said, seen a picture of her in the newspaper at an art party. She had looked beautiful.

Alice had not replied. She had got Caroline to text him and ask him to leave the flat while she came back to collect her belongings. Caroline had come with her; Alice feared encountering him, and feared even more being disappointed if she didn't. But in the event he was not there and she had felt nothing. It was over.

'Long time no see!'

Alice almost fell over the person on the pavement in front of her. She recovered her balance just in time to see that it was Mrs Nutt, coming out of the flats with her trusty shopping trolley. She screwed up her wrinkled yellow face at Alice.

'Your young man's very quiet these days,' she reported.

'He's not my young man,' Alice said shortly.

Mrs Nutt nodded. 'He told me.'

'Told you?'

'He told me all about it when he came to pay the rent. Seemed pretty shook up about it. Gave him a sherry, I did, and told him he was a blithering idiot. Girls like you don't come along very often.'

'Thank you, Mrs Nutt.' Alice was surprised and touched.

'Doctors, though.' The old woman shook her head in its knitted hat. 'Two a bleedin' penny. And they all think they're blinking marvellous.'

Alice went on her way, grinning.

There had been changes along her old way to work, as there always were in London whenever you turned your back for five minutes. Nonetheless, she was unprepared for this one.

Walking down the street where Palladio was, she first thought she had taken a wrong turning. There was no sign of an art gallery at all. But then she saw Tomley's, and Bella Umbria, and realised that the shop between them was indeed her former place of employment. Palladio's peeling yellow exterior had gone, however.

It was now painted bright pink and appeared to specialise in retro cooking equipment.

Alice stared, bewildered, at the piles of red and white spotted pans where the Hogarths had been, the flower-sprigged aprons where the Victorian lady artists had hung and the green enamel breadbins in place of the Nicholsons. There were Paisley-printed rubber gloves decorated with black rubber flounces at the wrists. The girl inside – Alice went in to check – had never heard of Palladio, and indeed, Alice found herself thinking, it was tempting to wonder whether she hadn't just imagined it all, so completely and so quickly had the old place gone. It was as if Adam and his pictures had never been.

But they had been. They lived on in her heart, if nowhere else. She wondered, not entirely comfortably, what Adam would have made of Zero. Of the Nothingness exhibition. Would he think it amusing? She could almost hear his voice, full of mild dismay. 'Oh *Beatrix*!'

The mobile in her bag rang. Alice fished it out, wondering if it was Angelica. There had been a call yesterday; someone shouting from what sounded like the bottom of a deep well, drowned out by a deafening hiss. It had been impossible to make out any of the words, but Alice had a feeling it was her employer. Would she return in time for the party? And if so, what would she think?

'Alice? It's modern art's Mr Mystery here.'

Alice gave a whoop of excitement. A couple of passing men, their suits stretched and creased with rucksacks, stared at her.

'Big day, Dan. Or should I say Zero?'

'What?' she said next. She frowned. Her nerves were playing tricks with her ears now. 'It might just be the line from Suffolk, Dan, but I thought I just heard you say that . . . you can't do it.'

'That's right. I can't do it. I can't be Zero.'

'But . . .' Alice spluttered, as her chest constricted and she felt herself gasping for breath.

'I've spent all night thinking about it, and I just can't do it. I can't do Nothingness, Alice. I'm sorry.'

Alice was still fighting for air. But she could tell by his voice that there was no point in arguing, even if speech had been an option.

'But don't worry,' the voice from Aldeham continued.

Alice's head spun. 'Don't *worry*?' she managed to grind out between gasps. 'You're pulling out of my gallery, on the most important night of my life, and you're telling me not to *worry*?'

'That's right,' came Dan's reply. She noted with fury that he sounded happy and excited. 'I've got a . . .'

But what Dan had got remained a mystery, as he had disappeared into the ether. The phone at Alice's ear buzzed emptily. She staggered a few steps across the pavement and slumped against the wall.

'You all right, miss?' Someone took her arm. Hopelessly, Alice looked up into a face she recognised. The waitress from Bella Umbria, who had always made Adam his ham on white bread.

'Signorina Alice!' she exclaimed with obvious pleasure. 'You OK?'

'Fine,' said Alice thickly. She allowed herself to be led to the nearest outside chair, where she spread out her elbows and slumped her head on her hands.

'You drink too much, huh?' chided the waitress indulgently. 'I get you cappuccino. On the house. Is nice to see you, Alice. The people next door now, they not so nice. Not like you and Signor Adam. Spotty pans! *Pah!*' She thumbed her nose at the kitchenware establishment and flounced back into Bella Umbria.

Through the decorative holes in the metal table, Alice stared down at the black circles of chewing gun on the pavement. Zero was just that – zero.

She closed her eyes and groaned, not caring if the morning sun was feasting greedily on her exposed neck.

The great joke was over. Over before it had begun. And that was a joke in itself. The gallery was a joke. The fact that Angelica was away was a joke. Her career was a joke, her romantic life was a joke and due to all of the above, she herself was a joke.

'Thank you,' she muttered, as a cappuccino was gently positioned at her elbow.

'*Prego*,' murmured the waitress. Alice, still not looking up, could feel her hesitating. 'OK? You want me call you doctor?'

Alice sat up abruptly at that. Her red hair made a wild curve through the air. 'Ha. No. No thanks. A doctor's the last thing I need.'

The waitress, evidently relieved at this proof that life still ran in Alice's veins, smiled and went back inside.

Alice sipped her coffee, her eyes turned regretfully on the zinging pink façade of her erstwhile place of employment. She knew, as surely as if he were sitting opposite her and telling her, that Adam disapproved of Zero.

Art was not a joke. Palladio had not been a joke. It had been real, earnest. She had been wrong to lose sight of that, to use the apparent frivolity of her new milieu as a weapon, as revenge.

Art was art. Bad art, good art. In the most basic of analyses, you needed the former to define the latter. The former to *finance* the latter, too. Alice swallowed. Contemporary art might not be her particular preference, but there was no doubt that it kept the art business going. Interest in what the cutting-edge got up to fuelled interest in all the other branches, provided money for them too. Who was she to laugh at it all?

She had been cruelly deceived by David and Suki, but did that give her the right to try and deceive the art world? Even in jest? And how funny had it been anyway? Her intentions had been cynical. At the very least, should she have kept Caroline, a good woman who had helped her, in the dark about what was really going on?

She felt disgusted with herself, but also relieved. Zero had not happened. She had been saved, not damned.

Her mobile rang again. It was Dan, full of apologies. 'My phone ran out at the crucial moment,' he explained. 'I was just about to say that I'd got a replacement.'

'Replacement?'

'For tonight. To take the gallery space.'

'It's OK,' Alice said hurriedly.

'Why?' Dan sounded alarmed now, for the first time. 'You've got someone else? Already?'

'No. I haven't. But I don't want one. I don't want to do the Zero thing after all.' Alice laughed, slightly bitterly. 'You could say that at the last minute I realised I had principles.'

'No, no, I'm not talking about Zero,' Dan assured her excitedly. I've got someone else. Some*thing* else. Someone brilliant and new and completely original. Something fantastic.'

'Can you see it?' Alice asked wearily.

'You bet you can,' Dan enthused. 'And you can see her, too. Siobhan O'Sullivan. We're on our way, on the train. I've got the answer, Alice. She's the real deal. A new and truly amazing contemporary artist who really isn't a joke.'

Chapter 69

The Gold Street galleries were getting into party order with a vengeance. From the vantage point of the OneSquared front window, Alice had already seen a truckload of tree trunks grinding heavily up the street towards the Rabid Gallery, where it would shortly be turned into a birch forest. Ten minutes later, rather to her surprise, she saw it grinding back down again, still fully loaded with trunks.

'Too tall,' Caroline snorted, coming into OneSquared as the truck turned the corner. 'Whoever ordered them got their feet and metres mixed up. They're going away to be reduced by a third.'

Caroline seemed to Alice extraordinarily calm. But then, the fate of an art gallery, an artist and a gallery assistant did not depend directly on the decisions she had recently made. Whereas, for Alice, what happened tonight at the Gold Street party would shape the future not only for herself, but for Siobhan and Angelica too. If the latter ever returned.

Caroline had, anyway, the enjoyable distraction of her documentary, which had seen her dashing up and down Gold Street all morning, interviewing everyone from proprietors to contractors. Left in the gallery, having hung the sole artwork OneSquared were displaying during the party, Alice found herself regretting her decision that their catering should be only champagne and sausage rolls.

She had bought the latter at Marks and Spencer on the way to work; the champagne, delivered that morning, was augmenting the bottles already in the fridge. The glasses, delivered along with the wine, stood gleaming in the kitchen, ready to be transferred to the desk at party time. There were no waiting staff to organise – Alice had decided to put the bottles on the table and let people help themselves. Simpler that way. But simpler, it now struck her, left more time to worry. Had she, like Rabid, to concern herself with an entire supersized birch forest, the day would have passed much more quickly.

'And I'm not sure the ham theatre's going all that well,' Caroline added, pausing by the door, apparently about to rush out again. 'Rabid's whole pata negra ham, to be carved to order by Cossack swordsmen,' she explained, as Alice looked blank. 'The caterers sent ready-sliced roast beef.'

'Oh dear.'

'It gets worse. The Cossack swordsmen thought it was their breakfast and ate it.'

Cossack swordsmen, Alice mused. She remembered seeing some wild-looking creatures with elaborate mustachios and baggy trousers walking down the street earlier. They had been laughing uproariously at the artworks in the various gallery windows.

'Although it's hardly going much better for poor old Miroslav Butterworth.' Caroline gave a comic grimace. 'You know they're having this Venice theme and were supposed to be flooding the gallery to create a Grand Canal effect?'

Alice nodded, wondering what could possibly be coming.

'Well it seems no one thought about the gaps between the floorboards. All the water's drained away; they're having to send for a special lining. Oh, and one of the gondoliers has a sore throat and can't sing. Oh well.' Caroline grinned. 'I'll see you later. I'm going to recce with the film crew. We're interviewing Dystopia's reverse stripper, although I hope she doesn't give us a demo. I've only just had breakfast.'

As Alice raised her hand in a weak wave, Caroline's grin faded slightly. She put her head back round the door. 'Are you OK? You look a bit pale.'

'Fine.' Alice nodded hard. 'Um, well,' she added, swallowing, 'possibly a bit nervous. Actually.'

Caroline shook her head in mock exasperation. 'Come on, Alice. Nothing to be scared of. Siobhan O'Sullivan's a towering genius, and her work's going to be a sensation.'

'Yes, but there's only one of it,' Alice quavered.

'So what. Less is more,' Caroline retorted with robust good humour. Watching her leave and stride confidently past the window, Alice wished for a quarter of her friend's conviction. She wished she could be Caroline full stop, actually. Capable, clever, good-humoured and generous. It did not seem to have occurred to her to be angry about the deception practised on her over Zero. 'All's fair in love and art,' she had said breezily. 'Forget it, Alice. It's not life-threatening.'

While it was not meant to be, it was exactly the kind of remark that David would have made. Alice turned her thoughts from him determinedly. Dwelling on what had happened only made her feel bitter about the past, and just now, with the party imminent, she needed all her energies to feel positive about the future.

She looked around the quiet gallery, with its empty white walls and uninterrupted stretch of floor. It was hard to imagine this space, later on, packed and bustling with the cream of the London art world. But what if, she thought with a sudden frisson of fear, OneSquared was not packed and bustling? What if no one came in at all?

She swallowed, feeling suddenly, utterly sick. Perhaps it would have been better to stick to Zero; interest in him had been enormous, after all. Once people got here and saw that he was not, after all, to be unveiled, that the show in fact consisted of one small painting, might they not just turn their backs? Be angry, even?

No. No. Everything would be fine. Failure was not an option.

A breath of fresh air, on the other hand, most definitely was an option. Going outside would also be an opportunity to assess the impact of Siobhan's work from a distance.

On the pavement, Alice realised the degree to which the thick glass of the window had insulated her from the noise and action in Gold Street. The throbbing engines of various delivery vans filled the air; looking down the road, Alice could see gold cages – for the dancing under the tsars, no doubt – being delivered to Rabid. And some silver poles – presumably for another kind of dancing altogether – being delivered to Dystopia, home of the sex party. PA systems and DJ turntables seemed to be going in to most places, as were boxes of champagne.

A great, gold-sprayed Lion of St Mark was swaying across the street towards Miroslav Butterworth. People with spiked, neon-sprayed hair were carrying glasses; someone had opted for the punk waiters, Alice guessed. Beside various of the street lamps, ladders were positioned, at the top of which workmen were stringing bunting with Andy Warhol screenprints. If she squinted, Alice could see, at the far end of the street, the unmistakable figure of Penelope from Diamond Snail strutting up and down in a hot pink wrap dress, barking out instructions, her arms full of ring binders and accompanied by a bevy of assistants.

Watching it all, she felt a wave of great, unexpected fondness for Gold Street. There was, for all the risible aspects, something moving about the excitement, care and effort being put into this, the biggest night in the street's collective calendar. There was a sense of everyone pulling together. Of community, even.

Excitement possessed Alice at the thought that she, too, was now a part of this world – a significant part, too. Had she not, through Angelica's absence, been forced to take a leading role? And she relished it, too. If all went well, when Angelica returned, talk of promotion would not be inappropriate.

If all went well. But would it? Her exhilaration was followed by a cold wave of terror. What if the Siobhan show flopped? What if, after all the laughing Alice had done in the past at the other galleries, they all now laughed at *her*?

She forced these thoughts away.

Blinking in the bright morning sunshine, she walked slowly across the road from the OneSquared Gallery. She stood outside Sump and looked back, assessing the effect of her own window from afar.

She shifted from foot to foot and crossed and uncrossed her arms. She put her head thoughtfully to one side and then to the other. She turned round and looked at the picture over both shoulders and then, on a sudden impulse, bent over and viewed it upside down, through her legs. It was at this point that she stopped. Short of standing on her head – not a good idea, as she was wearing a skirt – there was no other angle from which to look at it.

But from every angle, only one conclusion could be drawn. Siobhan's painting, *View*, was a triumph. Its soft, bright colours glowed bewitchingly; it looked entirely beautiful, despite – or possibly because of – its simple presentation.

The unframed canvas – there was no time to have it professionally mounted – hung against a small white wall, about three feet high by five feet wide, which Caroline had found in the storeroom. As the wall was made of polystyrene and had a small stand beneath, it was perfect for the purpose.

The door of the Sump Gallery opened behind her; Alice guessed from the wave of perfume and the scrape of high heels that it was Portia, rather than Cornelius, emerging.

Affecting not to have noticed, she kept her back turned. Portia was, after all, the woman with whom, before Alice's very eyes, Ciaran O'Sullivan had cheated on his wife. The wife who was now OneSquared's star artist. And while Alice was unable to think of Portia as the enemy, exactly, displays of friendliness were out of the question.

Her eyes on her shadow stretching out into the road, she hoped Portia might go past, or go away altogether. Her hopes were dashed as she saw the other girl's pneumatic outline pause directly behind where she stood.

'Wow,' said Portia. 'Radical.'

Alice turned. Portia was staring across the street at the OneSquared window. 'How do you mean, radical?'

Portia gave a lazy grin and tossed back her thick black hair. 'Well, it's a *painting*, isn't it? Canvas, oils, er . . . you know. That sort of thing.' Her large black eyes glowing with a kind of awe, she crossed the tight black arms of her tight black dress. 'I can't think of the last time I saw an actual painting in Gold Street.'

Alice felt her defences lowering slightly. 'Do you . . .' she ventured, looking back at *View*, 'like it?'

'Like it?' Portia sounded surprised. 'Well,' she hedged, 'I don't know much about paintings. We don't tend to have them at Sump . . .'

Alice was certain, to the depths of her knotted stomach, that Portia was making excuses so as to spare Alice her real opinion – that *View* was rubbish. Had she, Alice wondered dejectedly, allowed desperation to sway her better judgement? Was Siobhan's only real virtue that she filled a space? Would her unveiling tonight, before the entire art world, result not in a new art star being born, but in failure and humiliation?

Portia was still talking, Alice realised. 'But for what it's worth,' she was saying, 'I think it's pretty good, yes.'

Alice gasped. 'Really?' She whirled round and caught Portia by the wrists. That the first independent opinion on the work was positive sent joy shooting to all points of her body.

'Mmm.' One of Portia's magnificent dark eyebrows was magnificently raised. 'But actually, if you don't mind me saying . . .'

'What?' Alice braced herself in dread. The other remarks had obviously merely been polite.

'Well, after all that Zero stuff. I wasn't expecting him to come up with this sort of thing.'

Alice laughed in relief. 'Oh, this isn't Zero. He's . . . disappeared.'

'*Disappeared?*'

'That's right. Into thin air. So, um, we had to get a replacement, pretty fast.'

Portia, however, was still musing on Zero. 'But what about his work? Did he leave all that in the gallery?'

Alice looked at her. Was Portia joking? It seemed not. 'No,' she deadpanned. 'He took it all with him.'

Portia looked satisfied at this. 'So who's the new kid?' she asked, waving a hand at *View*.

Alice debated whether to tell her, then realised she would find out soon in any case. The information was, after all, stencilled in large red capitals across the front of the gallery window. *SIOBHAN O'SULLIVAN. NEW WORK FOR A NEW ERA.*

She watched Portia reading the name. It didn't seem to ring any bells.

'Well, see you later,' Portia said cheerfully, as she turned back to the doorway of her gallery. 'I only came out for a breather. Now it's back to Barbie on the Beach.' Alice frowned. 'I thought you'd changed it to Glitter.'

Portia shook her hair back over her shoulders.

'Double bluff. You can't be too careful.'

'Back to the mobile shucker, then,' Alice remarked.

Portia rolled her eyes. 'I've got a ton of sand to spread on the floor, and various barbecues to set up.'

'*You're* setting up the barbecues?' It was hard, Alice thought, to imagine the glamorous Portia red-faced and sweating over sausages.

Portia rolled her eyes. 'Building them, would you believe. Cornelius got them mail-order. We didn't realise they'd come as flatpacks. Luckily, our very sexy mobile shucker's got an entire tool kit with him. They're supposed to be for oysters, but he tells me,' she added with a giggle, 'that he's got some simply *huge* screws.'

Alice was looking behind her, into the Sump Gallery window. She could see the bags of sand lying about, as well as some large white cardboard boxes with pictures of sizzling grills full of hamburgers. At the very front, next to the window, was what looked like a supermarket trolley, sprayed gold.

Alice blinked. But it could not be a Zeb Spaw. He had, or so she had heard, cremated all his work. Perhaps she was seeing a ghost; given her occupation and strained nervous condition, it was not surprising that the unquiet spirits of hastily dispatched conceptual art were appearing before her.

Portia saw her looking. 'Sharon Aura,' she remarked. 'Our chosen piece for party night. It's her new direction.'

Alice was amazed. 'But it's . . .'

'Exactly like Spaw. I know. Sharon says it's an ironic *hommage*, but I think she's just run out of ideas. Already!' Portia shook her head and looked, for a moment, almost wise.

She undulated back indoors, her tight dress striking Alice as most unsuitable garb for the erection of barbecues. The mobile shucker was going to have his work cut out.

Alice crossed the road back to OneSquared, only narrowly escaping the truck returning with the Rabid Gallery's reduced birch forest.

Chapter 70

In the short space of time Alice had been out, the answerphone had taken ten messages. All were from disgruntled OneSquared artists furious to have been passed over for the prestigious party-night slot.

'. . . your criminal dereliction of artistic duty . . .' ranted Cruz Backhausen.

'. . . I don't mind telling you, when Angelica comes back . . .' fumed Hero Octagon.

'. . . outrageous insult; never in my artistic career have I . . .' raged Balthazar Ponce.

'. . . wouldn't recognise a masterpiece if it grabbed your arse . . .' snarled Empathy Collective.

Alice had reached the last of these when she saw, out of the corner of her eye, a shadow fall across the glass front door. She turned apprehensively; had the artists now decided to come in person and vent their anger?

With enormous relief she recognised the tall, friendly form of Jasper and hurried to let him in.

He stood awkwardly in the doorway, as if suddenly forgetting what he had come for. Alice felt a rush of fondness; his diffidence was so attractive to someone previously used to David's bombastic self-confidence.

'I was just passing and I thought I'd . . .' Jasper began, then stopped mid sentence. His eyes widened. 'You look, um, wonderful,' he blurted.

Alice grinned. 'This old thing?' she teased, sweeping a hand down the front of her outfit. Nonetheless, she felt excited. The clothes were new, very grown-up and, Caroline had assured her, very glamorous. It had been Caroline, in fact, who had insisted that Alice's first public appearance as artistic director of OneSquared was accompanied by as much chic as possible, and to this end she had supervised the purchase – at dizzying expense – of a fitted black shirt worn with a tight-waisted, billowing black satin skirt. 'Like a sort of Gothic Princess Margaret,' Caroline had remarked approvingly. Opaque black tights and some narrow high-heeled black shoes, borrowed from Caroline, set off Alice's slender legs.

'Not too . . . black?' Alice had queried, twirling before the full-length antique mirror in Caroline's glossy-mag fantasy of a bedroom.

Caroline had shaken her short dark bob with vehemence. 'Would be on me. But not you, with that glorious red mane. You look amazing, like some fabulous, sexy Celtic widow or something.'

Jasper seemed impressed too, it had to be said. As well as slightly abashed; his colour had risen, making his boyish face more boyish than ever. He had a tan, too, she noticed, giving him an attractive outdoorsy air, which the white of his shirt and the soft grey of his suit only emphasised.

'Thank you for the flowers.' She smiled. 'I love peonies. They spent a few days here, I'm afraid, because I was sort of . . . well . . . between flats, really.'

She was gabbling, she knew, but found it impossible to stop. 'I've, um, split up with my boyfriend, you see,' she finished, looking into his face.

'Oh,' said Jasper, in surprise. '*Oh*,' he repeated, in evident relief. 'That's great. Well, of course, not great,' he added hurriedly, purpling with embarrassment. 'I mean, that sounds awful. It must have been very difficult for you . . . erm . . . oh dear . . .' He looked down and shifted awkwardly from shiny black shoe to shiny black shoe.

'Not really,' Alice said. 'It was, well, a relief really.' She smiled. 'So if that offer of a drink is still open, I'd rather like to take you up on it.'

Jasper's face was transformed, she saw. A great grin stretched from ear to ear and his eyes were alight with pleasure. 'That would be wonderful.'

'So we should make a date,' Alice suggested.

'Are you free tonight?' he asked immediately.

She bit a regretful lip. 'Sorry. I've got a party.'

He looked her up and down, curiously. 'You don't look like you're going to a party, I mean, not compared to the last one.' Then he blushed. 'Sorry. Didn't mean to sound rude. No offence.'

'None taken,' Alice muttered, trying not to squirm at this reminder that the last time they had seen each other she had been wearing thigh-length patent boots and her nipples had been more or less in her eyes.

'You can come, if you like,' she offered suddenly. 'To the party. It's being given by the whole street. Every gallery's *en fête*, including us.'

She found herself crossing her fingers behind her back. It was dawning on her that Jasper's kindly presence, not to mention his sheer size and breadth, would be a source of reassurance on this night on which so much depended.

'I'd love to come,' he said immediately. 'Matter of fact, it would rather suit me. I haven't got very far with my art investment plan, you see. Been a bit busy. Another look round would be useful. Although I must say, that picture you have in your window is really special. That's why I came in . . .' He stopped and grinned. 'Well. *One* of the reasons I came in.'

That was, a relieved Alice noted, two independent votes in favour of *View*.

'Glad you like it,' she told him. 'Let's just hope that the rest of the art world agrees. Because if they don't . . .' Her glance fell to her shiny black skirt. Dread squeezed her insides. Might her sexy Scottish widow look be hideously appropriate – for the death of her gallery career?

'What do you mean, if they don't?' Jasper now lowered his tall frame on to the edge of the empty front desk. 'How could they not?'

Alice looked at him fearfully, her carefully maintained poise crumbling. 'I don't know. I don't know what people think is good art. I only know what I like. But the thing is . . .'

She told him what the thing was. That if Siobhan O'Sullivan's one painting failed to capture the imagination of the art world, she was finished herself.

Jasper listened to her carefully.

'You've got to visualise,' he said decisively, when she had finished.

Alice stared. 'Sorry?'

His arms were folded, his face serious, and he looked and sounded altogether different from the blushing, shuffle-footed Jasper of earlier. 'Whenever you've got a tricky situation in front of you,' he told her earnestly, 'you just have to imagine the ideal outcome. You have to really, really believe that it will happen. Then there's a good chance that it will.'

Alice looked at him quizzically.

'I know what you're thinking,' he said. 'That it sounds very psychobabbly. The odd thing is, though, it works. I've found it a great help throughout my business life.'

Alice felt her doubts fade. If someone as sensible, kind and normal as Jasper did this visualising thing, who was she to dismiss it out of hand? She needed all the help she could get at the moment.

'So,' Jasper said, leaning in close to Alice so she could smell his cedary aftershave. He reached out and took one of her hands, the touch sending a judder of delight along her nerves.

'Tell me, Alice,' he said gently, fixing her eyes with his own. 'What's the perfect outcome for you for tonight?'

Chapter 71

Starved cheekbone hit surgeried temple as fake air kiss met fake air kiss. Celebrities and socialites had fought capped tooth and tipped nail – and that was just the men – to be invited to the Gold Street party, the art world's most exclusive summer event.

Flashbulbs were going off like gunfire; champagne corks fired volleys in return. In the background, the pulsing sound of music vied with the non-stop roar of high-octane gossip.

Expensive scents mingled with the smell of food as the most powerful people in the art business made their way slowly through the heaving, brightly lit street. The crowd stood back to let them pass, as well as have a good look at them.

These were, after all, the market-makers, the movers and shakers. There was Fuchsia Klumpp in black leather, her hair cut short and dyed platinum to match that of her companion, her latest protégée, Sharon Aura. Some said Aura was her lover. Others said Klumpp was already tiring of the affair and was considering another dump on the market.

There were film stars, rock stars, models, celebrity hairdressers, aristocrats, plutocrats and technocrats. There were teenage scions of the famous, people famous for being famous, has-beens and yet-to-comes. There were reality TV stars, celebrity chefs, footballers, WAGs and even the occasional artist. There were billionaires, zillionaires and gagillionaires. There were collectors, thieves, connoisseurs and ignoramuses. There were perfumed men with slicked-back hair and expensive watches. There were women with cheekbones almost as high as their high beige hair.

Hundreds of preternaturally perfect teeth stretched in hundreds of preternaturally sincere smiles. People were schmoozing, networking and giving and receiving face time. Some were even enjoying themselves: flirting, joking, chatting, exclaiming, insinuating and hugging each other carefully so as not to dislodge any make-up. Sunglasses were de rigueur, even though the sun was now setting. The rich shaft of light it sent down the street picked out a dazzle of diamonds, plus glints of gold everywhere from necks to wrists to ears to teeth.

Some people were even looking at art.

Alice, circulating round the packed floor of OneSquared, was holding her breath so hard she suspected she was blue in the face. But Jasper's plan seemed to be working. She had visualised success, and so far everything had gone well.

There had been a difficult moment at the very beginning, though. The crowd of partygoers had headed straight for OneSquared, expecting to witness the unveiling of Zero. Widespread and audible disgruntlement had set in at the news that the enigma, far from being revealed, was not even present. As the boos gathered momentum, Alice, cowering in the gallery with Siobhan, Dan and Jasper, realised she had to take charge. The future of other people beside herself, not least the terrified artist, hung on what she did next.

'Just visualise,' Jasper whispered, and Alice visualised, with all her might. She visualised convincing all present about the brilliance of Siobhan O'Sullivan. Then she went outside with the front desk stool.

She had stood on it as best she could, given its asymmetrical and sloping-seated nature. Wobbling but determined, she had begun to address the crowd.

Her words had been received initially in stony silence. Dread had gathered in her heart and nausea in her stomach as the silence slowly became low mutterings. People began to talk behind their hands and gesture angrily at Siobhan's picture.

Then the miracle had happened. A large and excitable man with thick black hair had pushed to the front of the crowd. Alice, recognising the famous art critic, had looked at him in mute appeal. He had stared back, his eyes hard and unyielding. Then he had opened his mouth and declared, in booming tones that could probably be heard all the way to the river, 'My dear, congratulations! A star is born!'

Alice had promptly fallen off the stool; Siobhan, who was beside it, had fainted. Fortunately Dan was there to catch her, and Jasper, hovering at her side, had managed to catch Alice. Caroline, waiting nearby with her camera crew and a mischievous smile, managed to catch it all.

But the tide had turned. Amid a growing murmur of appreciation from the crowd, the art critic had continued to lavish praise on Siobhan and Alice. 'A brilliant run-up campaign,' he had boomed. 'Pretending to launch Zero, when all the time you were about to spring *this* delight.' He beamed at Siobhan. 'A PR stroke of genius. Even if,' he added, regretfully, 'I was rather looking forward to meeting Zero.'

Siobhan, sick with relief, did not notice Dan wriggling beside her at this point, as if he was very uncomfortable about something.

Alice, meanwhile, wanted to laugh, cry and shout, all at the same time. It was like being in the happiest of happy dreams. With the art critic as cheerleader, the crowd were hip-hip-hurraying, over and over again, for Britart's brightest new star. Everything had worked out perfectly. The moment, finally, was how she had visualised it.

Siobhan was launched. Her own career was saved. The OneSquared Gallery had a bright future – the brightest future on Gold Street if the fact that there were more people here than anywhere else was anything to go by. Angelica, when she came back, would be amazed. Thrilled. And, most importantly of all, grateful.

'Thank you, Jasper,' Alice murmured, turning to him and flinging her arms about him.

She felt his back stiffen suddenly and pulled back, disconcerted. She looked up at him, but his head was turned away. For a fleeting second the hideous suspicion that she had read him all wrong, that he was not in the least romantically interested, swept through her.

Then she realised that his attention was elsewhere altogether. On the woman in tattered clothes and matted dreadlocks forcing herself through the crowd towards the gallery.

She wore no make-up, and her creased and angry face had the colour and consistency of a particularly fine pair of brogues. Yet Alice recognised her immediately. 'Angelica! What . . . I mean . . . how . . .'

'How what?' came the familiar irate tones, as Angelica shoved herself to the front. 'How come I look like this? Because I've been on a bloody bus from India for the last three weeks, that's why.'

'Well, um, it's great to have you back.' Alice felt for a grip on the situation. Visualise. She must visualise. Visualising Angelica's impressed delight at the recent triumph, she went straight to the point. 'The party's been a success, Angelica. We've got the hottest new star in Gold Street. Look, there she is, over there, with all those TV crews round her.'

She pointed eagerly to where poor Siobhan, looking quite overwhelmed and squeezing every last drop of blood out of Dan's hand, was, indeed, staring like a rabbit in headlights into about ten news monitors at once whilst being jabbered at in several different languages.

'It doesn't make any difference,' Angelica declared. 'I'm shutting the gallery.'

Whenever Alice, in later years, looked back on this moment, there was never any sound. The noise of the crowd faded to nothing and all movement slowed to a halt. All she could ever hear was her own voice saying, very quietly, '*What?*'

'Nick's divorcing me,' Angelica announced. The nostrils of her sharp nose had a bitter, triumphant flare that reminded Alice of a witch in a fairy tale. 'On the advice of his *doctor*,' Angelica added viciously. 'I'm getting bugger all in the settlement. I'll hardly be able to support myself, let alone a bloody art gallery.'

As Alice stood, thunderstruck amid the ruin of her dreams, there was a wail from the crowd. Followed by several boos and some shouts of 'Shame!'

'But . . .' Alice forced out desperately. 'But we've got a future here, Angelica. Siobhan is going to be massive. We've tried so hard . . .'

Under Angelica's contemptuous stare, she felt, for all her efforts, her conviction fading along with her voice. She tried to visualise, but could not summon up the energy. All she could see now was the end. The end of everything they had worked for, and which had seemed so tantalisingly close.

'Please,' she begged, with a last desperate effort. 'You can't pull the plug on it now.'

'Can't I?' Angelica snarled, pushing her face close to Alice's, the movement releasing a malodorous wave of patchouli and sweat. 'Well I am doing. It's all *too late*. What have you got to say to that, eh?' She stabbed Alice in the chest.

Alice had nothing to say. Speech was beyond her now. She collapsed into Jasper's arms, racked with heartbroken tears.

Chapter 72

Three months later

As the *Romeo and Juliet* Fantasy Overture reached its sombre conclusion, Siobhan, looking up from her canvas, saw a handful of bronze leaves swirl past the window of the big, sunny white room. It was autumn; the summer was over. But it still felt like a new beginning.

Dan was looking across at her from his own easel.

'How's the Prime Minister going?' Siobhan smiled. He had recently been commissioned to paint the first official portrait of the newly elected leader. A prestigious assignment, and one that reflected the way their careers were taking off in tandem. As well as the six commissions Siobhan was working on, and Dan's five, there had been a number of magazine features about the husband-and-wife artists. There had been even more solely about the wife, whose career had launched so spectacularly at the Gold Street party in the summer.

'Come and see,' Dan invited.

Siobhan put down her brush and went round the back of his easel.

The politician looked out, feet apart, arms folded, expression belligerent. It was an excellent portrait, as Dan's portraits always were. Not for nothing – although he scorned any form of hype – had he been hailed as the most exciting portrait artist working in Britain today.

But Siobhan, who knew his work so well, could read the prime ministerial picture like a book.

'You don't like him.' She grinned.

'He was very arrogant,' Dan agreed. 'But it gave me more scope. More interesting than painting someone nice, in a way. I can leave clues for posterity.'

'Like that sludgy background,' Siobhan teased. 'Are you saying he has a murky past?'

'Sludgy? You think so?'

She watched him looking anxiously at his work, head on one side like a bespectacled bird with a shock of dark hair. A flood of love washed through her. Everything had turned out so well, and it was all because of him. And Alice, of course.

Even now, the memory of the dash to OneSquared to meet Alice made her tremble. The rushing through the London Underground, bubble-wrapped canvas under her arm, because Dan insisted it was quicker than a taxi. The lung-bursting run through the blazing heat to Gold Street; the flinging open of the gallery door by an Alice who was clearly all impatience, and a Caroline scarcely less so. The subsequent sweating, heart-hammering, weak-limbed wait for their verdict. The joy when it had come. 'At last,' she had heard Alice say, in tones that had been almost tearful. 'Something good.'

Then there had been the party, all the drama . . .

'What are you thinking about?' Dan looked up from his murky background to see a dreamy-eyed Siobhan, her brush lifted aimlessly into the air.

As she looked at him, he blinked with pleasure, as always.

'I was just remembering the party; Angelica coming back,' Siobhan said in the low Irish voice that never failed to thrill him. 'Her saying to Alice that it was all very well her producing a hit artist, but she couldn't afford to run the gallery any more.'

Dan grinned as he took up the story. 'And then Alice bursting into tears and saying it was just so awful, after all her work, especially now that there was so much interest in Siobhan O'Sullivan . . .'

'And then,' Siobhan broke in excitedly, 'Jasper stepping forward and saying . . .' she grinned, and assumed a toffish accent, 'that actually, he'd been thinking about investing in an art gallery for some time . . .'

'Just as long as Alice ran it,' Dan chimed in. 'It was sweet the way he insisted on naming it the Wonderland Gallery on the spot. Everyone cheered.'

'He's crazy about her,' Siobhan said happily.

'As I am about you,' Dan assured her, coming over and pulling her into his arms. Siobhan squealed as the paint from the brush he still held in one hand smeared stickily across her cheek. Dan had not noticed, however. His eyes were on Siobhan's now-empty ring finger, to be replaced by his own once the divorce from Ciaran came through.

In the end, Ciaran had come quietly. He had been amazed to find Siobhan at the party, more amazed still that she was the focus of so much of the excitement. The fact that he had arrived at the celebrations flushed with success himself, fresh from his well-received performance on *Brilliant Britain*, had, Dan suspected, helped a great deal to oil the wheels. A poor start to the reunion tour, watched by an audience of twenty million or more, would have been hard – impossible – for him to bear; as it was, he had been able to watch his wife's triumph with relative equanimity. They were clearly going in different directions; Ciaran quite literally, with the start of the Japanese leg of the Boyfriend tour.

Siobhan's thoughts were going along the same track. That Ciaran, too, wanted to keep the business amicable had been a great and unexpected relief. He had offered her Aldeham Manor as her settlement; she had accepted and sold it immediately. Now she looked happily around the garden studio of their new home, the tall, elegant Georgian house in Richmond she had bought with the proceeds.

Dan's thoughts had moved on to Aldeham. Part of him missed

it, despite everything. He would never have met Siobhan without it, for one thing. And matters were certainly more pleasant there now that Roger had replaced him as Birgit's housemate, especially as he insisted she actually did some housework. Meanwhile, the repulsive Kevin Swift had been forced by the local council to reinstate his rose arbour, plant new trees, grass over his helipad and generally start behaving like a human being.

The pair of them returned to their painting. After a while, Dan looked up, having remembered something.

'Alice tells me she's thinking of getting Zeb back on the Wonderland gallery list,' he said. 'Apparently some of those etchings he's done of Bo are really exceptional. Very Schiele.'

'Another happy couple.' Siobhan smiled. 'We just need to find someone for Mrs de Goldsmith now.' She reached up to the shelf near her easel for a fresh brush, then withdrew her arm suddenly as cramp shot through her.

'You'd better sit down, darling,' Dan said, seeing her hand hover over the small but definite bump below her breasts. 'You need to relax whenever you can, the doctor said.'

'But I've got a whole exhibition to paint,' Siobhan fretted.

This was true, Dan knew. The Wonderland Gallery had received offers of more commissions following the show than Siobhan could probably manage in five years. Yet however eager she was to make up for lost time, a baby on the way meant that she had to pace herself, like it or not.

'You can take your time,' he assured her. 'Alice will find a way to stave off your fans and keep them on the boil at the same time.'

'Just as long as they're not Fuchsia Klumpp,' Siobhan returned.

Dan raised his eyebrows. The London art world had rippled with astonishment at the news that the Wonderland Gallery had refused to sell a single Siobhan O'Sullivan to the powerful collector. 'They won't be. Alice is protecting her assets. She's not risking you being dumped like Zeb was.'

'Although Zeb now says that Fuchsia's dumping him was the best thing that ever happened to him,' Siobhan reminded him.

'The best thing that happened to all of us, really,' Dan mused thoughtfully. 'We owe Zeb a lot. Perhaps if the baby's a boy . . .' He looked questioningly at Siobhan.

'I am *not* calling it Zebedee.'

Dan held up his paint-stained hands. 'OK.'

'Anyway,' Siobhan said. 'The person we really need to thank is Zero. He *was* a real person, wasn't he?'

'Apparently,' Dan mumbled, lowering his head to hide his red face.

'Alice always changes the subject whenever I bring it up.' Siobhan frowned. 'I'd *love* to know who he was . . .'